How to Sacrifice Your Lover

A Tale of Gaslighting and the Cult of Borderline Personality

Ada Loveless

DEDICATION

Dedicated to all who just want to be who they are and feel loved, and to she who knows who she is, and dumps this dedication into a bottomless abyss

True as Remembered

Contents

Foreword

You are one of the very first people to honor me by reading this book. Even if this book were *never* written, this story, on its own, took a lot away from my soul, sanity, prosperity, and wallet. Publishing it simply puts it to bed. It may be understood by very few.

I am not sure how this book will be received by many readers. You may think the main character, Yuki, is a **villain**. You may think he is a **hero** or **victim**. All of those things are likely true. This book may *validly* read, to some, like a pathetic 450-page **love letter** from a whiney nerd to a prom queen. It might *validly* read, to others, like a 40-year-old virgin man trying to mansplain sex and relationships to adult women. But really, to me, the author, this book is about **psychology**. It is about what happens when people with opposing life experiences, become intertwined and their **personality disorders and defects** get the best of them, causing them to **tangle** in ways that are both **beautiful** and **horribly abusive** at the same time. It doesn't matter if you think of any character as a hero or a villain, what matters, is that these characters exist, as real people, and experience life in their unique ways.

It may not be an easy read. It may make you **cringe**. If any of those statements are true of your experience reading this, then this book is a **success**, in my opinion. Not everything about art and music and cinema and literature is created with the intention of invoking pleasant feelings in those who experience it. Some art is intended to invoke *unpleasant* **feelings**. I merely hope that, when reading this book, you'll feel the feelings that I felt as I wrote it, and those feelings are often unpleasant, frantic, chaotic, loathing, lovesick, and even, frequently, pathetic.

Chapter 0

"FUCK YOU! FUCK YOU! FUCK YOU!" Amber screams as I stand in the entryway of my house. I take one step back as paper plates of pizza fly at my feet with each "fuck you" she delivers with increasing fury.

"Why are you speaking to me like this in my house?" I ask politely. I am calm and collected, yet Amber is completely off-the-handle.

"ALL I WANT TO DO IS SMOKE THIS *FUCKING* BOWL AND GET DRUNK!! IT'S MY BIRTHDAY, AND I JUST WANTED TO GET THROUGH TONIGHT WITHOUT ANY FUCKING DRAMA, BUT I'M TOO SICK TO EVEN DRINK MYSELF TO DEATH!!!"

"Why are you speaking to me like this in my house?" I ask again, now beginning to boil.

"FUCK YOU! I hate you!"

My resolve to keep my cool begins to crumble. *"Why are you speaking to me like this in my house!"* I ask again - my voice building into a low growl. I grit my teeth. I clench my fists.

Amber leaves the kitchen area attached to the living room, walks past me, and storms up the stairs that wind from the entryway up to a loft that overlooks the entryway and living room. "FUCK YOU! I'LL MOVE OUT TOMORROW!" she snaps just before she slams the door to "her" room. She lets out a loud screech and I hear the dull thump of a heavy object being thrown. A thud reverberates through my house as loud as her screaming.

I finally raise my voice, "NO, YOU'RE MOVING OUT TONIGHT!"

"I'M NOT LEAVING WITHOUT MY STUFF!" she shouts back, her voice sounding muffled from the other side of the closed door. Amber always cared about her "stuff".

"I'll gladly put it out on the curb for you!" I return, now with a cocky swagger. I'm high on myself, a little shocked, but feeling righteous. I'm proud that I was finally able to stand up to her. I had bent over backwards too many times for her; I let her bully me around; but for once, I was flexing my muscles and letting her know that I demanded respect.

Her butch, rainbow-haired friend Beth sighs and follows her up the stairs, entering the bedroom. "I've never seen her like this," she says as she passes by.

"Well, I have," I reply. "This isn't the first time."

Amber almost sprays Beth with mace as she enters the bedroom. She must have thought Beth was me as she entered. I am a little angry about the events that just transpired but more depressed than angry. I generally don't get angry about things. I just stand in the entryway, stunned, for what feels like a few minutes, but is probably just a few seconds. Upon reconnecting my brain to the motor functions throughout my body, I go through all my kitchen drawers, find all my knives, and take them into the basement where I hide them in an old blue suitcase. It wouldn't be the first time a girl violently chased me through my own house with a knife. I decide it best to take precautions.

I go outside, peer into the darkness, and find my good friends and houseguests for the week, Techna and Daedalus, are cowering in near-pitch-blackness. They're put off by all the screaming and shouting. They're in town visiting from out of town and travel here to stay with me often. They don't go by their real names. Few people I know use their real names in the Goth/Cyberpunk scene.

"I'm not impressed, Yuki," says Techna. "You asked me to size-up this girl, and from what I've seen all night, I just gotta say that this snotty, spoiled party-girl attitude she has is super immature! She's pushing 30 years old but should have outgrown this attitude when she was a teenager! You really should be with someone grown-up!"

"I know, I know. But I just really want to be a kid again myself.

You know, I didn't really party when I was younger, and I lived a life of isolation and boredom in my 20's, so I suppose I love a hot mess! I just find this party-girl raver vibe super-attractive," I reply.

"But she's clearly just using you because you have money and a nice house! I care about you, but I don't think you have any business being with her!"

"Well, as you get to know someone, you never really know how it's going to unfold as you peel back all the layers. It was good in the beginning, a nice time, but over time she just got more and more demanding and mean. I didn't want it to take these turns, I hoped she would prove to care, but now, clearly, this is scorched earth! I can't fix this now no matter how much I want to," I reply.

Techna and Daedalus are good friends, but I think my neighbor, "Neighbor Mike", thinks that they're hired prostitutes every time he sees them. Most people in Minnesota are plain and boring, and I have an incessant need to be in the company of freaks. Techna is wearing her favorite tight silver sequined dress, a pink wig, and her favorite "hooker shoes". She loves her pink wig because when she goes to the gay clubs, the gay men all think she's a man dressed in drag. Her shoes are knee-high platform heels with straps strewn with bullets twisting up her leg and with heels shaped like revolvers. They make her look like a sex worker, but Techna is none of that. Techna is just a beautiful, classy, fun girl who loves to shock people, and maybe do a little cam work on the side for fun.

Daedalus is her flamboyant bisexual boyfriend, a tall, hairy, effeminate, panty-wearing, Goth man with long black hair, black fingernails, white makeup, and painted eyebrows. Techna loves how bizarre Daedalus is. They both dress in ways that would make "normal" people uncomfortable. Shocking other people is regarded to be one of Techna's great pleasures. Yet, *even if* she might think it is funny to tell dead-baby jokes at an infant's funeral, Techna and Daedalus are two of the most morally centered people I know. They're good friends, my best friends.

We're all on the fringes of the "Goth" scene in Minneapolis. It is a scene characterized by men and women into vampires, black clothing, and industrial music. I say we're on the "fringes", but others might say that we're at the nucleus of it all. You see, in Minneapolis, you don't have to be obsessed with the dark side to be welcomed in the Goth scene. You don't have to love Trent Reznor or be into bondage sex to be welcome here. You can be whoever you want to be. In fact, the one thing that sets us apart in our community is that *anything goes* here. You are respected, and as long as you're open-minded and not a pedophile, rapist, or murderer, you can be whoever you want.

I was drawn to the scene because I'm a bit freaky myself. At 34, I am still learning to be "myself". I am currently sporting long hair colored green and purple which changes on any given week. I never had the guts to dye my hair until this year. I worried about the public scrutiny I would face when I dyed it for the first time, particularly as a professional software engineer. I never had the guts to do many of the kinds of things that other kids did when they were in high school. I missed out on all the kissing games, wild parties, and binge drinking when I was younger. I didn't start drinking until I was in my 20s. Some might have called me a good kid... but to my peers... well... maybe I was just a spineless prude. I am scared of many of the things that ordinary people endure regularly. I'm uncomfortable expressing my sexuality, or talking about sexual things in general, being in the presence of drugs, even pot. I want a wholesome environment to live in, but also one that fulfills my urges. I imagine others out there looking at me as emotionally and socially immature, and I might be the first to admit that I am. Maybe I'm just trying to fix that by gaining experience that I was missing earlier in life, trying to live the lost years of my life in my middle age. Really, I just want to be a kid again, but I see the clock of life ticking, and the burdens of old age on the horizon.

I expected negative reactions from people when I first started expressing myself outwardly but was surprised to learn that being unique on the outside starts many friendly conversations. I exercise what I call "fashion freedom" in the way I dress, taking fashion risks, bending gender norms regularly, but compared to most in the scene, I'm pretty "normal". I'd always been an outcast, even in a scene full of outcasts, and sometimes I feel like I might not be *bold enough* to truly fit into this scene... even this... decidedly open-minded scene, which is full of bold people into leather, bondage, assless chaps, kilts, whips, chains, piercings, tattoos, transsexuals, and transvestites. I'm plenty crazy, mind you, but at this point in my life, I keep most of my craziness "in the closet".

Amber and Beth are also on the fringes of the scene, and, as a result, we share many common friends. The Goth scene is like its own little small-town inside a big city. Everyone knows everyone. There are only a few hundred of us and we frequent the same clubs every week.

But Amber and Beth don't fit the Goth standard *at all*. They don't champion the color black like most in the scene. They don't listen to depressing, dark, music. They don't collect novelties celebrating The Addams Family, The Cure, Hellraiser, or Dracula.

They're just club girls... stoners. They don't care who they hang out with, just as long as there is pot involved. It just so happened that in recent months, Amber had been living in my house at my expense and relying on my money for her weed habit. She had no job, and no real job leads; she didn't pay any bills or buy herself food, but I didn't mind. Amber was fun to be around... most of the time. We had fun, even if I was paying. Amber's hair is long and dyed pink and black, which I had funded not even an hour earlier. She's petite, not too shy to wear thigh-high stockings paired with extremely short skirts, and tops cut low enough to expose her breasts just beyond the areolas. Her eyebrows are painted because she recently shaved them for a fetish website when she needed extra cash.

Beth's hair is always a rainbow of colors, which is the only feminine thing about her. She is a "tom-girl", sporting tennis shoes, knee-length cargo shorts from the boy's department at Walmart, and a cheap white T-shirt with some random dive bar's logo on the front.

They love going to dance parties that play dubstep music and do party drugs like ecstasy and whatever new drug is hip. I first met them at a party hosted by my old friend Echo. I thought they were lesbian lovers, but they soon proved to be more bisexual than gay. Amber quickly took a liking to my hair which, at the time, was colored a deep purple. Purple is her favorite color, and my hair matched her purple stockings. I am a sucker for a girl in long stockings. I found it difficult to resist her. At first, it seemed like she couldn't resist me either. She could be a fun girl. In many ways, she was a geeky guy's dream. She played "Magic" and kicked just about anyone's ass at Halo on Xbox. We had plenty of fun playing video games together or watching childish cartoons. Most of the time, I enjoyed her company.

I quickly found out that weed fuels Amber's lifestyle and also fuels Amber and Beth's friendship. They love weed like no two people on planet earth. Together, they probably smoke more pot than the entire Minneapolis Goth scene combined and are connected to the fringes of the scene because… well… Amber had many "roommates" in the past.

I, certainly, am not the first person she had been freeloading off. She seemed to bounce around, freeloading off one geeky guy in the scene until her terrible attitude got her kicked to the curb, at which point she would quickly just find another one. She admits, bluntly and openly, that things for her are just "too easy".

On many levels, we got along very well. I cared about her deeply, but, unfortunately for me, Amber's only care in life is pot. In 2011, pot is just starting to become politically accepted as harmless, and therefore there is talk of it becoming decriminalized in some states. The popular consensus is that it is far safer than alcohol, which is already legal everywhere. No one can deny that alcohol is far more destructive than marijuana, but when you smoke as much weed as Amber, even *she* fully admits that it causes *some* problems. Even the most obsessed stoners I know smoke only a tiny fraction of the weed that Amber does. She smokes and smokes all day and all night, every 15 minutes it seems, at a cost of several hundreds of dollars every month. She couldn't quit if she tried, but she doesn't *want* to quit anyway.

Today is her birthday, June 12th. She is mostly recovered from her most recent hospitalization. It has been 14 days since I took her to the ER. The doctor's diagnosis was "acute THC intoxication". They pumped her full of all the anti-nausea meds they could fit into her veins, but none of it could stop Amber from vomiting every 30 seconds (literally). The vomiting, they said, was psychosomatic. It was paired with constant panic attacks and an unceasing compulsion to take showers. The doctors had never had a patient with higher levels of THC in their bloodstream at any time in their careers. They were legitimately concerned that if she couldn't keep food in her body, she would possibly die.

I stayed by her hospital bedside for the duration of 4 days until we managed to get her to stop vomiting *just* long enough to get her discharged. The nurses were refusing to let her shower on doctor's orders after she took 24 showers in just one day in the hospital, a directive that she thought was cruel. I thought it was rather cruel myself. If she gets relief from the simple act of showering, why would the doctor's order be to deny her that relief? How much are we paying for this hospital anyway?

We eventually figured out, out of desperation, that if I rubbed her back, she wouldn't need to take showers as often. Armed with this knowledge, we managed to fool the doctors long enough to get her discharged. I rubbed her back when the nurses were gone, virtually all day and all night for days, and on the final day, just moments before the doctor came in for her obligatory $400, 4-minute morning visit. Once the doctor left, Amber immediately vomited, but eventually, the discharge came. I put her in a wheelchair, and we bolted out of there as if we were running for our lives.

We came back to my house and, immediately, she began vomiting again. This continued for another 10 days. Despite claiming that she'd stop smoking pot as soon as she got out of the hospital, she had smoked her first bowl as soon as I left the house to go pick up her prescriptions. I spent the next 10 days massaging her back, arms, feet, hands, and legs for 6 hours a day on average. If I wasn't rubbing her back, she was showering or running the jacuzzi jets.

As I sat behind her, massaging her back, my hands turned to mush, but when my fingers grew weak, she'd shout at me in violent fits of rage things like, "What the fuck are you doing?!? You're doing it all wrong!" She'd treat me like a slave when my technique was incorrect, or my focus was on the wrong part of her back. Yet, there was never a *correct* answer… the proper technique and location changed by the minute. There was no way for me to know what was or wasn't correct… all I knew was that if it was wrong, I'd get her wrath.

My ability to tolerate Amber seemed to depend on what part of her brain the cannabis decided to affect at a given moment. Sometimes it would make her fun, sometimes nervous, sometimes angry. But *most* of the time it made her lethargic, slow, and dumb. She was unable to complete complex tasks or form complex thoughts, and her perception of time was way different than reality. She basically sat around the house all night watching Ren and Stimpy and slept all day until I'd get home from work at 5:30PM. She paid me very little respect. I didn't ask her for rent money… mostly just respect.

Despite her obvious flaws, I wanted her to be my girlfriend. Anyone impartial to our relationship would certainly ask, "Why?" I guess the short answer is that I am a man who just wants to be a kid again. I want to kiss the hot girl under the bleachers like I never got to do when I was younger and bullied.

Amber knew how to give me just enough of a taste to keep me paying. Initially, she led me on to believe that she wanted me to be her boyfriend. We went clubbing together. She dressed all hot in her thigh-high fishnet stockings and knee-high boots, short skirt, and colorful hair. She stayed with me at the bar and let me put my arm around her. I paid not only for her drinks, but for the drinks of several of her friends every night, and to an uninformed observer, we were together.

We were intimate, but it was the worst sex I ever had in my life. The first time she critiqued my performance, "Have you ever gotten a chick off before?" she asked.

"Um, I'm pretty sure I have, actually," I replied, stunned.

"Well, apparently those girls don't know how to *fuck!*" she snapped back.

I rolled off her, offended, and gave up. I figured we could try again some other day and figure out the right rhythm.

I figured there would be plenty of opportunities to figure it out. She wanted to move in with me. I wanted a companion to come home to every day. But once she moved in, she changed. She was completely turned off like a light. She became increasingly rude. She immediately declared one room of the house to be hers and forbade me from entering it without her permission. She disrespected my dog. She started having video chat conversations with her ex-boyfriends, carrying my laptop around the house giving them a tour of her "awesome new pad" gloating to her friends about what she managed to acquire with $0 and her gamer-girl hotness.

Despite her sudden changes, I still paid her way; I bought her all her food; I bought her weed. If I protested spending incredible amounts of money on weed, she said she could get the money in "other ways", but I didn't like them. They included things such as selling nude photos of herself to nerdy guys or going on fetish websites to make videos. I felt pressured by my emotional desire to win her loyalty… and in the 2 months she lived with me I drained my bank accounts and ran up my credit cards trying to make her happy.

I cared about her. I cared about her for reasons that seem completely illogical as I now write this. She was a clever manipulator. She didn't declare that she *didn't* want me… she simply declared that she wanted more time. "Maybe in the future" she'd want me for her boyfriend. And I, well… I was just an insecure, gender-confused, nerd who for the first time in a long time got to sit close to a girl he really cared about.

But the time was here. It was now time where this relationship had to become "real", or I had to go my separate ways with her. I decided that I'd perform one more act for her; I'd throw her a party for her birthday. If she didn't want me after that, it would be over.

I had built a reputation for throwing some of the best parties in town. Amber had never even been to one of my parties, but she had definitely heard about them... oh yes... she had *definitely* heard of them. In 2011, *everyone* is talking about them.

But as of this moment, as she throws pizza at me in a tirade of profanities, there will clearly be no chance of Amber having a legendary birthday party in my house. Illegitimate relationships like this drive me crazy, and after slowly losing my cool for weeks, I lost my ability to be cool with her completely. So as Amber volleys her anger at me, is it really *she* who lost her cool? Or was it me? I really wish I had the self-control to just be "cool" about it. I wish I could say, "Hey, babe, it's alright, let's just be buddies, friends," but I'm not some hardened emotionless brute like most men. I'm an emotional, gender-confused man. She cornered me against a wall, and I crawled up the wall to get away from the sound of my heart-shattering. The incidents of tonight cancel everything. She moves back in with her father and moves her party to her father's garage.

She hates living at her dad's place. It isn't good for someone who smokes as much weed as she does. Sometimes, when you're high and the cannabis lands on the wrong receptors, you need the ability to find silence, and her dad's house is not such a place. If you're nocturnal, it is not a good place when you're trying to sleep in the daytime either. She didn't want to be there. I thought I had leverage to get her to shape up her act, but two days later, she throws herself a quaint little party in her father's garage and photos of her and Brad (the "douche bag ex") appear on social media as she wears clothing I had bought her just days earlier, clearly as a direct insult to me. They get back together, officially, as a couple, immediately. She moves in with him just days later so she doesn't have to stay at her dad's place. I figure half the reason for it is so that she can say one last "fuck you" to me.

I did "love" her. I loved 95% of her... but the remaining 5% was straight out of the Jerry Springer show. She was white trash. She was a stoner. She was a bitch. She was a con artist, a survivalist, and a thief.

But as I've written in songs, "I can love a thief, as long as she loves me."

I cope with my loss by focusing on the negative. I'm down in the dumps for a little while. Eventually, I decide that I'll do what I always do when I'm depressed. I'll throw a wild, destructive party and invite everyone I know to come over for a night of debauchery. Maybe at the end of the night, I'll have gained a bit of social equity... and maybe I'll even meet someone special. I decide that "Amber's party" will happen, but just without Amber being invited. It will be spectacular. Maybe I'll even send her some video of the party she never had. I schedule it for 3 weeks out. As the RSVPs roll in, it is immediately clear that it is going to be a big event.

Before I get in too deep, I must convey a message to my friends. This story, including this chapter and the chapters following, is a TRUE story. But please understand that it is a story about PERCEPTION and not necessarily a story about FACT. It is not important whether these PERCEPTIONS are accurate. But what IS important is the simple fact that they were PERCEIVED. But as you breathe a sigh of relief, having just been given an easy way to call me a confused liar, this book is also about how the perceptions of an intelligent mind can be rewritten, bent, and twisted through psychological and emotional manipulation. One thing is for certain, confusion is a powerful weapon. This 90-day period of my life was confusing. I was confused... emotionally confused... mentally confused, intellectually confused, and physically exhausted from lack of sleep and constant demands for favors, deeds, labor, and attention. I felt like a child in a cult. A confused mind can be warped into accepting, believing, and parroting the lies of a powerful person with a sinister agenda.

So, therefore, I might say, "This is a TRUE story... if you believe the gossip." The fake names have been changed to *other* fake names, and the *real* names have been changed... to *fake* names. Let's say that similarities to real people are "coincidental" and if you recognize some of yourself in this book, it might be actually a composite of multiple people you know. Consider this a work of fiction if it makes you feel better. Even my own name is not my own in this book, but I wrote this book with the best intentions of being accurate in my perceptions of actions, words, thoughts, and feelings

I reveal this to you as honestly as I possibly can. You'll find this story to be abnormally honest as I recall not just my good deeds, but my bad deeds, thoughts, and feelings as well. "Honesty" is a terrible card to play; I realize this. Therefore, understand that I reveal all this to you because I'm sick of relationships being a game of cards. By the end of reading this, you'll know my hand, like playing poker with someone who refuses to hide his own cards... and that hand will be as valuable as folded. And once you've seen my cards, you'll be able to make a clear choice to make a bet on me or take me for everything I have. You'll know all my "tells" … my bluffs ... how scheming and manipulative I can be. You'll know how bitter and jealous I can be. You'll know my motivations for the months of the past, and for the future.

But we're all human. We're often victims of our own impulses. I try to be understanding when others fall victim to their compulsions and impulses because I can fall victim to my own.

I will, years from now, reread this story whenever I'm feeling nostalgic as an old man. I perceived these episodes to be the most beautiful and romantic moments of my life so far... but again, what is "perception" when your lights have been dimmed and you are told that you are blind instead of in the dark?

Chapter 1 - Act I - The Love Bomb

I've always lived a decent life in many respects. I've taken care of myself... I was never handed anything of significance... I worked for it. But I've always had a great job that paid a decent salary. I've always been intelligent, talented, moderately creative, and a decent human being. I live a life that many envy, working as a software engineer for a video game and music company. This brings me to all the exclusive trade shows that the gamer fans wish they could attend, as well as the music trade shows where rock stars are so common that you basically just look right past them.

People want my job.... but I have it. I have a beautiful house, a nice car, all the guitars, synthesizers, drums, and recording gear I ever wanted as a musician, and, really, all the material crap I ever wanted to buy in my life. But none of it ever meant much to me because what I envy are things completely different from what I have. We all tend not to envy what comes easy and covet the difficult things.

I am successful because I had no strong human connections growing up outside my family and found myself isolated and playing with my father's computer scraps as a kid. In isolation, I never really learned to bond with people very easily, but at the same time, I am a lover... an intense lover. All this made me into someone who would do just about anything to fill the hole in my heart reserved only for one special girl. I've dated some beautiful women in my life and had strong relationships with a couple of them. One girl, for impractical reasons, became my fiancée, and we bought this beautiful house together and a lovely puppy named Ada. Ada, bless her heart, had medical problems and when she died, I took her name to be my hacker alias and pseudonym. Some people know me as Ada, Ada Loveless, but in 2011, Ada is still alive, so for now we will just call me Yuki.

As for my fiancée, by the time we bought the house... things just weren't "right" with the relationship. The passion had long since disappeared, along with most of her politeness. She wanted a dog, a house, and a "Smart Car". Upon acquiring all 3 of these things, she left me, her partner for 8 years, just 4 months later. I bailed her out of her financial obligations to the house and took her dog to be my best and sometimes only (it seemed) friend.

I'd never been strong at forming relationships... and I realized that maybe I stuck with her for so long because I had "settled". She demanded that I take on an appearance that wasn't who I was, with short hair, boring sweaters, ugly shoes, and uncomfortable textures. I couldn't be that person anymore. This time... I needed someone to love *me*, not this facade! But finding myself was tough, considering I struggled with where and how I fit into my gender roles in society, every day of my life.

Being a man, who rejects masculinity, seeking a woman, makes things complicated when you're looking for love. When I look at adult male stereotypes, with their pickup trucks, tool belts, boring fashion, and misogyny, I see nothing of who I am on the inside. I see myself as a kind, loving, and emotional person who wants to treat people with kindness and admire flowy and fancy dresses. I looked in the mirror at my male body and wished it had a more feminine shape so that I could embrace that shape, and dress it in fanciness, but I am not a transgender person. I am just a man who wants to be beautiful, more than anything in the world.

So, this pursuit of a soulmate is a difficult one. I have been looking for a soulmate since I was a child. Finding someone to "settle" for is hard enough... let alone finding someone who actually appreciates all of me.

But even if I found someone perfect, I would have to be perfect for her as well, and how can I be that as a man who rejects masculinity? My chances of finding her would require finding her at exactly the right time in her life when she was single, available, and ready to meet me. I knew that when I found this girl, I had to leap headfirst at the chance to grab her while she was ready.

In the past, I did what my pathology compelled me to do as a misfit of society... I gave in to these imperfect relationships with excessive amounts of compromise... and just completely and fully and loved all my girlfriends to the best of my ability while not really giving myself what I wanted. Regardless of my compromises, these imperfect relationships eventually collapsed. At the age of 34, I was ready to go big or give up.

I began one last big push to find someone perfect for me. I called it a "kamikaze ride". I was going to give everything I had... my entire life and wellbeing... my *soul... everything...* to find my dream girl. And in pursuit of her, *I would crash and burn and destroy my life in the process if needed!*

Money is material... money is worthless... I envy those of you with LOVE in your lives. With this new mission in full force, I give my money to "social investments". I throw huge parties and build a reputation for myself in a humble campaign to win the hearts of my peers. I invite the entire city of Minneapolis to come and join me, and even start to become a bit of a local celebrity.

Now that Amber has moved out, it is time for another party. The RSVP list reaches into the triple digits, which is a lot for a house smaller than a mansion. These parties, for me, are about efficient people-meeting. I don't really want to be friends with all these people, but they are a logical means towards a goal of finding a handful of good friends and one super special friend that I would hopefully marry. I always throw a party with a personal goal in mind.

My house has a small but tall dance floor connected to a long kitchen counter, great for stacking lots of alcohol, connected to a dining room which is barren of typical dining room furniture. There are few walls, giving it a nightclub-like feel. One of the two bathrooms sports a small Jacuzzi capable of entertaining 2-3 drunk and horny party goers at a time if they really wanted. Then there's a loft that overlooks the dance floor with a couple of private bedrooms upstairs which I've converted into space where people can lounge in comfortable chairs. I've developed a key set of principles for throwing a great party, even if you're an unpopular nerd.

1. Never throw a party for yourself. Throw a party for someone else who is more popular than you. In fact, throw a party with multiple "guests of honor". These people are responsible for making sure their friends show up.
2. Free booze if you can afford it.
3. Everyone is invited, but make sure they know a "password"
4. Lock away anything valuable because someone you didn't invite is inevitably planning to rob you.
5. Volunteer security, or if you're rich, hire security.
6. Inspire people to dance, my secret sauce.

A day before the party, I finish a laser and light gig at First Avenue. The timing of this gig is unfortunate because the 25 or so lights that I just tore down from the club now have to come back to my house and be set up on my dancefloor. I spend all day rigging and wiring trusses, lights, and video screens with the intention of proving to people that this will be the greatest house party they ever visited in their lives.

In the final moments, I fashion a makeshift DJ booth out of a TV box I had laying around, because… well I'm not very good at furniture, and I rig up a PA system optimized with professional audio mixers. The labor is intense… I look like hell… I've got bags under my eyes. I wonder whether anyone will actually show up at 9:30 when the party is scheduled to start. I need more time, but no one ever shows up to a house party on time, right? Maybe I'll have time for a proper shower before the patrons arrive. Unfortunately, as 9:30 comes around, 15 people show up at my house almost as if they were waiting outside in line for the party to start. I panic to get the music going at the last minute. People start drinking and dancing almost instantly as the lights, lasers, and strobes shoot beams through my fogged home… sucking people into the dance floor. The mood is infectious, and I, at the center of it all, feel "popular" for only the second time in my life.

The party grows into an intense affair. The guests number in the hundreds and people who I barely know are in my house and strewn about my lawn. At the peak of the night, I step up to the DJ booth and put on a track that is arguably the anthem to the Goths of the world: "Closer" by Nine Inch Nails, a slow grooving, sleazy, industrial track which bears a chorus containing the words "I want to fuck you like an animal..." The dance floor lights up. The crowd sings along. The lasers, fog, lights, and music are all perfect.

As I stumble around, drunk. I take a video on my phone. "Was this your birthday party? Wait... no it wasn't... oops!" I bend down as I shout into the phone to get maximum output from my lungs as if I am singing passionately in an arena-rock band, "Fuuckkk youuuuu!" shout as I conclude the video. Before I can think twice and stop myself, I email it to Amber then go about saying my standard 3 sentences to each guest. "Hi, welcome to my Party! Help yourself to anything on the counter. Coats can go upstairs in the guest bedroom."

Things eventually get a bit out of hand. Techna informs me that an uninvited neighbor was bounced. Zak, a prominent member of the scene who could win a Professor Charles Xavier, lookalike contest, had taken him out in a headlock and, with much fanfare and showboating (as he is known to do), dragged him out my front door, across my lawn, and out of the picket fence gate at the end of my driveway.

I appreciate that Zak took the initiative to take care of someone who was clearly uninvited, but I'm not terribly fond of Zak as a person. He's popular in the scene, but I don't think too many people truly respect him. He's dramatic, a showoff, selfish, and immoral, not to mention, one of the most sociopathic and narcissistic people I know.

I brush off the incident... It sounds like Zak had it under control. I go about my business and wander around, saying my hellos to everyone in attendance, but, as I venture out onto the front lawn, which is now strewn with 50 or so friends. The uninvited neighbor is still outside my gate, and now Luna, my long-ago ex-girlfriend, is caught up in the mix.

I approach to find her infuriated. She's tiny, measuring just 5ft tall, but her personality is volatile and explosive. Her boyfriend is up in the uninvited guest's face. As they invite each other to brawl, Luna shouts profanities.

The uninvited guest is a "bro" and clearly doesn't belong with us Goth freaks, nor does his friend, a fat, bearded man in a white and green farmer hat. Richard quizzes them, "Do you even know whose house this is?" he asks.

"I don't give a *fuck* whose house this is!" the fat one says.

I step in. I am indignant, not because there's a fight about to happen, but I am insulted by the fact that the fat one would disregard my hunger for popularity, "Well, you better care whose house this is… because this is MY HOUSE! And you are clearly not invited and need to leave!" I steam.

I look to my left. Luna is still pissed off. Her boyfriend looks ready for a fight, his shirt removed and muscles showing, but Luna herself is far more agitated. Despite being held back by 4 mutual friends, she gets an arm free. She steals glass bottles from other partygoers and tosses them at the uninvited neighbor and his fat friend. The muscle-bound jock's legs begin to bleed as they are cut deeply by the broken glass.

"You fucker!" she screams. She breaks free and leaps the fence. I barely have time to blink before, Luna, weighing in at a mere 100lbs, is up in the face and ready to fight this 6ft 2in, muscle-bound guy, who is drunk out of his mind, stumbling. I have my phone in hand. I press "911" in anticipation of hitting "send". But I think for a moment. Cops tend to ruin parties. I stop myself at the last second. Things calm down, for now. I guess I'm not too drunk to not think twice about *everything*.

I ponder for a moment on Luna as the neighbors trudge away, egos shattered, throwing hand signals and insults. Luna… heh… that's a long story. I guess I've dated my share of firecrackers. Being a shy person, it is difficult to meet women who are not aggressive.

Just as I turn away from my fence, which is now broken and in need of repairs, I see a man stumble out my front door and fall into my mailbox. It is ripped off its post and falls to the ground, spilling its contents all over my grass and shrubs. Then, the music stops. I go inside to find my DJ booth toppled over along with my PA speakers. The mixer is full of dents from hitting the floor and the speaker needs repairs. I am stumbling drunk but manage to get some duct tape and repair the speaker enough to get the music and lights going again as everyone cheers for the return of dancing. The makeshift booth would get knocked over 6 times tonight.

The night is dramatic, intense… but fun. At some point, I need to just take a break and sit down for a bit. By this time, all my friends are hooking up with each other... making out... or worse… it's like a fucking high school kegger in here, but I'm not looking to "hook up" with anyone. I'm not interested in any fleeting one-night bullshit sex. I threw this party with a goal.

My simple goal was to take a step towards establishing myself as a "hub" of the scene. With myself as a "hub" of the scene, I now have the social equity to move forward in my social life with confidence. I have faith that this will ultimately lead me to meet someone I can spend the rest of my life with. I don't expect my journey to end tonight. I expect that the journey is just now reaching full stride and that the coming months will be exciting and fresh now that I'm "somebody".

Despite all the drama, I feel great. I pause and take a break. I find my dog, Ada. She is a very sweet, sociable, 100-pound Greater Swiss Mountain Dog who loves mingling at the party, but now appears to be partied out. She is looking for a bit of love, showing her belly, as I sit on my beer-soaked floor for a moment to pet her. Feeling like my day's work is done, I have no desire to meet or hook up with anyone.

I rub Ada's belly. I scratch her ears. I love that it is so easy to make her happy. Dogs, unlike humans, are so simple to please, and when they smile, it reflects onto you. They don't judge you for your politics, sexuality, or religion. They don't care if you're ugly or smelly. They just want to be with you, and they're happy to be by your side. I know just the spot to scratch to make Ada smile, and as someone who derives his self-worth from his ability to make another happy, Ada's ability to be satisfied by the simplest of things is instant gratification for me.

"Did you have a good time, Ada?" I ask her. "I hope you had fun tonight, sweety. I love you so much. Someday, we'll find you a new mommy."

Out of nowhere, a girl who I've never spoken to sits down to pet Ada with me. Her beauty is shocking. She's 27, stunning, with dyed red hair in streaks of varying red tones, black and white extensions, and perfect red lips to match. I quiver when I look at her with her black goth boots, red over-the-knee socks, short petticoat, and smooth leggings. She's clean... slender... beautiful... refined down to every little detail. Her name is Inari. I'd seen her in photos before as she was a model in an old friend's fashion show, but to see her now in person was a whole, new, unique experience.

I thought she had a boyfriend, and naturally, I figure, she's way out of my league. But as she speaks to me at this moment, I feel like a peasant being spoken to by a goddess.

"I'm Inari," she says. "I sent you a friend request earlier."

"Yes, I definitely remember you from photos. I saw that you modeled for my friend, Echo, but I've never actually met you."

"I just wanted to meet you before I left. It would be a shame if I left without meeting the host," she says.

"Well, it is very nice to meet you," I reply.

"I love doggers," she says. "I have a couple of my own. They're the best." She rubs Ada's belly and Ada smiles happily.

"Sometimes I ponder how a dog's love is so simple," I say. "Offer them hugs, treats, and walks and they return you kisses, smiles, love, excitement, and complete devotion. Compare that to the love of humans who demand chiseled bodies, sex, money, fame, success, youth, beauty, sometimes drugs and booze and expensive dinners, rides in jet planes, exotic vacations, fancy cars and houses, and in return, they sometimes seem to offer just mind games, emotional trickery, lies, and deceit. Why can't human love be as simple as a dog's love?"

"I know what you mean. Aww, she's so cute! She clearly loves coming around and meeting everyone; we had lots of fun with her upstairs," she says.

"Yes, Ada loves people and therefore loves parties. Half the reason I throw parties is just to make her happy, otherwise, it is just me and her here alone."

"Wow, you live here alone then?" she asks.

"Yeah, well, I had a fiancée, and recently, well I guess I've been going through some shit. It's tough to find love when you're a nerdy guy like me." I suddenly feel glum and self-conscious. "I'm sorry I look like hell… I've been up for practically 2 days straight prepping for this party."

"Aww no. I think you look fine. Is that a Jacuzzi in there? I totally wish we could jump in," she says. She leans over into my ear, "I think lasers are sexy," she whispers.

I feel a jolt of euphoria as if I'm the most important man in the world. "Aw… you flatter me," I say.

She leans over again, "I think nerds are sexy too."

I'm normally intimidated by women and would never sit next to a girl I just met normally and tell her she's beautiful… but in this case, her eyes *beg* me. "Wow, you're really beautiful," I say. But to be polite, I say it in a way that is not sleazy but as-if simply stating a fact.

She smiles bright, pausing for a moment, "Thank you, I don't get enough of that."

"Really? No way. I don't believe it," I say. "Well, you *are* beautiful, you know…" I declare again, "…and I'm really glad I met you."

She smiles bright and pauses. I see her chest rise as she breathes more heavily as if I'd just reached in and made her heart pump faster with my bare hands, and as I bask in the glow of her beauty, she gazes at me like a girl who's just met her true love. "I'm glad I met you too," she says.

Her sweetness is so intense it makes me want to cry. But we both just sit, with Ada between us, and gaze. I think of nothing. I am simply enjoying the feeling of the moment like one enjoys the rays of the sun on a beautiful day. She's an angel. What is such a sweet girl doing in a scene like this?

"I have to go now though, my 'ride' is leaving," she says.

"It's okay," I say. "I'm glad to have met you, I'll talk to you online, okay? Do you ever go to Hard Mondays?"

"I love Hard Mondays," she says. "It is my favorite place to be."

"Me too, I'm always there. I can't believe we haven't met before now."

"Yeah, I don't know why we haven't."

"I'm really, really glad I met you," I repeat again.

"I'm really glad I met you, too," she replies, again with the sweetness and passion of the kindest and most sincere girl, touched by angels.

Our conversation is tragically short, and as she walks away and I'm left sitting on the floor with Ada, alone again, my thoughts become more sober than my blood-alcohol level would indicate. She is clearly taken, although she clearly referred to her boyfriend as her "ride" with emphasis as if she was mocking him with a demotion. But still... no way. I could never win the heart of this girl. My thoughts are now completely out of the realm of fantasy, yet I am enthralled to meet someone so beautiful, and especially enthralled that she'd reach out to me with what seemed like genuine admiration and affection. I am fulfilled... a bit turned on... but I know the odds... and the odds of us being a match are slim. There are so many tests to pass, so many gates to travel through before I feel like I mutually connect with anyone. I bask in her glow for a bit. It is about 3:30AM and the night for me is only half over.

By sunrise, there are still dozens of people in my house. My lawn is strewn with bottles, cans, cups, and cigarette butts. 5 people are passed out face-down on my driveway. The hardwood floors are covered in a layer of beer and soot that takes several scrubbings to remove. A few people, including Techna and Daedalus, stay back until the next evening to help me clean up and fix the fence after the fight with the neighborhood douchebag. I feel like it is my best party yet. My optimism is recharged, but in between these exciting times I often revert to loneliness, so I worry that the glow that I feel is temporary.

If I start to feel down, I remind myself, "I've done the work. I've made lots of new acquaintances and look forward to all my new potential friendships." I now have new things to hope for. The party is a great success. Hope is the zest of life, not accomplishment. It is about the ride, not the reward.

Chapter 2 - The "Ride"

The party, a success, was not possible without the help of many close friends. I go online to reach out to all the people who made the night special. I tag Inari as well as a bunch of people.

Wow... just wow.

Thanks for the great weekend, everyone. It wasn't enough to just throw a party... you guys all had to SHOW UP to make the weekend amazing.

Without the help of so many of you ... this party wouldn't have started.

There were some damages, but they're all fixable.... a little superglue, a couple of nails, a good scrubbin'...

The party wouldn't have been a party without everyone who showed up... we are good people... unfortunately, some blackout-drunk, uninvited neighbors showed up as well.

But, let me be clear... the guy who got bounced was NO FRIEND of ANYONE invited to the party. We may look like scary darksiders to boring, normal people, but we all know that the only problems that ever come to our clubs come from the tourists who come to gawk at us.

Be assured that the next party will have bona fide security, and this may require some volunteers and/or donations to pull off.... but you all know that these nights are worth it. We need to work together to keep them safe. How about Halloween!? That would be completely, completely, totally off-the-hook.

We went through at least 13 cases of beer plus gallons and gallons and gallons of hard liquor, vodka, gin, rum, wine, Triplesec, Jagermeister, whiskey... hell, I even bought some "Cupcake" lol. Thank you to those who contributed additional alcohol and/or funds to help cover costs at the end of the night.

Also, I'd like to give out a big thanks to everyone who stayed behind to help clean up. We didn't finish cleaning up until 9PM the following night. I ended up mowing my next-door neighbor's lawn just because she was so cool in putting up with our noise.

I didn't throw this party to make superficial connections... I threw this party to make lasting connections with people. I considered it an investment in social equity. A worthwhile one indeed! Many of you know me well enough to understand that. Money never meant a whole lot to me, but the companionship of GREAT people has always meant EVERYTHING.

It was great to see everyone and great to meet all the new people I met. If you ever want to buy me a drink ;) come find me out at the clubs on a Monday or Wednesday.

I'm going to tag an awful lot of people here for special thanks... whether you contributed hard labor, good deeds, crowd control, or just made an effort to get to know me as a friend... a big thanks for everything everyone... you guys all mean a TON to me! I apologize if I miss anyone... call me out if I forget you!

~Yuki

I tag a long list of people for thanks, and Inari is on the list... simply because... well... she made me feel amazing for a moment. I pause for a moment and ask myself why it is that I'm including her. These other people actually *did* things to help make the party happen. Am I insulting them by putting Inari on this list when in reality, she didn't really do much of anything but say a few kind words to me? I almost feel sleazy about it, as if I'm just tagging a "hot girl" whose attention I want. I ponder for a moment how often and easily I put my back and shoulders into tasks for the mere exchange of words -- not exactly a fair transaction in many cases, but the party I just threw for a bunch of strangers wasn't exactly a fair transaction in and of itself.

Regardless of what my motivations are, it isn't long before Inari and I find ourselves chatting online... and through the course of events she shows up for a Monday night at "The Saloon", one of the most famous gay bars in all of Minneapolis. The Minneapolis Goth scene goes hand-in-hand with the Lesbian, Gay, Bisexual, and Transsexual scene (LGBT) scene. In later years they would welcome queers into their culture by adding a "Q" or a "+" to the end of LGBT, but this is 2011... we're not there yet. As a clearly queer man, this is just another one of many ways I feel like an outsider, just like I feel like an outsider in the Goth community already.

Goth nights are typically hosted at gay bars in Minneapolis-- Monday nights at The Saloon, Thursday nights at "The Bolt" for a night they call "Chamber", and Fridays and Saturdays the scene has its own dedicated club, Ground Zero, one of the most famous and original Goth clubs in the United States, running for 20 years or more.

"Hard Mondays", is arguably the best truly Goth night in the town, if only because it is "tourist-free". To be called a "tourist" is a stiff insult in the Goth community. It refers to someone who comes to the Goth clubs just to stare and laugh at all the patrons as if they're animals in a zoo. These people make the devoted regulars feel less welcomed and, whereas we all would certainly love it if a "dress code" were enforced, the club owners cannot agree to turn potential money away at the door. The Goth clubs are all struggling, and the once-mighty "Ground Zero" has been weathered and neglected in its 20 years of operation. The club that used to make me feel like I was in an exotic world where all my sinful thoughts were celebrated in all forms of art, dance, music, and other forms of expression, has now been reduced to a rotting shell.

The Saloon is considerably more upscale but caters to Goths only on Monday nights, which is enough for us to love them for it. The bar is known for making notoriously stiff drinks. One mixed drink, as we say, is like *seven* anywhere else. It is decidedly a "gay man's" bar, and its décor is almost blatantly sexist. They might as well put up a sign that says, "lesbians stay out", but instead they choose to express their bias in less-verbal ways. The women's restrooms are so pathetic, small, and unclean that women habitually just use the immaculate men's room which is clean and lit with romantic mood lights. The walls throughout the club are plastered with elegant portraits of muscular men in their underwear, and posters promoting their "shower contest night" sport muscular hunks lathered up with soap and water. The main dance area features a small stage with a glass shower cage where the audience can watch the shower contestants. On Monday nights, it typically features a dominatrix who, for a fee, will invite you up on stage to be whipped, spanked, and tortured. There's also a "fire bar" featuring an elegant fireplace, a "video bar" which plays music videos all night, and, my favorite, the "movie bar" which plays "bad" movies all night.

Inari said she loves Monday nights at The Saloon. I can't believe I've never met her up until this point. In fact, it is almost *suspect*. She tells me that she loves Monday nights here, but I am absolutely positive that I have been the most regular patron of Hard Mondays now for the last several years, and if a girl like that ever showed up anywhere in this club, I would have noticed her. I almost wonder if she's trying to inflate her status by playing up how active she is in my favorite club.

She shows up with her "ride". Now she cannot easily declare her "ride" is anything other than her boyfriend. He's a sturdy gentleman, not exactly a hunk, but well dressed and polite. As I have now physical confirmation in the flesh that she is very much "taken", I am polite and careful not to encroach on her relationship. I don't believe it is right to come in-between healthy relationships and I talk to Inari with no intention of "hitting" on her.

The conversation turns to subjects that I normally wouldn't talk about to someone I just met. Past relationships are discussed... it had only been a few weeks since Amber's eviction, and it is still on my mind, and Laura, my ex-fiancée has also been dragging me down lately with her overbearing requests for money. I could use a good friend who would listen to my stories. Inari is a great listener.

"You know, people have so much fun at your parties that you don't need to spend $500 on booze for everyone," she says.

"I know. The next one will probably be too big for me to fund on my own, so I'll have to get others to contribute to the alcohol supply. This time around, however, I just wanted there to be absolutely no excuse for someone to not show up. I wanted to meet as many people as possible in a short time."

"But people like you the way you are, regardless of whether you're spending all your money on them. You don't need to flaunt your money to make friends."

"Well... maybe people like me... I dunno. I've got a very deliberate plan with what I'm doing here, you know. I'm looking for a special someone... and this was just the first step. In all honesty when I find this person... I'm going to get the fuck out of this scene. I don't need nor want to be popular nor rich. But what I *do* want out of life is for one person on this planet to love and understand me exactly the way I am, and for me to love her in return. I don't have the capacity in my heart to love more than one person, I give myself completely to only *one* and *one alone*, all the polyamory and swingers clubs really turn me off. To not love your partner exclusively is greedy if you ask me."

I am pleased that Inari has wholesome things to say. "Yeah, I don't really like sleeping around," she says. "So many of my friends have caught stuff, it's not funny at all. It's unclean. I won't ever date anyone unless they get tested for STDs... herpes ... I don't want any of that crap."

Since Jin seems rather quiet, merely nodding in attention, I make a point to ask Jin about his hobbies. "I've been studying martial arts, Taekwondo," he offers.

"Oh yeah? Are you like a blackbelt or something?" I ask.

"No not yet, but I'll get there. I study every day," he says.

"I really wish you would just spend more time with me, Jin. You don't really need to study Taekwondo every day!" Inari lightheartedly complains.

"Yes… I do," he says firmly.

As he says this I get a hint of an impression that he feels the need to study martial arts if only to get away from Inari's smothering grip. But at this point, I know nothing about either of them, and I cannot pass judgment and write it off as playful banter.

"So, I mean, can you kick some ass?" I joke.

Inari interjects, "Yeah, Jin, go ahead and tell the story about how you kicked 3 guys' asses at one time."

Jin almost seems to blush, but Jin seems too sturdy and polite to blush. Instead, he merely pauses, calculating his thoughts like an old computer rendering its next brilliant chess move. "Well, 3 guys surrounded me on the street and I took two of them down. I knocked one out, subdued one, and the other ran off. The cops told me that the way the law works is that they could technically take me in for assault with a deadly weapon, since I know martial arts, but they weren't going to do that because they didn't believe I was in the wrong."

Inari smiles in a way that seems cartoonishly fantastical as if she thinks his story is a hilarious fantasy. Jin merely keeps a steady, expressionless face and the conversation continues. I don't really care that much about what Jin has to say, because I rarely find interest in men as friends or interests in regular masculine things in general. Certainly, martial arts are not in my realm of interest. Karate seems like a waste of time to me. I turn my attention to Inari instead for most of the night. She is the charismatic one.

Jin mostly just nods his head in attention as Inari and I have enthusiastic, emphatic conversations about everything from the music we like to our favorite TV shows. Jin is polite, of few words, but attentive and agreeable. He seems self-assured, confident, and unthreatened by my presence, but either he is barely participating in the conversation, getting steamrolled by my fanatic connection with his girlfriend, or maybe I just simply don't care about Jin enough to remember anything he said… any of those three scenarios could be true.

Maybe it was a mutual connection, or maybe it was entirely just *her* extreme charisma that carried our conversation. She had so much charisma which, combined with her beauty, made her a potent potion when you had her attention. After a while, even with Jin sitting next to her, I start feeling us getting physically closer, and I stop myself from getting too close… too friendly. To make it appear less like I am flirting, I start to talk about Amber. I don't know if it is a mistake, but I thought it might be reassuring to *him* to hear me talk about drama with another girl.

Inari laughs with me, as she knew Amber from the "dodgeball" scene. People used to make fun of her because she was a generally awful person. They called her "herpe trap" because she would get nerdy guys to buy her things, and when they thought that they might eventually "get some action" she would tell them that she had herpes and refuse to sleep with them.

As Inari and I laugh and joke and poke fun, with Jin *only occasionally* chiming in and nodding by her side, I find myself bringing my body closer and closer. It starts to feel a bit too friendly, even to the degree that Jin seems a little startled and taken aback. I notice him slightly agitated with how animated we are with each other… like he's feeling left out of the conversation. He puts his hand on her leg and strokes her thigh over her petticoat. It seems to be a signal for me to "back off". I look down with my peripheral vision so as not to make it obvious that I am reactive to his move, and I almost feel like maybe he's giving *her* a signal too.

I'm disappointed that I can't get as close as I want to her, but it's all good… I don't intend to attempt to mess with what I perceive to be a good relationship. Good, happy relationships deserve to remain happy without interference from me. When two people are good together, I've always maintained that it is best to leave them be.

But I keep in mind that there have been many times in the past when I wish other men would have followed my own rules of engagement. I think to myself, *"What kind of pussy am I? There isn't another guy in this room who would back away from a girl so gorgeous and sweet just because she had a boyfriend, and if she were mine, I'd have to fight tooth and nail to keep her by my side from all the vultures who would seek to steal her upon any sign of weakness from me."*

Regardless of whether it is fair or not, I consider that it is never a good moral choice to try and steal someone away. I *try* to live by the golden rule, even though I fail sometimes.

Even if her admiration of me is totally platonic... I feel admired by her, and I certainly admire her myself. I keep in the back of my mind how blunt she was with me at the party... she was, after all, quite forward with me. But maybe she was just being friendly and playful. I've been misled by a few "flirts" in my lifetime. I've been around the block. Nevertheless, I'm not giving up on this girl. If anything, she's just too damn nice to ignore for any reason. I have no choice but to continue contact with her.

As the week continues, I invite her to go out to the haunts I love, but it is all in vain, and although I expect nothing more than friendship, I certainly hope she comes out one of these nights if I simply keep insisting. She is rare, very rare. It is already apparent.

Chapter 3 - Save the Princess

Although my expectations are low, I can't get Inari out of my head.
I am hypercritical of the conversation choices I made when we
were talking, and I worry a bit that I talked too much about the past
and too negatively. Whereas the conversation of the other night
was intense in a good way, it also dove quite a bit into the past,
complaints, and condemnations… and that's invariably a mistake
when meeting new people. Maybe that's why I didn't see her the
rest of the week. Maybe she saw the cracks in my smile, saw that I
was dwelling on past issues, and figured I wasn't into her.
Regardless, the past is still resolving itself. The whole drama with
Amber weeks ago resulted in conflicts with other friends.

Enter Echo. Echo and I have a long, long, history. I met her when
she was just 15 years old. She was a cute blonde punk rocker back
then. Back in those days, we hung out in "indie" coffee houses.
Coffee houses were where people went to meet people before
social media existed. Inspired by the Seattle grunge craze of the
'90s, "Cosmic Charlie's" became my favorite haunt. I don't even
drink coffee, but it was just a place to go to meet people outside of
the bar scene. I was in my early 20s and made friends of all ages,
from age 15 - 70. I met people very slowly most of the time and
might not have met *anyone at all* if I hadn't offered free rides to
everyone. Eventually, people figured out they could trust and rely
on me for transportation and my network of non-paying customers
grew over time as Cosmic Charlies became a booming scene,
swarmed with regular patrons every day. Sometimes, I'd drive a
dozen people in and out of the coffee house every day, yet I was
still lonely, girlfriendless.

Echo hung out with homeless punks. They wore matching leather
jackets strewn with metal studs and crudely painted white lettering
on their backs. She might have even been homeless herself for a
bit, but I don't really know. But I know she and her friends didn't
really get to eat good food too often. I would take her away from
the coffee shop and offer to buy her lunch at a fancy Italian joint in
the neighborhood on the occasion that I needed some company.

When we were done eating, we'd go back to the coffee house. I'd bring a little extra for her punk friends, and they would devour it within seconds as if they hadn't eaten in a year.

Echo had a typical broken family life. Her mother and father were divorced, but from the little bit that I knew of them, they seemed to love their daughter very much. They maybe just kept her on a leash that was a bit too long. Her mother would lose track of where she was because Echo could just tell her that she was staying at her dad's place or vice versa and her mother and father didn't appear to want to communicate to each other about her whereabouts.

Echo and Luna, the 5 ft tall, fence-leaping, blonde ex-girlfriend, would become best friends by the time they were entering their 5th and 6th years of their 4-year high school education. During this time they were often spending their weekends in my St. Paul apartment.

I used to fix Echo's mother's computer all the time. Her mother used to complain about how Luna's parents weren't keeping track of their daughter as good parents should.

"They should be getting her to finish school and not letting her stay at your place on the weekends," she'd complain. "Do they really have any idea what their daughter is getting into? Where's the parenting!? I am glad she's staying with you, though. If I didn't trust you so much, I'd be inclined to chat with them."

"Yeah, I try to motivate her to graduate, you know. It shouldn't be all that hard to graduate. I don't endorse her laziness. We fight about it from time to time and she just lashes out at me for being some kind of 'know it all'."

Echo's mother, however, seemed not to acknowledge that her *own* daughter was in the same boat, unable to finish school, and seemed completely unaware that her *own daughter* usually stayed over with Luna and me every weekend. We even floated the idea of becoming a 3-some on a few occasions, but Luna and I both had feelings of jealousy and agreed to stay exclusive.

Luna had barely half the credits she needed to graduate by her 6th year of high school. Every semester she dug herself a deeper hole, constantly skipping school. The Goth scene was sucking them in. Despite enabling their bad behaviors, I was ultimately the only person keeping them somewhat honest... holding them back from diving into the deep end of the party scene, where orgies and hard drugs were commonplace. All this was happening less than one block away from my apartment, in another basement apartment on Cathedral Hill, heavily driven by Zak, one of my least-favorite people in the scene.

I enjoyed the company of Luna and Echo, but deep in my heart, I knew that they were eventually going to get sucked into the mindless self-indulgence taking place up the street. The parties promised free love and free sexual expression in all forms, and Luna's mother was dying of lung cancer, causing her to have a need for distraction and instant gratification. Her need to escape was incessant while she dealt with the pain of her home life. As they got closer to all the temptation, it was inevitable that Luna would break my heart. I could no longer keep her away from Zak's events. She wanted to be free while she was still young and beautiful. She said it "wasn't fair" of me to take that away from her. I could write a whole book just on the events surrounding our dramatic and explosive breakup, but instead, I created a musical tribute, a sad, beautiful, concept album that I called "Luna and the Destroyer".

We'll revisit this story later, but for now, let me just say that when it was done, I could not be anywhere near her, or *anyone* associated with the scene. I would have nightmares at night wondering what she was getting into over there, but the worst nightmares were actually happy dreams. I would dream that she and I got back together, that she loved me, that we were enjoying good times like we always did. I dreamed of her looking up into my eyes, twinkling, with her rainbow hair, in a beautiful white dress, and telling me she loved me just before she kissed me. These dreams were the worst of all because when I would wake up from my sleep, I would realize that it was just a dream. Every time this happened, I would feel my heart shatter all over again, and I would start my days feeling like I was dumped by the love of my life, nearly every single morning.

I had to break free. I had to go… fast. All my friends were at these parties, however, and I couldn't keep my composure with Luna around. Out of mad desperation, I used some vilification and manipulation to ensure that Luna was uninvited from the parties so that I could attend them without having to see her. I tried a number of things that seemed to have no effect. Zak didn't really care that she slept around, that she was getting in too deep with drugs, being horrible to her mother, or being unfair and unfaithful to me, but Zak knew that I had money, and Luna had none… and that by inviting me, I would contribute booze to his parties, whereas Luna would just "mooch" and consume the contributions of others, being a jobless, high school dropout.

Finally, I mustered up the courage, went into the Portland Ave, basement apartment, armed with a large contribution of booze, and was greeted immediately by some girls playing a kissing game where the objective is simply to pass an ice cube from one person to the next. I more or less latched onto the first girl that would pay attention to me at the party, a Goth girl named Laura. Beautiful she was, by any standard. By the end of the night, we were making out in a corner, despite the fact that I knew basically nothing about her. She was intensely shy, but not opposed to shoving her tongue down my throat all night. Eventually, she and I ran away from everyone, went one block over to my apartment where I took her virginity. Thereafter, she and I became reclusive. Laura's shy personality was ideal as we spent 8 years happily isolated from everyone, essentially just watching Lord of the Rings on repeat, studying, and working on computer software. I had little desire to reconnect to the fringes of the sex-crazed club scene during this time.

While Laura and I tried our best to get along and build a life together, away from them, Echo and Luna continued their friendship over the years in my absence. I talked to Luna on average, once a year. When we talked, we never brought up our relationships. We barely got past small talk. We seemed to be completely, emotionally blocked off from each other.

As I write this, however, Laura and I have recently separated ways. It took me the last two years to break out of my social coma and meet people again. I began by shyly peering into the old haunts that I used to love, trying, carefully, to contain my emotions as I got closer and closer to the nucleus of the scene that betrayed me so severely a decade ago, still hoping to never have to see Luna again.

Echo, now an adult in her late 20's is still a mere 4ft.-11in. tall. She abandoned her punk friends in her teens and now is one of the most classically Goth girls I know. She wears colorful hair extensions, corsets, and fancy dresses, and aspires to be a fashion designer, occasionally putting on runway shows.

There are several fashion designers in the Minneapolis Goth scene. They make the many exotic articles of clothing that the kids wear in the clubs and at parties. So much of the scene revolves around fashion. Techna and Echo are well-known fashion designers, and Amber, Luna, and Inari all model for their runway shows. Luna's brother takes care of photography, Jin does business management, and other friends take care of lighting and sound. I'd been getting to know the fashion scene more and more and would often help out Techna with her shows locally.

After a decade-long silence with Echo, in the lonely days after Laura moved out, Echo and I reconnected. We got Italian food, like old times, flirted, but we never really made it past friendship… so having turned over that stone and finding nothing, I began turning over others. One night I found myself at her place for a party. That's where I met stoner party-girl Amber, who latched onto me and moved into my house just 2 weeks later.

News of this shocked Echo, because Echo and I were sort of

dating… well flirting at best. Echo was just hurt that Amber blocked her from getting to me, and, in truth, Echo had rejected me already. I would have given Echo more if she wanted it, but she didn't. Regardless of whether there were any official contracts signed between us, feelings of jealousy arose anyway. Maybe it hurt her extra because Echo had been betrayed by Amber multiple times, and Amber had a routine of stealing Echo's boyfriends… Echo's specifically! I questioned why Amber would even be invited to a party at her place if she had done that even *once*. In a nutshell, Amber's brief invasion of my life left wounds that needed to be mended with Echo, and tonight, at The Saloon, Echo and I agreed beforehand to chat frankly about mending things.

Amber's leaving hurt me more than it hurt Amber, and naturally, I sought out emotional support from friends, including Echo. But for some reason, Echo liked to take both sides of any argument. In emails and texts, I called her out for being "two-faced" earlier in the week. I told her that if she took both sides of an argument, she was taking *no* sides at all! I thought it was slimy and dishonest to pretend to agree with one friend while simultaneously telling your friend's enemy that you agree with them at the same time. Furthermore, the "enemy" in question was Amber, who betrayed not only *me* but *Echo* as well.

"Why the fuck won't you take a side, Echo?" I demand to know of her. "Amber has routinely targeted your boyfriends and stolen them from you. It is like she is doing it out of spite for you. If there's any time that you should be taking a side, it is *now!* If you're not on my side, Echo, then you're not my friend."

"It is not my business to come in between friends," she replies. "I just don't do that. It is not how I operate."

In the middle of our serious conversation, Inari and Jin arrive.

I am happy to see both of them, but it awkwardly cuts off the argument I am having with Echo. I can't help but pause for a moment to take in Inari's beauty… as she is more beautiful than anyone could ever dream. The four of us stand in a circle for a few minutes making small talk until Echo decides to go out on the patio to smoke.

"You'll have to excuse me for a moment. I should go check up on Echo," I say. "We were just resolving some personal issues."

"You're going on the smoking patio? But you don't smoke, do you?" Inari asks.

"Oh, no... not at all! I was just going to check on her... we're resolving personal issues," I reply.

Inari leans forward into my ear and speaks in the most sultry, seductive voice she has used with me yet. "You have no idea how much more I love you now," she says.

I'm shaking in my boots as I walk away. I retreat to the smoking patio, but there I do not continue my conversation with Echo. Echo has found other friends to chit-chat with. Instead, I just stand out there, alone, pondering what Inari's words, spoken moments earlier, and their inflection, could mean.

What is with this sideways declaration of love? Is it sarcasm?... no way. A joke?... no way! Am I just overreacting to this word, "love"? She didn't say it like brotherly-sisterly love, friendly love, motherly love... it was straight up, seductive, like "my god I'm so 'in love' with you 'love'". Am I just being too sensitive? But really, even though it is just a sideways statement, nobody has ever said anything to me like that in that voice, using such a strong word, "love", with such an inflection... and yet in reference to something seemingly mundane, like smoking. But maybe it isn't about something so simple. Maybe she is referencing something way bigger. Maybe she is trying to tell me that she's been dreaming of me while we were apart and wants to make it obviously clear to me that she loves me. I ponder, wildly confused. As you will learn throughout this entire book, Inari had a spooky way of getting me to second guess the meanings behind her blunt statements and accept her own realities regarding minor or even major events… but I don't want to give away the story. But let me just say, be on the lookout. It is easy to deny the meaning of a sentence if you have the power of her radiance, shine, and interpersonal charisma, especially if you leave a dash of plausible deniability in every grandiose thing you say. This scene is full of incestuous people who cheapen the word "love" and casually fornicate with each other, but I do not believe Inari to be a casual fornicator.

Since she had shown herself to be a woman of choice, abnormally strong words, who shows me unusually strong affections, as I ponder on the patio, I think to myself that maybe her use of the word "love" in the fleeting sense is a signal to me. Whatever she is doing, whatever her intentions, I'm going to find out!

This is a motivational turning point for me. She is, after all, the most beautiful and kind girl I've ever met. For the rest of the night, I begin to see how far I can push our conversational boundaries. I had been politely restraining myself during our earlier encounters. But now I need to see how far down this rabbit hole I can go.

When a girl this amazing shows affection to a geeky guy like me, I simply *have no choice* but to see where it leads. If you frown upon my actions from here on out, just bear in mind… I, in no way, had a choice in any of this. I *had* to see where I could take my relationship with this girl. If I didn't walk this path, I would have regretted it for the rest of my life. And if I *did*, I might *also* regret it. But, either way… it would be exciting!

Something in my brain snaps and I just let loose. I say to myself, "Fuck it… I'm all in," and… the rest of the night is … absolutely amazing. The electricity between us lights up in a way that I've never experienced in my life. I emotionally charge at her with my eyes, locking eyes, squaring shoulders, and she charges right back, placing her face inches away from mine as I praise her beauty and sweetness interweaved with small talk and sweet nothings. She just soaks up everything I say and returns compliments, whereas any other girl I interacted with this way would have certainly been uncomfortable to have a guy like me so blatantly and bluntly "hitting" on her. The ease at which she allows me to get close to her makes me feel at peace. I find the confidence to gaze into her eyes, and she gazes back into mine and smiles deeply. I begin to think that this girl might even "love" me. I find confidence in myself that I've never felt at any other time in my life.

But Jin is there. Jin is talking to other friends just 5 feet away from us in this noisy club, possibly able to see our body language, but not able to hear us. It is not my intention to hurt Jin or come in between a good relationship. Yet as I boldly stand across from her, literally holding both her hands and gazing into her eyes, I wonder…

"I'm sorry, I'm getting too close," I declare.

"I don't have a personal space bubble, really. You can't get too close to me," she says.

I cock one eyebrow and think to myself that no girl wants some guy she just met in her face so much that if he moved his nose 2 inches closer, he'd be making out with her in front of her boyfriend. I owe it to her to back off.

"I shouldn't be getting too friendly with you," I repeat.

"Trust me... you cannot go too far," she reaffirms.

"But you know… this…" I gesture to Jin, "this is a good thing… right? I don't want to feel like I'm encroaching on something good."

This is a signal for her to tell me what *is not* good about her relationship with Jin. She seems to understand this because she follows suit.

"It's not all that good at *all*," she says. "He's dumped me twice already and didn't even give me a reason! The last time was just before Con which really hurt because that's where we met." She sighs and looks away, "He loves me about as much as a robot can love someone."

And there it is. Her relationship with Jin is clearly on the out-and-out. If he dumped her twice, certainly a 3rd dumping was only just around the corner. Their relationship clearly isn't going to last. I am straight with her, even as Jin is no more than 5 feet away from us. "You deserve better," I say. "How on earth is it remotely possible for anyone to not be madly in love with you? You are the kindest, most beautiful, and sweet girl I have ever met in my entire life. If he doesn't love you, there's something really wrong with him!" I hold both her hands again. I gaze into her eyes again. "I'm *really* glad I met you," I say.

She pauses, blushes, and smiles as-if soaking in the warmth radiating from my heart. "I'm really glad I met you too," she says.

In my own mind, I now commit myself to her emotionally. There is no girl on planet earth I want more. I see no reason to devote myself to any other pursuits. I faithfully commit myself to getting to know her better. Operation "Save the Princess" has begun.

I honestly believe that our feelings for each other are mutually intense. My blood is replaced with heroine.... we talk and talk and talk until the bar closes about all the things people talk about. She is kind and sympathetic when I tell her of my dog's health struggles, struggles with people, growing up, and how I became the person I am. It is incredibly rare that anyone ever shows this level of interest in anything I had to say. Knowing that she will allow it, I become more and more comfortable touching her hands. I caress them again and again. Our eyes lock and stay locked for what seems to be an eternity, and this feeling alone is better than all the sex I've ever had in my life. I am instantly addicted to her eyes and would do anything to look into them again, and I feel compelled to foreshadow that, 10 years later, I still regard these very moments to be among the happiest memories of my life.

At the end of the night, I am glowing. The bar kicks all the patrons out onto the sidewalk, and everyone loiters for a while to say their goodbyes. Inari reconnects with Jin after hours of intense conversation exclusively with me. I look over at her. I can't hear what they are saying, but their body language gives off vibes like she's trying to find a reason to stay out longer and ditch him for the night.

"Could this really be happening?" I think to myself. I cannot hear what they're saying but they're visibly arguing. She has a sad expression on her face as he tries to talk to her. She seems almost angry; she doesn't want to go home with him. He pressures her. She wipes tears from her eyes, and as she does this, I catch her glancing over at me.

I find my friend Maddox, a long-haired, kilt-wearing, bearded, lanky man who, being a complete sociopath, often offers me unsolicited sage-like advice. We both lean up against the building and simply absorb the scene unfolding in front of us.

"I think… I think that girl is in-love with me," I say, in an uncharacteristic cocky tone. "What do you think?"

"Well… well… well, I must say she is looking over at you awfully strangely," he says with his characteristic stutter.

"It almost appears to me like she is trying to stay out with me and ditch her boyfriend."

"It… it would appear that your assessment is possible from what I can see from this angle," he stutters. "But… but be careful. If she's willing to do that to him, what might she do to you if you were together?"

"But I don't think it's like that. Sounds like they're on the out-and-out and a girl like her is going to be single for like… 12 hours… we see this kind of thing happen all the time."

"True, maybe. All I can say is, good luck!" he concludes.

Maddox and I pause our talking and sit on a public bench. People bounce between groups to say their final goodbyes… yet no matter in which circle she stands, I find her glancing over at me again and again and again.

I believe in my heart that she is torn between staying with her boyfriend or staying out with me, and God, I don't want this night with her to be over. As Maddox and I continue to monitor her body language as we sit, I decide to perform a cocky experiment.

"Watch this," I say.

I give her a special glance, not a beckoning glance like you might give to a friend you want to come over, but a deep, longing, loving stare. I let her know with my eyes, and my eyes alone, that I want her. We lock eyes… and all it takes is this single look and she instantly comes over and kneels next to me on the concrete at my feet. She grasps my leg as I put one arm around her. Her touch fills my body with warmth and electricity.

"You should come over and hang out with us!" she declares, "I want to stay out later, but Jin says it would be rude because we have Hugo over as a house guest. Still, you should come over and hang out with us. Please?"

"I dunno if I'd totally feel welcome, is Jin okay with that?" I ask.

"It's okay, you should come, you need to come! Please, Yuki!"

"Okay, but I don't know where I'm going. Do you have an address?" I ask.

At this moment, Jin approaches to steal her away from me and her voice becomes more urgent, "Well, just find Hugo and follow him!" she says. Jin pulls her away. He practically drags her by the arm, and, as she scurries away with him, she looks back over her shoulder, and repeats, "Find Hugo!" she says.

I look around me. Hugo is nowhere to be found, and I realize that all of the people loitering have now suddenly gone as if they vanished, and since I can't find Hugo... I don't know where to go.

I resign for the night, sending her a text, apologizing, and asking for the address again... but she never responds to any of my texts. It is confusing because I would figure that if she really wanted to see me, but found me absent, she might check her phone to see if I tried to contact her. Unfortunately, this night... is done. I want to be with her more... but it is just not possible in this physical universe. I have absolutely no idea where she went. Instead, I go home alone with this feeling of love sickness weighing on my heart, but with hope for the future.

Chapter 4 - Love Letters

Since I am unable to reach Inari at the end of the night, my love sickness gets the best of me. I feel compelled to write to her. The next day, I send her a long love letter. I spill my guts to her. It is full of sappy, blunt stuff... tons of it.

Inari,

I am so very glad I met you, and I am so very glad you've made such an effort to get to know me. And let me say that I know in my heart that you are a great, wonderful person who cares about others and that makes you such a rare, rare gem.

So let me just say.... the thing I want for you more than anything in the world is for you to be happy, no matter what the cost is to me. I always feel a bit out of line getting close to someone unavailable, and I would feel selfish if I corrupted something good for my own personal gain. But there are undeniable truths that I cannot let slip away whenever I interact with you, and I feel compelled to lay my cards down on the table.

I believe that those who know what TRUE love is... deserve the TRUEST of love... and deserve to have that love reciprocated. You told me repeatedly last night that no matter what I say, I can't cross a line with you... so I'm going to go a bit heavy here and simply hope that you appreciate what I have to say.

I've always observed you to be shockingly beautiful... but it wasn't until you reached out to me personally that I even understood just how beautiful you REALLY are.

And last night, I have to say, was intense for me... I was glowing... I was beaming... I was smiling... I was happy... all night. I slept like a child last night. I felt like I poured my heart into you, and you poured your heart back in return... and I've never met anyone so willing to do that for me.

I realized that you're not just another shallow face in a sea of greedy manipulators. When I look into the eyes of even some of my most cherished friends in the scene, I see darkness in them. I see darkness all around me. This darkness has always made me sad and, at times, a little bit angry.

But I don't see that same darkness in you. When you even so much as glance at me, it hits me like a bullet.... it communicates to me that you care like no other... and strangely, instead of the panic that I might feel if a girl even 1/10th as beautiful as you looked at me across a room... I am instead overcome with peace, calm, and confidence.

I am self-realized at that moment. My insecurities become meaningless... and I just think to myself that you are the most beautiful, kind, and genuine girl in the galaxy. At that moment, the rest of the world evaporates, and all that's left are me and you, standing in an empty, black space, lit by a lone distant star.

All the unhappy memories of the past are completely forgotten, meaningless, and insignificant... it is as if I have found my first love again or experienced my first kiss... there is only the future and no past... because whatever happened yesterday is meaningless... yesterday? What was yesterday? I don't know. Life begins again at that moment. I feel like life is beginning again for me now.

My #1 mission in life is to love someone who loves me in return... someone who loves every single aspect of my being... despite all my flaws. If I have found that girl, I will love her until the end of time all the same. I have loved those who are far less worthy. I have loved those who are not worthy at all.

But until I met you, I never knew that anyone could be so worthy... but I don't want these feelings to be a burden to you.

I believe that you're perfect... and I can't imagine why anyone would think otherwise. So, whatever results from this crazy, wild, love letter, just know that I am here and will always consider you in the best of light. I will always be absolutely enthralled to have met you... you have brightened up my life significantly already.

I obviously feel like I have so much more to say and share with you, and I want to get to know you on the deepest of levels. We share an invisible energy... I think others see that in us.

I'm sorry I didn't come over last night. I couldn't find Hugo at the end of the night... It was probably best that I stayed away last night to let things simmer for a bit. There will be plenty of time to figure this out... and just know that I am looking forward to whatever comes.

~Yuki

If I said any of that to a girl who wasn't ready to hear it, I'd likely never hear from her again... and... unfortunately... I don't hear from her for about 1.5 days, in fact. It is a little bit jarring. If there truly was as much electricity between us as I thought there was, wouldn't a normal person be eager to check out their social media for love notes from the person they had a mesmerizing experience with the night before? Wouldn't she be eager to send me a message of her own?

The waiting is intense. My brain is on fire and time cannot move fast enough. 1.5 days is a long time to wait when you're madly in love.

Eventually, she calls me. I thought that normal humans didn't use phones these days in favor of less-personal methods of communication. I'm flattered that she'd be so bold as to call me. We make small talk, but she does not acknowledge anything in my love letter, yet I don't really even care as I am just so delighted to hear from her and be able to hear her voice on the other end of the phone.

"I'm really sorry, Hugo had a health problem and we had to take him to the ER," she explains. "Then I fell and scraped up my legs pretty badly. I am supposed to model for a show next week, and now I have to walk the runway with cuts and bruises."

I am delighted that my crazy love letter did not scare her off, assuming she read it. Did she read it? I don't even know. I am so elated to hear from her that I forget to ask.

"Why don't you come out to the North Loop club on Wednesday? I'll buy some rounds, and we'll get to know each other better." I ask.

"That sounds great, I'd like that," she says.

Wow, can this be happening? This girl... this angel... she's calling me! Is it possible she will keep pulling me in? The future appears to be full of magic.

Suddenly, the 1.5 days of waiting all makes sense, thankfully. I'm no longer languishing and confused, but confident again. I totally understand if there were medical emergencies distracting everyone from reaching back at me. I get it.

Chapter 5 - The North Loop

Every Wednesday, I go to the North Loop. It is packed with scenesters, punks, goths, and a whole mix of "dark siders" for a popular 80's dance night. It draws a crowd of generally good people who are respectful of each other. Wednesday nights at the club draw even more people than Fridays or Saturdays. The DJ likes the fact that his night is not on a Friday or Saturday as a weeknight gives him more freedom to play all the retro music he wants. On a Wednesday he's not forced to cater to suburbia. He's not forced to play popular music.

Inari is coming tonight. I am excited. I anticipate her arrival nervously. I can't wait to introduce her around. My old friend and bandmate, David, is there. It is rare for me to see him out on the town so we spend some time catching up, but having toured the country doing hundreds of gigs with David's band, he and I are extremely close, and David knows me better than anyone else in the club.

"I can't wait for you to meet this girl! She is so sweet and I'm so in love, you have to talk me up like I'm some kind of great amazing dude or something, please! It is super important to me! More important than anything ever!" I beg of him.

"But dude, doesn't she have a boyfriend? Isn't that a bad sign? Would you want some guy falling in love with your girlfriend while you were dating?" David asks.

"No, man, but when you see this girl, and you see how she is with me… you just watch. When I get a moment alone with her, things will change between us, our body language will change, we will square up our shoulders and gaze at each other. Things will become instantly intense. She's on the out-and-out with him. It is very apparent. A girl this shockingly beautiful isn't going to stay single for long! I have to make a move! I am going to catch her… I know it, I feel it, intensely!"

The dynamic of this club is unfortunately different, however, and I made some miscalculations in how I imagined this night going. The biggest problem is that the club's outdoor patio is far quieter than The Saloon's noisy indoors. Jin comes with Inari, of course. If I'm to say to Inari what I really want to say, I must pull her away further from everyone, alone, and the intimacy of the outdoor space makes all that virtually impossible. I desperately want to continue whispering sweet nothings to her, but it's not loud enough around us, I have to pull her away.

I am, therefore, forced to find mundane things to talk about. I am talking to Inari and Jin together, therefore, I'm unable to truly say what is on my mind. Jin wants me to help him build a computer. Blah blah blah... I've built hundreds of computers in my life. I talk a bit about how to build a fake Macintosh computer, a "Hackintosh" as they call it, blah blah blah. Jin offers favors in return, but I don't like accepting favors. I have an itch to drive the conversation towards subjects that are more emotionally deep. It is difficult to talk to Inari about deep subjects when her boyfriend is standing next to her.

I elect to talk about this "concept album" I'm working on, but I fear it is a mistake. I love sad music, but other people don't typically share my love of dark depressing songs and don't, especially, want to hear dark depressing concept albums about personal events from my past. I'm told I dwell too much. People just want to hear songs that make them smile and dance, but I'm not a smiley, dancy person. Nobody wants to hear me talk about songs of heartbreak involving an ex-girlfriend, in this case, Luna. But god, I want to talk on a deeper level with her, and it is my only option to emotionally connect to her that I can think of. I want Inari to understand what makes me tick, and I demand to be loved the way I am, gloom and doom and all.

The events that inspired my concept album, which I've entitled "Luna and the Destroyer", occurred 10 years ago and surround my painful breakup with Luna. And whereas, yes, they were deeply troubling to me at the time, I am careful to note that I find it therapeutic to complete the album *now* during a time when I've forgiven the past and moved on.

"I don't think it is unhealthy to reflect on the past and learn from it, and one of the reasons that I was able to escape from being trapped by a girl like Amber was because I had similar experiences of being trapped before." The person I was 10 years ago would have let her run me into the ground for years, but this more mature version of me doesn't take that kind of crap anymore. We all learn from our experiences." I profess.

The album starts with a song written around a love poem I wrote for Luna when we met.

Hope And Ignorance – by Luna and the Destroyer
[hear it at adaloveless.com]

The sky has stars,
the moon an edge,
you see clearly now,
it has come to this,

we walk the mirrors of the skies,
with sandy stars beneath our feet,
fireflies fall from the night,
but our love rises up,

and we know more than mothers,
who are bedridden and sore,
or miles from home,

great days may come,
if we can hope,
for time to confirm,
what we already know,

we take such consequence in stride,
we reach across this new divide,
we whisper only in the dark,
and care not of whose hearts we broke,

and we know more than mothers,
who are bedridden and sore,
or miles from home,

It should be noted that Luna hated the poem because she expected it to be about how beautiful she was and how in love with her I was, but instead I chose to write a poem that plucked out the darkness lurking in the shadows surrounding our meeting. The album as a whole follows the collapse of our relationship and the death of her mother and all the lies and manipulation that ensued during our breakup. I joke, "My album starts depressing, then goes downhill from there. Some people might find that disturbing or pathetic... but I love sad music. The world wouldn't be complete without sad songs. I wanted to write an album that is *all* sad."

"When it is done," I joked to Luna recently, "I'll tie you to a chair and make you listen to it. Then we'll be even."

I made it my summer mission to finish the album. Working on the music helped divert the feelings I had about other recent negative events surrounding "herpe trap" Amber. I really shouldn't have brought it up... The fact that Inari is unavailable, and with Jin, puts me more into a ruminating mood though. To break out of this gloomy spell, I need to *reach* Inari again, like I did the other night. I desperately need to look into her eyes like we had done before! I want those awesome blunt euphoric exchanges that we had been volleying at each other on our previous encounter... but I can't reach her, but I try, but I can't reach her, I can't reach her... I just feel more and more glum, more alone, more frustrated.

Eventually, after hours of drivel... mundane conversation about stupid nothings that random people talk about in bars, I finally get a lone, single moment with her. Jin leaves us alone to grab a drink... our body postures change... we square up shoulders and gaze into each other's eyes and talk immediately about things that he would certainly find inappropriate.

"Did you get my email?" I ask.

"Yes," she replies… "I don't know what to say; I get things like that all the time…you know… Amber…" Inari looks away and to the side and towards the ground.

I cut her off, frantically spouting words in a whisper so as not to let my words travel beyond her ears. "Wait wait wait," I say, frantically manic. "Why are you mentioning Amber at all? I meant what I said in that email… Amber doesn't exist to me anymore… there's only *you*. There's only future, no past… no one else matters! If you ever catch me talking about Amber, you understand, it is just a diversion… I'm just trying to make it seem to Jin like I'm not chasing you."

She gives me some taken-aback, confused looks, but doesn't have time to reply. Before I can press the subject any further, Jin returns with her drink, and I am flustered and frustrated that I made it appear that there were cracks in my love for her. I am unable to clarify or plead with her as we must immediately change the subject to simpler, shallower things.

As my two minutes of alone time with Inari has now expired, I skulk over to Maddox and David, standing by a Greek stone statue on the patio. I say nothing, frustrated, and simply lean against the wooden fence looking back at Jin and Inari, continuing a group conversation in a small huddle on the other side.

"I'm looking very forward to living vicariously through you!" Maddox says.

I simply smile a frustrated smile. But even if I only had a couple of minutes to talk to her alone and the 2 minutes felt incomplete… It was a beautiful 2 minutes of complete embarrassment.

At the end of the night, standing on the boulevard, Jin is busy in conversation a few feet away. Here, I get a few last words. Feeling the night winding down, I tell her that she can call me any time, day or night, and she says that I can do the same. She warns me that she's terrible about answering her phone and I may have to call her 12 times before she answers, but she assures me that it is okay to call 12 times in a row. "Just keep calling me until I answer," she says. "I sleep like a brick but it's okay to wake me up."

"Okay, I'll call you 12 times, but I'll stop at 13. Okay?" I say, semi-joking.

As she's about to leave I stroke her forearm, gently, slowly scratching her with my fingernails as I gaze into her eyes, telepathically communicating "goodbye". She smiles brightly and strokes my forearm in exactly the same way. These 5 seconds would be the highlight of tonight as she leaves without words, but just a smile, a touch, and a glow as she steps away from me backwards, still gazing, being dragged by her other arm... by Jin.

Chapter 6 - 1993

I really hope she isn't serious about making me call her 12 times in a row because that would make me feel like some kind of creepy stalker. But I suppose if I have her permission, what can I do? It's my only option.

Thankfully, when I call her the next day, she answers on the first attempt. It seems like I'm waking her up from a nap, but she says she's not napping "yet". I apologize and say that I can call her back later, but she stays awake, and we just start chatting. I take this time mostly to chat about small talk.

I learn of her infatuation with foxes and wolves. "I wish I were a wolfer or a fox! I just want a fox tail. Maybe I'll dress up as a wolf for Halloween, but most years I just end up spending so much time helping Barry with his costume that I don't have time to work on my own. Maybe this year will be different!" she says.

"I'll help you with your costume," I eagerly reply, knowing that whereas I love Halloween and costumes, I'm actually terrible at dealing with my *own* costumes. I'm not crafty, but I'll pretend or try to be if it results in quality time with Inari. "I think I've seen pictures of you and Barry online, didn't you used to date?" I ask.

"Yeah, but that was a long time ago. Years ago. Now we're just roommates and he's my best friend," she says. "We were working together, managing a kitchen for a catering business, but I got laid off, and I'm in between jobs now."

I think to myself that, gosh, Barry must have some serious self-control to be living with an ex-girlfriend like Inari. I would be tortured with jealousy to be so close to her, yet watch her drift off into relationships with other men. I just couldn't do it. I would go insane. I wish I had such poise and self-control, but I do not.

"Well are you looking for a new job then, how are you making money?" I ask.

"Well, I live really cheaply. I don't own much and I don't need much to survive," she says.

"Yeah, but you have a house and rent, right?" I question. "I mean I pay $90 a month just for a cell phone, and you have one of those! You can't survive without a job!"

"If you're paying that much for a phone you're getting ripped off. I got a special deal on mine for $35 with unlimited talk time," she replies. "You should look into it."

"Hmmm, maybe. I shopped around and they didn't offer me a deal like that," I say. In 2011, most people still have limits on the number of minutes the phone company will offer for free. I had been bouncing around from company to company to try and find an "unlimited" plan. Many companies simply didn't offer such a thing until recently, and even now that those plans are available, they cost a premium. $35 is quite surprising to me.

The more I talk to her about financial stuff, the more I get the impression that possibly someone else is handling her finances for her. Maybe she leans on Barry for such things. Maybe she gets her cell phone from a family plan, or by piggybacking on a friend's account. Her hair is immaculate, professionally done, probably at a cost of hundreds of dollars every month. A girl can't have hair like that and not be making any money, and there's no way she can maintain all the weaves and extensions and color of it without regular appointments. There's no way she can do it all herself, there's just too much going on there, too much to perfectly tend to, and no way for her to properly maintain the parts that are in the back of her head. Maybe she has some money in savings, but she worked in a catering business, and there's no way she wouldn't be living paycheck to paycheck, living in a house on her own, paying for expensive hair appointments on top of utility bills. It doesn't really make sense, but I don't really know anything about her situation, and I'm not judging.

I brush off the inconsistencies. In some ways, I find her naivety to be adorable. I want someone in my life for whom I feel good doing things. I want someone who finds value in the skills that I bring to a relationship, and her kindness and sweetness are more valuable to me than anything.

As the conversation turns deeper, I learn of her "fucked up" family life. She says she's the "fuck-up of the fuck-up of the family", borne out of wedlock to a mother who was more of a big sister to her than a mother. Her family was full of uncles and aunts who were "successful" as she called it. They raised their noses at her mother and therefore raised their noses at her. She grew up with her grandparents as if they were her parents. Her mother was a defiant young teenager when she gave birth, and a defiant, underachieving tween as she became older. Inari was never her mother's priority and caring about her daughter was far from the first thing on her mind.

Her mother refused to tell her who her father was growing up. She promised to tell her when she turned 18 (when she could no longer be the subject of a custody battle) but when the time came, her mother *still* refused to tell her who her father was. "Your father doesn't know you exist," she said. Inari felt awkward seeking out her father. She feared that if she introduced herself to him that he'd ask her how big of a check to write and send her on her way, but Inari didn't want money; she wanted a father.

Inari's grandparents were her saviors. Her grandparents loved her growing up and still love her now. Except for one uncle, they are the only oasis of affection in a family that she feels looks down upon her.

"I find it difficult to believe that anyone would look down upon you Inari. You are the most kind, caring, and sweet girl I've ever met in my life and that includes all the pastors and ministers I've ever met," I assure her.

Jin is cooking food while she and I talk. He has been cooking for maybe an hour and interrupts our conversation to tell her that food is ready. Whereas she acknowledges him, she continues talking with me as if addicted to our conversation.

We talk quite a bit about religion and atheism. "I acquired quite the stack of books outside my bedroom door," she says. "My grandparents were always pushing books on me because they thought I was turning to the devil or something."

"I'm definitely not a religious person," I state, believing her to be in agreement. "I spent many years researching cults, mystery cults, religious cults, and secular cults. At this point in my life, I am convinced that any dogma not rooted in science is dangerous to society. Do you know what organization, government, or other entity has murdered more people than any other organization in history?" I ask.

"I don't know, but I'd imagine the Nazis… Hitler?" she replied.

"No. It's actually the Catholic church. The inquisition not only murdered but *tortured* millions of people with horrible devices, like 'the rack'! Have you ever heard of 'The Judas Cradle'? It is basically a spike that they ram up your butt. The 'Spider' rips your breasts apart. But sometimes they'd just hang you upside down and saw you in half, beginning with your crotch. Why? Because you didn't believe in their version of the bible. Maybe you were a protestant, like a Lutheran or a Presbyterian. Anyone who didn't join the Catholic church was essentially a heretic, and fair game for torture. All this nonsense because people want to force everyone else to believe their own versions of some old ghost stories."

"Yeah, that's no good," Inari seems to agree. "I believe in respecting other people's spiritual choices, as long as they don't impose them on others."

"Well, I subscribe to what is called 'militant atheism'. Which is that religious dogma needs to be called out and banished for what it is. It is all a bunch of fairy tales and lies that don't deserve to influence governments or critical thinking establishments, schools, science… You should read this guy, Sam Harris. He basically wrote the Atheist's bible and opens his book by challenging the very definition of 'belief'. It is very enlightening."

"I suppose I'll have to check that out… interesting," Inari agrees.

I don't try to profess my love to her at all during this call. Instead, I just try to use this time to take another baby step in building a lasting friendship with her. I am happy that she would award me so much of her time. Her fashion show is the next day. I look forward to seeing her there.

20-30 minutes have now passed since Jin summoned her to dinner. He returns, a little bit annoyed. Her food at this point is probably ice cold. She finally concedes that she should have been eating right now, so I say my goodbyes and tell her that I'll see her tomorrow. "I'll be there for *you*, ya know? I'm going to support *you*," I say.

It was the longest phone conversation I've had with anyone since I was in high school. I didn't think kids talked on the phone these days. Everyone is so paranoid about running over their minute allotment for their cell phone plans; no one ever talks on the phone for extended periods. They chat online, they text, and then they get together in person, but no one talks on the phone. The fact that Inari is so up-front and personal with me is flattering. I love it.

Maybe it is just her way of doing things, but I feel special. She is personable and beyond charismatic. I look forward to the show the next day and I make sure I get to the box office early enough to get a ticket before they sell out.

Looking back, I probably should have steered the conversation into the deepest, blunt, relationship subjects that I couldn't talk about when Jin was around. I should have just professed my love to her right there and overtly. But I guess I felt it appropriate to make sure I *knew* the girl I was falling in love with, and we talked about all kinds of things for over 2 hours.

Chapter 7 - The Fet Ball

The Fet Ball is a major event for Goths and anyone open and honest about their sexuality. Hosted by a world-famous dominatrix, its magnetism attracts all the regulars from our haunts. They come dressed as gimps, in formal Victorian gowns, dapper suits, adorning lace, sporting whips, chains, diapers, heels, leather, spandex, latex, dressed in drag, spikes. Whatever your kink, there's no shame.

The Varsity Theater is decked out with elegant fixtures, lighting, and artwork. Even the restrooms are a work of art, featuring a grand co-ed wash area where men and women congregate together around elegant brick architecture, beautiful faucets, and indoor foliage, lit masterfully and romantically.

Our friend Wheels is a feature of the sideshow. He has no legs, but instead of getting around in a wheelchair, he chooses to roll on the floor and get around using his hands to scoot his body around. He is high-spirited, especially considering his condition, and enjoys working the sideshows and enticing attractive young ladies to stand on his chest. He is well-loved in the scene. A mutual friend even gave him a T-shirt that says "Welcome" on it in the form of a welcome mat, which he wears to every special outing. Wheels has many friends and is popular with the girls who sit on the floor to have eye-to-eye conversations with him.

A whole variety show on the main stage features fire dancers, sword swallowers, magic shows, and a man who cuts himself for dramatic effect. This night is full of all kinds of freaky fun for any dark sider, but the real reason I am here is to support Inari. Inari is modeling latex… this should be interesting. Latex is a very exotic material. Getting into one of these outfits is a crazy fight involving talcum powder and lube, often requiring the assistance of multiple people. I stand around waiting patiently for the fashion portion of the show to begin. I love all the fashion, but I really just want to see and talk to Inari again.

Unfortunately, she is mostly unavailable because she's backstage earlier in the night... so Jin and I spend some time getting to know each other... getting chummy... I guess I'm sizing him up. I quiz him on his career as if to make sure that I am unimpressed by his prospective future; I look for ways to boost my own confidence and convince myself that I am better than him. He's got an MBA. MBAs (Masters of Business Administration) are some of my least favorite people in the world. A whole degree with the word "Masters" in it, yet is no more significant than going to a tech school to learn to fill out forms. It makes for some arrogant "businessmen" who like to puff their chests and pretend that they are cooler than they are.

I am fully unimpressed with Jin as Inari's wave of the fashion show begins. She is wearing the most beautiful gold latex dress I've ever seen. I expected her to be dressed in some boring, black bodysuit, but this dress is beautiful, gold, elegant, with flowy, flirty, latex details. You could wear it to a cocktail party. She is easily the most gorgeous model on the runway, and the most beautiful model I've ever seen... the queen of all supermodels... and her presence in the flesh reaffirms my opinions of her... wow... she is gorgeous.

She inspired confidence in me every time she stood near me in the past, and as I see her approach, my confidence does not wane. With Jin standing immediately next to me, unimpressive, I feel further emboldened. I position myself right up at the end of the catwalk where she would do her final pose. I stand proudly, confidently gazing at her. With photographers all around, she gazes back at me, directly from the catwalk as the clicks of the cameras all fire off in rapid-fire. She continues to gaze at me as she positions her body in multiple poses to offer multiple angles for the various photographers crowding her. She looks at no one else but me. Only me. Directly. I imagine Jin to be completely emasculated as his goddess stares me down from her pedestal on the runway. My eyes were not fooling me. This was really happening.

After the fashion portion of the show, I wait patiently for her to come out and say hello to a handful of friends standing by the catwalk. Jin is of course hovering most of the time, but when Jin moves even 8 feet from us… as if on cue, she immediately knows what to say.

"They coached the models not to look at the photographers, so I chose to look at you," she says.

I'm not sure if she's making an excuse or a proclamation of love. But Jin, upon seeing us alone, feels compelled to hover closer, and she can say no more. For most of the ball, he hovers and hovers. But at some point, he decides to go get a drink and leaves us. This is our chance… That is our cue… we square up shoulders and put our noses 3 inches from each other. We stare into each other's eyes. We stand so close that it causes a stir among our friends. I see them visibly flinch in my peripheral vision. Later they would even confront me about it.

"You're so very beautiful," I tell her sweetly, my heart pumping, my chest rising dramatically.

"Thank you!" she says with a bright smile.

I open my mouth to say more romantic, blunt things to her at this moment, expecting to have *more* than a few seconds to speak my mind… but Jin, hovering, comes back almost immediately. Either he managed to get a drink from the bar at light speed, or he abandoned his quest for alcohol when he noticed us locking eyes again.

The subject changes back to small talk. The small talk is frustrating. Hanging my head, I decide to walk away from the conversation, but before I do, I walk over to the side of her opposite Jin, give her a one-armed hug, and speak into her ear, "You have no idea how much I am in love with you," I say.

But what she said back confused and saddened me… "That makes me sad," she said.

"Why sad?" I inquire, taken aback.

"Because I realize that you have the capacity to love me so much more than a robot," she replies, as she looks at me with sweet sad eyes.

I leave, hanging my head...wandering over to the bar and making small talk with Tesla, the "Goth Mother", as she's referred to. She has a husband named Ratt, and when put together with their children, make up a family in the spitting image of the Adam's Family.

I stand with Tesla for a moment as I swim in my own thoughts and emotions, contemplating what the hell Inari's words could mean. Why should my excessive capacity to love her make her sad? Shouldn't my love for her make her happy?

Tesla had observed us getting unusually close, and she issues warnings to me. "Be careful," she says. "A good friend of mine fell head-over-heels in love with her and spent months and months professing his love to her. They became best friends. Eventually, he left the state to escape his emotional attachment to her, and became suicidal. It was a big ordeal. I asked her how she felt about him, and she said that, whereas she had feelings for him, she didn't believe that he loved her."

I am stunned by her story.

She continues, "You can profess your love for her all you want, yet she may not ever believe that you truly love her. Whereas I like Inari and I like Jin, I don't really like Inari and Jin together. Yet, I don't think she'll ever leave him after the way she crawled back to him at Con. You should really just get out of this state! People here are crazy! Minnesota is a magnet for crazy people!"

Tesla's words are grim and disheartening. I can't stand to leave so many questions floating around in my head... so I wander back over. Jin and Inari are still standing in the same place, at the end of the catwalk, where I left them.

"We should talk more sometime when I can get more than 90 seconds of your time. I'm sorry about all this drama," I say.

"What drama?" Inari asks, "There's no drama."

"There's no drama!? If you think there's no drama, then maybe I should be trying harder to create some drama," I sigh as if giving up. "You understand that this is hard for me, right?" I begin to stutter... "You know... you know... I just want you to be happy... so I'm going to go away for a while and, please, you know... just be happy".

"But you deserve to be happy too," she replies. She looks at me with puppy-dog-eyes as if to communicate "don't go" as I look back at her with eyes of sad longing.

I wish she didn't say exactly those words, with the vague inflection that she used, because I didn't really even know what the words meant. Was she saying that I deserved to be happy alone or with someone else? Was she pleading with me to stay and be *made* happy by *her*? Why did she put the word "but" at the beginning of her sentence? Her inflection and use of this word seemed to communicate extra urgency of "please, don't leave me!" Is that what she is trying to tell me? Why does everything profound that comes out of her mouth have to have so many potential meanings and be rife with plausibly deniable rhetoric?

I go away, with bad posture, visibly upset, and sit in the front of the Varsity Theater in one of the many colorful, plush, antique armchairs available in the lobby.

I felt in my heart that if this exchange were at all emotional for her, she'd try to chase after me in some tactful way, but I wasn't walking away in an attempt at manipulation. Yet, I feel like there's a psychological twist happening in this theater, and I am not at all surprised, in fact, I *naturally expect* her to come looking for me.

20-30 seconds after I sit down... exactly on cue... she emerges... without Jin... but in another twist, either she doesn't see me, or I've just completely misinterpreted why she came out in the first place. Instead, she goes up the winding stairs to the co-ed restroom area and doesn't even look at me. Maybe she just needs to use the restroom or check her makeup or whatever, but I think in my heart that she is emotional and needs to escape alone for a moment. She appears visibly disturbed, and, after all, it *was* right on cue.

But also, on cue, 20-30 seconds after Inari, as-if I were conducting an orchestra, Jin emerges as well, following her. It is almost in a steady drawn-out rhythm. I figure he thinks that maybe she is leaving to go find me. He can't have *that*. He wants to hover and catch her in the act of talking to me, but she doesn't find me. Therefore, his only observation is benign... me, sitting alone in the front of the theater. Maybe he thought he won. Up until now... I was 100% sure I was winning... but *now* I feel like the underdog. I'm losing the battle for her heart.

I leave them alone for a while, but I see them out front of the theater after it closes. I am resigned. I am ready to retire. I am ready to go home, but Inari presses me to come to the after-party. The awkwardness of hours earlier seems to have almost knocked me out of the game entirely, but she still treats me like I'm important to her. She presses me to come to the after-party until I finally agree.

"I'm going if you're going!" I say, faking to have energy with a smile.

Chapter 8 - The After Party

I offer rides to a few friends, John, Bee, and Clement from the
Varsity Theater to the after-party. We get an address from Tesla.
I'd normally trust Tesla to know the correct address for an after-
party. Strangely, we find a party at the exact address she gave us,
but it doesn't appear to be the right party.

"I have no idea who those people are, but they didn't come from
any fetish ball for sure," I say to them after scoping out the party
and retreating to the sidewalk.

We make some phone calls. We all get back in my car. John gives
me directions to a familiar place: Zak's place. I figure this *isn't* the
after-party we are looking for, but we are making our own, I guess.
On some stroke of coincidence, Inari just happens to be at the same
place... with Jin, of course.

Immediately upon entering the door, a girl I'd been getting
acquainted with in previous weeks, Fiera, makes small talk. I had
seen Fiera during my last visit to Ground Zero. She is very nice
and friendly, and cute, with long dark curly hair, wearing a long
dress she likely bought at the Rennaisance Fair. Last time I saw her
we stood at the bar for quite some time making small talk and
getting to know each other. I bought her a drink, and it seemed like
she might even consider going home with me. I so desperately
needed some validation at the time, as things in my life were
frustratingly lonely. But Zak, as usual, had no boundaries of
respect when it came to seeing a cute girl he might stick his dick
in. As I was talking to Fiera at the club, Zak used his narcissistic,
sociopathic charm and inserted himself directly between us while
we were speaking in mid-sentence, then he grabbed her by the arm
and pulled her onto the dance floor, ultimately taking her home at
the end of the night. Zak routinely did that kind of thing, and he
did it to me, quite regularly. Every time it happened I felt like an
emasculated nerd.

"That was an awesome party you threw the other week!" Fiera

says. "You really should charge for entry, or make people pay for drinks, or cups, or contribute. You don't really need to be so generous to people. People think you're awesome regardless of your generosity."

"I know, I know, eventually I'll get others to contribute in some way, but for now, it is working the way I want it to," I reply.

Fiera disappears with Zak into his bedroom, and the remaining 5 of us talk in the living room, sitting in the small room like it is a drum circle or something. Clement is a new acquaintance, recommended to me by a mutual friend, and it is immediately apparent that he and I share much in common.

He seems to support everything about me from my "way with words" to my eccentric style of dress, but mostly he and I share a deep appreciation for computer science that nobody in the room can match. Clement, half Japanese-pervert-businessman, half American-engineer-artist, is exciting to talk to. Everywhere I go, hanging out in a bar or club, I meet ordinary people talking about ordinary things, but Clement, Clement is a NASA Software Engineer, with a Ph.D. in Computer Science, and is fascinated and appreciative of the technology that went into making my parties happen in ways that nobody else in the scene is capable of understanding.

"You built that whole lighting system from scratch!?" he asks, fascinated.

"Not just the lighting system, but the audio system, audio mixing, processing, effects, and the video system," I reply.

"Are you serious? You didn't just use something like Virtual DJ or some MIDI-to-DMX bridge or something?"

"Absolutely not, I don't like relying on 3rd party tools, I like to build my own so that I can make them do exactly what I want," I reply. "Everything was written by me from scratch, including the video processing. It's maybe a half-million lines of code. I converted all the audio into my own formats and processed the video, extracting metadata about prominent hues used in each frame so that I had the option of creating color palettes across all the lights that matched the videos frame for frame, and then built a whole custom scripting language and sequencing system to rapidly come up with 6 hours' worth of compelling light shows, but when I say 'rapidly' I mean, I worked my ass off creating light shows for 6 weeks before the party staying up until 6AM every day," I said.

"Holy shit that's a lot of work! But what are you doing that isn't already done with some standard stuff?" Clement replies, astonished.

"Well, for example, the DJ works from a computer that controls the audio, but instead of just sending the audio out the computer's audio ports to a sound system, I have that computer multicast UDP packets across the network. With that process in place, I can just run a little tiny program on any computer in the house on which I want to playback audio from the dance floor and the same audio comes out of every computer running the program. So, the speakers on the dance floor are just connected to a tiny computer running a little service."

"Wow!" he says.

"The video is done in a similar way. I pull the video from a common repository, but I send out sync pulses so that I just run a simple service on the machines where I want the videos to show up and the videos stay synchronized across all the screens in the house. The audio and video aren't necessarily even running on the same computers. Furthermore, the lighting commands, again... just a little service, UDP packets... it just so happens that DMX is really just a real-time protocol consisting of frames of 512 bytes blasted over and over, 45 times a second, 250,000 baud... so it's really easy to just wrap that in UDP... then up in the rafters there's a small computer with a USB-to-DMX dongle that sucks up the packets and sends the data out over the wires."

"You need to show me some of this code! I can't believe you did all of that! That's a lot of work!"

"Yeah, it was, I put about two years into it," I reply. "I have a lifetime of study in music, and I became fascinated by how visuals in music videos could actually make you like music better, like there were some songs that, if I heard them on my own, I didn't like at all, but when that same song was visualized in a music video, suddenly I *liked* the song. I wanted to visually enhance the music with lights and lasers in a way to inspire people to dance and have a good time. In some ways, it's an armchair psychological experiment."

"Judging by how much people like your parties, I think it is a successful experiment," he says.

The prominent subject of discussion cannot remain computer science all night, the rest of the group would certainly be feeling left out, so we talk about fashion, style, and emotional things. Inari pours her heart and emotions into the group, and I feel like sometimes she is talking directly to me, in non-specific subtle ways. She seems to see and feel that I'm lonely, hurting, longing, and a true lover, lost and wandering. As she emotionally attends to me, I feel that she is without regard to how much she is neglecting Jin.

Meanwhile, Zak and Fiera's activities in the adjacent bedroom become more and more apparent. Zak is getting laid... loudly. Zak and I have a... complex... history. I knew Zak more than a decade ago. Zak was one of the guys who used to throw all the parties one block from my Cathedral Hill apartment when I was with Luna. They threw parties literally every Friday night. They were brothers in perversion. Over time, their parties got more and more raunchy. Harder drugs started coming in at higher quantities. Rampant sex was the norm. I didn't like the influence that Zak had on the scene, and I rather wished he wasn't a part of it.

Shortly after we took a "break", Luna got sucked into their parties and was lost from me forever. The sex and drugs consumed her; I'm not sure in which order. Luna soon decided that she wanted to be "free" and enjoy her youth while she still had it. She declared that she wanted to be with me, but she wanted to be free at the same time. She told me she needed a "break" but didn't declare that she didn't love me anymore. Quite to the contrary, she told me she loved me every day, and she expressly said that she didn't want to break up… she just wanted a "break".

It put our relationship in a vague limbo. It made our relationship illegitimate, and, as I said at the beginning of this book, illegitimate relationships make me uneasy… and sometimes… a bit crazy. She still told me she loved me every day. She would still kiss me, but nothing more. I questioned why suddenly I wasn't worth what I used to be worth to her, but she found ways to calm my nerves enough so that she kept me wrapped around her finger. I was unaware that she was seeing someone else at the time… and then someone else… and possibly even someone else. Things were heated and complex for 9 months following. I didn't want to go to these infamous parties because Luna would be there. She'd be there and I figured she'd end up fucking someone else in front of me.

Yet, my apartment was only a block away, so after getting dumped by one guy she was seeing, Luna called me and walked over. Immediately upon her arrival, I tossed out two female guests who were celebrating my birthday with me. Quickly, Luna got into her act, pretending like she wanted to fuck me as a birthday gift, but I saw right through her. I opted *not* to fuck her, as a gentleman should, and instead offered her a shoulder to cry on for the night. I recall how thin Luna had gotten. The drugs were causing her to lose weight. She looked like heroin addicts look in the movies, frail, skinny, bony.

I took care of Luna for the night, but one week later, I walked down to Morrison's apartment after making sure they uninvited her. I found Laura sitting in the corner, shy and alone, and after a bit of kissing, I walked her one block back to my house, and then took her virginity. Laura and I never went there again, and about 6 weeks later, I bought her a diamond onyx ring. Laura thanked me for "rescuing" her as we disappeared from the scene, and we moved out to the suburbs for 8 years together.

Whereas I blame Luna, and Luna alone, for Luna's actions, the party scene surrounding Zak and Morrison left a horrible taste in my mouth that I could just never shake. Tonight, the sound of Zak having loud sex with Fiera in the next room brings up bad memories.

"There is no love in that room," I say to the group, referring to the rampant sex occurring in the next room. "This scene is what you make it," I continue, "My intention with throwing these parties is to transform the scene into something different... something better. I threw this last party with a goal... an agenda. My goal was to put myself in a situation where I could make a difference here for everyone, and for myself. Ultimately, my goal for *myself* is to meet someone special that I could one day build a life with."

"Let me be clear," I say, pausing. I look down at the floor. I raise my eyebrows, and look directly at Inari, sitting next to Jin, before continuing, "I *met* my goal. Just because I didn't get laid that night doesn't mean that I didn't accomplish my goal. Things moved in the right direction because of that party."

I switch my words from past tense to present tense in a blunt attempt to send an even clearer signal to Inari as I say to the group, *"If she is really meant for me, I don't need to take her home with me tonight."* I hope that my language signals have reached Inari. It appears that she understands. I'm talking about her, to her. She gets it... she wipes tears from her eyes, which appear to swell with longing, contemplative sadness, or heartache.

Conversation continues, and Clement offers me advice on my choice of style. He is a man of creative opinions and loves to offer them. At this period of my life, I am not entirely content with my outward self-expression. I am very self-conscious. Dysmorphia makes me concede that I am "working on myself" in the style and appearance department.

Inari sees how Clement's words are affecting me, "Hold on Clement. Yuki, you are perfect the way you are! You don't need to change anything for anyone!"

Clement stops his criticism. I *so very much* needed to hear her words. I *so very much* seek a girl who loves me the way I am, who sees no flaw in my character or appearance, who thinks I am perfect despite my flaws. She says the right things. Only *she* says the right things.

This triggers memories from when I first met her... I looked like absolute hell that night... I had barely slept since the night before... I worked my ass off all day preparing for the party... I had bags under my eyes... I was sweaty... my clothes were falling off my misshapen body... my hair was greasy. The pictures that came out of that night of me are some of the most unflattering photos ever taken of me. Inari introduced herself to me in *that* environment, when I looked like *that*... and yet she *still* felt compelled to whisper things in my ear that made me feel wanted and sexy.

Upon hearing her generous words, I absolutely *melt* for her. She is, in effect, telling everyone at the party... "Fuck them... I love you the way you are."

Over hours of conversation, Inari and I seem to exchange sentences that seem to bear similar, subtle codes and signals, and, at times, Inari seems to tear up when I send the right signals. Then, at some point, the subject of "dumping" comes up.

"Well, I've never dumped anyone in my life, I'm really a one-girl kind of person. The feeling of being dumped is the worst feeling I have ever felt in my life, and I absolutely refuse to incite that feeling on anyone," I declare.

At this point, Inari makes a jolted verbal jab at her boyfriend. "I'VE BEEN DUMPED! I'VE BEEN DUMPED FOR NO REASON! I MEAN IF SOMEONE DUMPS YOU, THEY OWE YOU A REASON, RIGHT?!"

Jin hangs his head; of course, she's talking about him. I know this as well, but I don't think he knows that I know the whole story. He was out of earshot when Inari and I discussed her issues with him. The argument escalates and it is clear that Inari is hurt and in a tizzy over Jin's treatment of her. "I DESERVE A REASON IF YOU'RE GOING TO DUMP ME, RIGHT?"

I get nervous. I don't want a confrontation to happen here, so I try to calm her down. I simply assure her with an unconfident stutter, "Of... of course you deserve a reason."

Jin's ego must be damaged because he says nothing and just hangs his head. We just spent 3 hours praising me, Jin's rival, and just 4 minutes of the night focused on Jin and it was entirely a berating of him. Suddenly it is time to go home. Zak essentially terminates the party. Zak doesn't want us in his apartment anymore, and is forceful in his words, "Party's over, get the fuck out!" Zak barely talked to us anyway; he just fucked Fiera all night.

There are logistics to work out such as who is giving who rides home... etc. It is 5:30AM. It feels like it is supposed to be the end of the night, but Inari has an endless hunger to stay out even longer on the town.

"Let's all hit that place on Hennepin that does all-night-breakfast!" she pleads.

"I'm really tired, Inari, I can make you some food at home when we get there," Jin offers.

"But they have such good fries, I could eat 3 whole plates of fries and tots and pancakes and vegetables…" she counters.

"Alright, alright, it's fine, but then we go home," he declares.

"Yukiki! You want to come get some tasty breakfast foods with us?" Inari asks of me.

I want to but I'm forced to decline. "I have to take 3 people home, so it is going to take me at least a whole hour just to do that, so by the time I do that it will be 6:30 and Ada needs to be let out to do her doggy business. I don't really see how it is logistically possible. You'll be done eating long before I can even make it there."

"Please Yuki! You should come, it will be fun!"

"I really just can't, I want to though."

Jin goes to check and make sure the door is locked and walks away for another 30 seconds or so. Once again, I stand directly in front of Inari. My shoulders are proud, but my eyes are sad. As we gaze at each other, I say nothing. Instead, she just senses sadness in me. She knows I do not want to leave her. She hugs me.

Jin returns and she continues to plead with me to go with them. "Please Yuki! You should come, it will be fun! What's wrong?"

"You know I want to … but I just can't work out how that will happen. I need to let the dog out. I'm really sorry, I wish I could. There will be other days," I say.

She gets this look on her face like she's going to cry as I turn to walk away. Concerned, I look back at her over my shoulder again. The expression on her face has now morphed into an expression of *terror*. Upon seeing her face, I get chills up my spine. I suddenly feel guilty for leaving her. Maybe her relationship with Jin is darker than his and her politeness would suggest. I sense fear in her. I fear that maybe she really, truly doesn't want to be left alone with him after she berated him in front of her friends.

Speculating about things like domestic abuse is a serious thing to do. I need to be careful. I can't just go around to my friends saying, "I think Jin beats Inari on a regular basis." There's no way of me knowing. The only evidence I would have to suggest anything of the sort is Inari's frightened nature as she goes home with Jin alone tonight. But as I write this, I remember, she gave me similar frightened looks Monday night when she and Jin were fighting, and Jin allowed Hugo to join them at his apartment. Following that night, she showed up with fresh scrapes and bruises. Did Jin cause her scrapes and bruises?

It is a bit of driving to get everyone to their destinations. John and Bee are drunk and decide to fuck like wild animals in my back seat while I drive. Clement and I discuss Inari and her posturing towards me. Clement agrees that she acts as though she cares about me in an unusual capacity for some reason.

I dwell upon the events of the night. I dwell upon the look she gave me at the end of it all. At 6:30AM I send her a long text as I finally return to take care of Ada...

"Inari... just getting home now. This is the second time that I've felt that you wanted me to rescue you at the end of the night... the truth is... I would gladly swoop in and claim you as my own. But how do I do this without a duel? I had an immaculate night. You are the kindest, most considerate, generous, and beautiful girl I have ever met. I have never met anyone like you. I love you on so so so many levels it makes me glow and makes me so happy. It is YOU that I wish I could build a life together with. You are truly amazing."

As I continue to dwell, I decide to document the events that brought us together. I don't know where, if anywhere, my relationship with Inari is going. But all I know is that I want things to be documented. If I need to tell the story to any of my friends or file any legal papers, I want it to be in a format that is complete, concise, and consistent. I don't sleep. I spend all day writing. And from here on out, every chapter is a day, an encounter, an event, documented every day. This book grows entirely from this writing. As I write these drafts, I do not know what the next chapter will contain, so what happens next, is just as much a mystery to me as it is to you.

Chapter 9 - Dichotomy

Sunday night, after not hearing from Inari all weekend, she finally calls.

"I'm sorry I couldn't get back to you, I really wish I could," she explains. "I have an undiagnosed sleeping disorder. Sometimes I stay awake for two days at a time until my body gives out and I sleep like a brick for two days straight," she says.

I am just relieved to hear her voice again. I had worried that she was ignoring me or that Jin hurt her. I just wish she'd communicate with me and let me know that she is safe sometimes. We talk for a couple hours about nothings and whatevers until Jin complains enough to get her off the phone. She and I agree that we should meet up at The Saloon on Monday night.

The strange looks of terror from the other night are pushed to the back of my mind. She is safe and in high spirits. I have no real reason to be alarmed. Yet, since she and I had been getting along so well together, I worry that Jin is getting a bit jealous, particularly after the events of the other night. I figure he'll find polite, but subtle ways to keep us from spending time together when we see each other next.

I'm a bit stressed out as I anticipate her arrival. They'd arrived at Hard Mondays before me in the past. I want every second of face time I can conjure up with her, so I get to the club early in anticipation and *count the minutes* until they arrive.

Hours pass, however... it is past midnight... I figure if they're coming, they'd be at the club by now. I go out on the patio... depressed... wondering how I can possibly get close to this girl if she isn't even coming to the club. Luna, having agreed to be my "wingman" is there to help me keep my wits about me. I begin to give up my hopes of seeing her for the night when I hear…

"Your girl is here! Yuki, look over there... your girl is here!"

Kenzie, Luna's new roommate, points out into the intersection with excitement, where Inari's distinct silhouette animates under the hazy beams of the streetlights, her hair flowing like an anime princess. Beautiful. Jin is in tow.

My mind is on fire. I take a few deep breaths and get my game plan organized in my head... then I spring into action.

I race inside to place myself in a visible spot in the club and I wait patiently for them to come around as if I weren't anticipating her arrival at all. They find me soon enough, and, almost immediately, Jin excuses himself to use the restroom. I immediately jump at the opportunity to talk privately with Inari, manic, heart racing... I start *gunning* words at her... my god... the shit I said. I'm slightly intoxicated because I've been at the club for hours by this point...

"Oh my god, you are the most beautiful girl in the world, Inari... more beautiful than anyone who's ever been on the cover of any magazine, walked a runway, starred in a movie, or become a rock star." She seems to light up at first... but as I lay it on thicker and thicker and thicker, she seems taken aback... repelled. Luna, playing the role of wingman, has positioned herself to overhear.

"Yuki, Echo really needs to talk to you outside, it's really important. Right away, it's important!"

She pulls me outside and I realize what I have done. I bury my head in my hands... "Oh my GOD! I just fucked it up! I just fucked it up didn't I!?"

"No, you didn't, you've got her here... you just need to chill for a bit... gossip in this scene spreads too quickly and if anyone here for a moment even *thinks* there's something going on between you, you could have some serious trouble and she probably was just backing off because she can't let word get to him. Even *if* she *wants you*, she can't make it look like something is going on between you."

I make a point to appear like I'm just socializing with random people at the bar for a while, but I make a point to cross paths with her to briefly explain myself. "I needed to back off, because if we keep giving each other these 'googly eyes', people will start spreading rumors, I'm sorry."

"Yeah, I know, I get it," she agrees. Her eyes are still sweet, and her voice is charming and friendly, confirming for the first time, verbally, that these eyes are, and always were, being mutually exchanged. I felt better inside knowing that it wasn't just my imagination.

I keep my distance and cool for a while, but long before the bar closes, Jin wants to go home early. He needs to work early in the morning. He comes over to say goodbye.

"We should do a movie night sometime this week," he says.

"I'll walk you to the door," I say, making small talk. I don't want them to go so early, and certainly, I want to speak to her one last time before she leaves with him. My mind races with plots, scams, schemes, and diversions that I might be able to employ to grab her attention away from him so that I can gaze at her and profess my love for her again… if only for a moment… before she leaves. But as they approach the door, I have nothing. I turn and walk away feeling defeated. I love her, why is she going?

Naturally, I feel a compulsion to look over my shoulder, as anyone would do when walking away from love. I stop 10 feet away, and turn towards the door, expecting them to have vanished, but I see that they are still standing there. I cannot hear what they're saying... but I start to feel pain as she appears to be sweet-talking him, touching him, staring into his eyes, and kissing him, right in front of me after all the intense exchanges we had recently. I excuse myself and move a distance away... but I can still see them... they stand there for a few minutes... kissing... smiling. My insides boil a little bit. "Why do I have to look at this? This is *pain*! Why is she making me stare into my *pain*?" I think to myself.

Suddenly I am confronted by a seemingly random guy in a long black trench coat. His name is Aurthur. He's a long-haired, bearded, blonde guy, a mysterious metalhead, biker type. He had been "people watching" us all night and noticed something going on between us.

"Be careful with her," he offers. "Don't let her get too close to you. She's got a lot of damage."

I don't want to hear his opinions. My limbs stiffen and I clench my fists. "I *love* that girl," I tell him… while watching her flirt, twinkle her eyes, and kiss this man who doesn't love her. "That over there is a *charade*. She *wants* me! And I'm not sure what the *hell* they're doing!"

At that moment, in my amped-up mania, I get an idea. "Let me try something," I say to Aurthur as I briskly walk away from him. I walk a straight line directly towards Jin and Inari, my limbs still stiff and my fists still clenched. They are still flirting and kissing and smiling as I bring myself within 12 inches of their kissing faces.

"I thought you guys were leaving. What's up?" I say in an animated, almost squeaky voice with a Cheshire smile.

"Yeah, you know," Jin replies, "I've got to work and stuff, but Inari wants to stay out later."

"Well, you know, I could give her a ride home. I promise I'll give her back in one piece. I'll get her back to you *early*," I offer, when in fact I have no intention of getting her home early… at least in the most obvious definition of the word.

"Are you sure you don't mind?" he asks.

"No, not at all!" I say, now trying to contain my excitement. I flutter my toes repeatedly, nearly jumping out of my boots.

I excuse myself... I have to run away before I burst out screaming with euphoric excitement. I run outside... literally *run* outside… to the patio. There I find Luna smoking a cigarette and give her a giant hug from behind. She seems startled as if I were some stranger attacking her.

"Dude, what the fuck, you can't just come up behind me like that!" she complains.

"I'm sorry, I'm sorry, I'm sorry… You'll never believe what I just did!" I cry with glee, "I just got Jin to leave without her!"

She turns around and her face lights up with excitement. "Holy shit!" she shouts. She high-fives me. We hug and embrace as if we were just rescued from a shipwreck. "Great Job, dude! Nice work!" she says as I practically cry on her shoulder.

We dismount our embrace. I plant my feet firmly on the ground and get my bearings. I begin to wonder how the hell it turned out to be *that* easy. How was it so easy to get the most beautiful girl in the world to agree to leave her boyfriend behind and stay with me? As I replay the visions that had caused me pain earlier, I suddenly realize that it wasn't *me* that convinced Jin to leave. It was *her*. And… for the first time… I see darkness in Inari... a truly profound darkness. You see, she's got him to trust her. She stared into his eyes and pacified him. She told him that everything would be alright while gazing into his eyes passionately, using every ounce of beauty and charisma that radiated from her so naturally. But this act, this play, this theater, was as dark as her smile was bright. It was as dangerous as sweet cocoa made with hot magma. If she was going to leave him, this is what would ruin him in the end, and if I got too close to her, it might very well be *our* end as well.

But what choice do I have? Her energy is like heroin. Maybe I am just better for her than him and she would never do such a thing to me. But she is a goddess, and I am just a lowly nerd! I never get the opportunity to connect with anyone with a fraction of her radiance! I have *no choice* but to trust her. I feel powerless! I am powerless!

I force myself to ignore what I see. It was just a little "goodbye dance" to run off a man she had no future with. We all have a bit of darkness in ourselves… and this… it was just a *hint* of darkness, right? Fuck Jin anyway… He's already dumped her twice, and in Inari's defense, the darkest thing in this story so far is the fact that Inari is with a man who clearly doesn't love her. I endorse the idea of her getting free of him.

It isn't long before the bar closes. I prepare for an awesome night.

Chapter 10 - The Monsoon and the Flower

I drive a couple of friends home, and then Inari and I stop by her place to pick up some booze because, I guess, it is decided we're going to Echo's place for after bar. It is Inari, Echo, Luna, Kenzie, and I. There are no real secrets in this room regarding my love of Inari. I've spared Echo the details, simply because of issues involving jealousy in our past, but she will figure out soon enough who I am here for.

We go to Echo's basement-level apartment, a dingy, basement-level apartment that reeks of cat pee. As we enter, Echo turns on *Buffy the Vampire Slayer*, which I'm sure she simply has in a loop on her VHS player attached to a tiny old television. Everything here is either grey, or *made* grey, from layers of dirt on the walls and furniture. The five of us hang out and do the kinds of stuff people do during an after-bar party. They talk about simple things, their favorite kinds of booze, their wildest experiences doing drugs during raves, their favorite music and musicians. I'm not really feeling the small talk. I just want to be near Inari, but I get mixed signals... I'm not sure why. As everyone else talks and has a good time, I ponder my problem. Eventually, I figure that maybe she isn't aware that there are *no secrets* in this room. Everyone at the party is already fully aware of my intense love for her, and everyone in this room has already observed the sparks flying in both directions. But whatever the reason, I am saddened that she doesn't even choose to sit next to me most of the time. I get nervous and agitated and start to feel insecure. Sitting in this cat-urine-soaked room makes my nostrils hurt and clothes smell like gasoline.

Thankfully, we eventually move the party to the roof of the apartment building. The perfect skyline views of the roof make it a worthy place to be romantic. Inari finally lets me sit behind her and leans against me as she talks with our mutual friends about things that I wouldn't even remember had they been said to me only a moment ago. I have no interest in small talk, I only have an interest in being near her. She lets me stroke her hair and rub her back, and for the first time of the entire night, I feel like there is hope between us.

As people grow tired, Luna and Kenzie get ready to leave together and the 5 of us stand in a circle to say goodbyes to them for the night. Luna, my "wingman", has been super supportive of me in this endeavor, so I decide to "fish" for an endorsement from her. I hope that if my ex-girlfriend endorses my character, Inari will appreciate that and trust me.

I confidently put my arm around Inari and speak to Luna in the 3rd person. "Luna gives me glowing endorsements, right?" I give her a little wink. She knows what to say.

"Yuki is a good guy, and possibly the only faithful guy I've ever been with," she says.

My heart thanks her. I give her a smile and a nod. I just really needed a nudge to move us forward.

After Luna and Kenzie leave, it is just Echo, Inari, and I. We walk into Loring Park, the park across the road, which we had been looking out over from the rooftop during the last hour. It is an urban park on the edge of downtown that engulfs Loring Lake. It is scenic, but maybe more of a "pond" than a "lake". Cozy and tranquil, the water looks like fireflies as the amber lights of the skyline are reflected upon its tiny waves. The three of us wander down to the end of a nearby fishing dock.

It is 3:30 AM and suddenly it is pouring down rain. Echo and Inari dance and sing in the monsoon and get wet and crazy, jumping on the dock, singing songs, holding hands in a circle, and splashing in puddles.

"I'm free! I'm free!" Inari exclaims. She is happy as a child. She makes me feel young again, but I wished that I could share her energy. The mixed signals of the night have triggered my internal insecurities and I have difficulty believing that I can win her heart especially given the distractions of other people present. I'm struggling, but not out. I'm trying to find a way back into her view, which at the moment, as she dances with Echo, seems to be fixated, like tunnel vision, on Echo, as they frolic and dance and sing.

It is 7AM when we leave Echo's place. The night … is finally over. And for the first time, Inari and I are alone as we walk the few blocks across the park to where my car is waiting. She is barefoot and splashing in the puddles.

Finally, I can speak to her bluntly. "I want to steal you away," I say.

"Now you finally tell me!" she says. She comes over and locks elbows with me.

"Oh uhh... was I supposed to say that earlier?" Suddenly I feel like an ass. I wear my emotions on my forehead, and her heart seems to melt when I show her sadness. She's a caring person.

"I kinda' don't want to go home now," she says.

"Well… we can hang out more then," I say, knowing full well that 7AM is way too late in the night to find another adventure for us.

"Noooo," she says in a sigh.

"Well, we're going to do this again, and next time we'll plan some night out where we trample through puddles and make ourselves look like absolute hell. Then we'll go out into public places and scare off the public! Maybe some mud wrestling! Haha! What do you think?"

She laughs generously at my joke, which wasn't really all that funny, and lightens up. She picks a pink flower from a nearby flower bed. As I look at her face, she is glowing with bliss, peace, and happiness as she inhales a deep sniff of the flower's aroma.

I drive her to Jin's place... it is a long drive because it is now rush hour and people are hustling to get to their morning jobs. I deliberately take University Avenue, because I know that the construction of the new light rail line will extend the drive.

As we drive, the discussion turns more and more frank. I shower her with affection and compliments, and she returns many compliments as well and assures me once again that she likes me the way I am, weirdness and all. I express insecurities about my body shape, but she tells me that she thinks I'm perfect. I am not obese, but I'm not chiseled like an athlete either.

"You know, I wouldn't want you to be any thinner. Yuki, women don't want men who are skinnier than they are, because then they would feel fat themselves" she says. "Just be thankful that you don't have to deal with all the beauty standards that women have to deal with. As a female, it is impossible to keep up with society's expectations of perfection!"

"But Inari, you do so *well* with it. You don't have to work as hard as you do. You are beautiful anyway. You work so hard to look perfect, I would still think that you were the most beautiful girl on the planet, even without all your fancy hair and fancy makeup."

She looks in the mirror attached to the sun-visor and pulls and prods at her eyes and face. She had just been frolicking in the rain so her hair is all wet and heavy and her clothes are still damp and her face is dirty. "Ugh, I'm so ugly," she says.

But I see nothing ugly in her. She didn't put her boots back on after the rainstorm, and is barefoot in the car, legs crossed, and her toes are near the center where I often rest my hand. I reach over and hold onto her foot as if I'm holding onto her hand... even her toenails are meticulously painted as if done by Michelangelo himself. I think to myself that painting them was hardly necessary. She complains that her hair looks terrible as she checks herself repeatedly in the overhead mirror, but her hair is of such beautiful texture as if painted with the finest brush by an army of legendary artists. In a way, the dirt and sand and wetness make her even sexier. My heart pumps harder as I realize that I am touching the skin of this amazing, beautiful, angel.

As we round the final corner to Jin's apartment. I start to panic at the thought of leaving her for the night. It's now or never. I have to be brutally honest with her before she leaves the car.

"I was dead serious when I said all that stuff earlier," I say. "I might have been a little drunk, but I meant it when I said that you *are* the most beautiful girl on planet earth... more beautiful than anyone who's ever been on the cover of any magazine... a movie star... or a rock star... or a supermodel. But I imagine that if I were a girl and some random guy started spewing that stuff at me, I'd run as fast as I could from him," I added. "God, I'm sorry I shouldn't have said that," I said, looking visibly ashamed.

"No... don't apologize," she says, now gazing very longingly and intently into my eyes. We're parked in front of the door to Jin's apartment. I want to kiss her, but I figure Jin is probably going to emerge any second to unlock the door for her.

"The instant you leave, I'm going to start missing you," I say. "I wish I could make you feel as wonderful as you make me feel."

She smiles brighter. But it is certainly time to go. Once again, I resign for the night... err... morning... but only for the moment. As she is leaving, she takes the flower she picked earlier and brushes my nose with it, and hands it to me for safe keeping with a twinkle and flutter of her laser-beam eyes.

"I'm going to keep this with me all day," I say. "Call me later. Please? For me?"

I find a text from Luna asking me how things went as I watch Inari meet Jin at the door (after all she can't get in without a key).

I call Luna in lieu of a text reply... "I didn't get her home until just now… 7:30AM," I tell her.

"Well, I guess when you said you'd 'get her home early' that's one valid interpretation of it," she jokes.

"Yeah, I guess so!" I snap back, laughing, blissfully basking in the feelings of love, but mulling over the loss of giving her back to Jin just moments ago.

Chapter 11 - The Catalyst

"Call me later. For me? Please?" I begged like a pathetic, whiny little man as I left her with another man. I expected her to call me sometime Monday, maybe after sleeping into the evening, but I panic as multiple days pass and I hear nothing. I try to call her myself yet fail to reach her. I send her text messages and emails... but she goes silent. I worry that her late-night partying may have made Jin mad and caused a fight. After repeated attempts, I finally text her a basic question, "Are you alive? yes/no."

She already knows that Techna is coming to town, always a special occasion. I try to remind her that she might not want to miss her visit. I stress in voicemails that Techna is an important fashion contact and she'd want to network with her to further her modeling career, but I mostly just want Techna and Inari to become friends and for Inari to be near me. Every hour feels like a day. Inari ignores my invitations.

Another Wednesday arrives and neither Inari nor Jin come to our favorite club. At this point, I almost feel like they're dead... like Jin is hiding her from me... jealous... angry that she would stay out all night with me. Usually, Jin returns my texts, but even *he* is silent now. I feel completely forgotten.

Such a contrast, it was, from how I left her Monday morning. I imagine scenarios that would inspire such silence from her. Maybe Jin got angry, they fought, and he forbade her to contact me. Maybe their fighting got physical. Maybe her aloofness towards him drove him to care about her more and, therefore, they came closer together, overshadowing her interest in me. Maybe she used me to make him jealous and now they were repairing their relationship.

As time goes by and she continues to ignore her phone and my messages, the more I can only concede that she's just *not interested* in communicating with me. I am baffled. I did nothing wrong. Things were so magical and intense between us the last time we sat next to each other.

So, after 3 days of trying to verify whether she's *even alive* and receiving no indications. I started digging for answers... digging for patterns. I start... asking questions. I had never tried to dig up any "dirt" on her before. I could not fathom looking upon her negatively. And even if rumors were to exist, I wouldn't have cared. But in my isolation, all I have are unanswered questions swirling around in my head.

I talk again to Aurthur, who had spoken to me Monday night. He used to date her years ago. He'd been keeping in contact with me because he'd expressed interest in my friend Angela and sought assistance in getting close to her. Now that I'm isolated and alone, I decide to seek his counsel regarding Inari as well. This time, I don't push away his advice so readily.

My head is barely attached to my shoulders. "Okay Aurthur, spill it, I'm listening now. How long did you date her?" I ask.

"Long enough to figure out that the drugs she did when she was younger have had some lasting effects," he replies.

I get angry with him, "Wait a minute, that doesn't sound like Inari at all," I say. "She seems pretty level-headed to me. I love this girl. I don't think she's crazy, and she tells me she has never done drugs and doesn't want to. Be careful how you characterize her, man, I *love* that girl."

"She's always been rather flighty," he says. "You know, I tried being a gentleman, I tried being polite to her... but it didn't get me anywhere. So then one day I came over and she said, 'What, are you a fag or something?' It made me mad, so I *proved* to her that I'm a man... if you know what I mean."

He continues, "But as I continued to try and get to know her, I'd come over and she'd just talk on the phone for hours and ignore me, and if her roommate, Barry, was there, she'd spend all of her time paying attention to him and not me. Eventually, I just walked out and got in my car. She chased after me... but I basically just told her that I thought I'd get back together with my ex... and I guess that's the real reason we ended it. There's something strange between her and her roommate, and I always figured that there were other guys in the mix too. It was just too difficult to keep her attention, she always seemed like she was running away."

I leave the conversation at that. I can't bear to hear any more.

His words discourage me. I get real with myself. I figure there is no way in hell I can wield this girl. I give up. As I sit on the front steps of my house watching Ada play in the grass, I leave her a very respectful voicemail.

Look Inari, if you want me, you should let me know now, and I will sweep you off your feet, but at this point in time, I don't expect you to do this. Obviously, you would have been awake at some point over the last few days to respond to a single question with a yes/no answer. Look, I love you, and I care about you, and I hope to see you again. Maybe I played the wrong cards. Maybe I played the 'love' card when you really wanted me to play a 'different' card, but really... I fucking hate love games. I would like to tell you this all in person, but it would require you actually communicating with me, and I don't believe that you are all that interested in communicating with me anymore. I'm stopping this chase. You can chase after me if you want, but I'm leaving this up to you. I'm moving on.

Immediately after leaving the voicemail, I try to set my sights on looking forward. I still have things going for me. I need to take my social life by the reins and utilize my newfound popularity. Thursday night arrives and it is time to go out to "Chamber". Angela and Aurthur are planning to be there, but Chamber is stunningly unpopular. If they're there, and I'm there, the attendance for the night might be 3... 4 if we're lucky.

Chapter 12 - The First End

Before leaving for the club, I troll around online. I get self-destructive. I begin posting nasty, awful things online. I am depressed, and, when I'm depressed, I throw parties. It is time. It is time to declare another party. I create an event posting online and invite people to it. I subtitle the event: "The Kamikaze Ride Ends Here" and call it "a celebration of the end of the world and all that is evil and wretched and slimy about humanity". I schedule it for the Friday night just before Halloween. People start RSVPing for the party within minutes.

I meet up with Angela at the club and Zak, like Zak always does, tries to cut off my conversation with her so he can hit on her. I get angry with him. I want him to go away…we're talking about personal things. But Angela, like many girls in the scene, is for some reason drawn to Zak's charisma, even if he is a complete womanizing bastard in a top hat. Angela does not let me finish my story and instead, I'm left to simply ponder alone as to why every goth scene in every city I've been to seems to have a doppelganger of Zak, a womanizing prick in a top hat who thinks he's God's gift to women. What is it with top hats? Why does the most narcissistic attention whoring male in a 150-mile radius seem to a top hat like a 7th-grader in a Burger King crown? Angela pairs up with Zak on the dance floor, seemingly smitten, but it doesn't matter anyway… because before I can ponder any longer, Inari finally decides to call me after receiving my voicemail.

I leave the club and go sit in my car. I am delighted at how uplifting the conversation is. Even though the subject of the conversation is supposed to be dark and gloomy, she makes me feel special and it uplifts me. I feel like everything is going to be alright, but I feel like I need some answers.

I am quick to apologize to her. I grovel, "I didn't mean to posture aggressively towards you. I am just an impatient person. I have always been an impatient person. I hate waiting in lines. I hate waiting for things. I have all my purchases shipped overnight, and oftentimes even *that* isn't even fast enough. When it comes to love and relationships especially, I am extremely impatient. I don't like waiting. I didn't like waiting to see you again, and when I didn't even hear from you, I got nervous and worried and negative."

After all the groveling, I address the elephant in the room, and ask her, point blank, how she feels... most importantly... how she feels about *me*. She's heard how I felt about her a zillion times and accepted it and smiled graciously every time I told her how beautiful she was and how in love with her I was, but I never really truly heard how she felt about me, romantically, out of her mouth.

She says a few beautiful things that I don't remember at all, because... on cue... she pauses... and leads into "but..."

I am crushed.

At first, she writes it off as bad timing... that she wants to be faithful to Jin... etc., etc., etc. But I press her further and eventually determine that there's no way she'd ever want me even if she were single and available... it is done.

Like with every breakup/rejection, I turn over every stone to try and find the missing puzzle piece that will get me to the center of this maze where her heart is... it is like a math equation that I try desperately to solve, a logical means to an emotional end, and it goes on for a couple of hours. It must have been painful for her. But she is not like nearly everyone else in this scene; she really has a big heart that is true and pure, and she listens intently while having so many wonderful things to say. It is apparent that she cares about me, still, deeply.

"Why would you stay with a man who doesn't love you?" I ask bluntly.

"I see there being 3 pillars to a good relationship, the mental, the physical, and the emotional," she says. "Very few relationships seem to encompass all 3 of those things, basically none of them really. There's always one missing, and when that occurs you have to find support from somewhere else. Jin isn't perfect. He's far from perfect. But I love him."

I try to make the case that she deserves better. I want to fill all the pillars of her relationship requirements! I attempt to portray myself as a man of confidence and honor. I portray myself as a misunderstood savant. I portray myself as the best for her. I dig through all the poetic concoctions that I had been dreaming of saying to her but, until now hadn't the guts to say. I tell her I love her... and I tell her that I am *in* love with her. I replay all the events of the last couple of weeks... including all my interpretations of many of the events documented in this book and ask for her own interpretations, but she simply replies with phrases, like:

"Just because I did those things or said those things, doesn't mean that I want you romantically."

"You misinterpreted that, that's not what that meant."

"You didn't see what you thought you saw. That never happened."

"You're too sensitive and derive too much meaning from nothing."

"You can't have those feelings just because I said or did those things."

Everything I say is shot down with those phrases... until I just feel like God herself rejected me.

"I need to improve myself," I say. "All of this mess was my fault, I'm so sorry I burdened you. I'm so embarrassed."

Everything and anything I do and say, until finally... after 4AM... I am exhausted. Ultimately ... figuring it to be a lost cause ... figuring it all to be done and over... I conjure up the most grandiose thing I will ever say to a girl in my life.

"I want us to look at our lives 50 years from now, remember how you and I met, and remind ourselves that LIFE IS BEAUTIFUL. If I were king, and you were queen, our lives would no longer be about 'me and you', but about *everyone* around us.... because I would be *so happy* and, life would be *so complete...* that I would want to *share* all this love I have with *everyone else...* because you make me feel so *amazing*."

But even my best, most poetic words do not sway her. It is clear I cannot do anything to win her heart. She worries about me. She worries about my ability to cope with her rejection. She tells me that I should seek therapy. "There's no shame in seeing a therapist, you know. My therapist helps me through a lot of things," she says.

"Well maybe," I reply, "but you don't have to worry about me being suicidal or anything. I'm the kind of guy that would have to write a thesis before he killed himself. I wouldn't leave some little note crying about my afternoon, then go hang myself. I'd have to write a long detailed, persuasive essay explaining everything that is wrong with the world before I permanently decided to end my connection to it. Worry about me after I've written a book," I conclude.

Of all the people I've ever met in the world who are worthy of love... she is, to me, by far, still the worthiest. She is a myth to me, a legend, a true goddess. And these brief moments with her were like being touched by God herself.

After we hang up, she notices my party invite and comments: "I'll make cookies! Pumpkins, bats, etc. You = best ever!"

Chapter 13 - Act II - Working and Tasking

I work on putting my eggs back in other baskets all day the next day.... planning things to do for Friday night. At the end of my workday, I'm at the office a bit late. It is 6PM and a coworker inquires about my weekend.

"Any exciting plans for the weekend?" he asks.

I instantly break down. I can't help but start sobbing in front of him. "I'm just going to sit here and finish this work," I reply with tears in my eyes. I had not been productive in my job due to all my personal drama. I needed to pick up the pace. Things were getting desperate in my career.

I had planned on seeing Inari this weekend. We planned a group outing to an amusement park, for roller coasters. The event was still on, but it was debatable as to if I would go now that things had changed.

I start making other plans for the weekend. I plan to hit a club with Luna that night. I also get a random text from Elizabeth with whom I previously had a complicated relationship. Weighing my options, I decide to check in on Elizabeth. I'm a busy bee, juggling 3 sets of plans.

I'd been with Elizabeth for 6 months before meeting Amber. Elizabeth, a beautiful curly-haired singer in a heavy metal band, was very jealous of Amber, but Elizabeth had a boyfriend of her own and our relationship was an illegitimate affair. I couldn't handle being in a love triangle with Elizabeth and her boyfriend. I don't like imagining myself betraying another human in that way. I don't like imagining his reaction when and if he is ever confronted by the news that his fiancee has been unfaithful. I don't like the idea that the girl I'm with is going to go home and spend the night with another man. Yet, somehow, I endured it for 6 months. I suppose I didn't mind initially. As we got in too deep, we escaped together to stay in a 5-star resort hotel on a California beach for a week, parking our cheap rental car next to a bunch of Lamborghinis and Ferraris and enjoying romantic dinners when we bothered to leave the hotel room. Eventually, after months of sneaking out, Elizabeth told me she loved me.

"No, you don't, Elizabeth," I replied. "If you were truly single right now and had the choice to date any man you wanted right now, you wouldn't choose me. You get the parts of me that you want, and the only thing that has held us together for this long is the fact that you don't have to take *all* of me. If you had to take *all* of me, you'd choose *nothing* over me."

But tonight, having been rejected by Inari less than 24 hours earlier, I feel like I should keep my options open.

I call Elizabeth for a heart-to-heart conversation. I apologize for running away from her when she declared that she was in love with me. In mid-sentence, my "call waiting" fires off. It is Inari.

"I gotta get this!" I say as I rudely hang up on Elizabeth.

Inari answers, sobbing. "Hi," she says. She sniffles.

I understand her inflection immediately, despite having heard only one syllable from her, "You sound sad... what's up?"

"I had no idea. I'm so sorry," she sobs.

"No idea about what?" I inquire, although I'm fairly certain I know where this conversation is going.

"I had no idea how serious this was!" she says. She pauses for a moment, then continues, "I don't check my email very often and emails just pile up, and I just finally read all the stuff you sent me, and … I'm sorry… I had no idea! I really had no idea!"

I sent her songs, song lyrics, and long emails full of prose. I practically proposed to her in one email. By the time she called on this night, however, she had read everything and even listened to all the songs I sent her.

"Your music is beautiful," Inari says, still sobbing faintly.

I talk to her for a long time... longer and longer. I'm supposed to meet up with Luna... but somehow, despite having declared that I must go, Inari just keeps pushing the conversation forward... topic after topic... preventing me from hanging up. It is as if she fears that if we stop talking, that I will run away from her and never talk to her again. I don't mind one bit. This is, after all, what I want. I want Inari.

"Hey, I get it. Look, I'm sorry. I was overbearing. I sent you lots of stuff. I'm a romantic sap. Look, I think you're the greatest human on the planet, I will never, ever, ever look down on you. You're good, I love you ya know?"

"I love you too, Yuki. You're my friend, Yuki," she replies.

"Well, you know, I hate that word 'friend', and I will always hate that word, but what's going on this weekend, you still planning on rollercoasters n' stuff?"

"Yeah, I'm just waiting for Jin to call. He's been at his LARP group. He should be coming over to pick me up, we're just going to watch movies and sleep."

Certainly, I interpret none of what she is saying as a newly realized profession of love from her. She has still marginalized me into the "friend zone". I hate being here, but I'm also at this moment in time feeling confident enough to stop myself from making grandiose professions of love to Inari... or maybe I'm just still exhausted from all the volleys of grandiose overtures and prose I dumped on her last night. Last night... it was a battle... and a hard-fought one for sure. If anyone is going to fire a volley of grandiose overtures now, it better be Inari... and her use of the word "friend"... Is kinda turning me off... frustrating.

The next thing I know, Jin is calling. I put Inari on hold and switch over to answer. He is very formal. "I just wanted to invite you to come to the amusement park with us tomorrow," he says.

"Certainly, you know, I'm actually just on the phone with Inari right now. She's expecting to hear from you soon," I reply.

The timing of all this seems a little weird to me. Jin, calling me while I'm already on the phone with Inari. Did she text him and demand that he specifically call me and invite me to the park? Did she want to create a scenario where he would specifically call me while she was already on the phone with her? Such an act might be designed to invoke an emotional response in Jin. He might be taken aback by my declaration that I was on the phone with his girlfriend, but I made sure to assure him that she was expecting to hear from him... because I'm a decent fucking person.

"Maybe everyone should just meet at my place tomorrow," I offer. "My car seats 6, so it should be a good vehicle for carpooling."

"Yeah, why don't we do that," Jin agrees.

I switch back to Inari and speak with far more confidence than I did the night before when I was freaking out and she was telling me I should seek therapy. "Don't worry about me. I'm a popular dude. I've got shit going on. Things are happening. I'm just reconnecting with many of the connections I lost when I decided to focus on *you* entirely. Elizabeth wants to mend things with me. Luna has been demanding my attention and has been having issues in her relationship. I have options. I have people to hang out with. I'm a popular dude... things are okay here. But if you really think that I'm making any unhealthy relationship choices, I want you to *stop* me from going there okay? If you believe that you can offer me more than anyone, then I want you to offer it to me okay?"

We talk and talk. We really talk well together. It is an hour later when her call waiting goes off. It is Jin. "I don't feel like answering it," she says.

I only think, but do not speak, "Goddamnit, why do you have to give me these mixed signals?"

The next thing I know, it is 1AM and we've been talking for literally 3 hours. She's in bed... my throat is sore from all the talking. I've now clocked in 6 hours of phone conversations with her in a single 24-hour time period. I finally let her go. I figure she'll call Jin and he'll come over. That'll be that. At no point in our conversation did we ever talk about being anything more than friends. I said grandiose things to her like I always have. I let her know, point-blank, that I wanted her for myself, but I didn't think for a second that she wanted me. Am I in the place where I belong in her life? Well... no. I'm just in the place where she put me.

But I confidently declare, "There *is* a connection between us!" I declare it quite confidently. I leave her no option to disagree with me. "There *is* a connection between us."

The next day I call Jin in the morning about hooking up for the park. He is much easier to get a hold of than Inari, so I figure I might as well just call the easiest person to get a hold of. I inquire regarding what time I should expect him.

"I'm planning on heading over soon, but the problem is, I've been calling Inari all morning and getting no answer," he reveals.

I'm genuinely surprised; I even smirk a little bit. "What!? I thought she went home with *you* last night... that's kinda' scary. She says she sleeps like a brick... so maybe you just have to go over and pound on the door."

"I'm not worried," he says, "and that's probably what I'll do."

He finally gets her roused, but it is almost 5PM by the time she's ready. We decide that mini-golfing instead of the park is the order of the day. We'll try for roller coasters tomorrow (Sunday).

We go golfing... and I try to avoid eye contact with Inari the entire time. When I *do* look at her, she gives me those *eyes* again. I melt. I still long for her... I still do. I probably always will.

At the end of the night, I give Inari and Jin a ride back to Jin's apartment and check out Inari's new car...it cost her $380. It's a steal.

Strangely, Inari walks around the car dozens of times, criticizing all of its flaws, "There are scratches in the bumper," she complains. "It looks like somebody keyed the door," she complains. "What's this, there's a little stain on the seat," she complains.

"Chill out!" Jin complains. "It cost $380 for god sake."

Inari nervously laughs, "I'm just joking, you realize right, I'm just being sarcastic... it's fine. It's fine. It's a fine car."

I love Inari, but I simply observe this episode with my mouth agape, wondering how unbalanced her sense of entitlement must be. A girl this beautiful is probably a bit damaged by what I call "the princess complex". A princess, like Inari, simply doesn't understand the plight of the commoner. This behavior seems to indicate that she doesn't understand the value of money enough to understand that she got a great deal. This can be a problem, as she likely also doesn't understand when people are being generous to her. Inari likely won't be driving this car soon anyway, as she has never had a driver's license.

Chapter 14 - Bias

The next day, Inari gets up considerably earlier. Everyone manages to get to my place around 1:30PM. We're hours behind schedule, but still making decent enough time to hit the park. Inari is lagging for the second day in a row, holding up the outing, in a way, holding the plans of the group hostage. She seems grumpy during the 30-minute car ride and barely says a single word the whole time except for some grumbles and grumpy retorts. At the park, the group exits my van and huddles together, making small talk before heading up to the ticket booth. I look around and I notice that Inari is missing. She hasn't left the car.

I return to the car and knock on the window, "Hey you coming? You alright?"

Inari says nothing. I imagine her to be grumpy and not interested in participating. Maybe she is looking for someone to convince her to get out of the car. Maybe I'll take up the challenge. I knock again, but still no answer. I open the door to find Inari pantsless, changing her clothes in the back seat.

"Oh shit, I'm sorry," I say, surprised.

"It's no big deal, it's not like I'm showing you my vagina or anything, I really don't care," she says.

Obviously, my heart pounds at the idea of seeing more skin than I'm used to seeing of her. "Alright, well, I'll be out here, I'm sorry. I was just making sure you were coming," I reply.

I return to the group, "Oops, I guess she's changing her clothes in there and I accidentally peeked at her in her underwear."

"She doesn't care," Jin says.

Inari emerges from the car, "Yeah it's not like I'm wearing skimpy underwear or anything. Not a big deal."

Inari is very lethargic. She blames her sleeping disorder, but she seems unhappy at the same time. I'm unhappy too... because I have to watch Inari and Jin hug each other all day. Sometimes when we're waiting in line she sits on the pavement and rests her head on his leg and I imagine and wish that I was sitting in his place. But they're clearly not doing well in their relationship, today, or generally.

In the back of my head, I keep hope alive and remind myself of a verse I wrote in a song, once upon a time.

You cower on your knees on the floor
Clutching to my leg
And I believe you genuine
To all you've said before
If I had only known your motives
and who you'd been to see
the night before
I take that last piece of heart for me
The one I'd always kept for me

The verse was inspired by a day at the Foxfire Café, with Luna, just a couple of days before things turned to shit between us. She got very clingy in the end as if giving me her final hugs goodbye. I thought to myself... "Wow, this is nice," at the time, but after I looked back on it and asked some other people, a friend suggested that it is common for a girl to be extra clingy just before she dumps her boyfriend. It would add up...

When my mental concentration slips, I catch myself wondering if Inari was only backing away from me to keep this volatile interpersonal situation, this powder keg, from igniting. I sometimes worry that she may have an uncanny ability to manipulate men that is dark and dangerous, but, you know, I proved myself to have a knack for misreading situations, and I discipline myself to think nothing of it. I don't really have a choice. Turning against her would starve me of these powerful feelings she brings to me. I can either believe that she is a goddess of light... or accept that she is dark… upon which time, she will surely excommunicate me and starve me of the glow I seek from her. I stop myself from thinking dark thoughts about her. I keep my thoughts of her pure. She is just a girl who is in a relationship with a man who doesn't properly love her. I will show her true love if I get the chance.

We decide to go on an "easy" ride… the Tilt-a-Whirl, easy, but fun all the same. Inari, Jin, and I triple up in a car and, as we're getting in, they begin to argue about something stupid. I didn't even hear what it was, but the next thing I know, they're trading evil looks at each other. When the ride is finished, after several minutes of awkward silence among the three of us, Inari gets off and gets as far away from him as possible, storming off into the distance.

We walk as a group, six in total. It is a fair distance to the next ride. The awkward vibes floating around cause me to physically distance myself from what's going on by about 30 yards or so. I have no interest in confrontations, especially ones that are not my own, but Inari comes over and walks close to me. She looks over and smiles an obviously fake flirty smile. I'd love to flirt back, but I recognize that this is obviously just an attempt to piss off Jin.

I press her, "Obviously something is wrong."

"Nothing is wrong. Why would anything be wrong?" she says. There's not even a hint of sarcasm in her voice, and I take in for a moment just how brilliant of an actress she is. A bad actress would be compelled to emphasize her words in such a way that conveyed a degree of sarcasm, overacting, unconvincing. Clearly, she intends this statement to be sarcastic, but she demonstrates incredible poise in her ability to remove all sarcasm from it in such a way that an unskilled actor would be incapable of doing.

"Obviously this is a powder keg about to explode," I say, shaking my head with a painful chuckle. I look back at her with a serious look, directly into her eyes, and offer to man-up for her. "Here's what I'm going to do. I'm going to go talk to Jin, and then I'm going to come back and talk to you, okay?"

Her face turns serious again. She no longer fakes a smile. She nods at me while locking eyes, assuring me that we understand each other. Without saying any more, I alter my path towards Jin. In the few seconds it takes me to reach Jin, I ponder about how much I absolutely hate being the "good guy" in this scenario. I honestly just want to break them up and set up a scenario where she crashes into my arms, but my moral compass guides me to *not* be a complete, total, douchebag. "Do you want to talk?" I ask.

"Yes," he says definitively.

"Hang back," I command.

We hang back about 15 paces and talk out of earshot from the group.

"I told her I'd come over and talk to you, but she didn't tell me anything about what's going on, so... what's been going on?" I ask.

"I don't know... she's just been in a bad mood all day, I don't really know what's up with her," he complains. "She told me about how you came onto her, but don't worry about it."

I am surprised and a little angered by this news. "What exactly did she tell you?"

"Well, just that you expressed interest in her, but you and she talked and agreed to be just friends."

Based on what he said... I figured that she downplayed the extent to which I pursued her, but I still couldn't be sure. I suppose it would depend on whether she told him Thursday or Friday. If it was Thursday, Inari would have not yet have discovered my cache of long love letters, poetry, music, and prose, but by Friday, she was in tears while talking to me on the phone and refusing to take Jin's calls.

Before I can think to explain myself, he interjects, "It's fine, I'm not upset. I'm not threatened by it."

"The reason I started chasing after her was because she kept giving me these googly eyes," I explain.

"Yeah, she does that to everyone," he comes back, quickly, as if to convey to me that her treatment of me is nothing special. Yet his tone also suggests a subtle degree of annoyance, not towards me, but towards Inari. I get the impression that Jin struggles to accept that Inari is an incessant flirt but is trained and conditioned and built to be stoic.

It would add up, but again, I trust Inari. I have no choice but to trust Inari and let her take me wherever she chooses to take me. I offer my perspective on why she might be gloomy today, "I know she's bitter about the whole dumping thing before Con."

"Yeah, I tried to talk to her about that, but I didn't really get anywhere," Jin concedes.

"I know she loves you though," I tell him.

"I *hope* she still does," he replies.

"I *know* she does," I assure him. "Please don't tell her that you mentioned anything about me coming on to her," I conclude.

"This never happened," he said.

I walk up and talk to Inari, "We have to be careful... because he knows I've been chasing you." Having observed some brilliant acting earlier, I figure, I'll give her another "audition". I am curious as to how she will react. Let's see how well she lies, shall we?

She gives me a beautifully crafted look of shock and amazement... "He does? Really?!" she says. Again, I ponder how her facial expressions and inflection were crafted perfectly, without a hint of sarcasm or over-acting. If Jin hadn't just outed this lie 15 seconds earlier, I'd have believed her shock.

Having established for the first time that Inari can tell a benign lie when she has to, I decide to keep *my* little white lie under the table. "He didn't say anything, but I'm pretty sure he knows." A white lie for a white lie... no harm no foul.

She has all kinds of complaints about Jin, tons and tons. She spends the next 3 hours just complaining about everything she hates about her relationship with Jin.

"Jin only cares about social status," she complains. "He thinks that I'm worthless because I don't have any fancy degrees or a fancy job or make lots of money. That's all he cares about. I'm just a trophy that he shows off to his friends. He doesn't really love me."

"I'm sorry, Inari," I console. "That's really shitty. Nobody should judge you for that. All I really care about is that you're a nice person and that you're nice to me. Nobody should judge you based on your career status. I envy people with charisma, who are capable of forming social bonds. You are clearly far better than me at all that."

"Jin will only want me while I'm young and beautiful, and when I'm old he will want to get rid of me," she complains. "Jin seems to be capable of venting his problems with me to strangers but seems to be incapable of talking directly to me."

I try to rationalize, "Sometimes guys have difficulty talking about their problems with their significant others because they have so much to lose. Therefore, they vent with their friends and coworkers instead. It is safer to talk about your problems to someone who doesn't have a stake in them. You need to realize that it is because he *cares* about you, that he is scared to resolve problems with you."

"I think you're wrong," she replies. "I don't think Jin is scared of anything. He really has no emotions at all. He's just a robot."

"Well, I think he has emotions. He's just very closed off about expressing them," I offer.

"No, believe me, I know who has feelings and who doesn't. Jin has emotions, but only a little bit. Many people, like you, Yuki, have a very wide range of emotions that they feel, but Jin... Jin's emotions are very narrow in range. He feels, but only just a little bit."

She and I partner up on *all* the remaining rides for the rest of the night, while she and he barely say a word directly to each other. I just try to ease the tension in the group by telling stories to everyone while, at the same time, being attentive to her and promoting healthy group conversation. When we're walking, and not waiting in a line, she and I pair up away from everyone else. Eventually, I make it clear that I am biased, and I still want her.

"I still daydream about all kinds of things I'd love to say to you," I say, "and yes, I daydreamt about saying exactly that to you hahaha..."

Inari never tries to put up barriers to my overtures, but at the same time, I try to be respectful of their relationship. Although clearly, I'm slipping in the morality department.

I continue going back and forth, relaying information between the two of them... but admittedly, I put less passion into consoling Jin while offering much comfort and consolation to Inari. It is both the natural order of things and deliberate. I ponder to myself how overtly sleazy I'm being by so unevenly dividing my time. On some level, I want to be overt about it. On some level, it is a flex.

I compare Jin to my ex, Laura, but stop short of suggesting that they should hook up, although the thought crosses my mind... it seems so perfect... get Jin a better match... then steal his girlfriend.

Everybody wins! Laura was and is plenty beautiful and a little bit kinky, like Inari, but Laura is also something Jin seeks that Inari isn't. Laura has pursued higher degrees and is currently in law school. Laura is reliable and has a steady job.

For me, however, Laura was a good companion for a while, but she just wasn't a match. Our relationship eventually grew into a thorn that just *had* to be pulled. I warn Inari, "The longer you let your relationship with Jin simmer, the more it will become apparent that it needs to end. You will end up like me and Laura. It is inevitable."

I feel awkward pairing up with Jin's girlfriend initially. I feel him watch me with jealous eyes. But as the night progresses, the routine gets less awkward. She and I stick together, cut off from everyone. It eventually feels like the normal order of the universe.

Finally, it is time for the last ride of the evening, "Steel Venom". Inari and I ride in the very back of everyone. She even makes deliberate moves to make sure our friends get on first so that we get in the back seat. The ride is constructed in such a way that they wouldn't be able to see us even if they looked over their shoulders, with chairs suspended from a rail that launches you up into the sky and back down again, accelerating from a standstill to full speed in an instant. I look over from my seat. I gaze into Inari's eyes as intently as was always routine before, and as if we had never had any conversations about being "just friends". She gazes back at me.

"I'm sorry you're having a bad day, I wish I could make it better," I say with honesty, care, and love in my heart.

"You have made it better," she replies with a twinkle and a flutter of her eyelids. She smiles an angelic smile, and my heart glows for her, and when my heart glows she seems to feel it, causing her to smile even brighter.

The ride launches... we scream as we are launched into the sky...

As there is no more time for rides, we immediately begin the long walk towards the exit of the park. I suddenly realize that my time with her is coming to a close and feel an intense urge to conjure up some overture of romance. I have spent many hours of many days dreaming of words that I might say to her, so I pull something out of my back pocket. "You've made me feel more special than anyone ever has in my life... and I'm just a random dude... you have no idea how much I love and appreciate that. You deserve someone who has as much passion for you as you do for him."

"But, Yuki, I *don't* just reach out to *anyone*. I reached out to you because you are special," she says back... smiling... beaming... twinkling.

God, her words. Her words are so magical. I dwell and ponder about the beauty and inflection of her words. Why does she bless me with such beautiful sentiments? Why can't she be mine?

We arrive at my place, and I invite them in to see a little bit of the new laser code I'm working on, then, they're on their way home. Immediately after they drive away, I play the role of the concerned friend, and I text *both* of them, informing them that if *either* of them needs someone to talk to, I'll be up all night working anyway. "Call anytime," I say.

I eagerly await the results with anticipation, biting my nails. I can't handle the waiting... waiting for word back. Did they break up? What's going on?

I go to bed to calm my nerves. I sometimes employ sleep to make time pass instantly when I'm impatient about things. I wake up at 5AM and find that Jin had texted me at 3:59. It is just one sentence, "Yeah we talked forever and all is good now."

Fail.

I can no longer sleep so I go in to work extremely early... I'm there by 5:30. I'm a bit battle-worn... I've lost this battle. But I still believe that there is more to this story. Sure, they made up, but if their relationship problems are so chronic, how much longer can they last? Yet, on some level, I still have to remind myself that even if they split up, it doesn't mean that I win. It just means that I have an unobstructed shot at winning if I even have a shot at *all*. Really, I think I'm far better than he could be for her.... more stable... more grand... more affectionate... more successful... more loving... more talented... more intelligent... more fun... more creative... more stylish... maybe even more attractive... and furthermore, *I worship the ground she walks on.*

Go figure. I can't battle an army that won't come to the battlefield, so I'll have to wait for the next meeting. Neither she nor he wants to fight, so I won't be winning any hearts with swords. Her happiness is my #1 priority, and if she's truly happy with him and I truly love her, then I should support that, but... I don't think she is... at *all*.

"This is sort of like Final Fantasy VII", Maddox says to me. "You've fought this big war and think the game is done but realize that you've only completed Act 1 and that there's still 90% of this story to be told. Right now... you're sitting outside Midgar with a huge adventure in front of you. In the course of events to come, friends will become enemies... enemies will become friends.... at some point, the plot will change into something different... then change back to something different again. But in the end... if it is meant to be... you will find each other again... someday... and the ultimate battle will be what you always expected it to be... before all the twists and turns of the plot confused you."

Chapter 15 - Post

I figure Inari and Jin, having re-won each other's hearts and affections, will disappear from my view for a couple of days. I am correct. I don't speak to Jin or Inari again until Tuesday morning. I notice Inari is online, commenting on posts made by other mutual friends. I take initiative and call her. She answers. When she pays attention to me, she gives me her attention fully, and I really appreciate that about her. I seek a post-mortem with her regarding the events of Sunday. She seems to feel like she broke through to him at the end of the night.... but she continues to spout out a long list of complaints. I tell her some of the things I said to him when we were hanging back.

"If you talked, you *must have* talked about the 'dumping thing before Con', right?" I ask.

"No. He still won't say anything about that, other than that he was being stupid! He owes me a better reason than that!" she replies.

Just before Con, Inari had disappeared to New Jersey. A friend of hers, who, according to her, was one of her best friends for months, became suicidal and she and her roommate/ex-boyfriend Barry went there to stop him from killing himself. She was gone for weeks, and during this time, Jin grew weary and upon her return from New Jersey, broke up with her, just before Con. Inari was heartbroken, but Jin went about his life seemingly unscathed emotionally. She pleaded with him, she begged. She convinced him to still go to Con with her, at least. They shared a hotel room, and whereas he wouldn't commit himself to her, nor would he pose with her in photographs, nor introduce her to the people he'd meet; he still had sex with her in the hotel. Inari broke down, and eventually just wouldn't go back to the hotel room with him. Days after Con, they mended their relationship, but Jin never really told her why he broke it off with her in the first place. We speculated that maybe he just had a burst of arrogance and thought that he could meet a new girl at the convention just as easily as he met her, or maybe he had an interest in someone specific, or maybe, just maybe, rumors about what happened in New Jersey were weighing on him and he didn't know who to trust. The only thing Jin ever said about his reasoning was, "I was being stupid."

"If he really loves me, he owes me a better answer than 'I was being stupid'. Why would he give me up so easily?" she repeats, over and over, obsessed.

Thinking back... it might have been a good thing for me to know. Why did he break up with her? I know he's told someone. But it would be foolish to arm me with such knowledge. I would be too powerful with it, and it would have been a really bad thing for me to relay to her if I had such knowledge. I know that someone out there knows... and they've kept it a secret from her as well. Even if I knew the answer, if I were the one to drop the bomb on her, I would only end up looking like the bad guy... and I'm trying to be honorable... the best I can... again... clearly failing in the morality department these days.

She brings up many other complaints about Jin... the same complaints I heard at the amusement park. Clearly, whatever wounds they have just aren't healing. They're still hemorrhaging badly. It becomes more and more apparent that she feels like she is treated like dirt by him most of the time. She tells me, again, that he is "obsessed with appearances" and she feels like if she weren't beautiful and well-loved by her friends, then he'd have nothing to do with her. She's his trophy, his status symbol. He cares only as much about her as he gains social equity from her. Jin wants her to be more educated, more successful. He wants her to have a solid career path. Inari feels like Jin sees her as an embarrassment, just like her family regards her... an embarrassment.

I simply assure Inari that I think she's perfect the way she is. "I am in love with your *heart*, and your social status has nothing to do with it, Inari! You could work at McDonald's, and I wouldn't look down upon you. I think you should do as much as you can with your career and education to make you happy. If having a better job makes you happy, then have a better job, but I'd never look down upon you for being happy in a job that is less than a CEO. Even without education, a person with your brains and charisma could achieve much."

For the time being, I just hope that I can continue to be friends with them both... I'll buy a few rounds as an apology the next time I see them.... and I'll try not to poison what they have.

I believe in my heart that I have something that is truly valuable and rare to her, but I've already done more chasing than is appropriate... I must give her the opportunity to come and get it for herself. The ball, again, is in her court... Things are happening though... things are happening for me... and for her. I think whatever is right and natural will happen, and I don't think this is entirely done.

Still, I have a compulsive desire to be "heard", and an overwhelming desire to be honest with her. "I should let you read this short story I wrote," I tell her. "It's called, *Life is Beautiful*, and in it, I've basically chronicled every day that I've ever interacted with you, since the beginning. But keep in mind that I am scared that if I let you read this story, you'll be offended. You'll probably hate me afterwards because, in it, I not only chronicle every interaction I've ever had with you, but I also chronicle every *thought* I've ever had about you. And some of these thoughts might offend you."

"You could never offend me," she says.

"No... trust me... you'll be offended by this. I want to be 100% honest with you... so I'll... I'll send it. It would be worthy of discussion," I say. "I want you to understand me, even if parts of it expose my own darkness."

Before I start my workday, I immediately obsess over revising this story. I neglect my job in favor of writing. I rewrite parts of the story that may express doubt about her and leave only the version of reality that I believe will displease her the least. I hope she is pleased with it, after all, and will appreciate the honesty.

I attach a reminder to the front of the story that this story is about PERCEPTION, and not about FACT. It doesn't matter whether the facts are accurate... but what really matters is the simple fact, that the events were PERCEIVED. I send her this very story, which, at the time, is only 15 chapters deep. I eagerly await her reaction to it. I attach it to a one-line email with the words,

"Our morals, beliefs, and convictions don't always correspond with our actions."

It is intended, in a way, to call out to her... to remind her that I believe that she and I are both *good* people even if sometimes we do things that may cause others to question how good we are. We're human. We sometimes fall victim to our own lack of self-control. I want her to confess. I want her to confess that she has sinned. That even if her love for me is potentially forbidden, I want her to admit that, in fact, she *does* love me. I feel so much love from her... there must be *real love* in there somewhere.

Chapter 16 - Opaque Mirrors

It is Wednesday. I go to the club, picking up Luna along the way. Despite my attempts to get Inari to come out, I don't expect Inari nor Jin to come.

I, therefore, spend some time reviving my long-lost friendship with Luna a bit more. Somewhere, deep down inside, I believe that she still loves me, but it is so buried under all the years of experiences she's had since we split up. Every girl I've ever loved keeps just a tiny shard of my shattered heart with them, always. As a result, I have just a little bit *less* heart left to give the next girl that comes along. If any of these loves, no matter how long lost, were ever in peril and truly needed help from me, I would drop anything I was doing right now to come and rescue them.

Luna is no different. Luna and I have deep heartfelt conversations on this night... and I once again try to understand what kind of downward spiral she led herself into after we finally went our separate ways for good. She talks about how just after her mother died, her dad had an accident and severely broke his leg. Luna was left to take care of the things that both her mother and father took care of around the house. Her depression sucked her into Morrison and Zak's parties, deeper and deeper. The scene as a whole was bringing in more and more drugs and Luna got consumed by every kind of drug she could put into her body. You name it, crack, cocaine, LSD, ecstasy, heroine, meth... all were fair game. She latched onto the things that came easy and made her feel good while trying to forget the burdens of life.

Eventually, Luna became good friends with her now longtime boyfriend, Richard. Luna hung out at the clubs and earned a reputation as the "topless pool chick" because she and Richard would always play pool topless at the club. She and he were "just friends" for a long time, then friends with benefits, an open relationship of sorts... and eventually they made themselves monogamous to each other. They'd tell no one they were even dating for months after they became "official".

Luna, however, confides in me that things between her and Richard aren't going so well. She got a DUI that would force her to give up her job as a delivery driver. She wanted to marry Richard, but apparently, he wasn't too keen on the idea. Now, without a job, pending court dates, and with a boyfriend who she thinks may have had his "fill" with her, she is depressed; she is feeling worthless as if maybe she made some really bad decisions that were now irreversible earlier in life.

At the end of the night, I drop off Luna at home. It is 3AM and I'm just walking up to the door to let Ada out into the lawn when Inari calls. She is polite and I am happy to hear from her. I wonder for a moment if she's read the 15-chapter "short story" I sent her. but it quickly becomes apparent that she has and quickly the mood of the conversation takes a dramatic turn.

"Yuki, the fact that anyone might have read this stuff scares me!" she says. "This could severely damage my reputation!"

"I just wanted to be honest with you, you always inspire honesty in me, even when I behave badly," I profess.

"Did you talk to all these people about me? Yuki! You can't do that! You can't assume that you know what I'm thinking just because I look at you a certain way! And what on earth are you talking about when you refer to my 'laser beam eyes'!? I never looked at you this way!"

"Yeah, you did! And you whispered in my ear all these seductive things!" I counter.

"Yeah, well, when I told you I thought lasers were sexy, it just seemed like you needed a pick-me-up, you were all mopey and down on yourself! It wasn't because I wanted to turn you on!"

"Why would I have been down on myself when I had you sitting across from me! That doesn't make any sense!"

"Yuki, those words never meant what you thought they meant!"

"But what about when I told you I wanted to steal you away and you said 'now you finally tell me!' as-if you were really waiting for me all night, or when you whispered, 'you have no idea how much more I love you now' into my ear at the club."

"I didn't mean it like that! I just meant like 'friend' love. Just because I said all of those things, or did all of those things, doesn't mean that I had any romantic interest in you!" she continues, "I really wish there was another form of the word 'love' that could describe the kind of love that you and I have, but let me assure you that it is not romantic. I just thought you looked like someone who never really had a really good friend in the world, and I wanted to be your friend. It was never romantic!"

"But it *was*. And it still *is*! You understand that, to you, I've said the most grandiose things I've ever said to anyone in my life, right? I mean, I sent you love letters and poetry and music and rehearsed all the romantic things I couldn't wait to say to you for hours and hours so that, during our next encounter, I could speak them to you! I said romantic things to you *all night long* and you didn't stop me! You should have stopped me, Inari!"

"Yuki, I have been 100% mentally, physically, and emotionally faithful to Jin. Whatever you think you're hearing or seeing is all in your head! I never 'gazed' at you from the runway at the Fet Ball, I told you, they coached me to look at someone other than the photographers, but you were just there."

"Yeah, and Jin was standing right next to me, why wouldn't you just look at him?"

"Jin wasn't standing next to you, I don't know what you're talking about! If he was there, I didn't see him. I think you're misremembering things, Yuki! I get it, Yuki! You have so much love in your heart, and that's why I love you, but you can't assume because I did some of these things or said some of these things that

I'm in love with you! That's just *crazy*. You really need to see a therapist! They can help you! I talk to my counselor all the time and she helps me with things. They can help you. I reached out to you because I saw you as someone who deserved to be reached, but not as a romantic partner."

"I'm sorry," I grovel. "I didn't mean to hurt you. I didn't mean to spread anything to anyone. I can impulsively and compulsively seek to confide my feelings in others."

"Who did you talk to Yuki?" she asks forcefully.

I am bashful, I feel like a naughty puppy being beaten by his master as I confess, "Techna, Daedalus, Luna, and Maddox. I deliberately left Echo in the dark… also Aurthur, I guess."

"Yeah, I'm going to have to talk to Aurthur about that crap he made up! I don't know why he said what he did, but that was really shitty and disgusting of him to say! I don't want people to think that I'm the 'bitch who hurt Yuki'," she says.

"I'm sorry, I'm so sorry! The longer you're not around, the more I feel like I need to talk to my best friends about my problems, and Inari, you are my *number one problem*! I need to do better. I'm so sorry, I hurt you. Your happiness is my #1 priority, I just want you to be happy, even if it means that I have to take the fall," I grovel even more.

"Your own happiness needs to be your #1 priority," she says.

"Well, I need to have you, Inari. My happiness is tied up in *you*, Inari! And if I have to wait, and if I have to improve myself for decades, I have no choice but to work hard for you. I'm so sorry!"

"You need to work on your mental health, Yuki. I need someone strong. I've been through trauma in my life and your trauma is nothing in comparison! I've had my car windows smashed out and been dragged out by my hair! I've been raped! You have no idea,

Yuki! Even Barry did some pretty fucked up shit to me. I grew up abused by my uncles, who were essentially brothers and my mother's response to my crying was to come into my room and complain, 'if you don't stop crying, I'll come in and give you something to *really* cry about!' I became a 'cutter'. I used to cut my legs so deep I could almost see the bone, but I didn't bleed much. For some reason, I don't bleed like normal people."

She eventually calms down and we continue deep discussion, "I'd given up on men before I met Jin. I love him. But when he dumped me before Con, he seemed perfectly capable of moving forward in his life without me and left me feeling paralyzed and unable to function. The easiness of how he tossed me aside made me feel so worthless."

"I wish I could rescue you from all that," I profess. "I want to take you away from all of that. I could have met you at Con during that time. If I had known what was going on, and we were able to connect, would things have been different?"

"Our relationship might be different if you met me then," she confesses.

"I'm so sorry, I couldn't get past my own personal drama to come and find you, Inari. I'll do better. I have no choice."

I went to Con because Luna invited me out. Luna told me that Richard was not going this year and therefore she and I could have time to make amends. That is where Luna spent many hours apologizing to me for her mistreatment of me a decade ago. After 10 hours of apologies, I felt that we could *finally* forget our grudges and rebuild our long-lost friendship.

Con is literally a party that lasts 4 days straight full of geeky people into comic books, sci-fi, and fantasy. No matter if it is 6AM or 6PM... the party is going strong. The parking lot of the hotel is packed with tailgaters. Sex, alcohol, and drugs are rampant all over the place. 5 surrounding hotels are overbooked with attendees who book hotel rooms even if they live just a few miles away… because having a hotel room means that you never have to leave the party. Those who can't get rooms of their own will crash on the floor of their friends' rooms. I take a more relaxed approach to the party though… I'm not big into promiscuous sex, drugs, or alcohol for that matter.

But my primary obsession at Con wasn't Luna. I had yet to meet Inari. It was, unfortunately, Amber. Con was taking place just 2.5 weeks after I tossed Amber out of my house. Her eviction left me more emotionally shaken than it left *her,* it seemed. Amber showed up on the second day of Con at 2:30AM. She and Beth walked together, side by side. Trailing behind them 5 feet away is Brad, the "douche bag ex", who is now upgraded to just "douche bag".

Brad is short and looks like he has "short man's syndrome", a condition my friends refer to as when a man needs to compensate for his shortness by being an asshole to everyone around them. Asshole or no asshole, Amber has Brad *trained*. Amber has him put in his place. It is evident in how he follows 3-5 feet behind her at all times. She talks to her friends with her back to him, and he just stands around like her personal assistant, waiting for her next command, like a dog on a leash.

Amber notices me in the parking lot where people congregate to smoke. She looks over at me, so I know I've got her attention. Without words, Luna and I communicate through body language, "We should fuck with her."

It helps to understand that Amber is well aware that I had a history with Luna, and when I last saw Amber, Luna and I were long lost. Luna was the "one who got away" who treated me so cruelly years ago. Just to mess with Amber, Luna and I know what to do. With some brilliant acting, we square up our shoulders as we exchange small talk eye-to-eye, much like Inari and I would come to do routinely. We beam at each other as if this encounter we're having is filling both of us with bliss and euphoria.

I can feel Amber's eyes burning into the back of my head from 40 feet away. I sneak a glance and see her steaming angry, with a scowl on her face.

Just then, in a stroke of luck, a photographer comes by. He really likes Luna's Tank Girl costume and asks for a photo. Amber watches us from 40 feet away as this photographer takes 50-100 pictures of her. I tend to Luna as if she's a supermodel and I am her handler. As the photographer finishes, we just go back to beaming at each other with blissful smiles and rainbow eyes.

The photographer walks right past Amber in her club-girl rave attire and her short skirt, without even a glance. Amber scowls again and throws her cigarette on the pavement and stomps off.

"Happiness is the greatest revenge, right?" I joke to Luna.

But all that is past. I continue my phone conversation with Inari. She is so damn nice to me. Our conversation turns so deep that I, again, have to remind myself that Inari is not my girlfriend, even though I love her so much.

"Everyone, including Jin, is always trying to change me," she sobs.

"Inari, you are the most perfect girl on planet earth. *Perfect... exactly* how you are. I don't *expect* nor *want* you to change *anything* about yourself. You are perfect! Absolutely perfect! You have perfect hair, a perfect heart, perfect eyes, a perfect smile! There's nothing wrong with you at all. You are the greatest and most amazing person I've ever met. You are perfect, exactly how you are! Absolutely no one is more perfect than you! You are perfect!" I swear to god I used the word "perfect" a hundred more times as I just sang her praises for more than 5 minutes.

Despite my overtures, her focus is still on Jin, "Jin thinks that I need more goals in life, a career, money."

I say the same things I've said to her before, it is getting exhausting, frankly, "I think you should do whatever fulfills you in life. I don't judge you based on your level of achievement or status. It's your heart that matters, Inari. And you have the most *perfect* heart! Regardless of status, if you have love in your life, I absolutely *envy* you."

My onslaught of affection finally reaches so far into Inari's heart that she explodes into a tirade of tears, "I wish he loved me like you do!!!" she cries.

My heart melts for her like it never has before in this instant. I wish *she loved me* like *I love her.* But in all honesty, I love this girl more than any girl I've ever loved. I love her so completely that I will feel no jealousy at this time. Ultimately, I want her to be happy.

But I know... I KNOW... I *KNOW*.... that he's not right for her... and for the first time ever, I really reach out to her deeply and tell her this... I plead with her. I beg her to see the light. Jin may be a good guy to someone who is used to being beaten up by her boyfriends, but he isn't right for *her.* For the first time ever, I directly aim and attack her relationship with Jin. But I do this not for my own sake... but for hers. I love her to death... I want her to be happy... and even if it is not with me, I am dead sure I don't want her to be with Jin. Jin clearly does not make her happy.

I feel in my heart that I am so much more capable of loving her than him... a "robot".

Unlike most of our conversations, despite 3 hours and 47 minutes of deep conversation, I never get signals that she wants to be "more-than-friends" with me.

If this were another night... and I hadn't been scolded 3 times by her already for assuming too much... I might have found such signals in her words... but not tonight. Yet she touches my heart so deeply... so deeply. We laugh together... we cry together... even if our love is not physical... there is *sooo* much love between us...

there is so much love emanating from her... and from me.

"I wish the English language had more than one word for love," she states. "Love has too many definitions. There's no specific word to differentiate the kind of love *we* have from the love that a married couple would have for each other."

"My heart is in denial," I say. "My heart just can't believe this," I say. "I don't know what kind of love you're referring to, because my love for *you* is the most complete love I have ever felt, and whatever you gave to me felt *so very real* as well, if only it lasted for a few moments."

"What on earth are you actually looking for in a mate then, Inari?"

"I want someone who is kind, considerate, stable, appreciative, emotionally available, and attentive. Someone who will give me hugs when I am sad... someone who loves me the way I am... someone who will pet my forehead and just tell me 'everything is going to be okay' when I'm having a bad day..."

"You realize that you're describing me?" I tell her.

She does not respond directly but continues her description... more passionately... all her words describing me as I see myself with her... "Someone who will build a life with me... hold my hand while I sleep... protect me... take care of me..."

"You realize that you're describing me?" I tell her again.

She continues, with more words... words upon words... speaking faster and faster getting more animated and more dramatic in her cadence... "I WANT TO HAVE A DOG! I want to hold hands! Climb trees! Watch sunsets! Frolic in the rain!" She shouts so many things on and on, that I could not possibly list them all. Random fun things... silly things... happy things... peaceful things. As she does this I dream of myself happily doing all these things with her... I dream... I dream.

"You realize that you're describing me?" I say once again, more incessantly than before.

Normally I would be electrified by what seem to be blunt descriptions of me. I would normally take it as a signal that she wants more from me, but this time I am merely saddened. She sought all these things in a mate, but for some reason couldn't see or admit that her prince was standing right in front of her the whole time.

"I am happy just standing across from you, and I cherish every moment we have together, no matter what we are doing," I say. "We could just be sitting around watching paint dry... and I would be happy to be sitting next to you. I want to be with you always... I want to spend every minute of every day with you. Meeting you has been a fairy tale," I say.

Her voice suddenly becomes serious, "Yeah, well I told my ex that I wanted a fairy tale and he said 'What the fuck!? That's dumb! Fairy tales aren't real,'"

"I believe in this fairy tale," I say. "I want this fairy tale," I say, trying to change the tone of the conversation back to fantasy.

"Fairy tales aren't real. My ex is right," she says.

The battle for her heart is hard-fought... but futile. "You realize that I don't just say all these things to anyone right? I mean I've said more grandiose things to you than I've ever said to anyone... including my fiancé... and I mean... I *proposed* to that girl!"

"Really?" she says. Suddenly I've got her attention.

"Yes," I say. I tell her the story of how I proposed to Laura...which was done in an awkward random conversation barely one month into our relationship. We were lying in bed when I chuckled and said, "I was just thinking how strange it would be if we got married."

She replied, "I don't think it would be strange at all."

So, I asked her, "Would you marry me then?"

She replied as if it wasn't a big deal. "Yes," she said.

"So, I can call you my fiancé then?" I asked to clarify… as if it weren't real.

"Yes," she affirmed.

The next day I went to the mall and bought her a cheap ring. It was cheap, but it suited her. 3 diamonds on white gold with a prominent black onyx protrusion. The diamonds were so crappy that they were almost unnoticeable, but she wouldn't have wanted a more expensive ring.

Inari laughs at the story... it wasn't what she expected for sure. My relationship with her is so much different and I feel like telling her this story helps her understand the gravity she has to me. These feelings I have for her are *heavy* and I am *never shy* about expressing them. Inari is so rare. So rare.

"If I ever proposed to you... there would be violins and trumpets, and thousands of people clapping in Victorian dresses as we're whisked away in a limo...no actually a pumpkin carriage... and there will be a parade!"

She laughs. She giggles. She likes my story.

"There *is* a connection between us," I repeat from our previous conversations. "There *is* a connection between us... There *is* a connection between us.... it is UNDENIABLE!!"

She does not respond with any words... but I hear maybe a giggle of sorts. I imagined I made her smile... but only she really knows.

But after hours of venting about dark subjects and connecting with each other on the deepest of levels... she returns her focus to talking about the things that are great about Jin and begins listing all the ways that he is good to her... and I come to reality.

This girl just doesn't see it. She just doesn't see the magic that I can bring to her. She doesn't believe in this fairy tale.

"This conversation should be awkward to you, you know. You don't want me dumping all these compliments and love letters on you every day, do you?"

She begins to respond as if to ignore the question... so I ask her again. "Do you want me to stop showering you with compliments and love letters?"

She again answers the question with too many words in a manner like how a politician answers a question he doesn't want to answer. It is almost like she didn't even hear the question... like she blocked it out... blacked it out.

I stop her... "You still haven't answered 'yes' to my question," I say.

"Yes, to what??"

"Do you want me to stop showering you with compliments and love letters every day?" I ask again.

She hesitates... "...yessss," she says in a sigh.

I chuckle at how adorable she is, as her sarcastic inflection indicates that she is clearly lying. "I don't believe you," I say. "So, whenever you need to be bombarded with compliments and wonderful sentiments... you call me up okay?"

She pauses for a second, I feel that she approved of that statement. I feel like she might have smiled and blushed a bit on the other end of the phone. She says nothing in return... and then our conversation continues into lighter, friendly subjects. We talk for what seems like forever.

"So, when you read this story, how does it make you FEEL?" I ask her.

"Well... I guess I worry... I worry that people will think that I'm scheming to cheat on Jin, and that is not the case," she replies.

I counter... "Well when *I* read this story, without knowing the ending, it feels to me like a *romantic* story about two people *coming to terms with the inevitable.*"

She pauses again to digest what I've just said to her. I imagine she's attempting to imagine the story as told from my perspective instead of her own. I feel like she understands why I would call the story "romantic", but it never really got through to her up until this point, simply because she was too worried about her reputation. She doesn't object to my assessment of it. She doesn't ask me to stop writing.

It is now nearly 6:30AM and she is worried about me and my work performance. I am confident about a lot of things in life... and I am not concerned about my career or losing my job.

"I love myself, and I love my life," I say. "I mean these things that I say," I say with more confidence than I'm sure she's ever heard from me before. "If I ever appear down... it is just because I'm weathered from the battle of life... but I am a warrior in this life... I have fighting strength... you don't worry about me at *all*."

I call it a night. I have to be at work in a couple of hours.

I know I have to take her off this pedestal that she is on, but unlike girls, I've put on pedestals in the past... I didn't *put* her on this pedestal... she was *just there* when I met her.

But this love I have for her is unrequited. It... must... stop... she knows this.

"Two people… coming to terms... with the inevitable," this is *fate*.

Time will tell us. Patience, Yuki... Patience.

Chapter 17 - Beauty in Chaos

It is Friday night... Inari now has Chapter 16. I decide that I will continue to send her chapters as I write them, but I don't assume she's read chapter 16 yet. She makes me feel like I'm her #1 priority when I'm standing across from her, but when she's got other things going on, I feel like I don't exist. It is a pattern that I wish she could break. And I wish I didn't feel so alone when she does this to me. I cannot just turn my feelings and concern for her on and off. I worry about her constantly, and I know there's more going on with her emotionally than I've yet to understand.

But how I so *do* want to understand her. I love this girl like mad, and I seek the beauty in her chaos. I spend some time talking to Maddox at The North Loop, intending to hit Ground Zero later in the night. He always has sociopathic, but sage-like, advice for me.

"The minds of women are always full of such chaos," he says. "It can drive us men mad... because we're such simple beings. Men want sex when they want it, and then they want to be left alone to conquer the world until they get horny again. Men are simple. On the other hand, women want men to be able to do impossible things. The life of a man is a walking paradox. A man is typically expected to read the mind of a woman. He's expected to know her feelings even when she refuses to express them... he's expected to know what she wants him to *do* without her asking him.... he's expected to know what *she* wants *him* to *say he wants for dinner* and will demand he keeps guessing until he finally chooses whatever she always had in mind to begin with! He's expected to take charge... but is never allowed to have opinions or feelings. He's expected to open doors for her... but never make her feel like she can't open the door for herself. He's expected to spend all his money wining and dining her... but if he ends up broke because of it, he is simply irresponsible. He's expected to be indestructible. To show weakness to a woman is to *immediately turn her off.*"

"I am not indestructible," I offer. "I don't *want* to be indestructible. I try to dissociate myself from the male gender for multiple reasons. I support feminism and the rights of women to take charge of their own gender roles that society has traditionally imposed upon them, and I *also* believe that the world is *finally* ready to accept that men should be no more obligated to conform to their traditional gender roles than women should be. It is not all that fun to be a man sometimes. I've always been the 'provider' in my relationships. It is pressuring to be expected to 'win the bread' every day. It is pressuring to be expected to compete in society. Women expect men to work hard and compete... and win. Sometimes, just sometimes, I want a break! Sometimes I just want to crawl back up into my mother's arms and have her hold me and take care of me. I am *not* indestructible. I have feelings. Being a man with feelings shouldn't be unattractive to women should it?"

"But look at Inari," Maddox adds, "what does she really have going for her besides her pristine image? She hides behind her makeup and her hair extensions and weaves. She's scared of having a flaw!"

"But she is flawless!" I reply. "She is flawless in spirit as well as image, you know! I love everything about her, even her hints of darkness!"

"*No one* is flawless," Maddox stresses. "The best advice I can give you is to simply state that nobody is just a victim. Everyone is a perpetrator of something. If she appears flawless to you, then there's something wrong. She is hiding something from you. She needs to be able to show you her flaws before you can trust her. Be careful."

"Even if she has darkness and flaws, I want to see past them. To be human is to be flawed, and I love her like no other human I've ever loved," I say, "and even if she's got flaws, she is a work of life, nature, this beautiful universe... everything flawed in the universe is beautiful, simply because it exists!"

"Yeah, but, I know you don't like Zak very much. To you, Zak is a big flaw. Is he beautiful as well?" he asks.

"Okay, I see your point, fuck that guy," I reply, jokingly. "But really, I suppose on some level, he became who he is through some kind of beautiful process, involving, molecules, fusion, fission, and the universe. Maybe he's mostly composed of antimatter!"

After concluding our conversation, I finish my drink alone and ponder my predicament. Why is this such a battle!? I feel guilty for taking up so much of Inari's time. I feel like demanding her time is arrogant of me. Why do I deserve her time? This battle for her heart feels like good and bad are fighting with each other. I don't want to battle good and evil to be with her, I just want there to be good. This feels... like war. Wars may be won... but there are always casualties... and for those who lose loved ones in war... the sacrifice is never a victory.

I try not to assume that I'll ever see Inari again. It is a coping mechanism that I employ to deal with my impatience. Inari suggested the other night that I get together with our mutual friend Azena. Azena had just left her husband. He was a real douchebag who would hit on women constantly while they were married. My female friends thought he was creepy as fuck. Azena didn't know he was telling them that she and he had an "understanding" before he'd sleep with random women. This, apparently, was not the case. Azena was potentially looking for someone new... someone good.

I decide... if Inari truly wants me to explore Azena as an option, since I'm already loosely acquainted with her, I'll send her a text and see what happens.

"Inari says that you and I should get to know each other better... and I trust Inari with my life."

It turns into a casual conversation... an ice breaker... she informs me that she'll be at Ground Zero later... I casually suggest that maybe I'll be there.

It is all casual friendliness. She *does* show up... with a few other people I am acquainted with. I get some small talk in, but there's only so much small talk you can dish out in your first real conversation. She had other friends to attend to, another man in the group, John, seems to have taken a liking to her and is staking his territory, but, before she completely terminates our conversation, I feel the need to inquire more about Inari, so I throw her name into the small talk.

"Inari and I have become very close friends recently," I offer.

"I actually just saw her on the street going into a party in Northeast," she notes.

"Was Jin with her?" I inquisitively ask, as transparent as glass.

"No, he's at 'game night'... I saw him earlier too," she informs.

Azena pairs up with John, who seems like a nice guy, but I don't know much about him. John was a kind-hearted gentleman who seemed to have similar problems keeping the attention of women, much like my own. I ponder how, like many nice guys, he may be unattractive to a girl like Azena.

Our small talk concluded; I get an idea. I decide to text Inari, and let her know that I've been successful in connecting with Azena. "I'm hanging with Azena per your suggestion." In some ways, it was a psychological maneuver, a game, a test. I figured if she truly wanted me to hang out with Azena, she'd simply read my text and be proud of me for moving on.

But my heart wants what it wants. Like so many times before, the orchestra seems to play exactly the next chord that I predict. Upon receiving my text, Inari does exactly what I want. Remember, Inari rarely, if ever, answers my text messages... even if it is a question like "I'm worried... are you alive? Yes/No." But this time... within 10 minutes... Inari calls me up.

"Hey, Yuki! You should come to this party! Bring Azena if she's up for it. There are also some nice girls I want you to meet!" she says.

I know she wants me to be happy without her... but I sense emotional chaos within her... and I believe that this chaos of emotion compels her to play into my hand.

I tell Azena that Inari invited both of us out to the party. She simply replies politely, "I've already made other plans," and that is that. I say my goodbyes to her and I'm immediately on my way. Upon arrival, immediately, I'm greeted just a couple of steps inside the door by a gentleman.

"You're Yuki, right?"

"I am", I reply.

"You're legendary," he says back.

I'm flattered... "Well, I guess my reputation precedes me... I guess maybe you've heard about my parties or something... people randomly approach me about them all the time," I continue. "Inari invited me out... she actually met me at my own party."

"Yeah, I live with Inari," he says.

"Oh okay... you must be Barry."

Barry presents himself as a stand-up guy. Of all the people at the party that there are to get to know...I enjoy talking to Barry the most. Inari finishes a couple of conversations, says a few words to me, and then goes around telling a few people how awesome I am. I blush a little bit. She tries to hook me up with a friend and then disappears behind a closed door with someone else... I guess to deliver some relationship advice or something, but I am taken aback by how long they stay locked away from me. Her conduct at the party is flattering yet disturbing at the same time.

I hang out and eventually find myself playing Rock Band...

showing off. I feel like a douche showing off... but Inari eggs me on. She asks me if I can play the game behind my head and I reply, definitively, "yes". As I flail about like a glam rocker, she and her friend Kat cheer and clap and jump. Inari demonstrates that she is an even more immaculate human being than I ever knew her to be. She is so loving... so kind... so open... so supportive… that it intimidates me. I never felt intimidated by her before now, because she always gazed into my eyes with such confidence to inspire great confidence in *me*. But without the taming quality of her eyes, I am merely intimidated by her greatness now. She does not gaze into my eyes. I've scolded her too many times for doing so.

Inari compliments me to all her friends using words like "amazing", "awesome", and "legendary" as Barry had echoed as I entered the door, but I am quiet and reserved throughout the party. I am nervous and I need her eyes to tame me. I kinda feel like I look like some random idiot playing video games, showing off like a douche bag.

It is a hard night because my heart wanted so much to be next to her... but she had other agendas with other people and other friends. I discipline myself to be okay with that... and I *am* okay with that. But I guess the hardest part about it all was just watching her interact with others. In this room, I'm not her #1 favorite guy in the world... in fact... I'm probably ranked about #30. She loves everyone so much and is direct and affectionate with everyone at the party.

Never once does she give me those eyes of hers all night. I try desperately to make eye contact with her, but she never locks eyes with me. I sit next to Barry after getting burnt-out on Rock Band but mostly burnt-out from trying to achieve eye contact with Inari. Inari comes over and kneels on the floor in front of him… she rests her elbows on his knees… and she peers up into his eyes more deeply than she *ever* looked into mine.

It becomes apparent that her emotional connection to Barry is very complex and deep… deeper than her relationship with Jin…

deeper than her relationship with me. The beauty of Inari is now more and more and more chaotic... more complex... an equation more complex than the equation of life itself.

I'm no longer sure where I fit in, if at all. I feel like I don't belong here. I feel like a 3rd wheel. I feel like the hummingbird that creates enough chaos to start a hurricane… consequential, but trivial.

Inari is drunk and getting drunker. She is having fun and we're planning a group of 4 or 5 to go to another all-night diner. I'm looking forward to this adventure as it would get me a chance to become better acquainted with Barry, Inari, and Kat. Win, win, win.

Everything seems fine... we're ready to go.... but Inari won't put down her drink. The party is over... the host declared it. But 20 minutes pass and she still won't put down her drink. Finally, she finishes it in a big gulp... we all think we're walking to the door... but as our backs are turned, she quickly mixes herself up yet another... a tall one! Barry and a couple other people try desperately to get it away from her.

"But I bought this vodka. It's mine," she says in a whimper.

She gets visibly drunker by the minute... but as Barry tries to pull it away, she refuses to give it to him, "It only has a little bit of drinky in it," she slurs. She pulls Barry into the kitchen... she's upset about something... I don't know what.

I need some fresh air, so I decide to go outside and sit on the porch... I bring my car around and park it illegally in front of the house. Then, I go back inside to get the scoop.

"I don't think we're going anywhere," Kat says in a disappointed tone.

I understand, we all get too drunk sometimes. But Inari is now drunker than I've ever seen any conscious human being in my life, and I am worried... I feel compelled to take care of her, but I don't think that I am first in line. I've felt slightly unwelcome for the last couple of hours as if I'm just crashing a party I'm not invited to. I figure I'll say my goodbyes to her and Barry and be on my way.

But now, she is so mentally *gone*. She's unable to speak. She sits in a corner of the kitchen with Barry, holding his hand. I try to get her to say "goodbye" to me, but she just stares at me with a catatonic stare, as if she doesn't even know my face... she's clearly had *way* too much. Looking back, I probably should have stayed around in case she needed to make a trip to the ER. I, again, try to get her to say "goodbye" to me, but she mumbles half a syllable and ignores me. It is like I'm a ghost. Then she stands up... staggering. She almost falls and I help her keep her balance. It is clear that she's not going anywhere... I just want her to say "goodbye" to me... but she is incapable... or unwilling... or both... who knows how much of her brain is even functioning at this point. Did she even hear me? As I walk to the door... I try to get her to wave to me or something... to acknowledge that... yes... I am leaving... I look over my shoulder... she is looking over at me... so I wave... but she doesn't wave back. She just stares, catatonic and empty.

I trust that I'm leaving her in good hands with Barry. Still, I leave worried about her and I still worry about her as I write this.

It is the hardest goodbye I've ever said to anyone.

On some levels, I feel like I'm responsible for all of this. I can only speculate what she was feeling... I know she drinks from time to time...but I didn't think she would drink herself into such a state. I draw wild conclusions that maybe she got depressed because she couldn't make me happy and tried to stuff down her anxiety with alcohol. She clearly tried so very hard to do good things for me but was possibly emotionally frustrated that she couldn't make me happy. Maybe she wanted to drink to forget that I was there... I don't know... It was really wild. Most people would just pass out when they drank too much, but she was awake, yet catatonic, like a different person in her own body who didn't know where she was, who she was, who I was, or why I was waving to her. It's like she didn't even understand the gesture of someone waving to her.

But maybe it is arrogant of me to think that I'm so important in her life. How could little, insignificant me, cause her any drama? "What drama? There is no drama," she said to me on the night of the Fetish Ball. She didn't see the drama that I saw in her eyes… or at least she refused to acknowledge it.

Looking back there were probably as many signs to indicate that she had *no interest* in me as there were signs that she *did*. When faced with conflicting signals like this, which signals do you choose to believe? When someone says "yes" but actions say "no" which path do you believe? I guess you believe the path you want to believe, or you pick the path that is recommended to you by the person you trust the most. But the person I trust most… is Inari.

I owe it to Inari to stop dragging her down with my personal drama. I owe it to her to stop professing my love for her. I'm sure that knowing that I love her but also knowing that she cannot requite my love does *not* make her happy. I want Inari to be happy, and I simply know… and I simply know *now*… that I owe it to her to *stop* this bullshit… So, I conclude this chapter written not *about* Inari, but *to* Inari. I will be sending her this chapter as soon as it is written, just as I have sent her all the other chapters…

So once again Inari… I say to you…

I love you. I love you to death. I would take a bullet for you right now. I love you exactly how you are. I think that everything about you is perfect. I don't desire you to change anything about yourself. You're beautiful, you're kind, generous, and warm-hearted to a degree that I didn't think was possible in any human being. It is easy to be in love with you. And you, therefore, deserve the ABSOLUTE BEST and I want you to know that I'll ALWAYS be here for you. I will always fight for you and defend your honor to my OWN death.

But since I love you... I owe it to you to stay out of your way. To let you make your own mistakes. I owe it to you to try to move on. You want this for me, and I recognize that you want it not just for me... but for YOURSELF. You want me to move on. I am not helping you. I thought I could help you, but I feel like I am doing DAMAGE to you with all these letters and stories and text messages and compliments. I cannot damage a girl that I truly love like no other.

If saying this to you makes you feel abandoned in any way... then we once again MUST TALK. I would appreciate one last chance to talk to you like we always have. I LOVE our talks. It would really sadden me to end this all like this.

I don't want to abandon you, but I feel like I'm hurting you. I can't HURT you Inari. I can't live with myself if I know that I'm hurting you.

Don't worry about me though... as I said... I'm a WARRIOR. Maybe I'm a bit weathered... but I'm a WARRIOR. I'm going to continue to fight and claw my way through life... and I'll continue to protect the ones I love... and I'll continue to protect YOU.

I have a life that others envy... SOMEONE out there must want to share this life with me... and hopefully, when I meet her, she is every bit as amazing as YOU are. I hope I meet her soon... but I must say that no girl has ever crossed my path so worthy as YOU Inari. It puts all the other relationship battles of the past into a new perspective. This has been the hardest fought war of hearts I've ever fought in my life. All the other little battles seem like mere skirmishes compared to this... so now I, at least, know that if I can survive this... I can certainly survive these other journeys.

You've done well for me.

But I must emphasize... I must leave this book open. Maddox tells me, "17 chapters isn't a book. You need at least 30."

Yet I've written every chapter here as if it were the last, and, once again... I conclude this very chapter as if it is the last as well.

But you know... you KNOW... that I would love nothing more than to talk with you on the phone all night...every night... to sit next to you... to gaze into your eyes... to run through parks in the rain... to usher you confidently through the journeys of life... to build a life with you... to support your dreams... to build monuments for you... to make the world a better place... together... with YOU... for YOU.

But what I want is irrelevant... this is about YOU and what YOU WANT... DO NOT FEAR WHAT YOU WANT... You only have one life... live an immaculate one. You're an immaculate girl... but if you want me to move on... I'll do that... FOR YOU.

LIFE... in all its chaos... is FUCKING BEAUTIFUL, Inari. And you deserve a life that is the most beautiful of lives that can ever be achieved because you are the most beautiful human being I have EVER met. Don't let ANYONE tell you otherwise... if they do... I'll come after them.

Love, Yuki

Chapter 18 - A Mother's Love

The next day, Saturday, Tesla, "The Goth Mother", is throwing a potluck for all the Goths. It is a pretty major event, and attendance is expected to be over 100. I sleep most of the day. Having written off Inari the night before, my subconscious decides to dwell upon the girl it dwelled upon at the beginning of summer, Amber.

Amber appears in my dreams... nightmares. I dream that I am at a party very similar to the party I would be going to Saturday evening. In fact, it is spooky how this house appears in my dream. It was a house I had never been to in real life, yet I seemed to dream about it beforehand. I stand in a room of the house around a pool table. Amber flanks me and, without warning, hugs me and begins kissing my neck. I feel her arms wrapped around me, her breath, and her lips on my neck as if it were reality. But in real life, this is very uncharacteristic of her. She was rarely affectionate, and when I'd complain, she'd tell me I was too "clingy".

I suddenly know what she's playing, "Where's Brad? Didn't you come here in his piece-of-shit car?"

"Yeah... what else would I drive?" she cockily replies.

I push her away from me. "Get away from me and leave me alone!"

"Ha! What a dupe you are! I could never be interested in you!" She speaks to me in the most blatantly childish, shallow language, "I'm hot, you're ugly! What did you ever expect! I'm just not a good person!" she laughs, "I never intended to be a good person! I have no desire to be a good person! I am going to take everything you own and conquer you!"

I wake up from my nightmare. It is afternoon. My conscious mind gradually takes over, and I ponder over the events of Friday night where I watched Inari drink herself under the table, hold hands with Barry, and then disappear into a bedroom with him. I am still shaken by the drama of it all. I worry whether Inari is safe. "Are you alive? yes/no" I text.

Unable to reach her, I "friend" Barry on social media and ask him. Barry does not reply.

It is now 8PM and there is still no word from anyone. With no one left to call, I finally called Jin. "Have you heard anything from Inari?" I ask. "Last night she was drunker than I'd ever seen a conscious human being in my life, and honestly I'm worried about her. She might have needed to go to the hospital for alcohol poisoning!"

"Well that's not good, was Barry with her?" he asks.

"Yes."

"If Barry was with her, she'll be alright. He knows what to do."

I hear nothing for a time... until Jin finally texts me. "She's alright."

"Thank you! I'm so glad! Thanks for the update!"

I assume there's probably no way in hell that they'll make it out to Tesla's party. Inari will be nursing what is surely a monster hangover. I will have to go alone, and I dread the thought that Amber will probably be there. She is now living in Tesla's house with Brad. Tesla and Ratt often take in the troubled kids from the street, and Amber definitely qualifies, but I figure the chances of her being there are 50/50.

As I straighten my red necktie and try to erase the blemishes on my face, I think about Amber's mother. Her mother "loves" her all the same, but when I met her, it was the strangest mother-daughter dynamic I had ever encountered. Two months earlier, as I sat by Amber's bed in the hospital, her mother came to visit. Amber was sleeping. She had been sleeping since I arrived after stopping at home to bathe and change clothes. Her mother and I elected to leave the hospital room to avoid disturbing her and retreated to the hospital cafeteria. There, we talked, heart-to-heart, eye-to-eye. I didn't want her mother to worry that I was another drug-addicted, drug-dealing boyfriend. I emphasized that she and I weren't "together", but I informed her that I cared about her very much.

"Amber has always been a problem child," her mother said. "She has always been difficult, and she's always been a 'daddy's girl'. There was always only so much I could do to motivate her. In fact, I found that, really, the only way I was ever able to motivate her was with money."

"Well, I want you to know that if Amber has a problem with pot and drugs that it is certainly not due to my influence. I try my best to be a positive influence on her."

"Well, how is she even getting the money to buy pot?" she asked.

"Well uh… I might have given her money… and that money might have gone to pot…" I stumble. "It is complicated."

"Well… she's extremely motivated by money," her mother stressed. "Sometime, we should have a conversation about her and I'll give you all the dirt on her," she offered.

"Well, I don't want any dirt," I said. "Right now, I'm just trying to give her a blank slate. I'm trying to help her forget her past mistakes and move forward on a positive path. Reminding me or her of misdeeds of the past won't help her become a better person. I believe she wants to do better for herself, and that's why she's with me now."

Her mother chuckled as to suggest that I am truly naive. "She's *really* just motivated by money," she stressed. "Really… really… if you ever want to have a conversation about Amber, you can just call me."

Her mother left the hospital and I returned up to the 5th floor where Amber was in her 3rd day of admission. I entered the room just as she was waking up.

"You look cute today," she complimented.

I was taken aback... Amber never complimented me, ever. "Awww... thank you so much," I replied.

I sat next to her hospital bed. I held her hand, and she held back. "Everything is going to be okay. We're going to get you out of here. It'll all be over before you know it."

"I really appreciate that you're here. You have no idea how much I love you right now," she said.

Again, I am taken aback. If Amber is telling me she "loves" me, she can't be serious. I hesitate, but I reply. "I love you too. We're going to get you out of here... it'll be over soon."

As I suspected in my heart, as quickly as her affection came, it soon left. Soon after Amber was recovered, this supposed "love" she had for me vanished. On the day after her illness finally passed, I returned home from work, and, unprovoked, in reply to absolutely nothing, she simply pondered aloud. "Maybe I'll want to be with you in... a year."

"Well, that was out of left-field! I didn't even ask you anything... but... A year!?" I replied, shocked, but not necessarily surprised.

She backpedaled, "Or, maybe a month, I don't know."

It smelled of the kind of bullshit that Luna put me through a decade ago. Amber was intending to lead me on as long as she could. She had no love to give me. Had I not been burnt by Luna in the past, I might have let her play me longer. But I knew very well where this relationship was going... it was going *nowhere*. I knew it was going nowhere weeks ago.

I had been mentally preparing myself for what needed to be done. So there, standing in the kitchen, I set a time limit on the remainder of our "relationship". I told myself that if Amber recovered from her illness and her affections of me remained unchanged, even though I had done everything I could to take care of her, I'd make one last grandiose gesture towards her. One last gesture… then I'd change my *own* course and never look back. Amber wanted her birthday party under the laser lights in my house. I'd throw her this party, and if nothing changed between us, I'd tell her she should find a new place to live.

Monday before her party, she and I were discussing her birthday present (of course). Sitting in the Jacuzzi, massaging her topless back, I offered, "Maybe I could just treat you to an all-day spa where you can get massaged and pampered and manicured like a rich snob."

"That would be awesome," she said. After all, she was still compelled to take 24 showers every day.

"Are you going to be upset if my ex-boyfriend comes to my party?" she asks.

Brad had been drooling all over her in the clubs when I wasn't looking. He clearly wanted her back and was clearly willing to do anything to get her. I begin to feel more uncomfortable. "I don't know," I reply. "I don't really know if I'm comfortable throwing this party at *all*," I state in a mopey voice. "In general, you know, I have social anxiety, and filling my house with strange people puts me on edge a bit. Especially if there are creepy dudes bringing drugs into my house that want to fuck you. But whatever, it's your party."

Amber flips out, "FUCK YOU! ALL I WANT IS THIS PARTY! WHY WOULD YOU TRY AND DROP THIS ON ME AFTER I'VE ALREADY TOLD EVERYONE ABOUT IT!? YOU ALREADY AGREED TO IT! FUCK YOU! FUCK YOU!"

"Fine, you can have it. Have it here. It is fine," I caved. My shoulders hunched over. I wasn't happy to be bending over to her will for the zillionth time.

"I DON'T WANT TO HAVE IT HERE IF YOU'RE JUST GOING TO BE ALL GRUMPY ABOUT IT!" she counters.

"Look, I just don't want Brad to be at the party. He's not going to be there is he?"

"I don't want him there. He's not going to be there," she replied.

"I'm sorry," I said, "but just understand that I don't really know how to get any respect from you if I just give away everything I have. I feel like I'm making myself too cheap and that you don't respect me because of it. You can have your party… but just realize that I wish I meant something to you… because you mean so much to me."

Amber's eyes began to tear up and, in my heart, I felt that I had gotten through to her. I thought that maybe she had finally learned that my affections and generosity were human, and my human compassion was worth something to her.

Things cooled down, and, minutes later, we found ourselves in the back yard, talking pleasantly, sitting in my two-person lawn swing. Most of the time our interactions were quite pleasant, but when they weren't… they *really weren't*.

We soaked in the sun. Ada ran around the yard and played in the grass. Birds chirped. The breeze blew fresh air through the trees. We sat next to each other, enjoying the moment.

"This is nice. I like this," she said. "Someday I hope to have a yard like this of my own."

"Well, I'm glad you're here. You can live here as long as you want."

"I don't think I'm going to be living here much longer," she said bluntly.

"Well, that makes me sad," I said with a sigh. I added nothing more. I made no further arguments.

"I'm just being honest," she added.

I realized that, in fact, I had *not* made any new breakthroughs with Amber. She was never going to decide to love me. My heart numbed. I decided to walk a straight line and fulfill my promises to her like a robot lacking the proper programming to turn and avoid obstacles. I'd take her to the salon on her birthday; I'd buy dinner and drinks for her friends; I'd throw her one hell of an epic party, yet I approached these tasks with a new numbness in my heart. I was a dead man walking.

Two days later was Amber's birthday. It was Wednesday, two days before her Friday party was to take place. She wasn't feeling well enough for an all-day spa, so I had taken her to some expensive hair appointments and she spent hundreds of dollars getting foils and dyes. Afterwards, I bought dinner for her and 3 of her friends, but, as we returned home, she got a call. She was offering directions to someone.

"Brad's coming over. He just got a new car. He's just coming over to drop off some money and buy some pot from me," she said. "Don't freak out, I don't want him. He's a douchebag. He's an asshole."

As we rounded the corner at the end of my street, there was Brad in his "new" car, a piece-of-shit white 1978 Ford Thunderbird. I had a 1979 Thunderbird when I was in high school, 20 YEARS AGO and, even then, my car was a joke among my peers. Brad's car is 43 years old -- a beast that surely bellowed heaps of black smoke into the air when he drove it. It was a gas-guzzling, rusted-out, garbage truck... a boat... a barge.

Amber uncontrollably laughed at the sight of his car ... "HA! WHAT A FAG! What a piece of shit!" she gaffed.

I felt like she shouldn't be so harsh on him. But honestly, you couldn't *pay* me to take that car off your hands. And before you consider me a hypocrite, I'll remind you that my unforgiving literary descriptions of his vehicle are written having already known was going to come, and Brad... well... Brad can kiss my ass.

Because upon entering my house, Brad revealed that he didn't have any money. Therefore, the first thing that came to my mind was, "What the fuck are you doing here then?" He stuck around for a couple of hours and smoked up with Amber and Beth as I stewed around the house... cleaning... trying to calm my nerves. I was getting more and more anxious, angry, and worried by the minute. I felt like, at any moment, Amber was going to tell me that she was getting back together with him, and I'd have to listen to them fuck each other constantly in my house all night. Who knows, maybe they were already fucking when I wasn't at home!

"I'm not feeling well. Can I sleep in your bed, while you go to the club?" he asks her.

"No!" Amber replied forcefully, "you need to go home." A small victory for me. We drove off just as he was getting in his car, I made sure to lock up the house tightly. My nerves calmed, and we went to the club. Techna and Daedalus were in town. I wanted Amber to meet them. I thought Amber and Techna would get along. Techna has an explosive sense of humor. Techna, Daedalus, and I joked about gays, Goths, dead babies, and pedophiles like we never had before. Everyone, including Beth, laughed hysterically around us... everyone but Amber.

Amber's mood at the club was decidedly grim. She was gloomy and distant while I was hyperactive and bouncing off the walls. I thought that she'd be attracted to my newfound confidence at the club... but she stayed reserved... pissy.

I had a terrible feeling in my heart as we drove back from the club at 2AM, 4 hours later. I knew in my heart that Brad would still be parked in front of my house when we returned. I knew it. I knew it. And sure enough, his distinctive rusty old white 1978 Thunderbird was still parked in front of my house. And certainly, he was still in it. Now, this was serious. I wasn't going to put up with this.

"Why is your boyfriend's car still parked in front of my house?" I asked firmly without checking my emotions or words.

"He's not my boyfriend!" she snapped.

I took hold of myself, "I'm sorry… ex-boyfriend… but seriously… what's going on?"

"I don't know, I haven't even been texting him," she said.

We parked. We went inside. And I followed her up the stairs into the loft. She went into "her room", slamming the door.

"You don't think it is a little creepy that he's still here?" I asked.

"You're creepy!" she snapped from the other side of the door.

"Fuuuuck you," I said, shaking my head. I walked back downstairs to entertain the guests. Techna and Daedalus are spending the night as they always do when they come to town.

Upon hearing this interchange, they decide to pull me out onto my driveway for a private chat. There, they spent 20 minutes begging me to throw Amber out of the house. Techna pleaded with me as Daedalus went over to size-up Brad, who is still sleeping in his car. He's even cleverly put the hood up so as to suggest that his car is broken down.

"No girl is hot enough to treat you this way!" Techna pleads. "Seriously she's not worth it! She is not worth this kind of treatment! She contributes *nothing* to you and still can't even pay you a little bit of respect!? Get rid of her! You need to get rid of her NOW!"

"You're right," I conceded as I began to foam at the mouth. "I'm going to do it then. I'm going to do it right now! I'm going to throw her out of my house!"

"Really?" she asked in such a way to suggest that I shouldn't do anything too rash.

I took a deep breath. I calmed down and collected myself. "No…" I said. "Maybe I'll just go in and politely but firmly demand a resolution to this issue."

"That sounds a bit more reasonable," she concluded.

I walked in the front door and stood in the entryway. Amber and Beth were reheating leftover pizza in the microwave 15 feet in front of me.

"Alright, I'm sorry, but Brad has to move, there's no good reason for him to be parked out in front of my house for 6 hours," I said.

"Maybe his car broke down," she said. "Maybe he's sick. If you want him gone, you ask him!"

Her excuses perturbed me. Any response that was not in total agreement with me I considered to be completely out-of-line. I had bent over backwards to take care of her, and now this guy is stalking her, and she doesn't feel that it is even necessary to get rid of him? I felt like I was being used… played.

I manned up and did as she suggested. I went out to his car and demanded that he move.

He replied politely, agreed to move, and I went back into the house where Amber and Beth were still cooking pizza in the kitchen.

"I don't understand what the big deal is. You're kinda being a jerk," she said.

"I'm being a jerk? I think I'm being pretty calm about it actually. The big deal is that he's been there for far too long, and even if you don't think he's a threat, I'm not so sure that he's not going to come in here and rape everyone once the lights are out," I said. "But the thing that I don't understand is why the hell you're choosing to respect him more than you respect me right now. I've been *nothing but good* to you, and right now you're choosing *his* feelings over *mine*."

"Why don't you trust me!" she growled. Her facial expression had now morphed into anger. I can still see her face in memories as clear as day. She reminded me of a white, pink-haired, angry gorilla. She reached for plates of food, and one plate after another came flying at me as she picked them up from the base and tossed them overhand.

"FUCK YOU! FUCK YOU! FUCK YOU!"

"Why are you speaking to me like this in my house?" I asked.

"ALL I WANT TO DO IS SMOKE THIS BOWL AND GET DRUNK!! IT'S MY BIRTHDAY AND I JUST WANTED TO GET THROUGH TONIGHT WITHOUT ANY FUCKING DRAMA, BUT I'M TOO SICK TO EVEN DRINK MYSELF TO DEATH!!!"

The rest is history.

In the course of events, it is concluded that Amber would not be living in my house after tonight. I expected her to spend the night and leave in the morning.

Techna, Daedalus, and I retreated back to the driveway in the aftermath of the fight; Amber and Beth stayed inside. In the tizzy of the moment, I had almost completely forgotten about Brad. I finally looked out onto the street to find Brad's car had gone. Apparently, it *hadn't* broken down so badly that he couldn't drive it away from my house once things got heated.

The three of us agreed that it felt like he orchestrated the whole ordeal. He manipulated and crafted an explosive situation. We finished our post-mortem and reentered the house. Just as I opened the front door, I found Amber and Beth, walking the other way. They left without saying a single word. I have not spoken to either of them verbally since.

I knew at some point I'd have to actually talk to Amber like a human being, and I reached out to her via text messages and emails in the next couple of weeks. She, however, ignored me. Her ignorance of me drove me mad. Her ability to forget me and my *inability* to forget *her* drove me crazier and crazier with each passing day. I felt expendable and I began to interpret her aloofness as cruel until Amber was 100% a demon in my eyes. She and Brad got back together two days after her birthday, but I didn't learn of it right away. Instead, I tried to be kind and considerate and reach out to her with heartfelt apologies and sentiments.

Eventually, word inevitably got to me, and when I finally learned of it, I felt even *more* cheated than I had been before. I felt used. Amber was *surely* a demon now, surely. My respect for her had disappeared. The longer she continued to ignore me, the more worthless I felt, and the more she became a demon in my eyes. The only response I ever got from her was an email. It was only a few sentences… and in the email, she simply told me never to email her ever again.

I replied with the cruelest words I could think of. She aspired to be a video game artist, and I informed her that her art skills were pathetic and that no video game company, including my own, would ever hire her. I told her she'd never amount to anything. I told her that she wasn't even all that hot, and soon her looks were going to fail her completely. I told her that her breath smelled like dog shit. I told her she was fat. I warned her that she'd better learn to take care of herself because the day when no man would ever want to have sex with her was approaching fast.

It was clear that Amber and I would be mortal enemies for the foreseeable future. I developed a grudge. I don't form grudges easily, but when I do… they are quite hard to remove. Just ask Luna.

Therefore, tonight, I am a bit on edge at the idea that I might be forced to speak to Amber in person at Tesla's party. I arrange to meet Luna at the party in case a confrontation occurs. Upon arriving, I enter the house and I do a little recon. I only have to take a few steps around the house before I see Brad. I just smirk at him. He smirks back. I elect to stay in the backyard near the fire which is burning in a steel drum. I saw Brad, but I didn't see Amber, yet I assume that if he's there, she'll be there… if not now… eventually.

Tesla's party is full of tension, but I surround myself with enough friends that it doesn't matter that Amber, Brad, and Beth are at the same party. We manage to keep ourselves to one side of the house while they all stay on another side of the house. The rule seems decided without any verbal communication.

Luna, Echo, and I catch up on old times, remembering our times together a decade ago. We were much younger then, but we were all still the same people at our core. I believe that people, at their core, don't change. We spend a lot of time trash-talking Amber around the fire. And the consensus among the group is that Amber, at her core, is a rotten, despicable whore. Everyone around the fire shares their stories.

Amber was offered a job by Shannon but refused to take it upon learning that she'd actually be required to work and couldn't smoke pot on the job. Amber stole Echo's boyfriends on multiple occasions and seemed to get off on coming in-between healthy relationships. Amber coerced our friend Hannah's boyfriend into cheating on her and had unprotected sex with him to increase the chances that she'd give him herpes. Amber had earned the nickname "Herpe Trap" from the crowd she played dodgeball with because she tried to sleep with everyone and anyone and would inform them that she had herpes, just seconds before having sex with them.

Amber denied that she had herpes upon confrontation of her shady sexual practices, but I assured them that I picked up and paid for her prescriptions, and I had the receipts to prove that she took Acyclovir daily, an antiviral drug used to control viruses, such as herpes. I remind them, also, that I sat with her in the same room while she discussed her prescriptions with her doctors. Apparently, Amber's outbreaks are severe. It is theorized among the group that her generally poor health and addiction to pot exacerbate her outbreaks. But who really knows?

I remind everyone that having herpes is common enough that I don't look down upon anyone for having herpes. But she shouldn't be allowed to *lie about it* and have unprotected sex with anyone in the scene maliciously. People deserve to be forewarned. This scene, after all, is rather incestuous; everyone fucks everyone. Therefore, if someone brings something bad into the circle, it spreads around rather quickly. If she's trying to spread her STD intentionally by lying about it, it could potentially hurt a lot of people.

Eventually, I get sick of sitting in the same spot. I elect to just go home. Surely there needs to be a confrontation at some point... but I'm just not in the mood. Who knows if I'll ever be in the mood to deal with this issue? She is more or less banned from half the venues in town for all the crap she's pulled over the years anyway. My story of her is not unique. She leaves a trail of shit wherever she goes, so she rarely treads on my turf. She knows that she can't escape her poor reputation in my territory. On this night, I pity her. I leave her to have this party to herself. Saturday ends without incident. I simply go home and work on music. I've been inspired to write music lately.

Chapter 19 - Life is Beautiful

I don't hear from Inari for days. I worry about her, but she apparently doesn't feel the need to communicate with me. In fact, Jin was the only one courteous enough to inform me that she was okay the day after she practically poisoned herself with alcohol. Inari and Barry ignore me for the rest of the weekend entirely. I begin to feel like I'm not important. I feel like she has realized that we can't get any closer, or maybe she just doesn't care. I move forward as if any hope for a relationship with her is just a pipedream.

I cope with the loss in musical form. I begin a new track. This one is *not* for the concept album I keep telling everyone about… it is for a *new* concept album… an album about Inari. I record an initial demo for "Life is Beautiful" and I send it to her…hoping it will get her attention. The sentiments within it should resonate with both of us, I hope. It should represent where she and I both are in our lives. I have never written a "love song" for anyone. Granted I've written plenty of songs about "love", but usually only about the dark side of love. It is rare that I'd ever write a song "for" someone. This, therefore, is a strange, sappy exercise for me.

Life is Beautiful

Life is beautiful
in its fucked up way
and you are so beautiful
in every way
we take what's wonderful
and cast it away
but life is still beautiful
anyway

if I could paint this shell
and erase my years
and you could come to terms
with all your fears

155

we could transform this world
into a better place
and build a better place
for the human race

you can look alive
I can still look dead
but we can't deny
that we're meant for this life

I assume she will eventually read her email and listen to the song. I attach the lyrics so that there's no second-guessing the words. There are many ways this song can be interpreted... and how she chooses to interpret it will ultimately expose what she really wants from me.

It could be interpreted as a goodbye, a casting away. But it could also be interpreted as a coming together... as a realization that, inevitably, how she and I come together is beautiful even if it is our fucked up past that guides us in conquest for each other.

But regardless of which interpretation she chooses to apply to the song, one thing is consistent...

Life, despite all its imperfections, is beautiful anyway, and our individual lives belong only to us. And on a similar theme, combined with verbal sentiments expressed to her directly and indirectly... it is supposed to convey that Inari is *perfect* regardless of her flaws. Our chaos, flaws, and mistakes make us beautiful and perfect regardless of imperfection. Human imperfection is perfect.

I wake up pretty early on Monday. It is Labor Day. I have the day off work. I continue working on the song. Inari calls at 9AM but my phone is upstairs... I never expected her to try and call me at 9 in the morning. It is noon by the time I realize she's called. I call her back to no answer. I figure she's sleeping or something. I text Jin and tell him to come out to The Saloon, and I get no answer. I text Inari and tell her to either come out or call me at 3AM. I get no communication from either of them.

I post 12 revisions for the song on my website on Labor Day. I work hard on it until I am satisfied that it is just about perfect.

I begin to suspect that Jin is tactfully trying to prevent Inari from spending time with me. "Jin is not an idiot," Inari said to me the other day. "He sees what's going on." Jin clearly doesn't want me to spend too much time with his girlfriend, but his hands are tied by his own desire to be polite and his own desire to respect the sleeping disorders of his girlfriend.

I go to The Saloon... I don't expect them to show up.

Of course, Jin isn't an idiot... so, even *if* he trusts his girlfriend, He's not about to deliver her openly and willingly to a guy who wants to steal her away from him... that would be just dumb. Inari and I invariably always end up talking as if we're inseparable while Jin becomes almost a 3rd wheel whenever Inari and I are together with him.

I predict that Jin will put up convenient resistance to just about all my proposed outings going forward... I, therefore, text him and tell him that I'm buying the drinks if he comes out. If I cannot get through to Inari, I try to get through to Jin, instead. It is slimy of me, I know. I'm sure he sees right through me, but we're polite... it is a gentleman's duel.... this dance we do.

I feel all too conveniently ignored on Monday night... and eventually, Jin texts me… *way* late. He makes sure to subtly remind me that he's traded a night on the town for some form of quality time with Inari, as if to remind me that *he* has her and *I do not*. "Sorry I didn't get this earlier, drinks would have been lovely. Inari and I fell asleep watching a movie."

I show his text message to Luna at the club. She interprets it the same way I do. "Oooohh… that is subtle… Slimy!" she says.

It's all good and fair I suppose... I didn't expect them to come out, but I knew quite sure in my heart that Inari would call me after the bar closed. I was dead sure of it.

Chapter 20 - Asleep on the line

It is 2:55AM. I expect Inari to call by 3:00AM. I'm just about to doze off when surely… she calls. And like always, no matter what we say to each other, it feels wonderful to talk to her.

My brain is shut down... I am tired... but I never ever want to miss an opportunity to talk to her... so I struggle to form complete thoughts. She endures my flakiness for longer than she's ever endured me on the phone, 4 hours and 40 minutes. It is 7:30AM before we hang up.

"I'm really sorry about the other night," she says. "The nurses explained to me that the medication that I'm on should never be taken with alcohol and that even one drink could be enough to make me into a completely different person than I am. But I can't help but drink at parties, particularly when I'm surrounded by people. People make me nervous. Barry knows when I've had too much, and knows that when I've had too much, he should just put me to bed… and that's what he did."

"I trusted that you were in good hands. I enjoyed getting to know Barry. He seems like a good guy. I would have been more worried about you had Barry not been there," I agree. "You were really drunk, I had to catch you when you fell over after you stood up," I recall.

"I must have been *really* drunk then. I don't remember any of it. I'm rather strange… I never stumble when I'm drunk, nor do I ever slur my words. It can be quite difficult to even tell when I'm drunk, but Barry knows me well enough to know when to get me to quit. I trust him."

"Well, we tried to get you to quit, but you just kept mixing yourself drinks when we so much as blinked," I reply.

We talk for hours about anything and everything. Her sleeping disorder makes it difficult for her to function. She wishes she could sleep at night like a normal human being. "Usually, if I get a back rub, I can fall asleep quickly, but Jin never gives me back rubs. When I ask him, he just gets all pissy about it."

"Yeah, I don't understand why some people hate giving back rubs. It was a source of extreme tension between me and Luna. She would say, 'I'll give you a back rub when I *feel* like giving you a back rub!' like a total bitch. Yet I gave her back rubs every night for 1.5 years. If you truly need a back rub to sleep, your significant other should give you massages *every night* until you pass out. I figure it should be the job of any decent boyfriend. I'd certainly do that for any girlfriend who had an issue with insomnia."

I tell her the story of how I had to massage Amber's back for 4-6 hours on average every day for 10 days straight while she was having panic attacks after being in the hospital. I imagine Inari's jaw-dropping at the other end of the phone when I reveal to her how hard I worked for this worthless girl and how lop-sided my labors were towards Luna. My point was clear… "If you need a massage to sleep... I'd do that for you every night... no problem."

At times during the phone conversation, we elect to just pause for a few seconds, and we just listen to each other breathe. I imagine myself lying next to her... enjoying this moment... enjoying her presence... basking in her glow.

I struggle to conjure up charisma. I feel like I owe it to her to tell her what I am looking for in a mate. She had told me what she was looking for the other night. I owe it to her to tell her why she is so amazing to me.

I tell her that I am looking for someone with her own beautiful darkness, who understands and appreciates the pain of her life and uses it for good… someone who is faithful… someone imperfectly perfect, humble, selfless… a partner in life, strange, accepting, empathetic... someone who understands failure... someone who appreciates me the way I am... and whose life I can make better. If I weren't still on ZERO sleep as I write this... I could probably do better... another chapter... another chapter.

I stop *asking* her to get together with me. Instead, I begin to confidently declare... "We're getting together, just you and me... and you're going to the club this Wednesday... and... we're going to take Ada to the dog park. It has been decreed."

She seems to appreciate when I take command of her.

I argue with her that she should stop accepting my professions of love for her. She plays it as if she agrees... that it is the right thing to do. But ultimately... at the end of this night... she still accepts my gestures of love. The simple fact that she accepts my gestures makes me feel special enough to believe that there will be many more chapters to come in this story. I realistically concede that it is appropriate to step back... I can see this. But she worries that I'll try for so long in vain to win her affections that I'll just end up "hating" her in the end. I tell her that no matter what happens I could never feel ill of her...

"Inari... I'm following you for the rest of my life... until my grave," I assure her.

I wish I had the strength to get some of my points across in a more charismatic manner, but she seems to forgive me for being fatigued. And although she apologizes at times for keeping me up late, no apology is truly necessary. At times she scolds me for staying up all night on a work night, but I remind her that I do so willingly. She never truly insists on hanging up the phone with me. The mere fact that she would allow me to continue talking to her all night makes me feel special. She is there for me if I am there for her... at least on this night. This is the pattern with us lately. When we're together, we're practically glued together.

Eventually, time is no longer on our side. I *have* to go.

But it seems that just as I feel like the conversation is coming to an end, we just keep getting pulled back into conversation. As I start my morning routine to get ready for work, I am still on the phone with her, changing my clothes with phone-in-hand. Even as we say our final, final goodbye, I am never sure if this goodbye is going to be our last... it is a storm of goodbyes. Is it going to be her or I who hangs up the phone first? I don't know... it is delightfully... awkward.

Finally, as I am standing on my front porch with my car keys in hand, getting ready to drive to work... I say "goodbye". This time I truly intend to hang up the phone. I pull the phone from my ear and still I hesitate... pulling it back ever so slightly to check if she was going to say something more. But finally... finally our conversation is done. I drive to work... glowing. I love this girl so fucking much.

I tasted just a little bit of the same glow that came over me in the first days I met her. Back then, she radiated such beautiful energy and I thought and felt and I *truly believed in my heart*... "This girl really loves me." I was so sure of it then, "This girl really loves me." How can I be *this* wrong?

Chapter 21 - The Cold Shoulder War

Techna makes a surprise visit to town to scout locations for a future fashion show. I call up Inari, she answers.

"Techna is in town and you're going to come hang out with us," I say, offering her no option to decline.

Inari makes no attempt to decline, "Okay."

"We'll come pick you up in a couple of hours. Answer your phone, I'll be calling," I command.

"Okay, I'll hurry up and get ready," she says.

I hope that my commanding tone gives Inari a sense that this is supposed to be *our* time... not Jin's. Knowing that Inari can be difficult to wrangle, I continuously keep in touch with her, but it gets later and later into the evening, and Inari is still not ready to go out. We're all creatures of the night though, so a late-night thing is almost preferable. Techna and I kill time and shop for booze, assuming that Inari is working on her hair and makeup.

Eventually, Inari stops answering the phone... Techna and I end up sitting around my house, drinking alone. I obsess over getting in contact with Inari, but Inari fails to answer. We made no other plans but to hang out with her, so she's kinda messing up our night. Eventually, I do what I often do when I get impatient. I go to sleep. I sleep until something exciting happens. I am disappointed that Inari can't be reliable with me.

At 5AM, Inari calls. I am sleeping, but my phone is next to my ear, as it always is. Apparently, Jin decided to pick *this* night to finally give her a back massage and she passed out. He left her on the couch and then put a blanket over her and nobody told anyone that she wasn't going to make it out to meet us.

We were ready to drive over, pick her up, and whisk her away...

with or without him. If I weren't head-over-heels in love with this girl, I guess I would have just called it "rude". Regardless of it being 5AM... she and I talk for 40 minutes, joking about all kinds of stuff.

"Tomorrow we'll get together in the middle of the night and frolic through garbage because there aren't any meadows in the city," I joke. "I better save my strength, because some of this garbage is going to be heavy!" Don't let me ever become a comedy writer.

Even if my jokes really aren't funny, Inari laughs at them as if she is having a genuinely good time talking to me. It is always great to talk to her.

Even if we couldn't get together, it feels like a potentially good night that just had a small complication, to me, but Techna is less forgiving. She is still awake as I hang up the phone with Inari. "Inari can't possibly be this flaky and still care about you, Yuki! It all smells fishy!"

"Let's not jump to conclusions, Techna. After all, you haven't even met her yet."

"But that's part of the problem, Yuki," Techna replies. "Inari has now flaked out on meeting me *twice*. I don't like to put up with bullshit, and to me, it smells like bullshit."

"I don't think it is Inari's fault. She couldn't really help what happened. If anything, Jin should have called me and informed me that things got botched. He's kinda being an asshole if you ask me. He is playing games with *her and us*," I stress. "He's going to do whatever he can to stand in the way of us spending time together."

"But, if you were with Inari as her boyfriend, would *you* approve of what she is doing with you now... if she were doing it with another guy?"

"Well, no. Not at all," I say.

"Well then, you should tell Inari she needs to choose, she needs to make up her mind," she says.

"But it's not really like that. Jin doesn't appreciate Inari. He's dumped her twice already. Yes, I think she still wants him, but I think she just needs time to accept the inevitable. Things are changing... but they're not going to change overnight. I'm not worried about it. If we continue to get closer and closer every time we talk, I'm happy... and that's what is happening. We get closer and closer. Eventually, we'll either come together for real, or we'll split... I don't know. But right now... we're getting closer, and that's all that matters to me."

"But how do you know that Jin didn't dump her because she pulled this same kind of shit with some other guy?"

"I don't have any reason to suspect anything of the sort, although I guess I've heard some strange speculation about her and Barry, some guy who took her to Japan, and this guy from New Jersey," I concede.

"But I trust Inari," I continue. "I don't think the people who spread rumors and speculate about her know *anything* about her. Inari is beautiful and sought after by a lot of different guys in a scene full of people who aren't exactly model citizens. They all probably just stand around and cry that she won't have double-dick threesomes with them while assuming she's a stuck-up slut. I've spent more time with this girl than any of them. She seems pretty genuine. She's got some things to work out obviously, but I'll just let her work them out. I honestly care about her and I love her very much. There's no reason for me to have any ill feelings about her."

I really wanted Inari and Techna to hit it off. Techna is, after all, a fashion designer, and Inari has not modeled for her yet. I thought it would be win/win for both of them. Plus, I always go to Techna for my relationship advice. Techna likes to size up who I'm seeing/chasing.

But, thus far, Techna has only managed to talk down anyone I've been seeing. Yet in all fairness, I've been single now for 2.5 years and there have not been too many girls biting on the end of my line. But this time around, I want to make Techna proud. I want her to see that I've found someone worthy of my love and attention. I want Techna to endorse us. I want her to see that we make each other happy. And maybe, just maybe, Techna can be a catalyst that helps bring us together.

But the events of the night give Techna a rocky first impression of Inari. Techna's first impression of her is that she is flaky. "I don't know if I can have her model for me because Inari will have to show up... and show up *on time!*" she states.

"Just give her a chance, she'll come around," I beg. "I blame Jin exclusively for tonight."

Inevitably, I figure that Jin will become more possessive... and inevitably it will probably lead to confrontation. When the confrontation occurs, I imagine that I'll play the role of the guy who's not trying to tread on his turf... but that's so dumb of me. I should be sturdy and stand my ground and stand proudly with Inari. But I'll be dumb...I will assure him that Inari isn't interested in me and praise him for being such a lucky man... that will be that. I'll be a "pussy" about it.

This battle, it drags on. It fatigues me, but I do not tire of it. It is satisfying work... it is the zest of my life. I wish it were easier, but nothing good in life comes easy.

Chapter 22 - The Empathic

After flaking out on the previous night, Inari offers that we should get together. She even *texts* me her address. Inari loathes writing text messages. For her to stomach such a task is truly a rare occasion. It is Wednesday. Techna is still in town but will be leaving around midnight. It is the North Loop Wednesday club night.

We make plans for 4:30, but then she gets a migraine. I begin to think that this day is going to turn out the same as the previous one.

I call her up at 6. She does not answer. I call her more than the standard benchmark of 12 times before I give up. I think to myself about how calling someone these many times in a row is rather laborious. It takes 25 minutes to call someone 12 times. I write her off as a no-show. I'm sure she's sleeping. I begin going about my plans for the evening and just try to get her out of my mind.

But finally, she wakes up and, at 6:45, she finally calls me. Techna is getting ready to leave my house on an errand to deliver a dress to a client, while Inari and I talk on the phone for 40 minutes or so. At the end of our conversation, I agree to come pick her up. But just as I am about to hang up the phone, Jin calls on her other line. He tells her that *he* is on his way to pick her up and is almost at her house. Jin has suddenly invited himself along. It is not the end of the world, but I'd rather be with Inari alone for obvious reasons.

They are swift to show up at my door, unusually swift, maybe 10 minutes or so. After introducing Techna, I immediately start talking about evening plans, assuming we're all together for a long night of fun. But before I can get through a single sentence, Jin quickly interjects, "We have to hurry because we have to leave in about 40 minutes."

I feel like I'm hit with a brick. There was no mention of this before. I did not think they were just coming to "stop by", but to have a long quality night with us. He explains that, apparently, there's a meeting regarding a fashion show that Jin is managing. Inari either forgot or neglected to mention it.

Jin offers, "Well Inari, you can stay here and hang out with them, and I'll just go do the meeting myself."

"But I need to be there to keep you all organized and on the right track. I need to go with you. This show is important and you're going to screw it up!" Inari replies.

They continue to argue about it for some time, Jin insisting that she stay with us, and Inari insisting to leave with him for the meeting. Everything feels backwards to me. I believed in my head that if given the opportunity, Inari would choose me over Jin, when presented. Right now, she is proving the opposite and it fills my head with worry and dread.

With a sigh, burying the utter panic I feel, I accept that they are leaving, but I try extra hard to encourage them to come out to the club after the meeting. They agree. Without Inari, Techna and I decide to just hit the club early. There's hardly anyone we know there now. As we take in the early lulls, we talk about Inari.

"I don't get it, Yuki. I don't really see any unusual energy between you two. If she was into you, why didn't she stay with you when presented with the option?"

"I see your point. I am disappointed that she is not here. She didn't really *have* to go to the meeting, but wait until we're alone, Techna," I say. "When we are alone, or when we talk on the phone, the energy is *way* different."

"The fact that she didn't choose to stay with you over him demonstrates that she does *not* have feelings for you, Yuki. I'm just calling it like it is."

"Well. It is only one instance," I say. "She'll come around."

Whereas I worry that they will not come out tonight, I figure they eventually will. If anything, Jin wants to cultivate Techna as a fashion business contact, so he has a particular interest in being there.

Eventually, they come. I make a point to pay close attention to Jin for a while. I don't entirely dislike the guy. I suppose I even enjoy talking to him a bit. But my motivation for talking to Jin is to loosen his grip on Inari for a while. The happier I can keep Jin, the happier my night will be.

When I finally get facetime with Inari, I try my usual moves. I try to square my shoulders with her. I try to look into her eyes, but she resists. I still feel warm in her glow, and she is kind and affectionate, but for some reason, she won't look into my eyes. I contemplate repeatedly. *Why won't she look at me tonight?*

As the night winds down, we all say our goodbyes. Techna leaves on a long drive back to Wisconsin. Predictably, Jin is also looking to go to bed early as well. He makes plans to leave, and I figure he thinks he's bringing Inari with him, but I know better. I know in my heart that she's not going home with him tonight. Soon enough, they are standing eye-to-eye and she is talking to him... hugging him... and kissing him... there it is... the "goodbye dance"... I am of renewed confidence. She is coming with *me* tonight.

Once again, Aurthur is observing. It is his first time coming out on a Wednesday. I stand in a circle with him and a couple other guys as Inari appears to sweet-talk Jin. Aurthur just smiles at me.

"You know what's going on, right?" I declare with a smirk and a raise of my eyebrows. "You see what's happening, right?"

"Yeah... I know... I know," he says with a smile.

The rest of the circle appears confused, but we offer no hints as to what we're talking about... we keep it between him and me.

Sure enough, Jin soon comes over and pulls me out of the circle. With a sigh, he says, "Inari, wants to go to the after-bar."

I am prepared with my answer. "I'll get her home. It is no problem."

I say no more but turn around and rejoin my circle with Aurthur. I nod as I give him a "thumbs up" and a smirk.

"You seem pretty confident," he says.

"I just got confirmation. She's coming with me."

Aurthur and I lock eyes as he gives me another nod as if tipping an invisible hat. He is impressed.

Natalie had been throwing all the Wednesday night after-parties throughout the summer, so we find ourselves there. My friends, by default, always assumed that something was going on at Natalie's place after bar close on any given Wednesday.

We all congregate around a firepit in her backyard. It seems to come naturally that Inari and I are very close tonight. It is cramped around the bonfire. Inari sits close to me, shoulder to shoulder, temple to temple. We cannot avoid exchanging body heat as we sit close together. Despite our closeness, however, much of the night is difficult and uncomfortable as she argues with me about religion.

She and I had talked about religion before. I thought we were in total agreement, but, during this conversation, I learn that I offended her with my views on spirituality. Around the fire, I was having discussions about "militant atheism", Sam Harris, and his book *The End of Faith*, which is widely regarded to some as the "atheist's bible".

"Yuki, you cannot look down upon other people for having spiritual views," Inari snaps at me.

I am a little taken aback. She always acted offended that her grandparents were stacking bibles outside her bedroom door when she was a kid, but right now she is defending religion.

I try to explain how I got to where I am. I am often embarrassed to mention that I have my *own* history of struggle with spirituality. I came to this place in my life after some long battles attempting to find faith yet failing. At some point, I took on the opinion that religion wasn't serving anyone but the organizations that dispense it. Religion was creating dividing lines in a world where too many dividing lines, racial, geographical, social, political, and financial already existed.

"The world doesn't need another set of criteria upon which to divide people," I declare. "You may regard it to be a 'false idol', but Inari. 'Love' is my 'God'. That is all. Love is my God, and I love you. I did not find a lot of *true* love in this world. But I found you."

The neighbors complain that Natalie's backyard party is too loud, and she is forced to move it to the front of the house. As everyone is distracted and moving their beers and purses, Inari immediately takes the opportunity to get down on her knees in front of me and clutches my leg. "I'm so sorry I cannot be what you want," she pleads. "I'm so sorry we can't be more than friends. It hurts me to tell you this."

I just paraphrase what I've always said to her. "I just want you to be happy. I want you to live a happy life, regardless of whether it is with me." Maybe, looking back, I was completely full of shit.

But as we continue to discuss whatever our relationship to each other can or cannot be, it goes around and around in a circle... around and around. What starts off as a very blunt declaration of strict friendship becomes a reality that is far more confusing, complex, and borderline inappropriate as I shower her with an onslaught of blunt, romantic compliments, and she accepts them with a flirtatious smile, until, finally, Inari comes back around and reiterates that we cannot be anything more than friends. This paradoxical circle seems to never stop. We just keep circling around, declaring "friends only" while, at the same time, reaching deeper into emotional territory typically reserved for relationships that go far beyond friendship.

"I worry that if you don't get what you want from me, you'll end up 'hating' me like you hate Amber," she says.

"I could never hate someone so perfect and infallible, even if nothing romantic becomes of us, or if whatever we have ultimately ends. You're not Amber, don't even put yourself in the same league as her. Amber was attractive, but beyond that, her personality was complete trash. You're not Amber. You're a good person. You're the *best* person I've ever met. You are the most amazing girl I've ever met, and I don't take our meeting as just a trivial encounter with 'some girl'. There is always an energy being emitted from you. An unexplained energy radiates from you that I cannot deny or explain."

"I'm just a girl," she says, "and I'm a weirdo."

"I've meant everything I've ever said to you, no matter how grandiose. I don't just say these things to every girl I meet, you know. There's just some kind of chemistry that we have that enables me to open up to you, and I love it, I love you, and I'm addicted to you."

Echo, having moved to the front with the rest of the group, comes to the backyard to find us in the middle of an emotionally candid conversation. Drunk, she whispers into my ear, "If you get her over to my place, I think you've got a shot with her."

Echo wants to get away from the party... I get vibes from her that she's feeling that she can get the 3 of us alone for a 3-some or something. But to that proposition, I only think, "Noooo."

Inari seems to think Echo's intentions are dark and sinister and resists leaving Natalie's place. She doesn't want us to be alone with Echo, but she stops short of flat-out saying what is on her mind. Since I'm driving, and Echo has had enough to drink, I overrule Inari and I give Echo a ride home.

First, however, we need to stop at a gas station so that I can buy Echo a pack of smokes. I end up buying her cigarettes and she just helps herself, without asking, to enough cheap gas station food to last her about 3 meals or so under the assumption that I will just pay for it. Echo gets free stuff from me so much that it just feels like routine now. Half the time she doesn't even ask anymore. She'll maybe ask for a pack of smokes, then, at-the-same-time, she will walk around the gas station pulling sandwiches off the shelves to take full advantage of my generosity and gullibility. I don't really like the way she does this, but I figure, $20 means less to me than it does to her.

The 3 of us hang out at Echo's place for several hours, longer than I'd have liked.

Smalltalk ensues. Echo hasn't had a job for many months, maybe years. Somehow, she still manages to scrape by enough money for rent, most likely due to the kindness of family and friends. She gets free drinks from men in bars. She gets food from food stamps, cigarettes from mooching off friends, including my non-smoking self.

"When I get a job that pays real money, I'm going to pay back all of my friends who have helped me out over the years," she says.

"You realize that you're into me for about $40,000 don't you?" I ask with one eyebrow raised.

"Yeah... yeah... that sounds about right," she admits as if it is of no concern. "You're one of my oldest and best friends, Yuki," she says.

"Well, I don't really think that you're as good of a friend to me as you say you are," I bluntly declare.

Inari looks at me like I just hit her with a bullet and motions in such a way to urge me not to continue any further criticism of Echo. I admit that I was being blunt with her, and it needed to be said. I guess it felt like the right time to say it. I was trying to convince myself that the only way Echo's life was ever going to improve was if I got tough with her. Luna and I had even been talking about getting her friends together for an intervention. Echo had recklessly abandoned her own life and her rhetoric was demonstrating that she had no realistic plan for getting her life back on track.

Echo never lifted a finger for *me* in the 12 years I had known her. Any favors she did for me were in exchange for money and therefore couldn't be counted as "favors" at all. Therefore, I was recently coming to terms with the idea that any contact I had with Echo was never about "friendship" at all… it was about her getting what she needed and wanted from me… I just happened to be one of the most generous people she knew.

Nevertheless, I obey Inari's gestures and I call off my planned onslaught. Echo steps away for a moment, "I'm sorry, I wasn't trying to attack her character, I was simply trying to objectively define the status of our relationship. Really, we're not great friends. I want her to realize that, and if she does, maybe she'll try to be a better friend to me."

Inari assures me, "It's okay. I know you're a good person; you don't have to explain yourself to me. I *know* you're a good person. In fact, there's a reason I came to you the way I did."

She pauses and hesitates. She wants to say something profound but is scared to say it. Echo returns from the kitchen. Inari begins to stutter a syllable, "I'm…." but stops. But finally, she lets it out.

"I'm an empath, Yuki," she says. "I feel the emotions of everyone around me. The emotions of everyone scream at me, and I feel the darkness in their hearts. It drives me crazy. That's why Barry and I are so close, but it is also the reason that Barry and I cannot be together. We are both empaths. I'm drawn to you because I see goodness in you. You have a good heart, and your heart is good and true. But everyone else around us… they're all liars."

I truly believe her. But am I crazy? I just spent an hour earlier arguing against spiritual bullshit around the campfire, proclaiming myself to be a devout, militant atheist, yet here I am believing some spooky, ghostly, 6th sense garbage?

As much as I logically oppose this revelation, I acknowledge to myself that this is not the first time an empath has introduced herself to me. 2 years earlier, a girl named Katie introduced herself to me on a Wednesday at the North Loop club. She had been smiling and beaming at me for weeks even though we never talked. At first, I just thought she was smiling because she thought I was cute. I was shy, and I didn't have the guts to talk to her. Instead, she eventually came to me.

Upon introducing herself to me, she immediately told me that she could feel the emotions of everyone in the room. She was an "empath". Wednesday night was her favorite night on the town because the people there didn't have all the evil, dark, demons she sensed everywhere else… at least… not as much. She wouldn't be able to handle a typical club environment. A typical club would drive her insane.

"It's like I can feel everything that everyone is feeling around me all at once, and they're all screaming at me and I can't shut it off… and worse yet… they're generally selfish and evil," she said. I stayed with Katie most of the night and she offered a running commentary of the vibes of the room as the night progressed as well as the moods of the patrons.

Katie singled out individuals in the room and pointed out what they were feeling at the moment. They all started off happy and optimistic. Everyone was simply having a good time. Then as the men began to encroach on the attractive women on the dance floor the mood of the room turned darker. Then as the women danced with men other than those who were buying the drinks, the mood turned to jealousy, and when the women left early without them, the men were bitter and angry.

I thought of Katie when I first met Inari. I sensed an almost telepathic transference of emotion from Inari to me that I couldn't explain back then. When my heart glowed, Inari always got a special twinkle in her eyes in a way that was very similar to the looks that Katie had been giving me for weeks before I met her.

The way Inari lit up in my presence "hooked" me. I always said she had "laser beam eyes". It was as if she could see my heart glow for her. By this point, Inari had made me glow so much inside, that Inari could tell me she was an angel... I would believe it. She could tell me she was an alien... I would believe it... she could tell me she was a goddess... or from another dimension... or from the future even... and I would believe it.

She was *always* magical to me. She has a magic about her that I cannot explain. She makes me believe that there is something bigger than life... she convinced me that *she* was bigger than life... She compels me to perform grand gestures to her. If she's an angel, whatever an angel even *is*... I believe her. I believe *in* her. Maybe she is just a natural, logical evolution of the human species. She is an exception, a mutation. Her soul burns with a higher energy than most humans... in the most practical of definitions, Inari *is* an angel.

We continue to talk through the night. I bring up the incident where Inari got blackout drunk and passed out with Barry, scaring the hell out of me.

"I feel compelled to drink," she says, "even though my medications warn against it... because drinking is one of the few things that blocks out all the screaming that surrounds me in crowds of people. But I need to be careful... because if I get drunk… I can't read people most of the time… and I can be fooled. But if I'm sober, you can't fool me. You have to truly be an artist to fool me."

Conversation drifts in and out of various subjects, but it doesn't take too long for our conversation to turn into the vicious paradoxical circle it was earlier... one minute we're "just friends", and the next minute, I'm professing my undying love for her while she smiles and twinkles from all my flattery.

Echo is still mostly unaware of the depth of my feelings for Inari, or so I believe. Echo brings up the subject of Jin, accidentally or deliberately.

"You know what I heard while you were away in New Jersey?" Echo asks Inari.

Inari gives Echo her full attention.

"Jin said, 'I think she's the one, and I want to marry her.' He wants to marry you, you know."

I watch Inari's face immediately melt into bliss and happiness as if she is imagining the moment of Jin asking for her hand in marriage. Suddenly, I am depressed to a degree that Inari has never seen of me. I believe that Inari is the girl I've looked for my whole life, and I cannot stomach the idea that she might marry someone else, let alone this man. I am angry at Echo. This seems like manipulation. Echo's revelation immediately turns Inari's attention away from me, and Echo and Inari split off in the apartment, leaving me on the sofa to sit alone and just watch them interact.

She senses that I am agitated, stewing, waiting for my turn to talk. I sulk. I try to jump into their conversation, but Echo works hard to monopolize Inari's time and prevents me from speaking.

As they talk, Echo does her thing where she agrees with everything Inari says as if she's in total agreement and on her side with every opinion Inari offers about everything from the mundane to profound.

They bond over their history of being "cutters" and history of sexual assaults. She even claims to be an empath, a claim that just makes Echo seem like evil, dirty scum in my eyes. Then she decides that it is time to "make a move" on Inari... sexually.

Inari is drunk. I get concerned as Echo convinces Inari to show her pierced breasts. Echo kisses them. Then, she kisses Inari on the lips.

What I'm about to say will likely incite some triggers, but Echo is bullshit. She is just trying to get Inari to fuck her and steal her attention away from me. I know Echo too well. I'm not sure that Inari understands this because she's been drinking, but I'm sober, and I've known Echo for years and years. Whereas I believe the things Echo cried about were real, the rape, the abuse, etc., I don't believe Echo to be empathic at all. Echo told me the exact same stories of rape and abuse years ago with a different tone. They were a fantasy sex game with her boyfriend who would lock her in a cage for days at a time. Rape and self-abuse fetishes are common in our scene, and Echo never indicated anything to me that anything that happened to her wasn't protected with a safe word, and these stories seem to just be an attempt to bond with and impress Inari over a lie. Maybe there were other legit stories that Echo could have told that were *actually* true, but these stories are complete bullshit. I realize that there's no way for me to interject, interrupt, or disrespect Echo's stories of rape and abuse without coming off as a complete asshole. I ponder for a moment about how using such a lie, simply cannot be challenged. There's no way for me to call Echo out for being a liar without turning *myself* into an aggressor who doesn't "believe women". As someone who puts women on pedestals, sometimes without regard to how crappy they treat me, I absolutely want to cherish and respect women, and disown all types of toxic masculinity, but I am, right now, in a predicament. Regardless of the truth of the past, it doesn't change the fact that Echo is acting like a demon right now, and I worry about the dynamic taking place in this room.

Eventually, Inari confronts me about my emotional state. Echo, claiming to be an empath, tells Inari that she senses "danger" in my mood. "I see darkness in him!" Echo dramatically declares. "Don't go with him. I sense that he's going to hurt you!"

Now, I want a private audience with Inari. I demand it. I need to be alone with Inari before Echo corrupts and pollutes her and destroys my character in the process.

"Don't go," Echo whispers to her, acting all frantic... a poor actress, overly dramatic, like a twelve-year-old acting in a middle-school play about vampires. "I'm worried about what he'll do to you. I'm getting bad feelings from him."

Anger boils inside me as Echo continues to throw me under the bus. I think about saying, "Fuck you, Echo!", but I contain myself. Instead, I try to simply explain how I am feeling, but fail.

"My emotions are far too complex for words. I am struggling to find the words to describe them. It is a mix of a lot of things. But I really, really, urgently, feel like I need to talk to Inari right now... alone," I demand.

Echo acknowledges my request for alone time with Inari, but delays and delays to fulfill it, stalling our alone time with constant interruptions. I get more and more irritated and nervous as Echo continues to try and take advantage of Inari and Inari lets her. Echo continues to interrupt me as she continues her seduction of Inari, "Come on baby, stay the night with me," she says. I get more and more emotional, and Inari looks over at me.

"Yuki, I have never seen you like this before," Inari declares. She is confused about the emotions she believes she is reading from me with her empathic abilities.

"I am feeling a complex mix of anger, betrayal, worry, sadness, and impatience," I say. "I just need to speak with you alone, in private. Please. Now. Echo, leave us, please. Now."

Echo obliges by going into the bathroom for 20 seconds, but then again... *again... again...* she boomerangs back into the conversation before I can say an entire sentence. Finally, after nearly an hour of hell, we go out and sit on the front steps, thinking that she will stay inside and wait. But Echo... *sigh...* Echo follows us.

"Echo, you need to go back inside, and we'll let you know when we're done talking," Inari politely demands.

Echo tries to interject and mutters half a syllable.

"GO! ... NOW!" I demand.

"It's okay, Echo," Inari says. "We'll just be a few minutes."

Finally, Echo leaves for a period just long enough to let me say a few words to Inari. I figure I don't have much time before Echo comes back and reinvites herself into the conversation, so I get right to the point.

"Echo is just one of those people who just wants to fuck you. I've known her since she was 15 and can tell you, for a fact, that she never cared about *me*. She is just one of those people that have used me and abused me over the years and continues to do so. She is a liar, and I worry that she's trying to take advantage of you because you've been drinking."

"You don't think I know that?" Inari replies. "I'm surprised she hasn't been even *more* forward with trying to fuck me all night. But you have to appreciate that she *has* been through some serious shit in her life."

"The shit she's gone through in her life has largely been the result of her *own* choices though," I say. "I don't know how to get through to her without practicing some tough love."

"Well, the only way to practice tough love is to first let her get close to you," Inari says. "Only then, does tough love work."

It now is apparent to me that Inari knows *exactly* what she's doing with Echo. I am thoroughly impressed and feel no pain about the situation for the rest of the night. The night is coming to an end as the sun is high in the sky and Echo's neighbors are leaving the apartment building for work.

As we go back inside, Inari stops me again.

"There's still something bothering you," she says.

"I don't want to talk about it in the hall... can we please just go into the apartment?"

"No, Yuki. It's now or never."

"I don't like the idea of conversing outside another tenant's door. Please, I'll tell you the instant we get in the apartment."

When we get inside the apartment... despite constant distraction from Echo, who is listing off the names of her fish for the 20th time and competing for Inari's attention like it is a competition between gold and silver medalists in the Olympics, I have had enough of the distractions and pull Inari aside, grabbing her by the shoulders, and turning her to face me. I look into her eyes... 4 inches from her nose... and with complete confidence, I say, "What's *really* hurting me right now is that Echo told you that Jin wanted to marry you." I pause. "Inari... I may not have even kissed you... but *I* want to marry you."

Inari writes off Jin's affections. "Yeah, well he said all that stuff and we talked about it... then he *dumped* me," she says. "You think I'm crazy, don't you Yuki? You need to believe me before I can ever be with you."

Am I crazy? Is she crazy? I don't know, but I love her. I accept what she says to be truth. I believe her.

It is difficult to leave Echo's apartment tonight. Echo just keeps listing the names of her fish over and over and over and over as we try to get her to go to bed. Inari and I work together, as a team, to take care of Echo, and I feel comradery build between us as our newer, deeper understanding of each other is renewed.

Bedtime was long ago, but Echo wants to drink more, still listing off her fish, over and over. Fortunately, I am in possession of all the booze. She begs for another shot of my vodka. On any other night, I'd cave and let Echo drink more, but for the first time ever, I am tough. I refuse. "No, Echo! The doctor said you shouldn't drink at all... your liver is already fucked."

"Just one more shot. I'll put it in the fridge and save it for tomorrow. Come on, please!" she begs.

Eventually, somehow, we get Echo to go to bed. Inari accomplishes this by essentially seducing Echo into the bedroom and staying with her intimately until she falls asleep. I politely wait on the sofa for what seems like 30 minutes while the two of them do whatever they're doing in the bedroom. I hear murmurs of sweet talk. I imagine them kissing, but I don't really know. I remained where I was.

I had never stood up to Echo before. As we walk out, I thank Inari for making me a better person... she always does. By her side, I feel confident as I never have before. She and I have quickly formed the tightest bond I've ever formed with another human being in my life. She makes me a better person all the time. She makes me believe in myself like I never have before. She wipes my anxiety away. She brings me peace, calm, and fighting strength. She makes me a warrior.

But having left Echo's apartment tonight, this night still refuses to end, because now we finally have the time together that I've been so looking forward to cherishing. Every moment... every second... I cherish... every utterance... syllable... gesture... I cherish like no other.

For the first time, there's only us to judge us for gazing into each other's eyes. And gaze... we do... gaze we do.

I park outside Jin's apartment for a while. Jin calls... she sees his name appear on her phone.

"Aren't you going to answer that?" I ask.

She rolls her eyes and casts the phone aside. I just laugh inside... I smirk to myself. I've never seen her roll her eyes at anything before.

We talk for a long time in the car before we make our way inside, where we find ourselves sitting in a stairwell. There, sitting close together, Inari rests her head on my shoulder, and I reach over and confidently hold her hand. I pet her hand, assuring her I care about her deeply. We sit... bonding... talking... and just soaking up the warmth of each other for several minutes.

We continue further through the building and find ourselves on a couch near vending machines just outside Jin's apartment. It is a room with a glass wall isolating it from the rest of the hall. There we can feel like we're alone, even though Jin's apartment door is only 10ft away. The couch is comfortable; we spend another hour enjoying the presence of each other there without worrying that anyone will overhear us.

Jin, having not spoken to Inari since he left her at the club, finally emerges to leave for work. I see him through the glass wall, but he doesn't notice us. I point him out to Inari. She springs up and chases after him casually down the hall. "I love you," she shouts with a subtle chuckle. He comes back.

"Where have you been? I tried to call you," he says.

She kisses him.

"You have vodka on your breath," he says.

"Yeah, I had… uh… one drink after bar," she downplays.

He must rush off to work. He unlocks the apartment door for Inari.
She doesn't even have keys to his apartment even though they've
been dating for over a year. I expect that I'll leave her at the door
and go about my day, but after Jin leaves, she stands at the door
holding it open in an almost seductive stance, puffing out her
breasts to make them appear larger… and makes it clear with her
body language that I am invited in. Jin's apartment is very
minimalist. It has concrete floors, concrete walls, and stainless-
steel faucets. It is a modern loft in a building intended for artists,
but Jin is not an artist as far as I know.

Inari changes into pajamas. She's not shy at all about revealing
anything to me, but I am polite and look away when I realize she's
maybe more exposed than she would want me to see. Yet, I
incidentally get a glance at the back sides of her breasts as she
changes in the bedroom, making no attempts to isolate her body
from view.

We sit on the floor together and talk and talk and talk… I am late
for work, but I don't care one bit. We talk and talk and talk. I pet
her leg as we talk for a final hour together. I reassure her that she's
more perfect to me now than she was when the night started.

She sits up, and we are not shy at all about gazing into each other's
eyes. I gaze with more passion than I have ever gazed into her eyes
ever before. There's no one looking to judge us. It is just she and I,
alone… our noses 3 inches apart. We tilt our heads as if to avoid
noses for what would be our first kiss. So much love fills my heart
for this girl. So much love… SO MUCH FUCKING LOVE.

But…

I do not kiss her. I take her by the hips... I gaze into her eyes... I love this girl... I love this girl... and I will love her until my grave... but I do not kiss her... I do not try to kiss her... oh god how I want to... 'Love', after all, is my 'God'. I love this girl far too much to kiss her.

"You and I both need to learn to take a little. I'm not backing down," I say as I am leaving.

"I am a lost cause," she says.

"No, you're not a lost cause... I'm following you until my Alzheimer's is in such advanced stages that I can no longer remember you. I'm following you until my grave."

She takes my scarf and wraps it around my neck to suggest that she might possibly pull my neck towards her for what would surely be a romantic, passionate embrace.

"Don't worry," she says. "Things will work out."

I do not kiss her. I say goodbye.

Chapter 23 - Downtime

After being out all Wednesday night, I naturally expect Inari to be difficult to rouse for the next few days. I am quite surprised I hear from her *at all* on Friday. She agrees to help me out with my hair, but I expect it to be difficult for her to keep her plans with me. There are a whole bunch of different reasons. Her sleeping issues are just one of the reasons, but also because I've been spending an awful lot of time with her, and Jin probably wants his turn with a conscious Inari.

I am trying my best to be patient, and doing reasonably well with it, but I finally start to feel a little bit jealous of Jin. The guy doesn't want her as much as I do, but I don't think anyone can want *anyone* more than I want Inari. If I were a little bit bolder, I could have probably kept him away from her for longer the other morning. I didn't *have* to point him out when I saw him walking down the hall on Thursday morning, but I thought it was the right thing to do. If he had gone to work without letting Inari into his apartment, I would have had no choice but to take her somewhere else, as his apartment would have been locked, preventing her from getting inside.

When I feel impatient, I take long naps to pass the time. Sleep is great for making time pass instantly. Sometimes I just want to sleep until she calls. I get more and more nervous as the time in-between grows between each of our interactions.

I don't troll around online as much these days. This is usually a sign that I am feeling content with life. I tend to troll the internet when I feel like I need attention from people... but now I don't feel the need to socialize. I am content by myself.

I take a little time to stomp out a potential fire before it gets out of hand and write Echo an email. Knowing that Echo and Jin have been friends for years, I worry that she'll divulge information to Jin that she shouldn't. I'm not entirely proud of the wording of my email. I feel like I come off as scheming and manipulative. But maybe I *am* scheming and manipulative. Yet, I try to be honest about it… I continue to send Inari the chapters of this book as I write them. I will later send her this very chapter.

Echo,

About the other night.

You heard me say some things that are very blunt and VERY PRIVATE. I'm not entirely sure if you're aware of HOW SERIOUS THIS SITUATION IS. This is VERY VERY VERY VERY SERIOUS.

I didn't want to say anything too serious in front of you, and I apologize if you feel left out by anything. But I assure you it is FAR MORE SERIOUS than anything you might have heard through the grapevine. But at the same time… it is NOT WHAT YOU THINK. Inari is NOT CHEATING ON JIN WITH ME… and she is not cheating on him at all… many people think that she cheats on him with her roommate Barry all the time… I assure you… this is not the case. Inari is trustworthy and a serial monogamist. People say these things… but they are just rumors spread by people with black hearts who are simply unable to understand the heart of someone pure.

But at the same time, there are VERY VERY SERIOUS THINGS HAPPENING that are definitely NOT A GAME… and no one should be privy to some of the things I say to her except for ME and HER.

I beg you, PLEASE, as a friend… Do not try to change, alter, gossip about, or play games with the connection that she and I are making with each other. We don't play games.

Inari has quickly become my best friend and we have a relationship that is far deeper than ANY friendship that I've ever had in my LIFE. And that is ALL it is.

She knows whose hearts are good, and whose are black. She knows who is honest and who's a liar. She knows who is selfless and who is selfish. Believe me... she KNOWS. I had doubts until I talked to her privately on the steps of your apartment... there, I tested her, and she PASSED with flying colors.

We had a beautiful night that night... and I left her at Jin's apartment at 10:15AM... we had plenty of facetime to talk about what happened earlier in the night... and she and I are ON THE SAME PAGE about EVERYTHING.

But again... there are things that she and I say to each other that are very private and I didn't want you to hear. Please just keep the few things you may have heard to yourself.

Yuki

Echo replies in a typical fashion, riddled with typos, grammatical errors, and lacking all punctuation.

Yuki,

I never thought she was cheating on him with you and i realize its serious, but to tell you the truth i dont even remember everything that was said not to mention i would never tell anyone any thing about any bodies relationship. Thats not who I am. I dont gossip or spread rumors and love the both of you too much to want to destory anything about you two or even a friendship thats not who i am. I realize you are concerned and i understand that but I assure you the two of you are safe with me, and things will not be said.

-Sincerely Echo

Certainly, if Jin knew the exact extent to which I have been romancing Inari... he'd probably fly off the handle. Sometimes I think to myself that maybe I'm just a pawn in a game that she is playing with him to make him a more emotional person. I don't like feeling like a pawn... but I can't help feeling this way sometimes even if I think that my feelings are a bit irrational. I take time to frequently remind people that nothing is going on between

Inari and me because people *do* notice that she and I have become close in the clubs.

Sometimes, I daydream about coming clean with Jin, but I know it would be a bad idea. On many levels, I feel like I owe him an apology and I don't like having guilt on my conscience. But as I said to Inari Thursday morning, "You and I both need to learn to take a little. It is okay to take, every once in a while."

My conscience is weighing on me heavily right now. I feel like I need to come clean on a few little white lies and sins of omission in this story. Probably the hardest pill to swallow is that there's a substantial discrepancy between the number of people Inari *thinks* I've talked to about "us" versus that *actual* number. She may think it is 3-5 people. Luna and Techna and a couple others… but the number is probably closer to 50. Random people inquire about how things are going every night that I am out. I am not sure how many people have picked up on our energy, but when people ask, I am sure to always remind them that nothing is happening between us. If I admit to having feelings for Inari, I repeatedly remind them that she's faithful to Jin and that nothing inappropriate has happened between us… but I'm not sure how much longer I can keep this up without someone just flat-out disbelieving my explanation of our relationship.

People dangerously close to her are aware of our nature, and I remind them that Jin trusts her with me because she is trustworthy and that, just because I might have feelings for Inari, it doesn't mean that she is reciprocating anything.

But when Inari learns how far and wide people are talking, she'll worry about her reputation, certainly. Inari seems to care about her reputation immensely. I don't care about my reputation at all… here I am documenting the lying and scheming bastard I am.

As I write this, Jin has called me up and said that he and Inari are going to Echo's to deal with fashion show stuff. In what I would regard to be a huge gaffe in fashion show management, Jin has decided to make Echo his star designer for the show, and the show… is approaching… very fast. Echo is a talented designer, but also an unmotivated drunk who is spiraling out of control. The two of them are planning to go to her apartment to motivate her to "actually *sew* some shit."

Inari complains regularly of Jin's poor management skills and says that she does much to help Jin's supposed "fashion company" stay organized. Jin is forgetful and can't keep anything organized or get anything done on time. Yet, Jin doesn't make her a partner in his company and regards any opinions that come from Inari to be worthless without even considering them. Inari tests this theory by offering her opinions to other "partners" in the company who then, in turn, offer them to Jin. When the ideas come from sources other than Inari, Jin respects them.

I am legitimately worried that Inari and Jin are going to Echo's. My god, this could be ugly… way fucking ugly. If she gets drunk and lets information slip to Jin about what happened the other night… particularly after I just sent her this firm email regarding my feelings for Inari, this could get *very* ugly.

I now must show up just to run interference. I didn't want anything to be spilled in front of Echo… nothing… zero. I don't trust her. I don't trust her to keep her mouth shut. She knows too much.

Chapter 24 - Reds

Echo shows no shame in begging me to buy her a pack of smokes on my way over to her apartment. Echo has been drinking at home alone and is already a bit tipsy by the time I arrive at 9:30PM, but her supply of booze has now run dry. Echo never has money for cigarettes. She relies on friends and taxpayers to provide her with such luxuries as cigarettes, alcohol, and *food*.

I come early bearing a pack of Marlboro Reds. "I'm giving these to you with conditions," I say.

"What's that?!" she says in a perky voice as if she were excited to hear about what I was going to "make" her do.

"Not a word," I declare. "You heard some things on Wednesday night that I didn't want you to hear, while at the same time, I've kept you in the dark about how serious this is to me, but now that you've heard too much, you must understand that this is *serious*... at least to me," I say. "If Jin ever heard any of the things I say to Inari when he's not around, he'd probably fly off the handle and Inari would never forgive me if I came in between them. I have not had any inappropriate contact with Inari. There's nothing going on between us beyond simple friendship. I just want to make sure that I stop any rumors before they start."

"Even if you two were fooling around, it would be none of my business. You and Jin are both my friends, and I don't come in between friends like that... it is for you to work out," she replies.

We sit around and wait for Inari and Jin to show up. 12:15AM comes and they still haven't arrived. Echo is getting more and more stir-crazy. She wants booze. I don't tell her that I have a bottle of vodka in my car.

"Let's go to the bar on the corner and get some drinks!" she begs. "Please!" she begs... over and over.

"But, I don't feel like drinking," I say.

She presses on and presses on for nearly an hour. As I get fatigued from waiting for Inari and Jin to arrive, eventually I cave. I figure she's sober from her drinking earlier, so I can safely buy her one drink. We go to the bar and one drink turns to 2, but we're pushed up against closing time and I escape having to babysit a wasted Echo (again) on this night. I have little faith that Inari and Jin are going to show up after 2AM. I just head home. Inari calls me at 5AM. She, apparently, had a panic attack preventing her from going to Echo's. Whereas this would be an acceptable excuse, neither Inari nor Jin communicated that to either of us, so either way, it was still incredibly rude.

As I talk to her at 5AM, Inari's anxiety is still getting the best of her... she's out of meds. I don't want to heighten her anxiety, and I fully understand that going into Echo's place and dealing with Jin, Echo, and me in the same room was not going to exactly calm her nerves.

We talk for a long time. The subject, naturally, drifts to her empathic nature. She explains what life is like for her as an empath. It makes life difficult. She doesn't like having to feel everything around her, and whereas, to her, Jin may be a "robot" and narcissist, she finds his lack of emotional sway to be oddly comforting.

"Everyone has a range of emotion that they feel... it just so happens that Jin's range of feeling is very limited," she says. "But it is nice that I can be around him and not have to feel his emotions. It is quiet, peaceful."

Inari and Barry, both empaths, agreed that neither she nor he could get any emotional readings from Jin when they first met him. It was odd, eerie. He had dead eyes that Barry found disturbing, but Inari seemed to really appreciate. She was attracted to this sturdiness, this emptiness, and his unemotional response to things that might drive most people mad. Inari latched onto Jin in such a manner that, to a normal, unevolved, "well-adjusted" human being, would seem irrational. Even as Jin mistreated her during their first days together, Inari followed Jin around like a dog on a leash. His lack of emotion put a spell on her.

I worry that it is unhealthy. "When someone is unable to feel empathy for others, they are, by definition, a sociopath or psychopath. I certainly wouldn't accuse Jin of being murderous, but psychopaths are very often regarded as very polite and considerate to those close to them, yet their inability to feel empathy means that fewer emotional barriers are preventing them from hurting or even murdering people. I trust that you know Jin better than me, but, since I know you've had some problems with him, naturally, I worry about you, and I think that you deserve to be happy and cared for."

I offer to come over and sit in the hall with her like we did Thursday morning. I offer to help her get her meds, but we just talk on the phone. We talk and talk and talk about all kinds of stuff... nothing too deep... I get the idea that professions of love aren't going to help her anxiety tonight. After 2 hours on the phone, she agrees to let me come over. She tells me to take a nap and she'll call me once she's done her hygiene routines. Her hygiene routines routinely take hours. She buries her face in a snorkel for 15 minutes, showers, and then spends hours fluffing her hair, putting on her makeup, and deciding what clothes to wear.

I honestly don't expect her to stay awake. I expect her to crash. I don't expect to hear a peep from her until late in the evening Sunday... if at all. I go to sleep under the assumption that there will be no need for me to wake up. My desire to see her was a bit selfish of me anyway. Inari deserves a bit of time without having me bombard her with complex emotions.

As I lay in bed trying to fall asleep, I think about how our relationship has formed and how it ties in with her deity-like, empathic abilities. It all makes sense now. I have an intoxicating love in my heart for Inari and being near me must be like a drug to her. No matter how hard she tries to shut off this flame in my heart, it still glows for her... no matter what her intentions are with me... my heart still draws her in.... she senses its glow, and she simply cannot deny that she seeks it.

She has tried to push me away several times now but failed. Her failure to get rid of me was partly due to my incessant persistence, but also due to her own inability to give up the things she seeks from me. I was ready to tell her that I could accept that she had no love interest in me several times, but Inari always grabbed onto something to pull me back towards her. She couldn't let me go.

Whereas she berated me in the past for reading too much into the signals she was giving me, I would argue that the *real* reason I read into those signals was because there was *clearly* an eerie energy being exchanged between us... and I could sense this. I could sense her pulling at my heartstrings, and I could see her glow when I was happy. It was as if when my heart fluttered, hers did too.

Although I consider myself to have empathy for others, I'm not an empath on the level of Inari and Barry. I was initially disappointed that I would not be able to relate to her on this level. But, since then, I've come to realize that it is a blessing. Inari doesn't want to be with an empath. In fact, she would rather be with someone who feels nothing at all. That is why Jin is her man.

"Everyone has a range of emotions that they feel... it just so happens that Jin's range of feeling is very limited," she said to me.

I try to get her to understand that I constantly beam and glow and shine with all the happiness that is in my heart for her, and that should be *worth something* to her. I have confidence that this will work. It *will* work.

I keep thinking back to how she said, "Things will work out," as she gave me back my own scarf... romantically wrapping it around my neck as to pull me close to her.... my god how I wanted to kiss her then... my god.

Things *will* work out. It feels inevitable. I will give it all the time it requires.

I believe it is my duty to be honest with her. And in the spirit of honesty, I know I need to come clean about how much talk there is around the things that are happening between her and me, so I make a list of all the people I've talked to about us. It includes… 42 people. Ugh! 42 people! This is not good. This is not good at all. When she finds out about this, she is going to be very mad.

But she inspires such honesty in me, even when that honesty is dark. I constantly work to be the most honest version of myself, confessing my sins to her in the very text that you are reading now. Every time I write a new chapter, I send it to her, and I believe that she reads it. 42 people… she is not going to like that part, at all.

Chapter 25 - Fight or Flight

Inari calls me up at 5AM. She is pissed off. Rightfully so. Chapters 23 and 24 really pissed her off.

After getting my ass chewed out for a good 45 minutes, the conversation turns into yet another "just friends" conversation... and this time, Inari, still angry, makes it clear that she doesn't want me and probably never will.

I acknowledge that I needed to do a better job keeping my mouth shut, but in the gaps between when we saw each other, the silence was maddening. The longer the gaps, the more intense my obsession with her grew, and the more "free therapy" I needed from friends and acquaintances. If this were truly the end of us, I would walk away knowing and believing that it was *my* fault we couldn't be together.

"You realize that I've never told anyone about being an 'empath' but you and Barry, right!? You cannot tell people those things, and I feel really betrayed right now, and I worry that people will think I'm crazy!" she complains.

Suddenly I see the *real* problem. Inari is not upset that I wrote Chapters 23 and 24, she is merely upset at the idea that those chapters were shared with others, but I assure her that they absolutely were *not*. She seems to feel much better once she realizes that I hadn't been sharing crazy empathic stories with our friends. In fact, no one has read anything beyond chapter 15, but her.

The first 15 chapters were only ever shown to my closest and best friends and were originally intended to simply document the events out of concern for her relationship safety. And as far as they're concerned, the story ended on the day things got a bit crazy at the amusement park. Yet, if they tried to read those chapters now, they'd find them deleted.

But, regardless of my big mouth, my sins of omission are bad enough. Inari drills into me seeking details about what parts of the story I left out and what I haven't told her.

"There were tiny, but meaningful details that drove the story early on that I excluded from the story because if I included them, it would cast a shadow on your immaculate image," I confess. "On some levels, this writing was intended as a persuasive essay, a confession of my own thoughts and actions, and a profession of my own love, while also turning a mirror back at you for your own actions. So if I included some things that I heard you said one hour before I even met you, that would actually soil your immaculate image, and I'd have a harder time convincing you that I loved you and believed you to be infallible."

"What did I supposedly say!?" she snaps.

"Well, you told Kenzie that you thought right then and there that it was time for you to start cheating on Jin. You also told her that you loved him but weren't 'in love' with him."

"I have no idea what would inspire her to say something like that, and if she did say those things, I should have a talk with her," Inari defends.

"Well, that's between you and Kenzie then. I have nothing to do with it. I suppose it gave me a little extra confidence to know that you were thinking of making a move to something/someone new. All men understand that when you meet a girl so beautiful, charming, amazing, loving, and charismatic, you must insert yourself into their lives at exactly the right time, because if you wait too long, even a day or two, they are sucked up in a flash. As a 'man', your only chance of winning a girl like you is to be ready, available, and aggressive in your pursuit of her, the instant she becomes available to you."

"People are going to think I'm a slut, Yuki!" Inari complains.

"I wouldn't worry about it," I reply. "No one in this scene seems to care about anyone's drama but their own. The scene is so full of it that everyone lacks the emotional capacity to care. They are too busy dealing with their own bullshit. Regardless of whatever the dramatic 'story of the day' is, it is quickly forgotten and replaced when tomorrow's news comes to the surface."

It is a painful process to come clean, but by the end of it all, there are no secrets. And once there are no secrets, she and I are fully capable of moving past the drama and we talk as deeply and lovingly as we always have.

This story is for me and *you only*, Inari. For the last several chapters I've been sitting here asking myself why the hell I'm even talking to you like you're a 3rd person here. It seems entirely appropriate to just replace every occurrence of 'her' with 'you' in this story.

So... let's continue our story, shall we?

I breathed a sigh of relief when you calmed down upon learning that these writings have been private between us. If this story were passed around like a rumor, it would be damaging to you, and I don't want to damage you. Whereas I know that you want to be a good person, I think that, even more than *being* a good person, you want to be *seen* as such. You care about your immaculate image and reputation. Honestly, this is a tremendous difference between you and me. I don't give a fuck how other people see me. I just want them to know the *real* me. I am used to being an outcast who is stomped on and laughed at. What I *do* care about, however, is the freedom to speak my mind and tell the truth and be myself even if the truth makes me unpopular and even if the truth is incredibly dark. I know who I am. People who are concerned about image do not!

So... with this in mind... when I describe certain moments as "romantic" and you write them off as if they are the gross misinterpretations of a man with a sick, stalker mentality, I look back and think that maybe it was just a psychological game that you're playing. Because you often say these negative things about me and to me, but then you keep coming back and filling me up with such positivity and love. This roller-coaster of positive and negative is maddening and confusing. I'm just confused all the time because one day, you might say beautiful things into my eyes and then abandon me with your actions, and on other days you will berate me with your words, but then hold my hand and gaze into my eyes and let me tell you how beautiful you are and how much I love you.

The only time you seem to throw up boundaries between us is when others are looking. You worry that if we are close it will damage your image and reputation. We all defend ourselves vigorously when we know that we, ourselves, are to blame for our own actions. When you're painted into a corner, sometimes the only way out is to climb up the wall.

Even though there is darkness, deceit, lies, and trickery in this story, Inari. I believe that every bit of this story is beautiful, and I will love you to the end of the earth.

Yes, the other night, I wanted to kiss you... but I knew that if I tried... regardless of if I succeeded or if I failed... it would have ripple effects that were serious and far-reaching. If I failed... it would have hurt our friendship... if I succeeded, it would force you to come to terms with your relationship with Jin and it would force you to admit that you have feelings for me. I don't believe that you're ready to admit that to anyone... even yourself.

But that's okay... there are no pressing decisions that must be made *today*. I certainly love spending time with you. Every minute we're together, I feel this bond, building. Building to what? I don't know, because it isn't entirely up to me to decide how our bond is built and what our bond eventually becomes. But I feel it is building... and I feel that it isn't *only* my efforts that are contributing to this building. You're putting in your efforts as well as I am.

All the time, I ask you if it is time for me to call off this chase. You always confuse me with your reply. Your incessant lack of conviction is confusing. Am I supposed to be here? Am I supposed to go? I don't know at all.

I ask you if you want me to stop whispering romantic things in your ear when Jin is not listening. I ask you if you want me to stop writing you songs and stories... or saving the flowers you give me. If I ask you if you want me to stop *all of this* and you say anything less than a resounding, confident, "yes!" ... then I just don't believe you, and my heart grows more and more confused. And when I ask you a second time... and a third time... and you still don't answer "yes!" ... I believe you even less and less and I become even *more* confused. I'm confused, Inari.

But even though our 2 hour and 47-minute conversation earlier consisted largely of you telling me what an asshole I am, eventually, you ask me what I'm doing later... and I am quick to reply, "I'll pick you up at 5:30." And now I just bask in the warm thoughts of being near you again. Life... it is beautiful, isn't it?

Chapter 26 - GWC

Jin calls me up. He needs a photographer to shoot a photo that will appear on the posters and handbills for his impending fashion show. I am *not* a photographer. I am just a guy with a camera. I have a slightly nicer camera than your average photographer and some decent lenses, but I know half-a-dozen photographers that are far more talented and serious about their work than I am, and I wonder why he doesn't just call one of them. I'm not complaining though. Inari is going to be the model, so naturally, if I am invited to be near her, I jump at the opportunity.

Inari is worried that things aren't getting done in time for the fashion show. The show is less than 4 weeks away. Echo has yet to sew a single item, the flyers are not done, promotional work needs to be in full swing, and it all needed to be done *yesterday*. She convinces Jin to bash out the photo tonight. I agree to come by Zak's place for the shoot. His landlord, Sammy, is a friend of the scene and agrees to let us use a vacant, busted-up, apartment in the building as a makeshift studio. We'll get it done.

Zak's roommate, Shannon, is a hairdresser and another "partner" in Jin's company. She agrees to do Inari's hair for the shoot. They say they'll be just 15 minutes as Jin and I examine the site for the shoot, rig up lights, and take some test shots. I don't really know what I'm doing, but it will have to do.

15 minutes turns into 2.5 hours. I patiently wait, but I get more and more nervous as bar time approaches. I want to make an appearance at Hard Mondays tonight, but quite honestly, I'm not at all sure *why*. I just want to be near Inari, but sitting around, bored, I decide to check on Zak and Shannon's neighbor, Hannah.

Hannah is an old friend. I met Hannah a decade ago during the fallout with Luna. We became casual friends and hung out a few times. She was maybe a bit "too much" for me though. She was wild, and I was subdued. It made for an awkward dynamic when we'd go for long drives, and she would stick her head out my window and scream at pedestrians for fun. If she had to urinate, she'd jump out of the car and just let loose in the middle of a busy parking lot in broad daylight. Naturally, this didn't last, and I lost contact with her in the years I was absent from the scene.

Upon returning to my old haunts, I found myself at Ground Zero, where I met a burlesque dancer named "Magenta". Hannah had changed quite a bit in 10 years, and I barely recognized her in her burlesque getup. Her short blonde hair was now a long, crazy forest of colorful, braided hair extensions. Her septum was pierced along with possibly 25 other piercings around her body. She barely remembered me, but as we talked, her memories would eventually come back to her and we began to have deep conversations about our past lives and current problems.

At the beginning of summer, I was playing video games with Amber, as was the norm, when she got a call from her friend Dennis. Dennis claimed that his girlfriend, Hannah, just called in 3 thugs to beat him up and needed someone to come get him out of there. As we're driving, Amber is quick to offer without inquiry that "We're just friends... just as friends."

I, of course, oblige, but in the back of my mind, her jumpiness makes me immediately understand that there must have been more to their history than simple friendship. I brush it off as paranoia and just do my duty. We pick up Dennis from the very apartment building I am sitting in tonight where Inari is getting her hair done.

Dennis gets in my car, cut and bruised, but I guess I expected him to appear more beat-up than he was. He smells like absolute dog shit, but he thanks me for offering him a place to crash for the night. He's frantic. "Hannah is a manipulative whore!" he says. "I should have listened to everyone who told me to watch out for her. She is one crazy piece-of-shit."

I chime in and offer the few anecdotes I have regarding my experiences with Hannah. She was a bit crazy, certainly, but Hannah was always the first to admit that she is crazy. I think she had some schizophrenia. She would always claim to be a lesbian, quite vigorously, yet would have intense relationships with men who would torment her emotionally. Years ago I spent many hours offering her a shoulder to cry on when she would feel mistreated by them.

To find out she's dating a man is a surprise and *not a surprise* at the same time, but who the hell is this dogshit-smelling dude who's slithered into her pants? This seems gross and wrong. Dennis was unimpressive. He smelled like shit, literally. I mention this again, because really… he really smelled like shit. He was hideously ugly with a disproportionately large jaw and fucked up teeth (possibly from years of abusing meth). He probably hadn't bathed in 2 weeks, yet he was full of himself. He regarded himself as awesome, successful, and important.

Whereas I tried to be supportive of Amber's friend who had just gotten beaten up, I wondered why Hannah would be scraping the bottom of the dumpster for her latest boyfriend. She was far too beautiful and nice for him. He spent all night name-dropping bad metal acts that he supposedly was booking as a freelance booking agent, but he didn't realize that I, myself, played in a band with one of the biggest booking agents in the country so I knew enough about the subject to know that Dennis was a huge liar and exaggerator.

Dennis blames everyone *else* for his failures, including Hannah. He talks like he is flawless, but everyone else has just screwed him over. It was always "their fault". He is penniless. I offer him some leftover beer. I had a case of 24 unopened in the fridge. I wasn't going to drink it. I didn't like that swill. It was just a party leftover.

He and Amber seemed to bond as survivalists and just talked and drank while I went to bed, needing to work in the morning. When I woke up, Amber and Dennis were still awake, talking, and all 24-beers were gone, the cans strewn about around the sofa in the loft.

I never would have thought Hannah, let alone Amber, would ever have a romantic interest in this meth-mouthed sewer rat. But Amber would later reveal to me that she had sex with Dennis in the past, but only for the purpose of revenge. She always blamed her ex-boyfriend, Graydon, for giving her herpes when he cheated on her. She always believed that the stigma of having herpes had ruined her sex life. Amber was destructive in many ways. And one of the ways she liked to hurt people was to intentionally spread herpes to get revenge.

Dennis was one such guy. She invited him over to play video games and, of course, smoke weed. She was probably out of weed at the time and just needed someone to bring some over. Through the course of the events, they ended up making out, but Amber's breath was foul, as it usually was. Dennis told her that her breath smelled like shit and pushed her off him.

Amber didn't like being denied, rejected, so she waited to see him again until she was having an intense herpes outbreak. This time she fucked him. The only reason she did this was to give him herpes. It even turned into a pregnancy scare and the fallout from it became intense.

Having reconnected with "Magenta" at the club, the story of Dennis's 24-beer sleepover would quickly become a hot topic. I assumed she knew that Amber and Dennis had slept together in the past, but as it is casually brought up in conversation, it was clear that Hannah is upset by this. *Really* upset.

"He cheated on me! That fucking bastard!" she shouted.

"Wait, wait, I figured this was long ago, long before you even met him," I backpedaled.

"No, that's impossible, because I know exactly when this would have happened, as I got suspicious that he was sneaking around, but he denied it! That fucking bastard! I'm going to kill him! He's been freeloading off me. He is abusive, the cops are constantly coming over to respond to domestic complaints. It is so bad that

Sammy is threatening to evict me!"

After we went our separate ways, Hannah, armed with this new information, took it to Dennis. Hannah and Dennis split up. Dennis and Amber began harassing me, making threatening calls, and sending threatening texts. As it was getting heated, a depressed Hannah and I decided to get together in person, almost like a date. I bought her dinner at my favorite Asian restaurant. We caught up on old times. We went back to my house, and I showed her my laser show and played music videos. She cried on my shoulder. I held her hand.

"Look at me, I'm hideous," she said.

"No, you're beautiful," I replied.

"No, all of this is *fake*! It is nonsense. I've been raped. I've been psychologically tortured. I've been beaten. Look at me!" she cries. Hannah reaches into her mouth and removes her false teeth revealing that all her top front teeth are fake. "This is when my ex-boyfriend smashed my face into a curb!"

My heart sank for her. She did not deserve to live this trauma.

I simply held her while she cried until, somehow, she calmed down. We stood under the tranquil blue lights of my dance floor, her head on my shoulder, without speaking for a bit, until she broke the silence, "Do you think it is okay to seek revenge on people?"

"Well, you're a Christian, so it is not my place to offer you moral advice," I replied, "but when someone treats me unjustly that I love, and particularly when they leave me for good, I find that the only way I am able to cope with it initially is to focus on the negative. I fixate on the bad memories and remember them as vile, awful people... because, for me... it is easier to move forward believing that they left me because they were *bad people*... and *not because* I am worthless. It is far easier for me to hate Luna and

Amber than it is for me to accept that maybe I was just not *good enough* for them. Maybe I'm just stubborn in my assessments, but looking back, I brought them both a lot of love and generosity and they *never* really gave back *anything*. It was as if I was supposed to regard it to be a *privilege* just to sit near them! I would hang myself if I were forced to believe that I was not good enough for them *after all the love I gave them*. I *need* to fight them because I need enough adrenaline pumping through my veins to crawl out of this 'kill zone' to safety."

I continued, "I know you feel betrayed by Dennis. The best advice I can give is to simply remind you that 'hope' is the zest of life. I find that I can move forward if I have something to look forward to the next day. That might mean just a phone number from the right girl, an introduction, a new friend online, an email, an event to look forward to, or whatever. It shouldn't take long at all for you to find some hope. You're a beautiful girl."

"I know I shouldn't, but I really seek revenge on Dennis," she said again.

"Why don't you just tell them that we had sex tonight? I'll play along," I offered, jokingly. Hannah was gorgeous and all, but I regard sex to be an act of love, and I wouldn't want someone to fuck me who didn't love me.

Hannah lives literally across the hall from Zak and Shannon. Tonight, Inari's hair is taking *forever*. I check up on Hannah to see how she is doing. It has been a couple of months since she kicked Dennis to the curb. He'd been touring around the country in a beat-up van with some bad metal act which regularly threatened to pull over at the next rest stop and abandon him.

Hannah is having a bad day. Apparently, she was being generous to a friend from her church and was letting him crash at her place for the past few weeks, but unbeknownst to her, he had been stealing the keys to her safe. Little by little, he drained her safe of over $3500. She had only found out about it minutes earlier. I let her cry on my shoulder. I offer her free drinks at Hard Mondays after the photoshoot and she agrees to come along.

I treat her like she's my daughter and I'm her father trying to make sure she's behaving herself. I am inquisitive. Is she *really* staying away from Dennis? She loved Dennis because Dennis could quote scripture with her and he shared her liberal views about God. Hannah's version of spirituality encompasses evangelical foundations embellished with conspiracy theories surrounding the Illuminati, lizard people who want to take over the governments of the world. She believes that people in her bible-study group could cure her with a single touch if she came down with cancer. Regardless of their common interests, I tell her that I think she should love someone who treats her with respect. Fuck Dennis.

She spends over an hour trying to convert me into a spiritual person. I fight back, tooth and nail, in a respectful, sporting debate, trying to get her to abandon all faith in God. It turns into arguments surrounding creationism vs. evolution. Neither she nor I back down. She quotes the bible; I quote Sam Harris.

Eventually, the photoshoot happens. I take hundreds of photos of Inari in an adorable cabaret getup. She is shockingly adorable, as always. She is wearing a green corset; a short petticoat with a giant red bow on the back; long, black, satin gloves; fishnet stockings; and gorgeous black heels with faux diamond buckles. I wonder whether she's aware of how she makes me feel when she seduces the lens as I take hundreds of photos, 6 inches in front of her nose. In a rush to beat bar close, we hurry to get the photos done. By the time we get to Hard Mondays, there's just enough time to get Hannah one of their famous, notoriously stiff drinks and say "hi" to a few people before the bar closes.

Chapter 27 - Aussie

The next day, I send out samples of what I think are the better photos from the previous night. Inari hates them. She does not criticize my photography, but she is worried that the ribbon on the cabaret outfit is tied wrong and wrinkled. She wants to redo the photos with unwired ribbon vs. wired ribbon. I dread having to redo all the photos, but apparently, Jin and Shannon dread the idea *even more* and refuse to be involved in the redo. So, Inari and I decide we'll redo the photo together, without their help, alone.

I pick her up from Jin's apartment after work the next day, then, I take her to her house. I'd been to her house before, but never inside, so I have no idea what to expect. But even from the outside, it didn't look 'right'. It didn't look like the house that a 20 something and her ex-boyfriend/best-friend/roommate would live in. Something about the way the lawn was manicured… the lawn ornaments… the style of the chairs on the deck… didn't seem normal.

I am a bit nervous about entering the house. I am always a little nervous entering a new place, even a public place. An unfamiliar place always gives me unwelcomed vibes. Furthermore, this is also where Barry lives. Does Barry want me in his house? I don't really know.

I'd heard things through the grapevine that would suggest that Inari and Barry share a strange, abnormal, complicated relationship that always has everyone second-guessing. Even though they've been broken up for years, people in the scene don't trust that they've romantically split completely. People suggest that Barry even pays for all of Inari's expensive hair appointments. I don't lend any weight to their assessments; I don't think anyone knows anything about her in the scene, but something Maddox suggested to me on a previous night comes to mind as I enter the driveway.

He said, "I've heard that one way to tell if two ex-lovers who live together are truly split is to look in their bedrooms. If they're truly split, their possessions will not be mixed up in each other's rooms. But if you go into her room and you find his clothing and shoes and socks and underwear all over the place, then I'd certainly be suspicious."

I enter the house. It is a quaint but well-maintained house. But since Inari spends most of her time over at Jin's apartment, I assume that Barry is the one doing the maintenance. But, looking around, the decorations are very much a cozy country-style. I wonder if maybe the house was inherited from a family member, and no one has bothered to replace any of this stuff. But I don't really have time to examine things too carefully as we briskly rush past the kitchen and immediately go to Inari's bedroom. As Maddox suggested, I make a point to take in the items in the room. Are they all Inari's? At first sight, would appear to be largely Inari's room, although it lacks any sort of personal touch. It is lacking any posters for the things that she likes.

"I figured you'd have some posters on the wall or something," I say.

"Yeah, a tree fell on my house and destroyed everything I own, and I just never bothered to replace any of it," she explains.

"Oh man, that sucks. That must have been expensive. Even with the insurance, the out-of-pocket costs for something like that might be difficult to deal with," I continue.

Inari simply lets the statement hang in the air and says absolutely nothing in reply. I get the impression that she has nothing to really offer about how the house repairs were paid for or the work involved in dealing with insurance. The numbers don't really add up. I don't know how long it's been since Inari had a job, but I'm pretty sure it has been a long time, so someone else must be paying for this place.

As I continue to look around, eventually my eyes zero in on a man's suit coat resting on her chair and a man's running shoes on the floor. As I continue scanning, I find that items clearly belonging to Barry are scattered throughout the room. I write it off as only a little bit awkward, but I wonder if Maddox was right. I say nothing about the strangeness in the room.

Inari complains, "Ugh! Barry is always changing his clothes in my room! Am I the only one who cleans up things around here?"

Inari wants to find tape measures so she can visualize the posters we will ultimately be creating, so we soon visit a room in the basement with a workbench. It is strewn with baseball memorabilia, tools, and an old 8-track cassette player. I bask in nostalgic feelings about the old player. I didn't think she and Barry were old enough to remember, let alone, possess an old 8-track player. 8-track players were obsolete by the time I was a toddler, so they were *just before* my time, but with her being a few years younger than me, she would definitely know nothing of them. The baseball memorabilia seems out of place as well, as I didn't peg Barry to be a baseball fan. Just then Inari's grandmother enters the doorway.

"Did you feed Aussie," she asks. Aussie is Inari's dog, a cute, brown, terrier.

"Noooo," Inari confesses, "I'm sorry."

"Don't apologize to me. Apologize to Aussie," she returns.

I realize that I've imagined Inari and Barry's living situation to be different than it is. Inari and her ex-boyfriend, Barry, live in Inari's grandparents' house. I don't think less of her, but I wonder whether Inari's failure to mention this detail is the result of her own insecurities about herself. But maybe she thinks nothing of it. Maybe she is just trying to keep up the appearance of being successful and independent by failing to mention this detail. I wonder for a moment if she has entitlement issues, but I don't really care. I brush off any negative feelings because I love her so much. She really has no faults in my mind.

It isn't long before Barry comes home from work. He finds us in the basement. He is surprised and taken aback to see us alone together in the basement. She senses nervousness in him, and she asks him about it bluntly, "Barry, you're nervous. Why are you nervous?" she asks.

He offers no explanation. He goes back upstairs, and Inari continues to search for tape measures. Once she finds them, she lays them out in a square on the floor so she can visualize the dimensions of the posters she and I would be designing. Only minutes pass and Barry comes back downstairs into the workroom.

"I'm going out to Paul's," he declares.

"You're leaving already? But you just got here!" she says, surprised.

"Yeah, he's got a date tonight with some girl he met online, and I was going to give him a ride," he explains.

"With who? You? Are you getting gay with Paul?" Inari jokes. "But Barry, you have to stay here and motivate me to take a shower and do my makeup," Inari complains.

"Well… well," Barry stutters without saying anything more and just stands in the doorway.

"Barry, you know I won't be motivated to shower and shave and do my makeup unless I have you standing behind me, motivating me!"

"Well, you know, Paul's been depressed, and I already told him I'd do it. I'm just trying to help him out," he says.

"But Barry, please! I need you!" She continues to press into Barry. She inquires about all the details she can conjure up about this supposed "date" that their friend Paul is having. "How was he planning on getting there before you offered to give him a ride?"

"He was going to walk. But I told him I'd give him a lift already. I don't want to back down. That would be rude."

Inari continues to drill into Barry as if she doesn't believe his excuses for why he is leaving so soon. "You're nervous, she says. I know when you're nervous."

She changes the subject to jokes. "You're just going to get all gay with Paul, aren't you? How 'big' is Paul? Is he about average?" She measures out 6 inches on the tape measure. "So, this is 6 inches, eh? Supposedly this is 'average'. This shouldn't be too uncomfortable in your butt, should it?" She continues to joke, measuring out 4 inches, "What about this? This is no problem, right? You could take a 4-inch dick, right?"

Barry barely laughs and just nervously stands in the doorway. Inari fails to prevent him from leaving. Barry leaves us. Inari continues wasting time. She wastes much time mulling over dimensions and planning the shoot. I just want her to get dressed so we can shoot the thing, but it becomes apparent that this is not happening on this night. I want to go to the North Loop, but Inari is so unmotivated to change her clothes that we just end up talking for hours in her bedroom.

We both lay in her bed, but I am careful to keep my distance, careful not to invade her personal space. Jin eventually calls to check on progress. It turns into a long conversation and an argument. Jin seems all whiny and needy on the other end of the phone. Inari always portrayed him as an emotionless, sturdy guy, but he seems quite emotional at the moment. He tries to get her to spend the night at his place, but she refuses, and simply changes the subject and reminds him of all the things he needs to get done for the fashion show. Eventually, she gets him to cease his demands by firmly declaring, "Jin, I'm bleeding from my vagina and I'm in a bad mood and I just want to go to bed!"

It is after midnight when she hangs up. She still wants to do the photoshoot tonight. She offers to get ready while I make an appearance at the club. I try to get her to come with me, but I fail. She says she'll be awake after bar and ready to work. I am reluctant to leave her, I'm sure she'll be asleep when I'm done at the bar. I would rather be alone with her than at the club, but I also don't want to overstay my welcome.

I show up to the club, completely sober, to a bunch of drunk friends. It is 1AM. And much like Monday night, I waste no time making the rounds to catch up with friends. Tesla, the Goth Mother, approaches.

"Brad wanted me to tell you that he appreciated that you could be at the same party as him and act as an adult," she says.

"I don't care about Brad. He parked his shitbox car in front of my house like a creepy stalker, triggering a fight between Amber and me," I scoff, "If he was standing in front of me right now, I might be inclined to kick his ass."

"He's a nice guy, and she's just using him. She uses him all the time. He's a nice guy... and the reason I have money for drinks tonight is because he loaned us money until I get paid on Friday."

"I recognize that he probably is a nice guy," I say. "He just happens to be the guy with the greatest capacity to tolerate Amber's bullshit at the moment, but you must know that I'm still pretty pissed at him for manipulating an explosive situation that night."

"He was legitimately sick. I had to rescue him on the side of the road when he got heatstroke," she maintains. "I had to rescue him and drive him to your place that first day when he came over."

I pause for a second. As far as I knew, Brad had never been to my house until the day I met him, but Tesla is suggesting that he had been to my house before... when I wasn't there. This new information hits me a little bit, but I shrug it off because I don't really care about Amber anymore.

Well then, "You let him know that if he ever needs someone to talk to about Amber... I am certainly willing. We share a common bond, after all. And you can also let him and *her* know that I left that party early out of *pity*. There are *so* many places that Amber can't go without public ridicule, so I figured I would be generous and let her have her little party to herself."

I sit on a bench inside the club. It is strewn with various benches that look like pews from a church. A girl puts her arm around me and yanks me close to her and begins showering me with drunken but romantic compliments. Seconds later, a guy who I've never talked to, apparently bi or gay, or just having fun... sits down on the other side of me, snuggles up, and says, "Girl, what are you doing with my man!" In all good fun, we talk about life.

Without naming any names or getting into any specifics, I say, "My life is beautiful, full of romance, fantastic magic, but also full of conflict, peril, and lots of confusion. There is a special, beautiful, amazing girl who has become my best friend... and makes me feel so very illuminated."

The three of us smile brightly as we soak in all the romantic words we all hear.

"Unfortunately," I sigh, deflating, "she's unavailable."

"If she is unavailable, then she isn't worth your time!" the girl advises.

"It doesn't matter if she's unavailable... because what we have is beautiful anyway... and our bond still grows stronger and that's all that matters. Who knows where it will stop? Regardless of what may or may not happen, it is a beautiful ride."

There isn't a ton of time to enjoy the club tonight, but I get some fill out of it.

As I suspect, Inari falls asleep, and I am unable to reach her after bar. Natalie tries to get me to come to her place, but I elect to just go home. I've had enough. I am filled.

Chapter 28 - Inevitable Truths and Inevitable Consequences

Friday night, Inari and I decide we'll make one more attempt at motivating ourselves to take photos. Whereas I am willing to help get things done, really, this isn't *my* project; it is not my business to motivate her to be responsible. Therefore, I make no such effort. I just want to hang out with her. She doesn't seem too motivated to get the photo done either, so we just sit around talking about anything and everything. It is strange that I have this beautiful girl sitting next to me, yet I feel no immediate desire to rip her clothes off. Inari is my best friend and worthy of all my respect and her inner beauty is more perfect than her perfect exterior. But yes, absolutely, I want her to be my girlfriend and share all the romantic intimacies with her, I absolutely do.

I have never brought up the issue of sex with her. It wasn't a subject I really cared to discuss with her. I would have rather *she* brought up the issue of sex. It was a hurdle that needed to be jumped to get us to the next level. Over the previous days, I even made a list of these hurdles, confused by her signals. I figured that if these hurdles were jumped entirely, there would be no doubt that we would be together.

#1) Inari had to acknowledge and admit that my words were affecting her emotionally, that she was swayed by my words, and that my words inspired doubt regarding her compatibility with Jin.

#2) Inari had to drive a conversation towards sex. She was the kind of girl who wanted to discuss her sexual preferences before ever having sex with someone. I knew she would want to communicate specifics regarding exactly how she liked it. She'd want her partner to please her in a way that suited her preferences. She also would have to inquire about my own sexual desires to see if we might be sexually compatible. There would be no reason to gamble on someone new if she and he were not sexually compatible.

#3) Inari was scared to death of germs and especially sexually transmitted diseases. She'd want assurance that her partner is free of STDs before she'd ever consider having sex with him. She'd want more than an affirmation; she'd want a doctor's report.

#4) After all 3 conditions above were met, she would have to send me a signal, a clear-as-day signal, to let me know that it was okay for me to kiss her. Once we got that far, I figured there would be no more turning back.

We are again in the study adjacent to her bedroom. She starts off the conversation with her complaints about Jin. She can rant about what a terrible boyfriend he is for hours it seems. She never seems to tire of complaining about Jin. I offer my advice, trying to be as benign as to be polite, calling the situation honestly, with minimal bias.

Out of nowhere, Inari stops me in mid-sentence, "You... you're always making me second guess myself."

"I do? I didn't think anything I said to you was having any impact on you whatsoever," I replied.

"No, it does. You make me second-guess being with Jin all the time," she says.

Hurdle #1 was crossed. Not only was she second-guessing her relationship with Jin, but she acknowledged that *I* was affecting the course of it.

Our conversation continues. It is still early in the night when she brings up the subject of sex, hurdle #2. She asks about my own sexual preferences and experiences.

Talking about sex before the actual act is logically a healthy choice, but I'm rarely so bold. Plus, deliberately, I wanted Inari to bring up the subject. I wanted *her* to drive the discussion in that direction. If *she* brought it up, there was no way for her to accuse me of being creepy.

I say, "Sex, to me, is almost a crapshoot. All girls are different it seems. Some like it deep, some like it shallow, some want it emotional, some want it emotionless and mechanical, some want it happy, and some want it angry... some don't even want it at all. The angles and speed vary from girl to girl. I've brought some girls to climax simply by touching their breasts. Some have difficulty climaxing, yet some orgasm quite easily. Each girl is a mystery to me. Chemistry is difficult. Usually, the first time with anyone is terrible, but by the 2nd or 3rd time, I've figured you out and you can't get enough."

Inari says she wants a man to fuck her hard. She criticizes Jin's bedroom etiquette. She wants him to talk dirty to her, but he refuses. She tells me that one time he got mad and stopped simply because she said "fuck me harder" while they were having sex. She regards him to be selfish in bed. I am shocked to hear that Jin doesn't satisfy her in the bedroom. I figured that since Jin didn't emotionally satisfy her, nor did he intellectually satisfy her, she *must* be having some great sex with him or something, right?

"What the hell is it that you actually *do get* from the guy then?" I ask, quite frankly.

She offers no response or excuse as to why she is still with Jin despite all their dysfunction.

"It... it has been a while," she said, referring to the fact that they'd been sexually inactive for longer than she'd like.

We spend the pre-midnight hours in her room. She's lying in bed. I lie on the bed with her, but unlike the previous night when I shyly stayed at a distance from her, this time, I lie next to her... properly.

I am less shy about invading her space. I am less shy about getting close to her. I am in the middle of thinking to myself about how wonderful it is to be so close to my best friend when Jin calls. She answers. The volume on her phone is loud enough that I can hear most of their conversation. He learns that I am with her, and I hear his voice pause awkwardly. I imagine him thinking "What the hell is Yuki doing at your house?"

Jin and Inari argue on the phone as I lie on the bed next to her... eavesdropping, in a way... but Inari makes no effort to isolate their conversation from me. He offers that he should come over, but she makes excuses as to why he shouldn't. With each excuse she makes, Jin pauses, as if he is wondering why his girlfriend is so persistently preventing him from seeing her.

When asked what is wrong, Jin goes on about how his mother upset him today. His mother has some mental health issues. Inari offers him advice on how to deal with his mother, but I think that Jin never actually *sought* any such advice, nor did Inari truly *believe* he sought it. As I lie next to Inari, I only think to myself that Jin is using his talk about his mother to divert attention away from what is really upsetting him. Jin, in my opinion, is clearly upset that Inari is spending time, alone, with me. He doesn't understand how to deal with this emotion. He's not used to having deep emotions. He is a "robot" as Inari suggested. Feelings are new to him, and the physiological reactions that his body employs to protect himself from such feelings are foreign. They confuse him.

The situation that Inari has put Jin in is new and extreme. I wonder whether she's deliberately toying with him to teach him how to feel. I hear continued tremors in his voice to suggest that I am the source of his problems. He gets more and more agitated each time Inari reminds him that I am here. Inari seems completely unresponsive to his reactions.

At some point, my honesty and conscience get a hold of me and I politely suggest to Inari in a whisper, "You realize that Jin is upset because I am here, don't you?"

Jin, by nature, is compulsively polite. Even if he had an issue with

Inari, I doubt he would raise it. He sweeps his emotions under the rug and talks with Inari longer and longer about his supposed problems. Inari does not respond to his underlying emotional problems but dutifully responds only to the problems that Jin has presented as an affront to his real problems.

Eventually, he asks again if he can come over. He asks her to spend the night at his place.

She doesn't flat-out refuse to let him come over, but strongly suggests otherwise. She suggests that he take care of the things he needs to take care of for the fashion show going off on a tirade as she lists off a mental checklist of all the things that still need to get done.

Jin persists and persists on the phone for two hours as I lie on the bed, patiently observing. Eventually, Inari casually mentions Barry by name and Jin makes some comments that I cannot distinguish from my vantage point but are clearly condescending. Inari gets upset with Jin and vigorously defends Barry.

"Unlike most people, I don't just cut good people out of my life, Jin. Barry is genuinely sorry for the things he did. And as long as he is genuinely sorry, I forgive him, and Jin, when you talk down to Barry, you realize that you're talking down to me!" she snaps back. "Just go to bed, Jin. If I came over, you'd just fall asleep and then I'd be stuck awake and alone all night, and I really don't feel like sitting around alone and bored all night. Plus, I am bleeding out of my vagina. I don't want to deal with this right now. Yuki is still here; I am being rude to him by talking on the phone with you!"

"Oh, I didn't realize he was still there, I'm sorry," Jin says.

"Yes, he is still here and it is one of the reasons that I am upset... actually it is the *main* reason that I am upset with you. I'm being rude to him!"

Finally, Jin and Inari say their goodbyes and hang up the phone. There is no "I love you" at the end of the conversation. The conversation was cold. Very little love was flowing in either direction.

I confront Inari about her conversation with Jin and once again offer my perspective, "You realize that he is upset because I am here, don't you?"

"If he really wanted to come over, he could have," she suggests. "He didn't really want to come over; he was just trying to monopolize control over me... he does that all the time."

"But you realize that your diversionary attitude upset him. He *does* seem to have feelings from what I can see... I don't know why you don't sense it."

"He has feelings; he can be hurt and upset about things... but only a *little bit*. When you think he's upset, he really isn't upset like most people. His range of emotion is really quite limited," Inari replies.

I almost wonder whether she feels that Jin's supposed lack of feelings offers her a sporting opportunity to try and emotionally crack and abuse him. She seems to completely disregard that Jin possesses *any* feelings *at all* and therefore, to me, seems to think that it is okay to posture herself aggressively towards him. There is definitely some darkness in this girl. But we all have our darkness. And, as I've said before, the darkest and most tragic part of this story so far is that Inari has latched herself onto someone who doesn't seem to care about her.

We move to the study adjacent to her bedroom. Barry comes home and says a few words. He goes off to sleep. Inari and I watch videos on the internet. Eventually, we hear snoring from nearby. Inari tries to claim that it is the dog snoring, but it becomes apparent to me as I continue to listen, that it is the snoring of a human man. Barry is sleeping in Inari's bed. I think little of it, but it seems rather odd. I appreciate that Inari and Barry have a strange empathic connection and I doubt that they have sex with each other anymore, yet it seems inappropriate that Barry would just invite himself into her bed where he would pass out at the end of the night. I wonder whether she'd lie next to him and cuddle with him if I were to leave.

Jin and Barry hate each other. I can't be sure how much of it is jealousy if any. I make only assumptions, but I gather that Barry is still in love with Inari. Yes, this is pure speculation on my part, but, why wouldn't he be? Barry has not seriously dated anyone in the several years since he and Inari broke up. Barry and Inari still live together and share deep bonds... apparently, sharing the same bed sometimes.

Inari offers to show me email correspondence between Barry and Jin that she finds disturbing, but for some reason, Barry has changed his email password.

"Barry is plotting to abandon me," she says. "He's always got other things to do other than spend time with me. If I lose Barry, I'm going to be devastated."

Jin's inability to get along with Barry is fueled by Barry's past abuses of her. Jin cannot fathom why Inari still holds Barry in high regard after "all of the things he did to her". I don't know what those things are. Someday, maybe I will find out. It led to some scuffles between the two of them and some long hateful emails. Jin attacked Barry in the emails. He told Barry that he was "beneath" him. He proudly presented his academic and career achievements while cutting down Barry for his own lack of ambition. Barry showed the emails to Inari and it led to fighting between Inari and Jin. Inari regarded Jin's posturing to be an attack on *her* as well as Barry.

"If he thinks that Barry is an underachieving loser, what must that mean about how he feels about me?" she says to me. "I haven't done half as much as Barry with my life."

"I don't care how much you achieve, because you have the most beautiful heart I've ever seen in a girl. I hope my opinion matters," I say.

"Of course it does, Yuki," she assures.

Things eventually lighten up. We laugh and bond and hang out together. As the night progresses, she gets more comfortable getting close to me. We sit in chairs around the computer next to each other and she kicks her feet up and rests them across my body. I rub her feet and use them as a pillow. We stay up all night, entertaining ourselves. As she grows tired, she rests her head on my thigh and I pet her forehead. As the night progresses, we become more openly cuddly.

I eventually have to plug in my phone to be charged. This room is severely lacking in power receptacles. I crawl under a desk to find an outlet. Inari notices that my belt is not properly attached to the belt loops in my pants. She complains. "Yuki, you're not properly using your belt loops!"

I get back up from under the desk. She kneels in front of me. "Here, let me fix it."

I am shocked as Inari kneels in front of me as I stand up. She begins unfastening my belt. I can't help but become erect as quickly as an airbag exploding in a car crash as she places her face in perfect alignment as if she were about to perform dirty deeds with my man parts. I try to be polite. I have to cover myself while holding up my pants that are falling off my body as she slithers the belt back around to reattach it to the missing belt loops. My god… it is awkward. She says nothing about it. She goes about her business as usual.

We sit, once again, in the swivel chairs around the computer and watch funny videos from Japan where unsuspecting men sit in massage chairs only to have themselves unexpectedly launched down ski slopes, bare-assed naked. Inari knows Japanese and adorably translates what is said on-the-fly.

It is nearly 8AM before I leave her house. I'm getting accustomed to the rhythms of her sleeping schedule. She's now been up for two days straight; she's not going to be available Saturday night. I plan to go about my Saturday night without seeing her. I go to Ground Zero and catch up with friends.

Every day, the October party draws nearer, more and more people talk to me about it the clubs. Friends introduce me to new people being sure to inform them that "this guy throws the best parties in town" and people who would otherwise remain distant acquaintances now become openly friendly without any effort required from me,

"Everyone in the whole damn city is going to be at your party, I feel sorry for all the people putting on other events around town," would be a random compliment.

I cackle maniacally... "It is going to be crazy, I know!"

I spend Sunday thinking about the situation between Inari, Jin, and Barry. In my boredom, I write to her...

Inari,

I'm going to spit out some thoughts here.... and I will first lay down a disclaimer. I haven't observed nearly enough interaction between you and Jin or you and Barry or Barry and Jin or whatever to fully understand that dynamic that is among all of you. So, I'm going to throw out some opinions based on my limited observations just because... well I dunno... it's on my mind. I will fully admit that I'm probably just talking out my ass, so don't take any of this to mean that I'm Mr. Know-it-all... I don't want to sound pompous or like Dr. Phil.

But I must, I suppose, say, that Jin was quite diversionary on the phone with you earlier in the night, and you seemed quite

diversionary and withholding from him. He was not telling you what was really upsetting him. If he seemed at all surprised that I was still there I think he was just being a good actor. To me, the inflection and timing of his voice and his displeasure with many of your responses to things made it plainly obvious that he was just trying to appear like he had no jealousy. I think he believes that showing jealousy makes him appear like he needs you...and if he needs you... he is weak... and if he appears weak, you'll not want him anymore. I heard many of the things he said to you... and I heard your responses... and I gotta say... that I would have reacted EXACTLY the way he did in his situation. The situation being... my girlfriend... at home... in the middle of the night... alone with a guy who "wants" her... resistant to letting me come over... making weak excuses as to why I shouldn't.

I love to quote my own poetry because I'm an attention whoring douche bag...so here's a verse, part of a bigger thing, about being a "man" and sucking up the pains that you and others feel simply because you're forced to be "stable".

I fly, black wings spread
to catch the souls of the dead
as they're slaughtered below
because I must
to maintain my throne

When I read the verse, I think about finding the strength to "man up". Part of manning up is all about not showing anyone that you care. It could apply to how Jin feels. He's being a man because he's *conditioned to be a certain way. He's expected to be a hard-ass and* he's *been trained his whole life that being a wimp only gets you beat up.*

It's all a GAME that everyone plays a little bit differently. I play this game VERY POORLY in that I appear weak and needy all the time... and that probably makes me a huge loser to you... but I figure... at least I'm honest...

But back to Jin... he's playing a game of cat and mouse with you whether he wants to or not... our brains and emotions force us to play the game whether we want to or not. A big part of the game is played by withholding things. The person who keeps the things he/she wants for him/herself and doesn't let the other take ultimately ends up the happier person. I've seen it a zillion times. I've lived it a zillion times.

Inari, you and I play this game... we do this little dance. You maybe just don't realize it. You play this little game with Barry too... and with Jin. There's a game happening here.

In my limited exposure to Barry, my assessment is that... well... he's clearly still madly in love with you, but he can't have you. It probably breaks his heart every single day he is with you. Having me in your house clearly made him nervous because he was probably worried that I was there to replace him, and, even if what he has with you is limited, he cherishes what he has with you even though he wants it to be more. He basically has two options... 1) cut and run or 2) figure out a way to get back what is missing. The latter is probably impossible. It drives him crazy... so he will cut and run... trust me... he will cut and run. You know he's posturing to cut and run, don't you?

Our relationship is similar to your relationship with Barry in many ways. I feel like I'm providing you the same kinds of things that Barry provides, but Barry has been around longer... and Barry is getting discouraged... disheartened... he's looking for ways to escape. Barry talks about going out because he's withholding his time from you and THAT is the best power-play he has. If he sits around and does your bidding all the time, he'll have no power over you... but if he decides to go out and hang out with friends instead, you'll be left alone and potentially missing him. That gives him power. When he decided to leave the other night... you chased after him... you pleaded with him to stay... "You have to tell me stories while I soak my face," you said. You were submitting to his power... in this "game" he was playing... he made the right move... he went out for the evening... and left you alone.

You're withholding what he wants. He wants to be with you again. Maybe he realizes that he can't be with you... maybe his "control issues" have shamed him into believing that he doesn't deserve you... and maybe he doesn't. I don't remember if you told me exactly what happened between you... but regardless... you're there to remind him... like a scarlet letter... of the things that he feels he doesn't deserve.

Whatever it is that's going on between you, clearly, you have managed to put a spell on him that has reliably kept him posed in a specific position, perched a specific place, in your life.

Chapter 29 - The Loverboy and the Maid of Honor

I spend another night at Inari's place. This is becoming routine, it seems. What isn't becoming routine, however, is her hygiene. She hasn't showered in days, hasn't changed out of her pajamas, and she's frankly smelling with hints of rotten bananas, Asian food, and warm 3-day-old lettuce. Her hair is greasy, and her complexion is suffering. None of this deters me from wanting to be near her at all times, however. If she wants me here, and wants me near, I am absolutely enthralled to have her company.

At some point she makes me take an online personality test to determine my "dating persona". Inari, herself, took it. She also made Barry take it. The results were both insightful and humorous. Inari got the "Maid of Honor" personality type. It stated that she was a "perfect catch" but also "indecisive". Barry got the "Manchild" personality type and the results hilariously suggested, "We'd like to you seriously consider *not* using our service." My resulting personality type was called "Loverboy". It told me what I already knew about myself: I thrive in healthy, committed relationships, but it also warned that if I didn't find the commitment I sought, I would leave and find it elsewhere. Ominously, the description of the "Loverboy" personality type was the only result out of 16 possible results that did not offer any humorous wit. In my mind, there's nothing more valuable than love, and love is a dead-serious subject. It seemed fitting.

Everything about the rest of the night feels off balance and awful, however. My wit seems to fail me around every corner. I try to be funny but fail. I was in the middle of trying to woo her in the dumbest way I can think of by saying, "I'm awesome, you're awesome, and let's be awesome together!" a veiled, weak, reference to the classic 80's movie, Better Off Dead, when Lane tries to ask the roller skating cheerleader out on a date by saying "I was thinking, you skate, I skate, we skate, maybe we can get together and become a kinda.. skating team!" when Inari interjects…

"Yuki, there's one pretty major thing that disqualifies you from being able to be with me… you've been with Amber."

The mere mention of Amber's name sends me into a panic. My heart stops. I believe that the next words out of her mouth are going to be to permanently disqualify me. Maybe she was about to say "Yuki, I can't trust a guy who has been with a girl as dirty as Amber!" I had nightmares about this scenario. I thought that the mere fact that I had been with Amber would greatly dishonor me among my peers, and it would swing around and bite me eventually. I expected Inari to begin raining hellfire upon me, scolding every bad sexual move I ever made in my lifetime, but she stops short. "Yuki, you need to get checked for STDs. Go in and ask for a full panel."

I had never been checked for STDs, because, frankly, I've had next-to-no sex in my adult life. Before 2011 began, I spent 10 years with just 3 partners. 8 of those years were in a monogamous relationship with one person. I have never had unprotected sex, ever.

Inari, playing aptly the role of a hypochondriac, makes my nerves go wild. She fears for my health far more than I ever would. I am only concerned about how my health would potentially affect my *relationship* with her, caring little about myself, but she thought of germs like an army of rapists who were stalking her house every night, waiting for her to put down her guard and let them in. As she complains about dirt and dust and germs, I wonder, sideways, how someone so concerned with germs hasn't changed her clothes or taken a shower in several days.

"Herpes are viruses, so small that they can actually go through an unflawed condom. You can get them if someone just doesn't wash their hands after they pee and then touches something else that you touch. They spread like wildfire even if you're not having an active outbreak! They can travel from your lips to your eyes to your genitals without warning through your bloodstream!" she complains.

I had read that it was *possible* that you could contract herpes while using a condom, while not having an outbreak, but I'm pretty sure that her statement is an overstatement, and I'm pretty sure that 70% of everyone on the planet has them dormant, in some form. The common cold sore is just a form of oral herpes, and every kid I know got them growing up it seemed. I always read "possible" to mean "possible, but almost completely impossible". But the idea that she was calling me out as if I were a dirty, promiscuous man-whore stressed me out to no end. I always considered myself to be a sexually wholesome person, never having unprotected sex ever, and if ever having sex at all, very rarely and monogamously.

My eyes become vacant. Inari can tell I am worried. "Don't worry, it will be alright, you'll just get checked and everything will come back negative and then you'll know. Everything will be alright."

"But... what if it isn't?" I ponder out loud. "Monday nights... ug... Monday nights are the worst. It seems like most Mondays this year I end up going home with someone, and although I don't have sex with them, some kind of bizarre, embarrassing sexual encounter occurs. You see, it isn't just Amber that I've been with, I guess I've had a 'good year'. But, I've had sex with girls I wouldn't be incredibly proud to admit having sex with."

"Like who?" she asks.

"Like... uhh... Echo..." I admit. I stare at the floor with empty, depressed eyes.

"I wouldn't look down upon you at all for being with Echo," she offered.

"Really? Do you know how many people she's been with? Drug addicts? Do you know how many drugs she's done in her life? Do you know how many unclean people she's probably been with?" I look down at the floor. I'm not proud of myself. "I'm such a bastard," I continue. "You know, the day that Amber came back to my house with a truck to get her stuff, I called up Echo and asked her to be at the house when Amber arrived. Then I made it clear to Amber that I was going to fuck Echo that night, in my own little subtle way."

"How did you let her know?' Inari inquires.

"Well… through subtlety. You see, Amber knows my fetishes. So, to see Echo at my house dressed in such a way that she was catering to my fetishes would have been a major slight to her. Before Amber arrived, I made sure to dress up Echo in a short skirt and some purple and black striped thigh-highs. Amber knew my sexual weaknesses and would be greeted by Echo at the door (because I surely wasn't going to open the door for her) clearly dressed in such a way to send a clear signal that she was going to fuck me the way that I 'liked it'. My clear intention was to fuck Echo on this night… it always was. I needed to redeem my sexuality. I *needed* to feel like a woman could be sexually attracted to me."

"Did you then?" Inari asked.

"Uhhhgg… yes… I did… It was kinda awful though. I couldn't even keep it up."

Inari pauses and sighs as she touches my arm out of empathy. "Don't worry. I don't think any less of you," she says. "But you should be more careful of who you sleep with. Even if you get checked, some diseases have an incubation period that you have to worry about and may not even show up on the tests for six months. So many of my friends have caught things… it is not funny."

"Well, I *never* have sex without using protection, but some of the other encounters I had this year were potentially just as unclean as Amber and Echo."

I feel really off-balance about the STD talks, although I'm 100% sure I don't have any STDs, I'm one of the least sexually active people in the scene. But Amber was dirty, and Echo was probably dirtier.

I stumble in my confidence during the conversation for the rest of the night as I try to convince Inari that I am a man... a confident man... a man who could command her... but I fail miserably... groveling over her... worshiping her. I am lost. I cannot pretend to be a fun person or talk to her about happy, interesting things. I cannot be disqualified as a potential partner for Inari, I would feel like my life had just ended!

Even my usual talent for saying profound, romantic things to her is off-balance tonight. The things I say would make even someone numbed by 1980's love ballads cringe out of embarrassment. I say, "You're the closest thing I've found to a savior in my lifetime. Maybe that's idolatry, but who's really authorized to say what idolatry really is?" and "I'll follow whatever makes me happy I guess... and *you're* the best I've got," god the things I said were *lame* and *cringeworthy* and *utter shit.*

As the night progresses into morning, I leave her, assuming that it will be a while before I see her again. Jin hasn't seen her in several days. Instead, she and I have spent 3 nights together... up all night... talking... bonding. When we weren't together, we were on the phone for hours at a time. They can't possibly let this continue for much longer. I'd never go a week without seeing my girlfriend. I'd rarely even go a day.

As my time comes to an end, I, as has become a pattern, find more gaudy and sappy things to say to her, and as my remaining time with her dwindles, I find more bat-shit-crazy things to say to her... maybe the next thing I say will finally win her heart. Recalling so many times at the end of the night when I could swear that Inari wanted me to kiss her, I have a statement prepared, and I say it. "I'm only nervous when I'm walking up to the door and anticipating opening it... once the door is open... I'm quite self-assured. So Inari... all you have to do is let me know that it is okay to kiss you and you'll see a different, better version of me." We do not kiss tonight, and in hindsight, maybe I should have just said nothing at all... because that line was utter *shit*.

As I drive home, I contemplate my actions, my past, the unclean people I'd been with, and my inability to change my earlier decisions in life... they are done. Rush hour traffic grinds to a standstill, and as I am stuck in an ocean of cars that are barely moving, I have an epiphany. Suddenly... I realize... I just had a *good* night.

I was so blinded by the way she hit me with it, I didn't realize that Inari made a request that I knew was coming. Inari asked me to get checked for STDs. Once I had a negative result to show her, the only hurdle remaining was to get a clear signal from her that it was okay for me to kiss her. My confidence returns. The moment of my dreams was going to come!

Chapter 30 - The Second End

As I write this, I am still emotionally compromised, I feel like I'm about to crack. Dwelling upon my stupid decisions, including my decision to share too many feelings with Inari, I delete all the chapters from her view… except for *this* one. **Everything that has happened up until this point means nothing compared to what I am about to confess!** This is all that matters now. It is time to start forgetting things rather than remembering them. Let me rewind and document what has just happened.

It is Wednesday club night. I naturally assume that, by now, Inari certainly is making plans to see Jin, if not tonight, then tomorrow. I know she has plans to visit the Soap Factory for the "Haunted Basement" training. I naturally assume that Inari and Jin are doing it together. They hardly ever stop talking about it. It is a Haunted House that they are volunteer actors for.

This isn't your typical haunted house. This haunted house is so severe that if you want to enter, you have to be 21 years old and sign a waiver. Once inside, you're subjected to all kinds of very adult-themed scares. There's an area where Jin eats live cockroaches in front of you and tries to entice you to do the same. There's a "period room" full of women with blood-stained vaginas. There's a coffin room where you're blindfolded and locked in a coffin, for sometimes 30 minutes or more, sometimes *with* someone else dressed in costume, subjected to loud noises and awful smells as they simulate burying you alive.

I talk to Jin. He confirms that they'll be doing training for the haunted house together, and I just encourage him and her to come out to the Wednesday club. I don't expect them to come out. The weather has suddenly changed to remind us that a cold Minnesota winter is approaching fast. Inari will think it is too cold. I've seen her freak out upon exposure to temperatures far warmer than the 40-degrees we're expecting on this night. 40-degrees makes for a bad day in L.A., but it is a great day in Minnesota in the middle of the winter. Nevertheless, it is only September, and 40-degrees is a bit on the low side.

I write off any chances of seeing Inari tonight. I'll not be hearing from either of them tonight. Instead, Elizabeth contacts me. I am thankful that she's calling because I need someone to keep me from obsessing over a girl who refuses to admit that she wants me. Elizabeth informs me that she is planning to leave her boyfriend on her own accord... without any influence from me. My influence faded long, long ago. I tell her that if she's feeling up for it... she should come out to the club.

"Not my crowd," she says.

I casually leave an open invitation for her to spontaneously call me up for some Chinese food... whenever she's feeling up to it. She seems keen on the idea, but we don't make any plans.

Natalie also calls. She had been scheduled to work that night, but somehow found someone to switch shifts with her so she could hang at the club. She'll be out, so I guess maybe there's something to help keep my mind off this mess I've created for myself. Natalie is not for me. It is clearer now... yet it was never opaque to begin with. She's a nice girl, but it would never work out. I haven't had any one-on-one time with her since the springtime when we stayed up all night on her porch holding hands until sunrise.

The night is looking like a loss, but I'm looking at it as if a blank slate would be prudent. Maybe it is a good night to take an unbiased look at the scene and meet a few new people.

But then Inari calls. I am surprised to learn that she skipped training. Apparently, she's looking forward to coming to the club ... shockingly, she is not with Jin.

I immediately jump on the idea of coming over and picking her up. I LOVE spending time with her. And just to be out and about and enjoying a night on the town with her, without Jin, is an idea that I just cannot pass up.

I buy her a couple of drinks. We talk... we dance... we socialize. It is a good time. At the end of the night, we invite Echo over to my place. Echo tries to invite a 4th friend over, but I never learn of whom. We drink Crystal Head mixed with whatever we can find.

I queue up some tracks, the light show kicks on, arena-rock style, and the 3 of us dance under laser lights. As time progresses, Inari and I get quickly comfortable with each other. She sits in one of several bar stools around my kitchen and I approach her... standing in between her protruding knees and I gaze at her. Our heads travel dangerously close. Our foreheads meet, then our noses. I move my lips to be in alignment with hers... but she stops me...

"Nooo... Jin," she says. "I love Jin," she says.

I hang my head in shame. I should not have attempted such a feat. I move away from her and go over to the DJ booth to change the music and put on a song by The Cure that we can dance to. The Cure is Inari's favorite band. I want to please her. She talks to Echo as my back is facing both of them.

"I miss Jin," she says to Echo. "I haven't seen him in a week."

The next song begins, "Friday I'm in Love". Inari approaches me from behind with a sensual bear hug. It is like she's apologizing that she cannot be what I want her to be. The gesture doesn't numb the heartache I feel for her though. It only makes it hurt more. She is so sweet, and any further reminders of her sweetness just cause me further pain.

Time passes, and we find ourselves dangerously close again. Despite my failed attempt to kiss her just minutes earlier, we somehow find ourselves in the exact same pose as we were no more than 15 minutes earlier. I hold both her hands and rest them on her knees, and we, once again, get shockingly close, almost in a full embrace. I, once again, find my lips not even an inch from hers. I can taste her breath and feel its warmth on my face. But just then Echo begins to complain.

"Yuki, I'm drunk, and I need to go home now!" she slurs.

We forgot to watch Echo mix her drinks. She mixes them obscenely strong, and the stiff vodka makes it easy for her to get completely hammered. Inari and I decide to take her home. She can't stand on her own. I have one hell of a time getting her into my car. I feel like I'm carrying 90% of her weight. Eventually, I managed to stuff her in the back seat, then I go back inside because Inari is being slow to come out. A few minutes pass as Inari checks her makeup in the first-floor bathroom. As we exit the house, we find that Echo is delusional, has left the car, and is on her knees on the pavement of my driveway screaming and crying nonsense.

"My friend! My friend abandoned me! I invited my friend, but he abandoned me! This is awful! How could he do this to me!?" she cries.

As I approach her, she is confused about who I am, it seems. I get the impression that she thought that I was the friend that abandoned her and lashes out at me. "How could you do this to me!?" she cries.

We drive her home... she doesn't know where she is... she is really out of it. I double park in front of her place. Trying to park in Loring Park in the middle of the night is nearly impossible. All of the apartment buildings are high rises, and very few of them have proper parking facilities. Inari and I help her up the steps, walking past a dried-up vomit stain that I naturally assume was Echo's from days earlier. As we get to the door, Inari asks me to wait in the car. I question whether she has the strength to carry Echo on her own, but she assures me that she'll be able to take care of her.

I sit in my car and turn on the radio... a couple minutes later... I get a call... "Help, there's blood!" she says. I leave my car double-parked and walk back up the steps and find Inari and Echo in virtually the same spot I had left them just moments ago. They

managed to take 2 steps before Echo fell, splitting her nose open.
There's a substantial pool of blood in the hallway. I help her up
and we get her into her apartment. I go back outside to make sure
my car doesn't get ticketed or towed.

Maybe 40 minutes pass as I wait outside. I call only once to check
up on her and ask if I can be of any help. Inari gets Echo ready for
bed... apparently, it is quite the challenge.

Eventually, Inari emerges. Her face is covered in Echo's blood. I
ponder how her blood got there, but I honestly don't want to know.
I offer to help her wash her face when I get her home.

I drive... naturally assuming that the night is ending. I naturally
figure that Inari's house is the next waypoint. As I'm driving down
University, I inquire whether I'm making the proper final turn to
get to her house. Inari is *surprised* that I'm taking her home.

"I figured we were going back to your place," she says.

"Uh.... we can if that's what you want," I say.

"Whatever you want," she says.

I make a U-turn despite being only 1.5 blocks from Inari's house,
and when we arrive back where we came from, finally, we're
alone. Inari is more open with me now that Echo is gone. Our
togetherness feels like the natural order of the universe. She lies
down on the dance floor. I wash the blood off her face. She shows
me the scuff marks below her knees from where she injured herself
when Echo's weight carried her down to the floor. She pulls her
leggings down to her ankles to examine her knees, exposing her
underwear under her short black skirt. For the first time, I see
Inari's bare legs and the deep scars near her ankles that she
inflicted upon herself with razors when she was younger. It sends a
jolt through my body to see this, but I keep the composure of a
doctor who is simply examining a patient and offer to wash up her
scuffed knees.

It is 5:30 AM. It has been a long night. I would normally be dying for a pillow, but I cannot resist staying awake if Inari is next to me. The sky is starting to light up for the morning... just a hint of light. The lights and music are still going from earlier, I never turned them off before we took Echo home. I put on another track by The Cure... "Just Like Heaven". Inari comes up close to me. She swerves her body up to me and presses herself up against me. First, our hips connect, then our chests. She wraps her arms completely and fully around my neck. Alone under the lights we embrace... our noses flirt with each other for a time... then our foreheads... then finally... our lips connect... bashfully for a few seconds... until the kiss becomes deeper. This fairy tale... this dream... is it coming true? Is this the kiss I've been waiting for for so long?

I press my lips against hers more intensely, and then... as soon as I feel her lips return my engagement, I feel all her weight transfer into my arms. Her neck becomes limp, and her head tilts backwards. I think it is a joke at first, but suddenly I realize that she has completely fainted. If I didn't have my arms completely wrapped around her, she might have fallen and hurt herself quite badly, but I manage to get her to the floor gently.

I try politely shaking her to wake her up. It doesn't work. I try lightly slapping her face. "Inari! Wake up!" I shout. She stays completely motionless on my floor for what is probably a few seconds but feels like minutes.

I don't know what to make of the situation. I think to myself that maybe it is just part of her sleeping disorder... then I think that maybe she panicked out of guilt and the shock caused her to faint. I do not ponder the idea that alcohol had much of anything to do with it. Alcohol was on her breath and all... but not overly so.

Eventually, I decide to physically lift her by her shoulders, and she springs back to life, instantly. She is a bit loopy now... she seems out of it, not remembering things properly. She speaks only Japanese as she goes to the kitchen for another drink. She seems to act like nothing just happened. She doesn't even acknowledge that she fainted and just goes about her business. She begins to pour another drink, but I pull it from her so that I can police how strongly she mixes it. She says that she wants a shot and a chaser... so I give her just a couple of drops of vodka... I even pour some back into the bottle. She never slurs her words. She hadn't been drinking since before we took Echo home over 1.5 hours ago, and I typically stop drinking very early in the evening, before midnight, so as not to impair my driving, so I'm confused as to why her mental state seems so out-of-whack.

At this point, she realizes that she is missing her phone, so she must be somewhat functional, coming around. I agree to go back to Echo's to acquire it, but it would be impossible to get it until Echo wakes up tomorrow. Echo certainly will not be awake until the afternoon. We have what seems like coherent conversation... but she is confused and missing some details. She seems to have forgotten that I had washed the blood off her face... or even that I attempted to drive her to her own house. I need to take care of her as gentlemanly as I can. If she's not drunk, she's in some kind of bizarre, dissociative mental state. Maybe she had a seizure or something; maybe she fainted; regardless, it doesn't matter... I need to put her to bed. We will figure out what just happened tomorrow.

I help her up the steps. She could have done the steps on her own, but I help her anyway. She is clearly fatigued, and I can sense that she is going to sleep soon, if not due to alcohol, then due to her sleeping disorder.

I put her down on the futon in the spare bedroom, "Ohhhh... sure... you're not even going to let me sleep in your bed?! This isn't where you sleep!" she says.

I pick her back up like a man, chivalrously sweeping her off her feet. I bring her to *my* bed, and she is snoring within seconds. She sleeps on my shoulder all night, with one arm draped across my chest and one leg wrapped around my lower body. Ada sleeps at our feet. I don't sleep a wink. This is all too intense for me.

Occasionally, she wakes up from her slumber and looks up at me, directly into my eyes. I try to find meaning in what her eyes are telling me, but they disappear from me as fast as they come. She returns to sleeping… on my shoulder… in this embrace. I do not want to move a muscle, concerned that it would disturb her, wake her, fearing that if she woke up, she would stand up and walk out of the room, never to be so close to me again.

Proper morning comes. At 9AM I call my boss and tell him I am not going to make it to work today. I tell him that a friend of mine had a medical emergency the night before, and I have personal errands to deal with surrounding the incident.

Mostly, I don't want to put Inari in a situation where she might wake up in my house, not knowing how she got there, with no phone. I imagine that she would be scared shitless. She would have no way to contact me... no way to contact Jin. She would be trapped in my house. I decide that it is imperative that I stay with her.

Inari sleeps into the afternoon. I spend the day taking care of the dog and doing housework. Eventually, I come around to check on her and I find her sitting on the edge of the bed.

"What happened last night?" she asks.

I ask her if she remembers fainting... or if she remembers the car ride... Through the course of the conversation, it becomes apparent that she remembers nothing that happened after leaving Echo's apartment.

I tell her *most* of the story.

"You're not telling me the whole story, are you?" she prods.

"No, I'm not," I sigh.

"What are you not telling me then?" she asks with a curious smile.

"Something... something that will probably wipe the smile off your face," I say.

She leaves the subject alone for now. She is hungry and thirsty. I offer to get her a sandwich at a nearby sub shop and disappear for 20 minutes. She is, again, sleeping like a rock. I cannot wake her. I put her food in the fridge. After a while, I finally get a hold of Echo and arrange to get Inari's phone. I want to invite Inari to ride along, but Inari is still sleeping so deeply that I cannot rouse her. I go alone.

Echo is groggy, but okay. She gives me Inari's phone. I inquire how she's feeling... "I'm just groggy and I want to go back to bed," she says. We talk about nothing more. I just go on my way. I return home and simply leave her phone next to the bed. I continue to do housework.

Eventually, she wakes up, and I offer her water and the sandwich I got for her earlier. She eats half the sandwich and feels a migraine coming on. She has a long history of migraines. She can tell when she's about to have one. She gets nervous. "I might be vomiting in 30-minutes," she warns.

She is right. Within 20-30 minutes she is vomiting. I do my best to act as her nurse. After vomiting a few times, I drive her to the ER. I take care of getting her checked in. I answer questions for her so that she doesn't have to talk or think as much. I deal with most of the hospital staff by proxy. I've been in this situation before... sick people don't like being prodded with too many simple questions... I take charge. I hold her belongings for her while we're in the waiting room and she holds my hand as she rests her head on my shoulder. I am proud to have her by my side.

I feel the warm eyes of everyone around us in the waiting room, composed, mostly, of elderly men and women. I imagine what they must be thinking. They, surely, must all be pondering how sweet young love is. In their eyes, we are a couple... young... in love... blazing with affection, trust, and desire. I imagine them thinking about their own younger years, and how they slipped away… remembering their first kiss… remembering the time when they thought that relationships were fairy tales that ended with "happily ever after" … before they turned into obligatory rituals, laced with quarrels, lies, obligations.

They call her name and the routine data gathering process begins. I answer as many questions as I can for her while she is having her blood pressure taken and heart rate measured. I enjoy being there for her. There's nowhere else I'd rather be. I love this girl with *all* my heart.

We're admitted into ER room #5, the exact room where I took Amber when she had THC poisoning. My experience with Amber in the hospital made me a pro at dealing with the hospital staff, some of whom even remembered me from months earlier. I try to help the best I can... taking care of acquiring what she needs, vomit bags, warm blankets. I sit by her knees next to her bed.

"Yuki, why are you way down there?" she asks. "Come closer! Keep me warm! It's cold in here!"

I move my head close to her. I place my forehead upon hers. I hold her hand. We hold hands until our hands become clammy.

"I hate needles. I'm scared of needles!" she says, as they come to draw blood. "You need to distract me!"

"I'll do m best. What should I do?" I say as I stare into her eyes, my forehead still pressed against hers.

"You're already doing a good job. Do just this. Just tell me everything is going to be okay."

"Everything is going to be okay, girl, you know it is. I'll get you home to Scruffles and Aussie and you can be healed with all the puppy love! I love you and I care about you and we'll get you out of here," I return.

The nurse announces in a peppy voice, "Oh look! We're all done! That wasn't so bad was it?"

"Did I help?" I asked.

"You did a better job than anyone ever has," she replies.

Eventually... they discharge her... they're slow about it, but they get around to it. They don't even do an IV, as Inari changes her mind just before they insert the needle and suddenly feels like she can cope with the migraine. We discuss what to do next... and I agree to act as her nurse and take care of her for the night. She is still not feeling 100%. I get her some flavored bottled water and I take her back to my place.

Jin finally calls. "You haven't been calling me lately," Inari complains.

"I have, but you haven't been answering," he retorts, but in his characteristic, polite, voice.

"You could get in touch with me if you really wanted to, but you just haven't," she replies. As she says this I ponder how Inari seems to give me and potentially Jin, impossible feats to accomplish to prove our love for her.

"Well, I was wondering if I could come pick you up, and we could spend some time together," he asks.

"I don't know, I have a migraine, and I feel like I should just rest," she says.

"I'm sorry, I didn't know that."

"Yuki has been taking care of me. He took me to the ER. He's been doing a good job," she says.

"I'm glad you have someone you trust to look after you," he says,

"Maybe I could just come over and visit you, then."

Inari suddenly becomes angry and cross with Jin, "Well it is Yuki's house. I think you need to ask Yuki if you can come over!" she says, annoyed.

Jin doesn't seem to appreciate that she's in a bad mood, and retreats in his attempts to spend time with Inari. She never passes me the phone to allow him to ask for an invitation to my house. Their conversation ends without any love exchanged.

I am feeling victorious because I figure he's not coming over. We begin to talk about other trivial things. She asks about finding pajamas... and I agree to look for some for her so that she can spend the night again. I am prepared to just run out and buy some new pajamas at a nearby store if that is what she needs to feel comfortable, staying over again. I am personally looking forward to the slumber party.

A few minutes later... Jin calls. I don't answer. I imagine him stewing in his apartment, concerned, worried that his relationship with Inari is falling apart and she's spending time with me, his competition.

He calls again, almost immediately... I sigh... I answer. He asks if he can come over. I try not to sound like I'm reluctant to allow it... but, despite my own selfish desires to be alone with Inari and continue building our bonds, I have no real moral choice other than to let Jin see his girlfriend. "Of course, you can come over, Jin," I tell him. I instantly hate myself and hate my life.

I hang up the phone. "Did I make the right decision?" I ask Inari.

"I don't really want to deal with him," she says.

"I will call him and just tell him straight-up then," I offer.

"No, it's fine. I don't mind him coming over under certain

conditions," she says.

I never ask what these "certain conditions" are. I am more focused on the fact that my night with her is ending. I decide that I need to come clean about the night before. I hadn't told her the whole story.

There were multiple reasons that I felt I needed to come clean. One of the biggest reasons was purely selfish. Selfish it was that I was rather emotionally hurt by the fact that she didn't remember our kiss from the night before.

I didn't know what her reaction was going to be... I figured maybe she'd be upset. But I *had* to know. I *had* to know whether this kiss... mutually exchanged... despite being forgotten in a haze of alcohol (or whatever that fainting, freaky, double-personality episode was all about) bore any meaning to her. Even if she didn't remember the kiss, would she have objected to such an act? After all, I want to kiss her again. I want to kiss her sober. I want to kiss her *right now*, in fact.

I didn't know what her reaction was going to be, but I did not think it was going to be what it *was*. As our time together appeared to be running out, I finally asked her, bluntly, if she remembered kissing me the night before. In my heart of hearts... I wanted her to say "yes, and I love you" ...

but...

instead...

She reacted most *horribly*, far, far, far, beyond anything I could have possibly imagined... she didn't remember, she blacked out... My revelations, cause her to spiral into a complete panic.

"This is a bad dream! This is my worst nightmare!" she cries. "How could you tell me this while he's just minutes away from arriving here!? I'm going to have to pull myself together and regain my composure before he gets here! How am I going to do this!? How am I going to do this!? How am I going to do this!? I'm going to have to tell Jin about this! He's going to break up with me! Oh my God! He's going to break up with me!"

My spine is stiff as a board as she unleashes her words upon me, "Let me take all the blame then," I offer.

"You! You did this on purpose! You want us to break up! You're evil!" she attacks.

I endure, as she takes verbal swings at me and lands them with the brute force of a prizefighter. My jaw hangs open. I am speechless. I don't know what to say. She is right about a lot of things; I certainly was trying to break them up... but I never really considered it to be a selfish act. To me, it just seemed like the natural order of the universe that we came together. It seemed just as natural that we ended up kissing under the lights after what was a lovely, romantic week.

Inari, despite worrying about her composure, is *quite* level-headed when Jin arrives. She proves herself to be a brilliant actress once again. But I... I... upon his arrival... I am unable to contain my *own* emotions.

I answer the door... distant... reserved... I can't look anyone in the eyes. I am barely able to speak; I am barely able to move. My voice has seemingly dropped two octaves. "You guys can hang out here as long as you want, but I'm going to leave," I say as he enters the door.

"Where are you going?" Jin inquires, "What's wrong?" I feel the glow of victory overcome him as Jin suddenly realizes he is victorious. He has defeated me.

"I'm going... ... somewhere... I dunno... um... Grumpy's ... karaoke... I think... I was going to meet up with Natalie there."

I retreat to a corner of the house... pretend to play music in the studio because it is the only non-bathroom on the first floor with any real walls. I sit in the dark, lit only by indirect light of the cocoon I sit in which is lined with computer monitors, piano keyboards, speakers, mixers, rack-mounted effects processors with dozens of colored light flashing and pulsing, computer towers, microphone stands, microphones, guitars, and random drums strewn about the room from a kit that hasn't been set up in months.

Jin, enters the studio to say goodbye, and, *glowing* at the idea that I'm distressed, seems to have figured out that something happened between our brief phone interaction and his arrival at my door. It must have been something that Inari and I had discussed just before he arrived. Clearly... whatever it was didn't go my way. I've felt this kind of victory before. It was the same feeling I had when I took his place by Inari's side at the amusement park. Jin shakes my hand to say goodbye. He shakes my hand confidently... like a quarterback who just won the Superbowl might shake the hand of the losing quarterback.

Inari enters. She gives me a hug. "If there's anything I can do, please let me know," she says.

"I appreciate the sentiment, but you're not the person to help me. You can't help me," I say. "You're not the one to help me."

Inari whispers in Jin's ear. And Jin seems to echo what she says to him. "Thanks for taking care of Inari in the hospital; she says you were very helpful."

"The pleasure was all mine," I say with a depressing sigh as I look down at Jin's feet... "The pleasure... the pleasure was all mine."

Chapter 31 - Act III - Alternative Facts

I go to bed. I leave the phone by my ear.

I lay in bed dwelling, thinking, and contemplating. I have a strong conscience. It is not unusual for me to toss and turn at night if I am stressed. On this night I feel like I am pure evil. I am generally *my own* worst critic; therefore, it is unusual that someone *other than myself* might make me feel eviler than I make myself feel. Yet, Inari echoed my conscience. Inari and my conscience seemed to conspire together to remind me that I am not so righteous. The wind is out of my sails; the soul drained from my spirit. Nothing is stopping my conscience from keeping me awake this evening.

Hours pass. 2AM rolls around and I haven't slept a wink. Inari calls me. I answer. I am worried that I have just ruined her relationship… not just her relationship with Jin, but her relationship with *me*. We say a few words…

"He took the news well," she says "He basically said, 'Don't let it happen again!' and left it at that." She continues, "It's strange that I never know when he's going to freak out about something. He seems to blow up at little things, but lets major things slide sometimes."

I, for the first time ever, don't feel like talking to Inari on the phone all night. I suffered a great wound earlier that night. I need to just be left to my own thoughts. I need to just dwell in silence. I keep our conversation brief. We exchange little formalities.

I continue to be restless in bed. I dwell upon all the bad things that happened, but I also remind myself that this has still been the most beautiful episode of my life by whatever fucked-up definition of the word "beautiful" you want to choose. I replay all the beautiful, romantic moments... the long conversations... the splashing through puddles... the pink flower she brushed against my nose... I replay every time she gazed into my eyes... I love it when she looks at me... I love the peace that she brings to my heart... no matter if it was intentional or not. If I can never have her... at least I have the greatest memories of my life to remind me... that this has been a *great* life. A great life... made so much *greater* having been so lucky to spend even 5 minutes alone with this girl.

I try to forget. I try not to dwell... but I suck at it. I try to come to reality, but reality never feels like reality.

I go into Friday afternoon assuming, believing, truly, that Inari and I are "done". I feel that there is nothing more to do than to write this off as a complete loss. I violated her. I compromised her relationship with Jin... and my continued presence, clearly, continues to compromise her relationship with Jin. Furthermore, her continued relationship with Jin continues to compromise my mood. Something must change. I volunteer *myself... I* will change.

She calls me while I'm in the office and invites me over after I'm done with work. We decide that we need quality time to work through our recent issues. Obviously, we need to have a talk about what just happened. I think she has a desire to establish that there are no hard feelings between us.

Inari had been meaning to help me with my hair. Over the summer my hair was dyed so many colors that it is now a faded clownish mess. It needs to be bleached and redone. I want a solid bright red this time… or maybe red and black streaks, much like Inari's hair.

Inari has been sitting around the apartment, procrastinating. She hasn't showered yet. She tends to procrastinate whenever she needs to get ready to go anywhere. I feel sorry for her. She is a slave to her compulsive desire to appear flawless. I know plenty of beautiful girls that have been known to put on their makeup in the rear-view mirror of the car while it is parked outside the club, 3 minutes before seeing their friends, but Inari is not such a girl. She spends hours on her appearance, even though I remind her that she is beautiful the way she is.

I wait patiently in Jin's apartment. I don't like being here. I want to get out… I want to get out quickly. It feels like a prison. I want to get out before Jin arrives and reminds me of my shameful behavior of the previous night.

"This place is a prison," I say. "You don't even have keys for the place, and you have no means to escape on your own… it is like you're locked in a tower or something… I feel like I'm supposed to rescue you from here."

Inari laughs at my joke, but my joke is half-serious. Whereas Inari finds peace and quiet in the barren, empty, emotionless, concrete, white walls and grey cement floors of Jin's loft, which features a giant concrete pillar, 4ft in diameter, in the middle of his bedroom and open, exposed piping throughout the ceiling… I find this place to be gloomy and cold, a reminder of how unloving the world can be at times. If Inari weren't within these walls, there'd be no warmth or compassion anywhere to be found.

I get anxious. I want to get out before Jin gets home. I don't want to face him. But since Inari hasn't even showered yet, I think it is going to be impossible. I make a futile effort to get her to forget about her appearance and leave with me *now* abandoning all this nonsensical ritual.

"You *know* you're beautiful," I say with nervous urgency, hurried. "Don't worry so much about it, you look fine, we should just go. I know what you look like after you haven't showered for a week… you were still beautiful then."

"No," she says. "That was not cool of me. I just get that way when I'm depressed sometimes."

"I'm sorry you were depressed, Inari. You know I love you and that I would have done anything to help brighten your days. I stayed with you those nights because I was trying to brighten your life, it's not just about me you know," I remind her.

"But you *did* brighten my life, and you *do*," she says sweetly.

251

Sometimes I wish she wasn't so sweet.

After some coercion, she gets in the shower, and I wait patiently in Jin's apartment on a long, curvy, dark leather sofa. I am stewing, depressed. I get more and more depressed as the time for Jin to arrive nears. I don't want to see him. I do not want to see him.

Inari exits the shower and begins to dig through her bag for her makeup. She digs for a minute or so. Then, she becomes quite agitated.

"No! It can't be!" she exclaims. "No! Oh my god! No!"

"What's wrong," I ask, coming to her aid. Inari is kneeling on the floor of Jin's bathroom burying her head in her purse so as to hide her face from me.

"I can't find my makeup!" she says. She is crying like it is a matter of life and death. "I can't be without it!"

I, obviously, think she is overreacting, but I offer to help however I can. "What does it look like?" I ask.

"Well... obviously it looks like... makeup... it is a little round thing.... Oh my god! This is bad! What am I going to do!?"

"Hmm... I saw something in my downstairs bathroom that might be what you were looking for. I don't know where it came from."

"You did!? Why didn't you tell me!" she snaps, as if I've offended her, and purposefully slighted her by not mentioning it.

"Well... I don't know... I just noticed it as I was getting ready for work, this morning, I didn't know if it was yours or Techna's or what. I didn't think it was a huge deal."

"Oh my god, I need it! You don't understand! I can't be without it!"

"Well, my house is across town," I offer. "It will take me a while just to go get it... and it is rush hour, are you sure that we can't just buy you some at a makeup store around here?"

"No! It won't work! I don't even know what shade it is! It is a special shade that they personalize to match my face! I can't buy the wrong stuff! I would have to read the number off the bottom of it to know if it is right!"

"Okay then," I sigh. "I'll go get it for you. It is no problem."

"Would you? Please! I can't let anyone see me without my makeup. You don't understand! Even Jin hasn't seen me without my makeup!"

"Really?! That's rather strange. I'm sure you look just fine!" Inari is still kneeling on the floor hiding her face from me. "You shouldn't feel like you need to hide anything from me or Jin or anyone else. Turn around... look at me. I'm sure you look just fine."

"YUKI! I DON'T WANT TO HEAR IT! I'M NOT LEAVING WITHOUT MY MAKEUP! JIN CANNOT SEE ME LIKE THIS! PLEASE! PLEASE HELP ME!"

"Okay, Okay! I'm leaving now. I'll be back in an hour."

"Please hurry!"

By some miracle, I manage to make record time driving across town in rush hour traffic. I grab a little round cosmetic gadget, doodad, or whatever it is... a little clamshell with an attached mirror. I return from my house 40 minutes later.

I call her on the phone and ask her to come down to the door to let me into the building.

Inari doesn't want to come down. "Is anyone around there? Can't you just wait for someone to enter or leave and then slip in?"

"Well... there's really no one around here. I don't see anyone in the parking lot," I shrug.

Inari is nervous to leave Jin's apartment, even if just to travel the halls long enough to come and open the apartment door. Reluctantly, she agrees to come down. I am rather curious as to what she will look like without her makeup. I eagerly await to get the first glimpse of her makeup-less hideousness.

She arrives at the door. She is looking down at the floor and has brushed her hair over her face so as to conceal herself from me... but I can see her eyes. She looks at me with sad, bashful, worried eyes. She is still beautiful, still... shockingly beautiful... as always. I don't understand what all the fanfare is about. Inari is beautiful. She keeps her hair over her cheek.

"You look beautiful," I tell her.

"No, I don't. I have a rash, and I need this concealer to cover it," she claims.

"I wouldn't judge you if you had a rash on your face... I'm sure most people wouldn't either," I assure.

She walks in front of me as we approach the elevators and I hand her the makeup case I found in the bathroom. She takes it from me without looking backwards. "Is this what you're looking for?" I ask.

"No..." she sighs. "No, it is not." Her shoulders sag, and she looks down at the floor as we ride the elevator up two floors. "I don't know what to do now."

I ponder for a moment, thankful that she isn't berating me as she did earlier when faced with the same crisis, as we currently have taken zero steps forward. Calmly, I play the role of a confident problem-solver. "Well, maybe I will just have to go buy you some then," I offer.

"Maybe I can figure out the correct shade if I look it up online," she replies.

We agree that I should go to Macy's and call her when I get there. By the time I'm there, she'll have figured out what shade it is, and I can communicate it to the employees at the counter.

Another 40 minutes later, I arrive back at Jin's apartment with some kind of concealer foundation that costs a ridiculous amount of money. Makeup, apparently, is super expensive, and as I drive I ponder for a moment about how Inari has no money, but mostly, I'm just relieved that, finally, Inari has everything she needs to finish her rituals so that we can leave.

Inari is happier now, but still procrastinates doing the final things she needs to do before we actually leave the house.

I wait... lounging in a beanbag chair just outside the bathroom door... becoming increasingly nervous and increasingly gloomy by the minute. "Jin is arriving soon," I remind her. "I don't want to be here when he arrives."

"What's wrong? What's on your mind?" she asks. "You can tell me anything."

I don't really have any real *words* on my mind... just a haze of feelings. I think for a moment about how to communicate this moody haze in words... I stumble through a few words. I spit out a bunch of romantic dross as if I am a dog... trained to compliment her upon her command, then I try to explain my gloom. "The thing that is eating me at this very moment is that you referred to something as a 'bad dream' which... to me... was a *beautiful* dream coming true," I say. "I wanted that moment to be real. And to find out that it wasn't, really hurt me. It terrified me that you didn't remember it. You know how I feel about you. I've told you directly so many times. You're so beautiful, compassionate, warm... the greatest girl on planet earth and you deserve someone who sees in you what I do."

"I'm nothing special," she says. "I'm just a girl."

I wish I could convince her how special she is to me. Eventually, I realize I just must give up. I can't continue to profess my love to a girl who doesn't want it.

"The only option I have is to learn to accept this. And the best way for me to do that is to find some alone time... I need to take some time to clear my head... away from you," I say. "Every day I spend with you is more intense than the day before... and I don't know when this is going to stop.... but it needs to stop at some point... if it doesn't stop... it will boil over. It needs to become real... or it needs to stop," I say.

She exits the bathroom and comes over to me. She sits directly on my lap and wraps both of her arms around my neck. We embrace, not kissing, but hugging, spooning, in such a way that a 3rd person would think we were seasoned lovers. Her positioning is truly shocking to me. What is happening here? Why is she doing this to me? I am filled with nervousness.

"Everything is okay," she says.

I contemplate what she means by this... I think to myself... "What is everything? What is okay? Is she trying to tell me that 'we' are okay?" I write my optimistic thoughts off as delusional. Then, out loud, I verbally reply. "Everything is NOT okay."

"Why wouldn't everything be okay? It is fine. Everything is fine," she says.

"I'm not sure what you think 'everything' is, but I assure you that my 'everything' is definitely not 'fine'."

Jin soon comes home. She decides that she's hungry, adding further delays to our "quality time" that we were supposed to be using to deal with my hair issues. She and Jin decide to cook some curry. Somewhat annoyed by the delays, I painfully inquire, "how long with this take?"

"Not long at all," Jin simply replies with his usual formal tone.

2 hours later, the curry is still not done, and Inari is still not changed out of her pajamas. Jin is supposed to go to his LARP game night. He is running 2 hours behind schedule. I guess in his fantasy LARP world he is some kind of important figure, but in real life, he's only important in his own head. Inari is resistant to change out of her pajamas... I'm not in a position to motivate her. She says she is almost ready, but I measure "almost" to mean... 30 minutes... and soon she stops what she is doing to help Jin with his LARP makeup. 30 minutes pass... she's barely started dressing herself. I am just sitting... stewing... the night is dragging.

I excuse myself into the hall so that I can sit on the sofa by the vending machines... the music in the apartment is getting to me... some Goth industrial stuff that just oozes sadness. I just can't be in the presence of this music... I can't be in the presence of her... with Jin... kissing him... hugging him... telling him that she loves him every 5 minutes. I can't be there. I need to get out. Her actions towards him feel fake to me. Their love for each other is bombastic. Inari, normally a brilliant actress, is completely bombing in this performance as she leaps on him while he's cooking, and straddles and kisses him in front of me. I feel like she's putting on a show, like she's trying to prove to me that she loves him to magnify the conflict that is so obviously already present in the room, or maybe she's trying to prove to *him* that she loves *him* in my presence, reassuring him that she wants *nothing* to do with the nerd sitting on his sofa. It is a parade. As he readies his makeup for his LARP group, they leave the bathroom door cracked, seemingly deliberately, so that I see them kiss all romantically in the bathroom mirror... He dips her down to the floor as they kiss... I just want to sprout wings and fly away from it all.

I sit in the hall for what seems like an hour, then I get impatient and reenter the apartment. They're both in the bathroom. I listen carefully. "Are they having sex in there?" I wonder. If they are, I'm clearly leaving. I couldn't possibly endure such torture. I am tortured enough already.

It all seems so deliberately paraded in front of me in such a way as to scare me away. I wonder why the hell it is so necessary to torture me in this way. The only logical conclusion I can come to is that her affection for him is *not* genuine. Or, *if* it is genuine... it is complex... a different kind of genuine. It is as if he's put some kind of black-magic spell on her, or maybe she has put a spell on *him*.

Jin eventually leaves to pass judgment on some hapless Klingon who broke some kind of law against stealing magical crystals or something... I don't really give a fuck where he went... but all I know is that I'm glad that he's gone. With him gone, this demonstration of how to make your male suitors jealous has ended... and I can finally breathe easy again. The tone of the room changes drastically once he is gone. Jin will be presenting his curry at a potluck birthday party for Maddox later, and Inari and I will be alone while Jin is away at his LARP.

We get ready to *finally* hit the road ourselves... but there's a problem. I didn't expect to be there for long, so I didn't even bother to think about reading the signs, what was supposed to be 5 minutes, turned into 6 hours... I was towed.

Inari is hesitant to call Jin for help. She and I seem to both agree that we don't want him to come back. She offers to call Barry. Barry does not answer. I call my sister. She's willing to help. But ultimately, Jin helps us, because he is nearer than everyone else. It is embarrassing and frustrating to have to rely on Jin in this way, especially when I am just trying to get away from him.

As we await his arrival, she and I use the very limited time together efficiently. She wastes no time sitting next to me on the couch and leans over in such a way that we're intertwined like a pretzel... together... embracing... She stares into my eyes.

I would have loved to kiss her at that exact moment, but I don't subscribe to any illusions that it might be what *she* wants despite the body language being so blunt. I still look back on this moment, this vision, and wonder to myself, "why didn't I kiss her then?" We just talk. Once again, she says, "Everything is okay," ... not ... "Everything is GOING to be okay," but, "Everything is okay."

What does she mean by this? I try to get her to explain what she means.

"I need to find a way to make this real... or I need to disappear," I say. "You know exactly what I've been feeling and thinking... I've literally told you everything I've ever thought... but I have no idea what you're feeling or thinking... all I have to go by is what I see in your eyes. You're always looking at me with these *eyes*. I can't resist you."

Inari's eyes change in such a way to mock me. She cocks her head and opens them real wide... she deliberately blinks them at me to call them to my attention. "Well, it is normal to look someone in the eyes when you're talking to them."

I laugh at her adorable skill in mocking me with her eyes. "You know, when cartoon makers record voice-overs for actors, they actually *film* the actors, just their heads... and it is all because they want to film their eyes. They take the expressions from the actors, recorded on film, and map them on the animated characters. This is because the eyes say so much. Hollywood knows this. When I look into your eyes... I want to believe that what I see is *real,*" I say.

She does not confirm nor deny that what I see in her eyes is real, but simply lets me ponder the authenticity of her gaze. I see so much love in her eyes for me. But when she gives her eyes to Jin... it feels like such a charade. It maddens me. It saddens me. It confuses me. I just think, "What the fuck!?" to myself.

Inari adjusts her positioning and sits on my lap. I suddenly get
nervous as I know that Jin will be entering the door at any minute.
But the energy in her body is building with heat and passion and I
suddenly feel confident that maybe just now, something magical is
about to happen between us as she wraps her arms around my neck
one more time and brings her nose two inches from mine. But
before that can happen, we hear the door handle turn and Inari
leaps off of me... I imagine her heart to be racing. She wouldn't
want Jin to see us like this. She is hyperactive as she knows she
was just microseconds away from getting caught in a
compromising pose with me. She overplays her enthusiasm to see
him... the public display of affection returns... and this time it is
fucking relentless... I fear he's going to smell that something is up
because of how overplayed her enthusiasm is for him and what a
terrible acting performance she is offering. Again... I just think,
"what the fuck?!" to myself.

We get my car, paying $280 to the impound lot for an experience
not worth another fiber of paper or drop of ink, then we go to
Maddox's birthday potluck as a group. As we arrive I am greeted
by a guy at the door, "You! This guy is fucking awesome! Yes!
You're fucking awesome!" Everyone is excited about my
upcoming party and dousing me with flattery. It is relentless every
night that I am out and it builds as the party gets near.

I put on a smile that is merely a charade. I pretend to be happy. I
pretend to be interested in other girls. There are a couple there that
I am curious about, but I wear my unhappiness so profoundly on
my face and in my eyes, that I can't make anything work. I do my
best. I do my best for *Inari*. Escaping her is the best thing I can do
for her. But why did she sit in my lap earlier and gaze into my eyes
again? Is this *really* over between us? Is there *really* nothing here?

Inari stays close to Jin and her closeness with him seems like
retaliation against my flirting with other women... or maybe she's
just feeling obliged... I don't know. I'm just really confused! She

sat on my lap earlier and wrapped her arms around my neck, like… what the fuck is happening! What the hell is reality right now!?

Eventually, I corner Jin by the liquor table, "We should talk sometime. I owe you an apology for my part in the shit that went down the other night... and I want you to be able to trust me... you know… sometime... when the time is right."

"It's all good, no worries," he says.

I continue to flirt with Fiera most of the night, although my flirting is ineffectual, composed mostly of complaints about Zak, who she loudly fucked at the after-party following the Fet Ball. When asked bluntly why she would sleep with such a man, her only reply is that it "was inevitable that it was going to happen." I don't know what she means by that, but frankly, I don't really care. Without Inari, nothing tastes the same. I cannot be enthusiastic about talking to other women.

Jin is getting sleepy. Normally, he would just leave her and let *me* take her home, and I get the feeling like she would love to try another maneuver to ditch him and spend time with me. But tonight... Jin, clearly, doesn't seem to trust us enough to be alone, late at night. He finds the strength, regardless of how tired he is... to stay around and wait for Inari to finish her drink. She drinks it so slooooowwwwwly. Hours pass and she still hasn't finished it. It is now 5:30AM and an impatient Jin finishes it *for* her.

We dilly-dally as we're leaving. Inari tries all kinds of stall tactics to continue staying at the party as the sun continues to rise. "I feel bad for Yuki, Jin!" she says, "He just seems so sad," she says.

"Yuki will be alright, why don't we just invite him over again tomorrow," Jin replies.

"But, we need to stay and help clean up!" she says. "Look at all these dishes, let me at least do the dishes! I feel bad! Or at least let me scrub the floor!" she says as she pulls a mop and bucket from a nearby closet and searches around for cleaning supplies.

Jin gets more and more impatient, as he just watched his girlfriend stall and stall, taking well over an hour to finish her last drink which he ended up just finishing for her out of frustration.

Her efforts to stay behind are in vain. She knows... she knows... it isn't going to work... not tonight. Jin wants to leave... and this just isn't the right night to stay out with me.

I mention nothing of the dynamic between us, among us, to anyone during the night but I wear my emotions on my sleeve. I sit on a bench on the front porch of Maddox's house. Maddox is a skilless person who seemed to inherit or acquire enough money to have a large, gorgeous house with a perfect skyline view available to him from his front porch. John sits next to me and we admire the lights of the city that still illuminate the dawn sky.

"How are things with Azena?" I ask John.

"They are... uh... not happening..." he sighs. "Why do these girls insist on dating these men who are emotionally dead rocks?"

"You ask the exact question I am currently pondering every day," I reply. With a definitive tone, I answer him confidently, "It makes them feel safe," I say. "All we can do is prove that we can take care of them, that we *want* to take care of them... that we want to protect them... and that they make us happy. That's all I can do... that's all we can do. I can be a rock, you know... I can be a happy rock with the right girl."

"Yeah, you're right" he replies with a "brofist". I stand up from my chair... we pat each other on the back ... "Hang in there, buddy... good luck," he says.

Chapter 32 - The Man with No Legs

The next day begins, Saturday. It feels much like Friday. My goal is the same as yesterday. My goal is to find some way to have a private chat with Inari regarding the nature of our friendship. I had hoped to accomplish this yesterday, but yesterday was just so chaotic with all the craziness with makeup and car towing.

I just want to be alone with Inari, and I want to explain to her what our friendship *should* look like. I also want *her* to explain to *me* why the hell she thinks it is okay to sit on my lap and put her arms around my neck while, at the same time, claiming she has no romantic interest in me.

I intend to draw a line in the sand. I rehearse all the things I want to say to her. I keep a list of all the points I need to get across in my head. When our conversation finally happens and ultimately concludes, I imagine that I will, even if I don't see my dreams fulfilled, *know* what the hell is going on. I have made my intentions with Inari very, very clear to her. Now, s*he* needs to make her intentions *with me* just as clear as I've made my intentions to her.

After the events of Thursday night, I figured that Inari's level of affection towards me was clear. She didn't want me. She'd never want me. We are done. I'm drawing a line in the sand. We cannot be more than friends. But I'm not so sure that Inari understands what a "just friends" relationship with me should look like. I intend to help her understand what kinds of things a man and a woman who are "just friends" can and cannot do with each other. I want to spell it out very clearly.

The night begins much like Friday. I meet Inari alone at Jin's apartment. We plan to leave the apartment before he returns. Tonight is Echo's birthday. I offer to Inari that we should go to Echo's party together… just so that we can have a friendly, brutally frank conversation beforehand. She agrees. We'll run off together, alone, and meet up with Jin at the party later. The plan seems clear. The plan seems feasible.

But just like the previous night. We fail to leave the apartment before Jin arrives home. Inari and Jin, once again, get all affectionate with each other in a way that seems to be intended to put me off. I endure similar pains for an hour or two. Eventually, I decide that I've had enough. I don't need to sit and watch them touch and caress each other. I could be spending my Friday doing productive things. I could be moving on with my social life instead of dwelling on a relationship that has clearly hit a brick wall.

I eventually conclude that the healthiest move I can make at this point in time is… to just leave. Sitting around watching the two of them be all snuggly and cute together is painful… dreadfully painful. Every additional minute I spend in their presence drives me further into my own personal hell.

I stand up. "I guess I'll just meet you guys at Echo's party," I say.

Inari, apparently deciding that she wants to keep me around a bit longer, finally decides to take her attention away from Jin, and offers it to me, "Why are you gloomy, Yuki?" she asks.

"I'm not really interested in having a group discussion about it," I reply. "I'm fine, don't worry about me. You can't really help me anyway," I say. "Don't worry about me, I'm a popular guy."

"But I'm going to worry about you," Inari replies. "You seem so depressed. You have a great life! You should learn to love yourself."

"But I *do* love myself, you must understand. I simply don't like how other people see me. My whole life I've always been the guy that girls didn't like in 'that way'. I've always been the guy who was apparently a 'great catch' but no one ever wanted to fish for. I love myself. I'm proud of who I am, and I'm not going to change for anyone. You know… I have a lot of things people want… a great job that is fun and pays great money; I've always been smart, financially stable, and had a great family who loves me. But none of that ever really meant so much to me. The only thing I *ever* really cared about in life was finding *one person* to share my life with. I've devoted myself to this task since I was a child. It is the *only* thing I care about. It is funny how the thing I care about most is the one thing that I cannot have."

"YUKI! I WANT A FATHER! I AM NEVER GOING TO HAVE A FATHER! WHEELS... WHEELS WANTS LEGS! WHEELS IS NEVER GOING TO HAVE LEGS! DO YOU SEE WHEELS WHINING AND COMPLAINING AND GIVING UP ON LIFE BECAUSE HE'LL NEVER WALK? NO! NO YOU DON'T! YOU CAN'T HAVE EVERYTHING YOU WANT IN LIFE! YOU NEED TO BE THANKFUL FOR WHAT YOU HAVE!"

A shock runs up my spine. I am stunned at the directness of Inari's attack. She's never talked to me like this before. But she isn't done. She continues... revealing phrases and words that I had hoped she kept private between the two of us.

She quotes my own, lame poetry in a condescending tone. "I KNOW WHAT YOU WANT! LOVE IS YOUR GOD! IF YOU DON'T GET WHAT YOU WANT FROM ME, YOU'RE GOING TO END UP HATING ME JUST BECAUSE I WON'T AGREE TO BE YOUR GIRLFRIEND. THEN YOU'LL TALK A BUNCH OF TRASH ABOUT ME, JUST LIKE YOU DID TO AMBER!"

Inari's heart is racing, and she retreats to the bathroom and stares blankly into the mirror. Jin seems as shocked by Inari's sudden passionate tirade as I am. He sits on the floor, stunned, speechless. I slowly stand up from the couch.

"I guess that is my cue," I say, in the tone of a weathered old man who has lived through one too many battles in his lifetime.

Jin tries to be polite. "Uh... I guess so. Uh... sorry, I didn't see that coming."

265

I put on my coat as I walk towards the apartment door, passing the bathroom along the way. Suddenly, Inari stops me. "Wait. Don't go," she says. "I'm sorry, I only talk like that to people I care about, you know… I worry about you. I care about you."

"You can't help me," I say. "You're not the *right person* to help me."

"But I want to help you, I worry about you. You can't stop me from worrying about you."

"You can't help me! You're part of the problem, Inari. I appreciate that you want to help me, but you're just not the right person. It has to come from somewhere else… from someone who is *not* part of the problem… all I really hoped to get from you today was a few private minutes with you so that we can be brutally honest with each other about a couple of things. Then I figured I'd go on my way. But I can't talk to you when Jin is around."

Jin chimes in, "Anything you say to Inari you can say in front of me. There are no secrets between Inari and me."

"No, Jin, no I can't," I firmly declare. "There's no possible way that what you say is true," I say with a nervous chuckle.

"Anything you say to Inari will eventually find its way to me though. We're completely honest with each other."

"Well… I really *hope* that is not true," I reply, looking at Inari with an accusatory glare. In my head, I laugh at his statement, but also, I am a bit terrified at the possibility that he, in fact, has been privy to more information than I would be comfortable with him having. But… clearly… there is *no way* that it is true. If he knew everything, there would be *no way* that I would be welcomed in his apartment at this moment in time.

I speak directly to Inari, "There are things that I just simply don't feel comfortable saying in Jin's presence," I say.

"You don't need to talk as if I'm a third person here," Jin says. "I *can* hear everything you're saying."

"Sorry, Jin, but there are some things I just can't say with you around. I'm just going to go. We can continue this conversation some other time." I move to the door. I open it. I walk through it.

I shuffle slowly through the hall, looking at my feet. My feet are the only thing I see as tunnel vision from stress and sorrow causes my vision to narrow. I do not expect what happens next. Inari chases after me. In the hall, she grabs my arm. "No, please, don't go. Let's talk."

She pulls me through the glass door, into the glass room where the vending machines are. Jin stays behind, lurking at his apartment door. I am relieved that Jin is no longer in my presence. Jin is just out of view and behind a glass wall. Inari sits on the sofa by the vending machines, next to me. She rests her head on my shoulder and cuddles warmly.

"We… we need to draw a line in the sand," I say. "We need to define what our friendship will look like moving forward. That was my only intention in coming to see you yesterday and today. I want us to agree on what our friendship will look like, going forward. We need to clearly establish some lines that we do not cross."

"Well, that's easy, we just simply cannot do anything physical," she says.

"But what we're doing right now is physical. And if you continue to encourage this kind of physical contact, you must understand that I'm going to continue to want more of it from you… and I'm going to continue to want you in a more-than-friend way… we need to draw the line *further back* in the sand. We need to always keep 12 inches from each other. Maybe you can give me a hug goodbye at the end of the night, but other than that, there should be *no touching of any kind*."

Inari complies. She moves her body away from me. She lies on the couch with her head resting on the end farthest from me. She curls her legs up so that her toes seem to be *exactly* 12 inches from my body, almost as if deliberately mocking my request, seeking to starve me of the physical contact that she knows that I love and want.

We talk about things for a while. The conversation turns random. She doesn't seem to like the new boundaries I've set. Of course, I *hate* them, but they are necessary. I try to keep the conversation away from romantic subjects. It stays benign, about boring things. It is quite possibly the most boring, pointless conversation we have ever had about mundane subjects that seem deliberately chosen to be completely unemotional. Eventually, we're both getting a bit fatigued from talking and my throat is becoming sore from all of it. I decide that I need to be closer to her face so that we can hear each other more clearly. Her head, being at the opposite end of the sofa, makes it difficult for us to hear each other. I take the initiative to reposition myself on the floor in front of her so that I can talk directly to her face and look into her eyes. I would love to gaze at her as romantically as we always have, but I trust her to hold up her responsibilities in light of the new rules. As I sit in front of her, I rest my forearms on the edge of the couch. My left palm is upwards towards my face. I stare at my hand as if I'm reading my own palm, ruminating.

Without warning, Inari takes her right hand and walks her fingers up my wrist, as if she is mimicking a spider. She clutches my wrist and pulls it towards her. She takes my hand; I take hers.

"My god, you are so damn beautiful," I profess, heart racing.

She smiles brightly.

"I love you so very very much," I say.

She smiles brighter.

"… more than anyone I could ever possibly love, Inari." I brush her hair away from her eyes and caress her forehead. "I will never be able to love anyone more than I love you! You are the greatest human that ever walked this planet, kinder and sweeter than any angel that ever came from heaven! Nobody compares to you. I want nothing more than I want you!" I continue to profess, faster and with increasing nervousness. With every compliment I volley, she smiles even brighter, until it is as if she is brighter than the sun. For hours I fill her up with every romantic sentiment that I can possibly think of saying to her, repeating many of the sentiments she has already heard from me dozens of times. Jin has, long ago, gone to sleep by the time I finish complimenting her. I spout hours of compliments and sweet nothings as she gets sleepier and sleepier. Eventually, she speaks a few sentences in Japanese before she falls asleep entirely.

I am awake. I watch her… sleeping… holding her hand, now clammy and sweaty from our persistent body contact. I never let go of her hand and have now held onto it for hours. I worried that if I let go, I would never get it back.

But, now, with her sleeping, there's nothing left for me to do but go. I can't just leave her here, sleeping in this hallway. I must wake her up and bring her back inside. At first, I attempt to wake her verbally. I shake her. I pat her cheeks lightly. But nothing stirs her. Eventually, just like on the night she fainted in my arms, I decide to lift her shoulders. She snaps back to life, confused upon waking up, just as she was the last time when I woke her in this way.

She wakes up as if she's in a nightmare, "Ah! Ah! Ah! Where am I!? Help! Help! What's going on!?"

"Shhh, it's okay, Inari, it's Yuki, you're in the hall, outside Jin's apartment by the vending machines," I reply.

"Oh thank god!" she says as she hugs me tightly. "My nightmares are really intense sometimes. I was chased by monsters and demons! To wake myself up, I typically just kill myself in my dreams!" she says.

"Wow that's pretty intense, my nightmares usually just involve high school gym class, or forgetting to do my homework," I confess. "Come on, you can't sleep out here all night, lets get you back inside."

I escort her back into Jin's apartment a mere 15ft away. She is groggy and in a daze. As I open the door to his apartment, it is lit only by the hallway lights outside, and Jin is fast asleep. Inari wastes no time disappearing into the darkness. I see faint glimpses of her moving around in the dark, as I close the door, seeing her profile in the distance, lit only by the lights from the hallway. We don't even say goodbye. I peer into the dark apartment, expecting her to say one final word, but she is silent. As I close the door, the light from the hall becomes narrower and narrower until it is just a sliver. I can no longer see her anymore. With a click, I shut the door completely now. As I exit the apartment complex I am, once again, recharged with hope… but completely, utterly, confused. My brain just does not know reality, but my soul is locked into her. What… the… hell… I… am… confused!

Things are… clearly… complicated… and messy… but… maybe it just needs time. One thing is for certain… I am now more confused than I have *ever* been in my life. I thought it was all spelled out in black-and-white after she freaked out about our first kiss, then berated me in Jin's apartment… but she now just made it perfectly clear… there's plenty of *grey* mixed in with the black and white.

Maybe it was a mistake. But… I don't want it to be a mistake. No. God no! I definitely do *NOT* want this to be a mistake!

Chapter 33 - The Feedback Loop

A few days have passed since I last spoke to Inari. Monday rolls around. I try to contact her but she is consistently unresponsive until I finally get discouraged by it all. I wanted to see if she would come out to Hard Mondays... but, having not heard a peep from her, I just go out by myself. I am not too torn up by it. I keep in the back of my mind that it must be hard for her to coerce Jin into approving her outings with me all the time. She'll need to play it cool after last week. Last week was intense for everyone involved.

I'm really, therefore, surprised to see her show up to Hard Mondays, unannounced, with Jin. She didn't call to warn me or anything. She just showed up. Standing next to her in the club oozes with all the electricity and romance that it always has. The simple act of standing next to her transfers vibrations through my bones, and I imagine that she feels it too. When I stand next to her... she is drawn to me like a magnet. I ignore Jin. I don't even say "hello" to him.

But I try to stay disciplined. I try to keep my distance most of the night. I don't want him thinking I'm making moves on his girl again... I have to play it safe and cool. I pace through the various bars of the saloon, exiting the "movie bar", walk past the pool table and into the "music video bar" adjacent to the main room. Maddox exits the double doors of the main room and strikes up a routine conversation with me. Over his shoulder, I see Jin and Inari on the far side of the main bar. The main bar is an island separating the dance floor from the rest of the main room. 20 feet separates me from them. They do not notice me.

They stand there, flirting... nuzzling. Inari smiles, and Jin's eyes relax into a haze of lovesickness as she tickles his elbow and kisses him gently.

I pay little attention to Maddox as he rambles something that goes into my right ear and out the left. My attention is locked on Inari and Jin. My heart fills with longing and jealousy. This is clearly not a show intended for me. It is unlikely that they notice me watching. I become slightly upset, seeing them… they seem happy, enjoying a semi-private moment together. It was simple and pure on the surface.

But then… I remember. I remember… it is "the goodbye dance". I don't know how I know this. Something in the posture of the act communicates to me with 100% certainty that this *is* the goodbye dance. My sadness is replaced with confidence. My shoulders perk up from their lethargic sag. I look away from them. I don't need to see any more. I know now.

Paying no attention to whatever Maddox is saying to me, I interrupt him… "She's leaving with me tonight," I say. "Mark my words… she's leaving with me tonight."

Maddox stops whatever he's saying and chuckles. I say nothing more to him and simply walk off confidently. I wander around the movie bar, no longer concerned with what is happening between Inari and Jin. I know with 100% confidence that she is leaving with me.

It seems to take only 30 seconds for Jin to come and find me. Jin asks me to take care of Inari after bar. It is Echo's birthday.

"Inari wasn't to make sure Echo gets home and into bed safely. It is her birthday, after all, and we're concerned that she's is already too drunk," he states.

"I'll take care of both of them, then. It's no problem. It's never a problem," I reply. I don't mind at all. This means that my night, which would otherwise be coming to an end, is now just *beginning*. I love it.

I get Echo and Inari sandwiches at an all-night sub shop. They are very sweet to thank me for them. Inari looks after Echo, making sure she doesn't get so wasted that she injures herself again. Echo's nose is still marked from the nasty fall she took late

Wednesday night.

After sandwiches, we make our way to Echo's apartment in Loring Park. Echo basically wants to go to bed immediately... I don't complain... this simply means that Inari and I can have more time together, and I, frankly, was not interested in spending another long dramatic night with Echo's interference. We head to Jin's apartment, and we hang out in the hall by the vending machines, enjoying the semi-privacy of it all.

Things between are just as electric as they've ever been. It's as if the drama of last week changed nothing. I send tingles throughout her whole body with a deep foot massage. She moans passionately... the sounds she makes cause me to dream of something more romantic. I put all my heart and passion into making her feel wonderful.

"You're an angel," she says in a passionate moan. "I don't deserve you."

"You're an angel... you are," I simply reply.

"I'm not wonderful at all... I'm not really that good of a person," she says.

I assure her that I think she is wonderful. But in my head, I feel like my sycophancy is preventing me from hearing what she has to say. I believe in my heart that what she really wants is to *confess* to me.

Clearly, she has love for me in her heart, but what kind of love? And what sort of dark and twisted things might she be willing to do to keep this love that I have for her?

When I think about things sometimes... I think that these fights that she and I got in were just part of the show. She needs to marginalize me with great fanfare in front of him, and by yelling at me the other night, in his presence, she was protecting herself, while at the same time keeping me at the exact place she wanted and needed me.

Missing the opportunity to hear her confession, she returns to sweet talk. "You're too sweet to me," she says. "You're too nice."

"I try my best," I say.

"People only 'try' when they're trying to 'get' with me," she says. "Once they have me, they stop trying… they ignore me."

"I'm not like that. I will devote myself to you long before and long *after* I would ever be required to do so. I'm *already* devoted to you, clearly."

We exchange much love on this night. I gain further understanding of her emotions as she tells me about her family life. A strange life it is… a life of confusion and misplaced parental roles… a father who doesn't know she even exists… a family that she believes looks down on her. It is from this fucked up family situation she derives her values and her insecurities… and knowing her family history offers me much insight into what makes her tick. She talks about how, at family gatherings, her aunt would make her sit at the "kids table" even though she's 27 years old. She talks about how she confronted her uncle Steven about how it would mean "so very much" to her if he loved her, but Steven only replied, "I'll love whoever I want."

"As an empath, you see, I *know* my family doesn't love me," she says. "Only my grandparents love me."

As the sun is completely lighting the sky and people are going off to work their 9-5 jobs, I declare that I must go to work. She and I pause for a minute in the hall. A railing separates a ramp from stairs intended for wheelchair access in the main hall. She stands on one side; I stand on the other, our forearms resting on the railing in front of us. We gaze at each other. She stands there for a moment, seemingly absorbing all the love that I have for her. She clearly doesn't want me to leave. I don't want to leave her either. She's addicted to my glow, and I am addicted to hers.

As she absorbs this happiness, I reflect hers, I absorb hers, and reflect it back at her. In this process, we both feel happiness swell within us. It continues, building and circling, into a feedback loop of emotion. I undeniably want to kiss her more than anything I've ever wanted in the world now. But I do not kiss her. I love her too much. I put two fingers together and mime a kiss on her cheek.

I give her a big hug. "I miss you already," I say. I've said this kind of thing to her before... but this morning... it really seems to touch her more than it ever has. It resonates within her... and she clearly doesn't want me to go... she finds a way to devote herself to me for as long as possible... standing by my side more faithfully and persistently than she ever has before. She even decides to steal Jin's keys so that she can walk me to my car. I need to give her some things out of it, anyway.

It is a two-block walk to my car, so I offer to meet her at the door to the building and give her what she needs, but she refuses to stay behind. "You don't have to walk alone," she says.

She is so very sweet to me.... the sweetest she's ever been as she walks next to me, glowing. After finding my car, I drive the two blocks back to the building, but she is hesitant to get out... we hug again... but she won't leave.... So we hug again... and again.

"I miss you already," I say again... "If you get lonely... you call me... don't worry about me... don't worry about what time of day it is or whether I'll be sleeping... just call me... I don't want you to ever be lonely."

"You're so sweet to me. You're too nice to me," she says with a bright, beaming smile.

"But... if we don't stop this feedback loop, it will reach a critical mass... and then it will cause a nuclear reaction and the *whole city* will die!" I joke. "We have to save the planet from our chain reactive love for each other!"

We both laugh at the joke... but I think we both understand what it means.

It means that there are omens. This path we're going down has a potentially scary future ahead... no matter what turns we take along the way... there are going to be some negative consequences... and someone is going to get hurt.

Chapter 34 - Man at Arms

I worry that all this… this writing… it is damaging myself and damaging Inari. But I just *can't help it. I have to be honest! Always! Even if the truth is dark… even if the truth is difficult for her to hear and relive.*

I struggle with my conscience. Is it really a good idea to posture myself towards her in this way? Does she even appreciate it? Does she even read this sappy, whiney garbage? I have no idea. I don't know if 100% honesty is really a good idea.

After worrying about the consequences of being too honest, and longing for her to love me… I begin pulling down writings that might be too honest. My obsession over her, I conclude, must not be attractive to her. Instead, I write her a long email, directly.

This is not an admission of defeat, but a call to arms.

With every additional word that I write here, I erode your perceptions of confidence in me… it is clearer and clearer now that I have, despite trying my best, left you completely unimpressed with my performance. Despite all my efforts… despite my complete devotion.

With every phone call I make to you, I erode your confidence in me. With every text message I send you… I erode your confidence in me. With every word I say to you in Jin's presence, I erode your confidence in me.

But every time that we manage to find ourselves alone together… away from the judgement of Jin or others… you and I are 100% confident together… 100% beautiful together… and everything is all magic.

Mark my words, I will bounce back… I will bounce back as you've never seen anyone bounce back. I had hoped that I'd have you by my side when I bounced back… but I guess I never really expected it.

So, I'll have to fight it alone. But it's okay... I've done it this way for a long time.

Jin and I still need to have our "man to man" talk... which... should... come soon. Rest assured that I have thought long and hard about what I would say to him. And some of the things I say to him are going to be quite blunt.

I'm sure there will be some things that shock him... but that's kinda' part of the idea... to shock Jin... to make him feel like if he doesn't treat you with 100% respect... he could lose you. If only these things are my own feelings, they will shock him... I will not tear down your character, because I don't see anything about your character to tear down.

But I've decided, despite my earlier intentions NOT to apologize to him... NOT AT ALL... and instead... I'm going to use the opportunity to be verbally tough and strong, and open the conversation with one VERY SIMPLE question:

"Jin, how did we get here?"

Asking him this will call into question all his own actions. I honestly believe that I got close to you, Inari, mostly due to Jin's own misdeeds. You fucking love him... I see that. He's #1... Barry is #2... and if I'm feeling generous to myself.. maybe I'll put myself at #3. My presence has been nothing more than a wake-up call to him... he knows now that he can't take you for granted. He knows that I'm watching and lurking. He knows that I'm standing guard.

Our conversation will wind and twist into another question.... "What happened between you two?"... I'll ask him. And maybe he'll be more honest with me than he has with you about why it is that he left you hanging so many times. I'll smoke out his TRUE feelings for you. Does he really love you? What are his worries? What are his reservations? How much does he really trust you? Does he trust you just as much now as before? Does he trust you with me?

Then, I'll reveal to him my feelings for you... to an extent... to the degree that I think that he won't explode. Be assured that he will get a small taste of the kinds of things that I really say to you when he's not around. He will be assured that I love the hell out of you and that I don't just want to "get in your pants", but that I have emotionally devoted myself to you and intend to continue on this path. He will know that I'm standing guard in case he fucks up and that I'd die for you... and I'm sure he'll even draw the conclusion that my feelings for you far outweigh his own because I know, for sure, in my heart, that I can out-love him. I can out-love Jin 10 times over. And, for you, I can out-love Jin 100 times over.

But rest assured that I'll never be more honest with Jin than I am to you, Inari, and that my intentions will never be to destroy your relationship but to make your relationship as strong and honest and open as it can be, because, if Jin is not honest with you, then, let me tell you... he does not deserve you. My #1 intention with this man-to-man conversation, is to make sure that HE KNOWS and that HE UNDERSTANDS 100% that YOU DESERVE THE BEST... and if he is to deserve you... he BETTER FUCKING BE THE BEST. He must be as TIRELESS, RELENTLESSLY LOVING, ATTENTIVE, AND DEVOTED as I AM... and THEN SOME. He BETTER be. Because if he's not... he'll be hearing from me upon the slightest infraction.

"I love Inari," I will tell him. "But you've got her... and you better damn well learn to love her more than I do. For the time being, I'm leaving her with you, because that is where she has chosen to be. Even if I might not agree with her choices, I respect her choices, even if it is just because she is confused or scared or whatever. I don't know how she feels... but obviously, she loves you."

I will finish the conversation... it will be done... and I will then let him decide going forward, how much he loves you, without any interference from me.

I will wish you the best, you deserve the best. I hope you've found your man... I hope for you. I will power through my own life, having been beaten by these battles... but made stronger and more resilient going forward.

Already... I take less shit from people now. Last night, a girl who shall not be named, approached me and told me that I could buy her dinner, just as long as we didn't call it a "date". I laughed in her face... "fuck you." She back-pedaled and offered to go "Dutch" with me... but at this point, I was like... "I don't need you" and blew her off. The funny thing is... a couple of years ago... I wanted to date her. I don't anymore. I want someone with a soul... I'm smarter now.

Natalie got all romantic with me last night as well. As she embraced me in front of the North Loop. She said, "I'm in love with someone else, who's not available..."

I replied, "Well... that's my story too."

"I don't really want to go to this afterparty but are you going?" she asked.

"I'm going home," I said, firmly. I was not impressed by being offered the second-place prize, so... I declined a night's romp and preserved what's left of my integrity.

"Maybe I'll go home too then," she replied, likely feeling rejected that I would not go home with her. But I went home satisfied. I didn't need these crappy relationships. I know better. I deserve better.

Chapter 35 - Reality is How You Perceive It

Techna returns to town. Her next fashion show is Friday. She arrives in town Wednesday night and works all day Thursday at my house, fitting models. She brings her sewing machines in and sets them up in my second-floor spare bedroom and works around the clock getting her dresses perfect for her next show.

I arrive home after work to find her stressed, busy, and surrounded by scraps of fabric, skinny girls, and boyfriends of skinny girls. I make a vain attempt to forget Inari for a few minutes and decide that I should flirt with the girls who happen to be in my house. One takes a friendly liking to me. We talk about music for a couple of hours, and I show her my studio and recording gear. I play her a little bit of my concept album, and she is interested enough in it that she offers to play in a band if I ever get around to forming a new one.

Whereas having a house full of models is a bit exciting, I don't assume any of these girls to be prospects. I consider myself monogamous, devoted to Inari, even if Inari is not mine. Mentally and emotionally, I belong to her. I really have no interest in anyone else. It is unlikely that I will take an interest in any other girl than Inari any time soon. Inari is modeling for Techna in her next show. I am excited. I am happy that I was able to connect the two of them together. I am also happy because, this evening, Inari will be coming over to be fitted into Techna's newest dress.

Techna's new line deliberately takes a bold turn away from her peers. Our friends' fashion lines have trended towards cyberpunk and steampunk mixed in with traditional centuries-old, renaissance designs. Techna is tired of the scene and deliberately sought to express it in her latest designs. Her dresses are inspired by New Orleans, full of bright colors and religious patterns featuring embroidered patches of Jesus and Mary.

She is tired of all the lame high school drama that goes on in the Goth scene. No one in the Goth scene wants to grow up. To "grow up" is to become "boring" in our circles. Techna is, by no means boring, nor would I ever suspect that she's looking to become boring. Yet, she's sick of all the promiscuous sex, the kissing games, the sex games, the lying, cheating, crying, back-stabbing rumors. Love and monogamous relationships are less common than open, free love, casual sex arrangements in our scene.

I have no desire to be in an open relationship. And even if both partners consent to the openness of the relationship, most of the time, one partner is far more open to the idea of an "open relationship" than the other partner. It inevitably leads to jealousy, which inevitably leads to volatile situations, destructive behavior, self-destructive behavior. Many people in the scene have unusually potent sex drives and if they can't get sex every night from their partner, they insist on getting it elsewhere.

Techna gets all of her models into their dresses, takes her final measurements, and works diligently to get her work done for her show. By 10PM, all of her models are fitted, except one. Inari has yet to show up. I call her and suggest that we pick her up. I figure, if we pick her up, then Jin doesn't have to come along. Techna needs to stop at a store near Jin's apartment, and I'm sure Jin would appreciate not having to drive across town anyway. Inari seems to buy into the conspiracy. We'll pick her up so that Jin doesn't come along, then she'll tell him that she's crashing at her grandparents' house. Then we can hang out all night.

We arrive at Jin's apartment after stopping at the store. Inari quickly gets her things together and we're out the door within 5-10 minutes, this is probably the fastest I've ever managed to get Inari to leave the house. We arrive back at my house on the west side and we congregate in the loft. The loft is adjacent to a bathroom, the master bedroom, and the guest bedroom where Techna has set up shop. A curtainless picture window exposes the loft to the outside world. I'd been meaning to put up some curtains, but unfortunately, the windows are not reachable from the second floor. They are above the stairwell and partially above the dance floor. The floor beneath the windows is 18ft down. I don't even have a ladder tall enough to reach the windows. The windows have remained curtainless since I bought the house 3 years earlier. I'm always a bit self-conscious, particularly at night when the lights are on. The whole neighborhood can basically see what is happening in my house on the second floor.

Techna comes out of the spare bedroom and shows Inari her dress. It is red and white, cut just above the knees, conservative, like something out of Appalachia. "You can use the bathroom up here to try…" Techna stops in mid-sentence.

Inari strips down to her underwear right in front of the both of us, right in front of the picture window, with all the lights in the house on. She's not concerned about the neighbors seeing. Certainly not shy about me seeing either. I'm sitting 2ft in front of her. My god, her body is amazing.

The fitting doesn't take any more than 60 seconds. Inari strips again and puts her jeans and t-shirt on. The night is young. It isn't even midnight.

I decide that we should watch Zoolander to get in the mood for the fashion show. One movie turns into two movies. I ask Inari how late she can stay out.

"Not too late," she says.

I get close to Inari, but not impolitely close. Inari sits on the floor, leaning up against the railing that looks over the dance floor. I grab a pillow and lay in front of her on my chest. She puts her feet under the pillow to keep them warm and I pet them under the pillow to let her know that I care. I remind Inari of the time. She said she didn't want to stay out too late. But she doesn't object when we start the second movie of the night.

Techna is running out of time to prepare for the show. "I hope you don't mind, but I'm going to go in the bedroom and shut the door. I have too many things to do."

"No problem," I assure.

"Remember, 1:00PM. DON'T BE LATE!" she says. "I won't mind so much, but the lady who organizes the show will throw a complete hissy fit and yell at both of us."

After Techna leaves us alone, we're less shy about getting close. Inari is all sore from working the Haunted Basement. I massage her feet, her calves, her thighs… her *inner* thighs. I keep thinking to myself that I could accidentally twitch and touch her danger zone. I massage within half an inch of it. I fantasize about twitching deliberately, but I stop myself. One dumb move from me would mean the end for us. No matter how much I might dream in my head that she wants me to touch her, I can't take such a risk.

The massage lasts deep into the night. 3AM rolls around…. 4AM… 5AM. I ask her again if she needs to go home… she says nothing… But when 6AM arrives… Inari suddenly snaps into reality. Getting home becomes urgent now, but not so urgent that her right foot would receive less massage time than her left. I massage her left foot some more to finish the job. She gathers her things. I drive her home. Throughout the 20-minute drive, she turns increasingly sour.

"I need sleep before a big day," she says.

I apologize as if it is my fault. I kept her out, despite the fact that I reminded her of the time several times throughout the night. Yet, my apologies do not pacify her. She continues to be grumpy about the time. We both worry that she'll not be able to get up on time to get to the show by 1PM.

By the time we arrive at her house, she is totally cross. "I should be starting to get ready at 9AM," she says. "It is now 7AM... I'm only going to get 2 hours of sleep! I'm not going to be able to wake up."

"I'll call you 50 times and make sure you get up," I offer.

"It doesn't matter. I'll sleep right through my alarm. I'll sleep through anything."

"Well… I'll come over and pound on the door if I have to."

"It's okay… Barry or my grandparents will make sure I get up," she says. "I'll just take a cat nap or something… I'll live. Uhhhggh… I *need* sleep before a big day!"

"Well, I offered to take you home several times throughout the night," I respond, no longer quite so willing to take 100% of the blame.

"Well, you always seem so sad when I leave," she counters.

"Well… I enjoy all our time together, but I'd rather get you home early than feel responsible for screwing up your day the next day," I say.

"I *need* sleep," she repeats again.

I go home and get a 60-minute cat nap before work. I end up being late for work myself and my boss is pissed off at me. Luckily, I have an immediate solution to the problem he and I were working on at the end of the previous day. I told him I'd "sleep on the problem" … and I did as I said I would… if only for 60 minutes. I slept on it, and I have found the solution. He is pleased that I've found the solution. I dodged a bullet, but my job is hurting due to all my personal drama.

I call Inari to make sure she gets up but I don't get any answer. I feel that things are going to get fucked up. I debate with myself whether I should inform Techna. I don't think Inari will be on time. Weighing the options of "panic" or "don't panic", I decide not to panic. I figure, maybe Inari is just pissed and doesn't want to talk to me.

At 1:30 Techna texts me, "Inari is not here. :(I'm going to have to find another model now," I call Inari.

"Well, I can't get ready to go if I'm talking on the phone with you now, can I?" she snaps.

"Well, you should at least communicate to Techna what is happening," I say. "She is really worried right now."

15 minutes pass. Inari calls me back and asks me to tell Techna that she's on her way over. I relay the information to Techna and leave it at that... there's nothing I can or should do at this moment. Any further participation by me would only aggravate the situation.

Only at 5PM do I even find out that Inari made it to the show and wasn't replaced by another model. The fashion show happens. Inari's tardiness is far less fucked up than the management of the show. They put the runway in a hallway of a building on the Minneapolis College of Art and Design. There's no room to stand. No one can see anything. The runway is only elevated in two key places, elevated by a couple of risers. The models have to step up onto the risers, then step down again, walk along a red carpet, step up to another riser, turn, step down again, and walk back the way they came without colliding into the next model coming down the runway. The building is huge... full of many large open spaces. Why they decided to put it in the hallway is beyond me.

Inari exits the doorway where the models line up before their walk. She is visibly unhappy. I try to make eye contact and give her a smile, but she just continues to frown. I figure she is unhappy about the events of the day, but I figure that maybe everyone is just confused about the runway situation.

The first 3 of Techna's models get confused and walk around the risers on their return walk from the far end to avoid colliding with each other. Inari walks the runway and seems not to notice me, even though I present myself confidently for her attention.

After the show I meet up with, Sally, the model I had been flirting with during the night of the fitting. "I think Inari is mad at me for making her late," I confess. "I feel awful. I feel like I messed everything up."

I make some rounds, just feeling dumb and lost. Eventually, I find Inari and Sally talking. It would appear that Sally had relayed my feelings back to her.

"Everything is fine," Inari says. "You worry too much. Stop worrying."

I stutter a single syllable. Inari simply smiles. Jin lingers patiently while several other men attempt to flirt with his girlfriend. Even I am fascinated by how he seems unthreatened by all the men who incessantly put maximum effort into winning Inari's heart. If I were to ever be that "cool" with it, I would have to have maximum confidence that Inari truly and faithfully loved me. Even, I, not being her boyfriend, am getting jealous that she spends so much time humoring these men who clearly want to sleep with her. After about 2 hours of this, we all decide to get Asian food at a restaurant on Eat Street.

We all settle into the restaurant, about 10 of us in all. Inari and Jin bicker and fight as Jin places an order for her that she doesn't like, and Inari is surprised when her food arrives.

"What's this?" she prods.

"It's the Pad Thai with tofu," Jin replies, "I thought that was what you wanted."

"I don't want this!" Inari snaps.

I am pretty sure they examined the menu together and ordered together. I find myself becoming uncomfortable, nervous. Jin sends her food back to the kitchen.

"You take too much charge over things that you have no business taking charge of, Jin! You can't just order for me like that! You always do that! Jin, you need to let me make my own choices!"

I become increasingly more uncomfortable.

"Look!" she cries, "You're making me embarrass us in front of our friends, I don't like this! This is horrible! Just let me order my own food, Jin!"

As the food is sent back to the kitchen, I ponder and contrast how it was handled with the way I would have handled it. I would have taken the completely opposite approach, and accepted the food, even if it was the wrong order. Being the spineless prude that I am, I wouldn't have wanted to upset anyone, including the waiter or the kitchen staff. I would have accepted it as my fault, possibly even if it was completely wrong.

This slight problem seems to turn Inari completely against Jin for the entire duration of the meal. She doesn't want to let it go. She complains and complains and they argue and argue as she criticizes his handling of not just the meal, but everything in life, including his management of the now-canceled fashion show with Echo.

After the night winds down, Techna and I return back to my house to discuss the events of the past couple of days.

"When I saw them fighting at the restaurant, I just thought to myself 'what the fuck!?'" she says. "It was kind of odd. I felt like I wasn't supposed to be seeing this."

I offer my assessment of their relationship. "You see, I think Inari is scared to leave Jin and simply needs to be 100% sure that I'm the right person. You saw a little taste of how we interact together last night. I feel like the tides are changing."

"Yeah, your relationship is fucked up. It is inappropriate, and she needs to decide between him or you and if she doesn't want you, she needs to stop leading you on," she says.

"Even seeing so little as you did, you think so? I mean, you didn't really see all that much, and you didn't see how we interact when we're alone. I assure you, when we're alone, it is far more intense. When you went into the bedroom to sew last night, we were a bit less shy with each other."

"Really!? From what I can see already, your relationship is inappropriate. You need to tell her to pick him or you."

"Well, I don't see that I have to do that just yet. Just as long as we continue to get closer to each other, there's no reason to put an ultimatum on her. Doing so would only undo all of our progress. I will give her time to figure things out. She needs time to wrestle with her emotions. I am fine with giving her the time. She is worth it. It is only a matter of time. Jin and she can't possibly survive."

"Yeah, in my limited observation, they're pretty screwed up. But your relationship with her is pretty screwed up too."

Techna returns to Wisconsin Saturday afternoon. I end up at my default Saturday night haunt, Ground Zero.

I don't see many friends there, but the bar is busy. The only person who is of much interest to talk to is Nikki. Nikki told me last week that I could buy her dinner as long as it wasn't a "date" a week ago, and my first reflex was to laugh in her face. Tonight, she is maybe a bit more understanding and seems apologetic regarding her posturing the week before.

"It is good to see you, but I've just arrived, and I need to get a drink."

"You can keep me company if you like," she says.

"Of course. I'll be right back," I reply.

I go to the bar with the intention of returning to keep her company after I get a drink, but the bar takes forever. Ground Zero is unusually crowded tonight, but with no friends of mine. Nikki is the closest thing I have to a friend in this place, and I, honestly, barely know her.

By the time I get my drink, 10-15 minutes have passed and 3 other people are hovering around her. The rest of the night progresses and I barely talk to her at all. No big deal. I get vibes that she's a bit mean-spirited. I don't have room in my heart for mean-spirited girls right now.

I leave the bar early out of boredom, at 1AM. I text Inari and tell her that if she can't sleep after bar close, she can call me.

She does... it is 3AM. We get to talking about small talk... dogs... stuff.

Out of the blue, she compliments me generously out of the left-field, "You're too nice to me, Yuki!" she says in a flirty voice.

Just then I hear a forceful whisper on the other end of the phone. "WHAT... THE FUCK... ARE YOU DOING?" Jin says. "You're treating me like shit," he says... pissed off, in a forceful whisper.

"I'm only doing to you what you're doing to me," she says. "You rolled over and fell asleep. I just didn't want to be alone tonight."

"I can't work with your schedule," he whispers. "You're treating me like *I'm* treating *you* like shit."

Inari returns to my attention. "Heyyy…" she says.

"Sounds like you have some things to work out over there," I say.

"Yeah."

"Call me if you need me, okay?"

"Okay."

I leave them alone. I wonder if she talked to me in bed deliberately to drive him crazy and randomly complimented me at that exact moment because she wanted to make sure he heard it after she finally woke him up. I worry about her virtually every hour of every day. This relationship of hers doesn't feel healthy to me.

I care about her too much. It is not my job to care, but I care anyway... it is in my nature. I know that she loves me and cares about me as much as she is able... and I care about her all I am able. I believe that it is fear that keeps her from accepting her own feelings for me. She fears ending her relationship with Jin because up to this point in her life he's been the best for her. I wish I were good enough for her. I am not even 100% sure I'm NOT good enough for her... I'm not 100% sure what "reality" is? Am I good enough for Inari? I am just a confused disciple, looking for answers that only she has.

Chapter 36 - Ladytron

I get a call from Inari on Sunday night. I fail to answer. I don't know how I missed the call. My phone is always by my pillow at night… always. It has been that way ever since I met Inari. But maybe it is just because she has worn me out to the point where my body finally gave out and demanded sleep. I don't get much sleep these days. She keeps me up at night, even if we're not together or talking on the phone. She occupies every thought I have. I hardly have room for any others.

My phone must be by my side at all times, charged, ready to receive her call. If it is not, my nerves will certainly sound the alarm. I don't know how I missed her call. I, of course, try to call her back the instant I realize that I missed her call. I call her once, to no answer.

I decide that I need something to lure her in. I need an excuse to make contacting her important and time-sensitive. There's a band in town that we both like, Ladytron. They're playing the Fineline tonight. I can score some tickets for her. Maybe it will be an excuse for us to get together. I leave her voicemails.

She returns my call, finally. She's worn out from last night. Apparently, she was calling me because she got in such a huge fight with Jin that she was packing up the things she had at his apartment and planning to leave him. She wanted me to pick her up and bring her away from him.

Of all the calls to miss… this was certainly an important one. I mentally berate myself for missing her call. How could I miss such a call!?

"I had decided that I had just had it. I couldn't deal with him turning tiny issues into multi-hour arguments. I was packing up my stuff. I needed to get out of there, but I tried calling you, and I tried calling Barry and I couldn't leave."

"I'm so sorry! I would have totally come. I don't know how I missed your call. My phone is always by my ear."

"Eventually things cooled down, but I'm still pretty upset about it all. I just want to get away from him tonight. Ladytron sounds like a good idea."

"Will Jin be upset if you go without him?"

"Jin doesn't even like Ladytron. I'll just tell him to save his money."

I walk to the Fineline to get tickets as I talk to her on the phone. I don't have free tickets, but for her to believe that they are free removes any opportunity for her to refuse on the grounds of money.

Once the tickets are in hand, the plans are set in stone. I tell her to get ready so that we can get out of the apartment before Jin gets home. We'll have to rush. The doors open early.

Upon arrival at Jin's apartment, she is not ready, as is to be predicted. She procrastinates like she always does. I nervously count the minutes before Jin's arrival home and try to get her to hurry.

She searches for ways to get me to stop rushing her. "There's usually like 4 opening bands, right?" she inquires.

"No, actually, tonight, I think there's just one opening band, then Ladytron. It is an early, all-ages show."

"Oh… that's lame. Fine, I'll get ready."

She picks up the pace, but not enough to get us out of the apartment before Jin arrives.

Upon Jin's arrival, Jin is unaware of our plans. Upon hearing of our planned outing, he tries to invite himself along. He seems offended that I am going to a concert with his girlfriend. He looks up how to get tickets online.

Inari comes up with all the excuses she can think of to convince him to stay away. "You don't even like Ladytron."

"Certainly, I like Ladytron."

"You've only heard that one song I played for you, and I thought you didn't really even like it all that much."

"Well, they're not my favorite, but if they're in town I'd certainly like to come along."

"But Jin," Inari diverts, "you should save your money. You have to pay your bills. You spend too much money eating out at restaurants with your friends. You should be saving your money."

"Well, just let me look up how much it is and whether there are tickets."

"You've been going out way too much. What you *should* be doing is saving your money."

I chime in, "If I had an extra ticket, I'd give it to you. But I got mine for free through my connections."

Inari and I seem to be unable to shake Jin's insistence on coming along. The conversation lulls for a few minutes as Jin clicks away at the computer in silence, digging up ticket prices online. Inari silently and diligently tends to her hair, working at a steady pace. It is quite the contrast from her earlier procrastination. It is as if she's working hard so that she can get out and get away from Jin before he finally purchases his ticket.

I think through the problem before me, trying to figure out a way to make sure that Jin stays behind. I get an idea…

"Jin, maybe we can just go to the concert and then you can meet up with us at Hard Mondays afterwards. We'll hang out, get some drinks and then you can just take Inari home from there."

Jin doesn't answer me directly but instead speaks to Inari. "You know, maybe you're right. Maybe I should be saving my money." Jin gets up from the computer and stands outside the bathroom door. "I'm sorry, you're right. I just want you to know that I appreciate you."

"We should be going, the opening band has already started," I say… now also standing outside the bathroom door.

Inari scurries to put on her shoes. I leave and exit the apartment into the hall. I leave them to do whatever kissing or whatever they do in private. I don't want to see it.

We park the car near The Saloon and walk the 4-5 block walk up 1st Avenue to find the Fineline. We arrive just in time. There are only 15 minutes before Ladytron starts. Once we're alone. The gloves are off. Inari rests her head on my shoulder, and I lean my head to rest it gently on top of hers. I put my arm around her back and tickle her elbow in a way that she seems to like. Drunken dildo asshole men try to hit on her even as she clearly seems to indicate that she's taken. I run interference with a guy who tries to grind on her in the thick of the show.

Ladytron, the band and the music, are everything we expect, but, regardless, the quality of the concert has little to do with the quality of this night. Inari and I are close… emotionally… and physically. It is everything I dreamed of. It feels natural. It feels perfect.

Afterwards, we walk across the street to Minneapolis's famous downtown punk rock pizza joint, Pizza Luce. I buy pizza and we share a giant plate of Spaghetti. Once we've gorged ourselves, we walk back to The Saloon for Hard Mondays. I buy us drinks, a couple of Vampires, vodka cranberry with a shot of grenadine -- a

Goth creation. We sit, chatting in the movie bar, enjoying the night, almost as if we've forgotten that we're no longer anonymous in this crowd. She sits close to me on the barstool to the right of me. Our legs exchange body heat, keeping each other warm in the chilliness of this September night, and I feel loved in the warmth of her presence. We silently drink our drinks, enjoying the companionship, and I meditate on the beauty of human contact, physical connection, and the beauty of being with the girl I love. I love this moment.

Suddenly, I realize that my head is in the clouds. I need to be careful. I realize that my hand is in my own lap, but in this dimly lit room, it might appear as if I have my hand on *her* leg and the fact that we're sitting so close will likely disturb Jin when he arrives. And even if he doesn't see us like this, someone else in the bar might see us and inform him. Just as soon as I realize our misstep, Jin appears from behind and sticks his head in between us. He looks down at how close we are. He is polite but clearly taken aback. He makes a double-take on my hand, and I think he breathes a sigh of relief that my hand is not on his girlfriend's thigh.

Inari turns around to say hello to him. But to my shock, she does not distance herself from me. Her legs are still exchanging body heat with mine. In fact, when she turns around on her barstool, she gets even closer to me. Her knees and thighs press up against mine with greater pressure and I feel my thighs become warmer from the increasing exchange.

She talks to Jin. Jin offers to get her food from the bar which is accessible from a counter in the adjacent "Fire Bar". She informs him that we ate before we came over here, but she's still hungry enough that she could eat some fries or something. She doesn't seem to pick up on the vibes I got from him. I worry silently that she needs to move herself a couple inches away from me so that our bodies are not touching. I get a bit nervous. They continue to talk about ordinary things. He inquires about the concert and Inari offers her reviews, which are far more generous than my own, but the continuing exchange of body heat reminds me that I need to correct our posture. I figure I need to say a few words to Inari, but I need Jin to leave for a couple of minutes.

"Jin, I thought you were going to get some food," I remind him.

"Oh! Yes! I was going to do that," Jin obediently walks away to the adjacent bar. I almost believe that he picked up that I was giving him a "hint" that he should disappear for a couple of minutes. He obeys my command/suggestion without objection, without saying another word.

Immediately, once he's out of earshot, I question Inari. "Do you think we're a bit too close? I feel like we're making Jin uncomfortable."

"He's fine. Don't worry about him," she says.

"Well, I was picking up vibes from him that he was a bit disturbed by how close we were," I reply.

"Jin doesn't feel things like you or I. Even if he is upset... you know... it's just a *little* bit."

I stand up from my stool; Jin has placed his order and is returning in our direction. It is time for me to politely return Jin's girlfriend back to him. "Well, I'm going to go find Luna. I'll leave you two for now."

Inari and I had discussed that he seems unable to interpret human emotions and is therefore unable to empathize with people. I think he is unable to deal with his own emotions as well. He feels these things he's never felt before... and jealousy is something new to him. I believe he feels jealousy when I'm around but is unsure of how he is supposed to react when challenged. I believe he feels that Inari and I are closer than he'd like, but he doesn't know how to challenge his own feelings... he doesn't know when his feelings are or aren't appropriate. I try to tell Inari this... but Inari thinks

I've got it all wrong, that I don't understand Jin. I'm sure she knows him better than I do... but I dunno... I see her emotionally challenge him all the time... and I see him react, but I don't really see her understanding how he reacts. Or maybe it's just that she doesn't *care* how he reacts.

But at this point in time, I believe that Inari is an empath, so if she tells me that Jin feels a certain way, I believe her. At this point, I would believe anything Inari says to me, even if it were a blatant, verifiable lie that I could quickly disprove with evidence in my own hands.

I wander aimlessly around the bar. Inari breaks free from Jin for a while. We sit together in the fire bar. She mentions that Jin is probably going to want to go home soon. I make no suggestion that she should stay out later. I have no intention of monopolizing her time anymore tonight.

We split and wander some more. A few minutes pass and Jin approaches me "Inari is wondering if there's anything happening after bar."

I think for a moment about what a strange, subtle dynamic they have. Like ... really... Can't Inari ask me herself? I think about the subtle hilarity of human nature that Jin is the one to ask me this question... as if he's in control. He has the illusion of control. Maybe Inari wanted to *give him* the illusion of being in control. Silly humans.

I don't know how I cram all those thoughts through my brain, considering the rapidity and decisiveness of my reply... "Always," I say in a confident proclaiming voice.

There's always an after bar. Honestly, where there's an Inari, there's a plan for me... always. I don't need any further plans.

After bar, we spend a little bit of time with Echo... just a little. Then Inari and I spend the rest of the night together. I buy her a flavored water from the hall outside of Jin's apartment and we spend the night on the couch by the vending machines again.

"When you're feeling down, do you have a 'happy place' you go to?" she asks.

I blush and chuckle at the question.

She eggs me on. "Come on, Yuki... where's your happy place!"

"Yeah... well... my happy place is wherever you are," I reply.

"Awww... that's so sweet," she says. "I love you so much! You're too good to me!" she says as she cuddles with me and brings me much warmth. Her head is now resting on my shoulder and her body is completely snuggled up against my side. We are closer than we ever have been before. I love this girl so much. "You're an angel. I don't deserve someone like you," she says.

"Well, I think you deserve the best," I reply. "And I am willing to admit, that *I* am not the best, but I don't think Jin is either. But we can't keep doing this forever. There's only so much heartbreak that I can take. You break my heart every day, you know?"

"OH DEAR!" she gasps. "I really hope I don't make you feel that way! I'm so sorry."

"It's okay. Don't worry. I'm pretty tough. I'm used to this kind of stuff. I'll find a way to move on," I say. After leaving for the night, arriving in my own bed, I loathe myself for backing away from Inari. Why did I back off!? Why didn't I demand, right then and there, that she love me completely?

Chapter 37 - The Curse of the Deity

The peaks of my loyou've, our love... they feel so high. But in her absence, the valleys are now so, so low. I am like a heroin addict, and she is my heroine. I just need another fix. As I starve for more of her attention, I question it all. In these valleys, I write about my doubts. I just keep writing. I'm just a rambling drone now. Lovesick. Missing her. Missing her touch. Missing her twisted confusion. I'll put up with her confusion if she would just sit next to me, but as I write this, she is not here.

Starving and in love, I don't know why I keep doing this. I don't know why Inari lets me stew like this, working away to both honor, expose, and even embarrass her. But as I keep saying, I am under a spell, hypnotized to be honest with her, and she knows that I am devoted.

I've sent Inari 36 chapters of which *she* is the main subject. I stop and pause to think about this. This is just obsessive. No normal human being just lets someone write a novel about them, for them, and to them without putting a dramatic, serious stop to it all. She *must know* it is obsessive, and for her to not stop me is, at this point, just *absolutely reckless* and borderline cruel.

I don't know why she continues to let me work this way. I constantly battle with my conscience, unsure of what is right and what is wrong, what is wise and what is foolish... unsure of what is real and what is imaginary... unsure of my interpretations of all these actions and events, that should seem to be blatantly obvious. Why is reality so hard to grasp? When she holds my hand and tells me she loves me, what does that even mean anymore?

Is this right? Is it wrong? Is it right for me to plot against Jin? Is it right for her to get so close to me while knowing fully well the intricate details of not just every action, but every thought and emotion I have ever possessed of her?

Is this honesty killing me or hurting me? I am a fool! I am only setting myself up for bigger disappointment!

After drafting chapters 35 and 36, I dutifully send them to her as I have all the other chapters, but all this work, this labor, serving her... Is it worth it? Am I reaching her? I don't know!

Days have passed. I'm not even sure if she's read my latest writings. I'm not sure if it is so wise for me to have posted them for her to see. Should I leave them there and wait patiently for my goddess to read them, or should I pull them down before she gets the chance?

Maybe they sound too whiny and needy. Maybe I need to rewrite them to portray myself as a more confident, hardened man... a man who can command her.

I don't usually care how I portray myself... but I obsess over how she is seeing me. What do I need to do? What do I need to do to realize and experience her love completely? I write every chapter as if it is my last... and I think, for the sake of everyone involved, that, maybe, *this* should be the last chapter I write.

Fuck this. Who is this damn book for anyway, Inari? I've taken down *all* writing... if you want to read them... you'll have to ask me for them... but I don't really expect you to ever ask. I expect you to care about your own agenda... and your own agenda consists entirely of finding a way to make Jin love you "as much as [I] do." You want Jin, the robot to love you the way I do. But he won't because he's Jin. He's not me. If you want my love, you have to get it from me.

But I did say, "you break my heart every night." And whereas, yes, it is true, and yes, it is sad; I do not expect a remedy. I love you, but the breaking of my heart is a simple reality that I will have to live with. My heart has been broken enough times to where it is numb to this pain. But it is so rare that I meet someone so special as you to make my heart come alive again.

I promised myself that going forward, I would look at my life... our relationship... and your relationship with Jin in a different, more mature light. And whereas I really try to stay on the right track, I continue to fall completely off the rails with every attempt I make to escape this incessant desire for your love.

I need to talk to Jin.

"Jin, how did we get here?" I will ask. Imagine all the paths our conversation could take if I simply asked him that. A stunning question it is. An open-ended question.

I refuse to apologize for any of my actions... or any of my posturing towards him... or any of my posturing towards you. I owe no apologies.

You have a curse. You have the curse of being a deity. But in this relationship, I am merely a disciple of you. As your disciple, I wish I could help you lift your curse, but lifting your curse would make you a mere mortal, and clearly, you don't want that. Everyone you meet falls in love with you, and therefore your interactions with virtually everyone you meet will always be extreme, and as a result, a goddess of your caliber cannot have a normal relationship with anyone! The women will hate you for your beauty! The men will kill each other to get close to you! The old will be jealous of your youth! The young will be blinded by your kindness, intelligence, and experience! You have it *all*, you see!? You have it all, but you also have this CURSE! You even have my broken heart!

But life... even a life with a broken heart... is beautiful anyway isn't it?

Chapter 38 - Three in the Dark.

It is Thursday. Techna has a fashion show. Tonight, she is not
showcasing her designs, but modeling for a friend. Inari and I
decide that we're going to go in support of her. I show up at Jin's
apartment and for whatever reason Inari has, once again, not
communicated to Jin that I'm arriving. Jin is surprised to receive a
call from me requesting entry into his building. It takes him several
minutes to come down and let me in. As I wait for him to come
down, I imagine the two of them exchanging dirty looks and dirty
words with each other regarding the uninvited guest at the door.

Finally, he comes down, lets me in, and I go upstairs, expecting to
take Inari with me, who is, once again, going about her beauty
routines more slowly than I would like. Fashion shows are
generally shamefully short. If you don't show up on time, you
might as well not show up at all. It typically only takes about 15
minutes for the runway show to happen, although it is typically
followed by an hour or so of socialization.

Jin has decided to come along as well, so it would seem. I imagine
that there's no stopping him tonight. He doesn't show it, but I
sense that he is clearly not happy with my presence. He's clearly
not happy that I attempted to take Inari away from him once again.

The event takes place in the St. Paul, James J. Hill Library in
downtown St. Paul. The room is immaculate. We all gasp at the
beautiful architecture as we enter the building.

"Wow, look at this place, these ceilings must be 100ft high!" I
observe.

The walls are strewn with bookshelves connected by staircases and
ladders piled up 3 stories tall. The marble floors and pillars look
like they've been polished by an army of orphans armed with
toothbrushes. A series of solid oak, antique tables, are polished
with a sheen and shine, reflecting all the colorful books adorning
the walls and the antique light fixtures above.

We show up a few minutes late after rushing Inari out the door. We would have been later had we not had amazing luck and found a parking spot directly in front of the main entrance. We get in the door just as the first models are hitting the runway.

The fashion itself is exquisite, easily the best I've ever seen in person. It is full of elegant steampunk designs inspired by centuries-old antiquities with black and gold colors prominently decorated with leather, fringe, capes, and mechanical contraptions.

The show, as predicted, lasts only about 15 minutes. Afterward, we stand around in the library and socialize as teams of photographers get the various models in poses for single, double, and group shots.

Inari finds opportunities to break free from Jin, as he socializes around the room, pretending to be an important person with a fashion company. Having received cold vibes from Jin earlier, I try to play it cool and keep my distance from her, but she continues to follow me around. We both get distracted with pleasantries as various friends pop in and out of various unimportant conversations. If I separate from her, I make a point not to talk to her again unless she talks to me first. Jin observes our interactions from afar and he tolerates our interactions for a little while but seems to get increasingly bitter as she continues to follow me around the library. On one occasion, I pause to take a break, sitting in the 2nd row of wooden chairs along the runway. Jin and Inari walk by together. Jin sits in the front row, expecting his girlfriend to sit next to him, but Inari swerves around to join me in the back row behind him, sitting next to me. Jin scoffs and climbs over the chairs, grunting, clearly annoyed that Inari is drawn to me again. None of us openly address the dynamic happening between us, but I'm pretty sure we all feel it.

After the show, we decide to hit another Asian restaurant. It is a place I've never been to, but one of Jin and Inari's favorite places. Once in the restaurant, Inari and Jin act like a proper couple. This is in stark contrast to their dynamic the other night on Eat Street, where they were at each other's throats all night, seemingly hating each other, bickering over the menu. Tonight, however, they are content together. I don't think I've seen them this close in public. They talk about their future together as if they both intend for it to be long and prosperous. When the food arrives, Inari requests that Jin figure out the recipe so that he can make something similar for her at home. As the conversation continues and Inari and Jin interact like they're hand-in-glove, my mood grows sour… and sourer… and sourer.

I don't want to hang out with Inari and Jin. I just want to be with Inari. But here I am, listening to them talk about their future together, and with every word she says to him, my future with her feels more and more empty. She *should* understand this. Why doesn't she?

Inari confronts me about my mood, "Yuki, what's wrong?"

"I can't talk about it here," I reply.

"Why not, Yuki?" she presses. "What's so awful that you can't tell me about it?"

"I can tell you about it, but I just don't want to talk about it here in front of everyone else," I reply.

After, in my opinion, an unremarkable meal, I drive a small group back to Jin's apartment. By coincidence Techna's car is parked only a few blocks away as they were fitting models in a warehouse in the neighborhood, so Techna wants to retrieve her car from the warehouse near Jin's apartment and follow me back home as I drop them off, since she, being from out of town, isn't as familiar with the city as she'd like to be. I drive up to the door to Jin's apartment building to leave Jin and Inari for the night, with Techna's headlights in my rearview mirror.

Inari, all of a sudden, doesn't want to leave me. She searches for excuses to come with us, but Jin finds equally appealing excuses to keep her with him. She's concerned about my mood and wants to find out what is concerning me.

"Yuki, you seem sad. I don't want to leave you in this state," she offers.

"Well, you're welcome to stay out later with us, Techna and I will just be hanging out at home, I assume," I reply.

Jin interjects, "You need sleep. You haven't slept in 2 days."

"But I'm not really tired," she says.

"We were going to volunteer at the Haunted Basement tomorrow, if you don't get some sleep, you won't be able to volunteer," Jin offers.

"But Techna doesn't come to town very often, and I feel like I should spend time with her," Inari returns.

This continues for over 10 minutes; they must have made the same arguments repeatedly dozens of times as neither of them seemed to be able to convince the other to see things their way. Techna patiently waits in her car behind us. Inari and Jin go back and forth. But it is clear that Jin feels the need to keep a stubborn grip on his girlfriend tonight, and his stubbornness wins out. It is clear, at least to me, that he's concerned about how much time we spend alone together, but all of this is equally twisted in my mind after listening to them talk about their "future" together over dinner.

I decide to "tap out" of this battle. "It's okay, Inari," I say. "I'd love to have you over, but we can just hang out another time. If you feel like talking, you can always call me."

Inari leaves me and goes with Jin… reluctantly. She looks over her shoulder as she walks away. I drive the 20-minute drive home with Techna in tow. As we exit our respective vehicles, we say our first words to each other.

"What the hell were you doing back at Jin's? You sat there forever!" she immediately complains.

"Well... that... was just an example of how things are between Inari and me. At the end of every night, she's always trying to find a way to spend more time with me. It is fucked up, I know. I am mind-fucked by it every time it happens. It is like I'm a drug to her and she's a drug to me, and I just can't peel myself away from her, and she can't peel herself away from me. I don't know what I'm supposed to do."

"Well, I'm tired, I haven't slept much the last couple of nights. Do you mind if I just crash right away?" she asks, "I'm sorry, I'm not really feeling up for staying up late."

"It's okay," I reply, "I am expecting a call from Inari anyway. I'm sure she'll call."

At that instant, Inari calls. She demands to know why I was so upset at the restaurant.

I try to blow it off. "It is fine, I'm fine. I don't want to burden you with any complex emotions."

"No one gets as upset as you were without a good reason. Did you get your test results back? Were your tests clean?"

"Of course, they were!" I reply. "I wasn't ever concerned about that!"

"Then why did I see 'syphilis' in your search history as you were poking at your phone?" she presses.

I was unaware that she ever saw anything on my phone, so this conversation is now taking a strange turn.

"Well, that would probably just be because I was sitting outside the doctor's office waiting for my appointment time and decided to look up articles about whatever it was that I was about to be tested for. That's all."

"Is it herpes, then?" she asks.

"Did you get a copy of your test? Can you show me?"

"Actually, they told me that they don't send out copies of anything unless there's a positive test. 'No news is good news!' they said. Are you actually familiar with this process? I'm not sure how experienced you are in these things, because the experience wasn't at all how you told me it was going to be. I asked to be tested for herpes, and the doctor simply asked, 'Are you having an outbreak?', to which I replied, 'No'. Next, he said, 'Well we're not testing you for herpes then!' I asked him 'Why not?' and he said 'We can't test herpes without taking a sample of a legion, and even then, we can't really do much about it, there's no cure, so there's typically no point in doing that. We can test you for antibodies, but that doesn't tell us if you have herpes, because it only really tells us if you've ever come in contact with the virus at any point in the past, and basically everyone has. If you're alive, you have antibodies, it's just how it is.' He kinda had a tone with me that was sorta like, 'Hey dude, where are you getting your misinformation from?' and I felt kinda embarrassed asking."

"Well, that doctor doesn't know what he's talking about and you should find a new doctor," she protests.

"I went to Planned Parenthood for god sakes, I'm pretty sure they know what they're doing, it's like 70% of their business according to the nurse. You know they tell you statistics like that to reassure you and make you feel comfortable, like 'Hey this is a common thing to do, we do this all day long.'"

She backs off, "So no STDs then?"

"No, not at all."

"Then, what's wrong?" she demands.

I pause, "I don't want to burden you with my complex emotions; it isn't fair to you. Everything is fine."

"You can tell me anything, Yuki, you know this," she assures.

"Well... fine then. I was just upset because you and Jin seemed so happy together in the restaurant, and I just wished that I could be sitting in Jin's place. That's all. You know, you keep saying that you wish that Jin loved you the way I do... but what's so wrong with wishing that *I* loved you the way *I already* do? Because... I *already* love you, Inari. You have feelings for me! I know you do! You can't fear your feelings for me!

"Yeah, well you know Icarus right? They say don't fly too close to the sun... you'll burn your wings. The higher I fly, the harder I'll fall. It happens all the time. People only want me until they have me, then once they have me, they don't want me anymore."

"I don't think the laws of physics apply to metaphors, Inari. I love you Inari! I'm not going anywhere! I'M NEVER GOING TO LEAVE YOU! I'm sorry, but it is true that you break my heart every day... that's just what unrequited love feels like... it feels like getting dumped at the end of every day."

I continue, "You know, I've been looking for my old engagement ring. I've been looking for it for weeks, tearing up every corner of my house, every drawer. I finally found it. I wouldn't burden you with a proposal... you would never respect me if I did that. But... I thought... that I could give you this ring so that you would know... so that you would know *for sure*... that as long as you have it, I AM STILL WITH YOU... even if I'm not physically by your side at the moment. If I ever leave you, you see... I'd have to come and get it back. It is not something I would give away on a whim."

Inari begins to cry on the other end of the phone. "Yeah... well... I'm nothing special... just a girl."

"No, Inari, you're not just a girl. Maybe Jin thinks that way about you, but I... I definitely don't! You're NOT JUST A GIRL! You're the BEST! And you DESERVE THE BEST! You should never settle for anything less!"

I sense that my bombardment is weighing heavily on her. "I'm sorry... you need sleep. You haven't slept in two days. I didn't want to burden you with this stuff, but you asked. Just... get some sleep."

"I do need sleep," she concedes. "I wish I could stay up later, but I am fading fast."

I tire of the battle for the night. Despite the battle being hard-fought... things feel just as conflicted, unstable, and unsure as ever. I go to bed feeling like all is ruined. I didn't want to make her cry. I didn't want to burden her with my selfish emotional needs. I'm not fighting anymore tonight. Maybe I'll just sit back and let things cool down a bit... at least to the best of my abilities.

Chapter 39 - Buckets of Blood

Saturday arrives after a couple of days of silence from Inari. I sensed that my phone conversation with her Thursday night weighed on her heavily. She, for the first time ever, seemed to want to get away from me. She, for the first time, did *not* keep me up all night on the phone with her. Normally, I'd let her keep me up all night, with total disregard for time and my work schedule, because I was just happy to be talking to her *at all*. It didn't matter if it was the middle of the night. I would take her time whenever I could get it and I would hold onto it for as long as she would let me.

I felt terrible at the end of the conversation. I naturally assume that she'll seek to escape me. She'll disappear and ignore me... at least for a couple of days. I send her texts. I call. I leave voicemails. All are ignored.

But it is as expected.

The day of the "Zombie Pub Crawl" arrives. I had never been to the event in previous years. This year a friend from Hard Mondays scores us free passes. People who know what to expect from the ZPC don't recommend paying for them anyway. It is more fun to stay on the street and out of the bars where no special bracelets are required anyway. This year's crawl is expected to set a world record. Over 25,000 are expected to be in attendance.

I make plans to meet up with Maddox at his place on the far side of downtown Minneapolis. A group of us are gathering there to put on makeup and have decided that, since parking is going to be impossible anyway, we'll just walk from his house through downtown to find the crawl. I try to communicate my plans to Inari with hopes that she'll meet up with us, but I don't expect her to communicate back. She doesn't, so naturally, I do not expect to even see her *at all* on this night.

After loosening up with a drink, I acquire the guts to resort to "plan

B" and I send Jin a text. Jin answers and quite willingly relays their plans for the evening. I guide him to meet up with us at the Cabooze where we end up just hanging out in the street. No one in our group is terribly interested in hanging out in the overcrowded, stuffy bars, anyway. There are just too many people -- an annoying quantity of zombies. Being in the goth scene I expected zombie enthusiasts to be as polite as the legit dark siders I interact with every day… but these people aren't really enthusiasts of any sort. They are rude frat boys who, at best, shout catcalls from the windows of party busses and, at worst, demand that the hot zombie girls show their tits as if it is Mardi Gras or something. It is rather disgusting.

It is after 1AM when Inari and Jin arrive, but it is better late than never. Inari is one amazing-looking zombie. It is clear that she's put a ton of effort into her makeup, which is done up like a professional in a horror movie. She has a giant gash across her cleavage and her skin is pale like a true undead. Her eyes are meticulously covered in red to appear bloodshot. Despite the gore, she's absolutely stunning… amazing… beautiful. She's possibly the most beautiful I've ever seen her.

The gloom I felt the other night at the restaurant returns as Inari and Jin seem happy together. Jin role-plays as a photographer, playfully enticing Inari to pose like a model in various poses. Jokingly, he turns to me and says, "Sorry, excuse me if I'm getting a bit all worked up over here, haw haw!" as he grabs his erection through his pants while he continues to take pictures of his hot girlfriend, 2 feet in front of me. He's fucking mocking me… he is.

After taking a dozen or so snapshots, he asks me to take a picture of the two of them together. I politely agree. Jin and Inari pose together, and as she looks over at me, she mouths without speaking, "I'm sorry."

I sit on the pavement, feeling a bit gloomy from the scene. Jin decides that his friends need to be tended to, so Inari turns her attention to me. She sits on the pavement with me and I turn my body so that I am completely facing her.

Lucas comes by, he's a white-haired, well-groomed, goth man, that we're all familiar with. He kneels down with us and speaks directly to Inari… "Your boyfriend sure is singing your praises over there. He keeps telling everyone how much he loves you, how beautiful you are, and how sweet and kind you are."

"I don't believe that. He never says things like that to me," Inari says in return.

"Well, that's what he's saying right now over there... I thought you looked like you needed to hear that."

Inari brightens up. "Thank you, I did… thank you," she says.

My mood sinks into a deeper gloom. Inari clearly approves of his message.

"It is sad that he would say all of those things to his friends, but he won't say them to me," Inari says in sadness.

As we all decide to take the light rail across downtown to Maddox's place, Jin decides that he needs to run back to his car, several blocks away. As he is gone, the train arrives and the group lines up to board. The next thing I know, Inari slows her pace, ensuring that all of our friends board the train before us. And once we are the only two people remaining on the platform, she locks arms with me, making a 90-degree right turn, and by the time I realize what is even happening, we are walking off into the darkness, down a paved bike path. I look over my shoulder as Maddox and our friends look over at us. Their mouths are agape as if their eyes do not believe what they are affirming. Surely, there's something strange happening between us. It is surely true now.

We don't even say goodbye. It was as if we were in a hurry to slip away and escape before anyone could object, at exactly the right time when the train doors were closing.

"Uh, what's going to happen when Jin wonders where you are?" I say.

"Jin doesn't care about me. If he cares, he'll call me. He'll come find me."

"But we just kinda wandered off into the darkness, alone, don't you think he'll be worried," I ask.

"No, like I just said, Jin doesn't care about me. He doesn't give a fuck. He just wants to show me off to his friends, but he doesn't care if I'm safe or happy." She continues ranting about every complaint she has about Jin. "He is a kleptomaniac who gets a kick out of stealing things," she complains.

"I don't believe in stealing, that's wrong," I say, to contrast myself from him.

"I'm pretty sure he cheated on me with someone from his Japanese conversation group because he wouldn't even invite me out to dinner with them. He made up some excuse like he forgot to get me a reservation and there was limited seating or something," she complains. "I'm pretty sure he cheated on me when I was in New Jersey too."

"Being cheated on is the worst feeling in the world, I would never wish that upon you," I say.

"All he does is practice karate, and leaves me alone and bored in his apartment all night," she complains.

I simply play the role of a sycophant, "You deserve better, Inari. I don't know what you see in him. I question why, if he practices karate basically every day... why is he not a blackbelt yet? Is he actually studying Taekwondo when you think he is?"

"He's a liar. He made up that dumb story about how 3 guys tried to jump him but he kicked all their asses using his karate skills. He tried to say that the cops could have taken him in for assault with a deadly weapon since he knows Taekwondo, but I know he is full of shit, the cops were never there. Show me the police report, Jin! He's a fake, a fraud. That didn't happen. Jin is just obsessed with appearances. He is embarrassed to have me because I don't have a fancy degree or fancy job, but he just wants to make himself look cooler than he is… a fraud," she complains.

After hearing her repeat the same complaints repeatedly, over and over, I push the conversation darker. "I'm concerned," I state. An emotionless robot, as you say, is pretty much the definition of a psychopath or a sociopath. I'm concerned that he could be violent and turn on you."

She gives a very long pause as she looks over at me with sad eyes. "Well… there have been some incidents," she says. "One time I was playing around and he got mad and foot-swept me and I hit my head on the kitchen counter. He just left me there bleeding on the kitchen floor and didn't even check on me!" she confesses.

"My god, that's no good! You need to get away from him, Inari!" I stress, "If he is willing to do that, it is potentially just the beginning!"

She pauses, then continues, "Then there was another time… when he pulled my hair out of my head while we were in bed together…"

"You don't deserve this, Inari. I'm going to pull you away from this!"

Inari has decided she wants to go to the government center downtown where an out-of-state friend of hers, Ziggs, is participating in the "Occupy" protests, camping out on government property until winter comes and it becomes too cold to camp.

Without leaving Jin any information, we've walked a 3-mile walk up Cedar Ave, across the 35W freeway, up Washington Avenue, past the Metrodome, and through several blocks of downtown finding the protest, still going strong at 3AM.

She continues to recount many of the same complaints I've heard from her over and over in previous phone conversations. By now these stories are painfully familiar. And she again recounts some of the more painful episodes of her relationship like a record skipping on a record player.

I relay the sentiments that I always relay to her, almost like it is second nature for me to compliment her when she's feeling down. I try to convince her that her relationship is doomed. It is a ticking time bomb about to explode.

Jin eventually calls. I expect him to be angry. He *must* be angry, but he doesn't show it. I hear him speak politely on the phone while she uses her usual diversionary tactics to keep him away. They are the same tactics she used when she wanted to stay with me the night she had a migraine at my house before I confessed that I kissed her. They are the same tactics she employed when she wanted to stay at her house all week without showering, and when she wanted Jin to let the two of us attend the Ladytron concert alone. She grasps for every straw she can think of to keep him away. She tells him to take the light rail to Maddox's place where we will eventually meet him.

Jin counters her resistance by conceding defeat. "I think I'm just going to go home," he says. By playing this card, he's managed to get Inari worried.

"But Jin, are you sober enough to drive? You've been drinking, you shouldn't be driving. Take the light rail, you'll find us," she says.

"But I don't know where you are," he says.

Saying nothing, Inari abruptly passes the phone to me.

I am not expecting to talk to him, so I scramble to come up with a solution that keeps him happy, but keeps us together. I didn't really want to be completely *dishonest*... that wouldn't win Inari's heart. I thought about playing dumb and pretending I didn't know where we were or where we were going... but... since we don't want him to drive drunk... I tell him to take the light rail. "You'll see the protest from the train, I say. "When you see it... just get off."

Inari and I don't find the person we're looking for... her old friend, Ziggs. We circle the grounds several times... asking questions of the protesters who aren't sleeping. "Do you know Ziggs?" we ask. Some of the people we question give us vibes as if they are undercover FBI agents. The ones who we don't suspect to be FBI agents give us vibes as-if they think *we* are the undercover agents, asking nosy questions about their friends. No one admits to knowing Ziggs. Inari is disappointed.

Jin shows up and we meet him at the station immediately in front of the government center protest. I get us train tickets out of there to Maddox's house, but the next train isn't coming for another 45 minutes. We kill time by hanging out with a guy who I believe is the most double-agent-like of anyone on the site. He stands alone, isolated from the usual band of hippies that dot the site. He claims that he's a bit of an outsider to the other protesters because his agenda is purely political and partisan, representing the 3rd party political movement. I'm not so sure I buy his cover story, and I'm not so sure that Jin and Inari buy it either.

Jin admits to having a flask of vodka on him.

"What are you waiting for, let's break it out then!" he says.

Jin and Inari make no move to unveil the alcohol they've stashed on their persons. For all we know, he's just trying to get us to break a law that we know nothing about regarding alcohol on public grounds. They clearly decide not to trust him but remain polite.

We pass the time by joking and speculating about which protesters we think are legit, and which we think are government spies. The train is arriving in 10 minutes. Inari declares she wants to make one more attempt at finding her friend... one more stroll around the grounds. I am nervous about her request because I don't want to miss the train. At the last possible moment... Inari finds Ziggs just two minutes before the train is scheduled to arrive. They greet as if they were long-lost lovers finally encountering each other for the first time in a decade. She hugs him by the neck, then pulls her head away from him and gazes into his eyes with longing and passion. I don't know what to believe at this moment. Are Inari's spooky laser-beam eyes casting a spell on him? I think for a moment how I felt when she did this to me when we first met. Her eyes... they just feel cruel to me at this moment. Cruel. Cruel.

The image of Inari and Ziggs is forever, permanently burned into my brain, but I have no time to ponder and dwell upon what I just saw because suddenly I hear the train coming... two minutes early... Inari hears the train coming too but refuses to stop gazing at Ziggs until she's delayed us just long enough to miss the train's arrival. As we sprint, we all hope that the train will politely stay for two minutes, since after all, it is two minutes early. Unfortunately, the asshole train director allows the train to leave as fast as it comes, two minutes early, as we sprint to catch it. There are no more trains tonight, we have to walk.

We decide to hoof it back to my car... another 3 miles across downtown. Inari and Jin are both drunk.

I'm gloomy again... because my time alone with Inari has come to an end. I feel like I don't matter. Inari acts like she belongs to Jin, almost as if she's his property. She does this willingly and honestly, or so I think. I don't really have time to ponder about how I am shaken by her greeting of Ziggs, because as we walk, Inari and Jin practice acting, and I am drawn into their improv.

They begin to bicker as if he's Irish and she's Swedish. They act in flawless, over-the-top funny accents, but as they continue to bicker, their bickering becomes more and more about real subjects. And as 20 minutes of this pass, the subject of their bickering begins to become *very* serious.

They bicker about all the subjects that Inari has complained to me about in private and then some... sexual dysfunction... his obsession with appearances... his lack of emotional responsiveness to her... his finances... and even the incident where he bashed her head into the kitchen floor comes up, all without breaking character. Inari begins to breathe more heavily as her character becomes more and more agitated and she becomes increasingly winded from the long walk through downtown in her clunky platform boots. Their wit in their improv is far greater than my wit as a writer, unfortunately, and I wish I had a complete transcript of their performance.

With about a quarter-mile to go, we come to the top of an overpass... where highway 55 crosses interstate 94. Inari and Jin's arguing is ceaseless and has now persisted during the last 2 miles of walking.

Jin deflects her verbal assaults while maintaining his character occasionally turning to me, "Ya see what I'm dealing with here, lad? Tha' woman's crazy!"

"You don' lov' me an' ya' don' lov' anybody! You!... You are a liar ... an' a thief!" she says.

"If ya hate me so much, why don't cha just push me down this hill then, lass?" Jin says.

Somehow, I knew she would. She begins flailing her arms at him angrily and violently like she's fighting a high-school girl-on-girl catfight. She pushes... then, she pushes more... angrily, more and more. Then, the next thing I know... they're tumbling down the steep side of the hill that was built up to support the overpass, together... rolling end-over-end. It was almost like a cartoon fight where the animators just draw a swirl of arms and feet protruding through a cloud of smoke. They roll and roll... down the hill... until they find the concrete at the bottom.

Inari sits up from the concrete. Now out of character and angry, she lets out a loud screech. She decks Jin in the face... three times.

I stand at the top of the hill... stunned... observing the events... not believing my own eyes.

Jin holds both of her wrists to stop her from continuing to punch him. "Yuki, help! Get her off me! I don't want to hurt her!"

I snap into reality. I run down the hill and pull them away from each other.

Inari stands up and begins stomping her clunky boots to the top of the hill... "YOU! YOU FUCKING MONSTER! YOU'RE A FUCKING MONSTER IS WHAT YOU ARE!"

"WHAT'S WRONG WITH YOU! IT WAS A GAME!" Jin declares.

"YOU BASHED MY HEAD INTO THE PAVEMENT!"

"You pushed me down a FUCKING HILL! YOU'RE DRUNK!"

"SO ARE YOU! IS THAT YOUR EXCUSE? DO YOU THINK IT IS OKAY TO BEAT UP YOUR GIRLFRIEND JUST AS LONG AS YOU'RE DRUNK?"

"YOU PUNCHED ME!" Jin complains.

"YOU THREW ME DOWN A HILL!" Inari snaps back.

"YOU PULLED ME DOWN THE HILL!" Jin snaps back.

"Oh really, my 110-pound self pulled your wimpy 200lb ass down a hill. That doesn't even make any sense! I *soooo* want to punch you right now," Inari growls.

I gently hold Inari from behind, bear-hugging her. I hope that by being calm and affectionate I can convince her to remain calm.

Jin is irate and eggs her on, "Come on, then! Hit me! GO AHEAD AND HIT ME! I'm *begging* you to hit me. Let's solve this with violence! Please. Come on. Let's do this. You hit me, and we're *done*. It's *over* between us. Go ahead and hit me. I WANT YOU to hit me!"

I hold tighter onto both of her arms. Inari does not hit Jin.

Instead, she spins away from me and stumbles across the 8-lane highway until she finds the dark parking lot of the Dunwoody Institute on the other side.

"YOU'RE A FUCKING MONNNSTER!" she cries as she runs away. Two police cars pass but seem uninterested in the drama unfolding in front of them.

"I'M JUST THE GUY WHO'S IN LOVE WITH YOU!" he says.

He begins to cross the street after her.

"Hang back, Jin," I command. I chase after Inari.

"Get him away from me! Please keep him away from me! I don't want to see him! I can't see him! Please! Get him away from me! I don't want to be anywhere near him! Please help me! Please help me!" she cries… over and over. She collapses into a ball on the asphalt. The parking lot is lit only by a few distant streetlights.

"Jin is across the street. He's nowhere near us, okay?" I assure her.

I console her the best I can, trying to take care of her. She is hysterical and doesn't seem to even hear the basic commands I give her. My words don't even seem to reach her. I find myself repeating the simplest commands. Very simple commands... calmly, politely.

"Can you sit up for me?" I ask her.

She continues to blabber nonsense... "please father, forgive me..." she repeats over and over... praying to God over and over.

"Can you sit up for me?" I ask her again. "Inari, I need you to sit up for me okay? We're almost to my car, but I need you to sit up for me."

"It hurts, it hurts, it hurts!" she cries.

"What hurts?" I ask.

"My head hurts! Please help me! Please forgive me..." she continues to pray.

"I need you to sit up for me so I can look at your head," I repeat. I repeat it at least 20 times before I am able to sit her up.

Finally, I examine her head in the dark... I cannot see very well... but it is clear that her head is wet with blood from what I can tell.

"We need to get to where there's some light so I can get a better look at you. I need you to stand up for me. Can you stand up for me?" I ask.

She continues to scream and pray and mumble incoherent words... or possibly Japanese words... regardless I simply cannot understand them. I have to repeat the request again another 20 times.

"Can you stand up for me please?"

"Can you stand up for me please?"

"Can you stand up for me please?"

"Can you stand up for me please?"

"Can you stand up for me please?"

On and on and on. When one command does not work, I ask another command 20 times to no avail, trying various words and phrasing to get her to get off her knees and stand up. We've now been in this vacant parking lot for about 20-30 minutes. Eventually, I get her to stand. I carry at least 30% of her weight on my shoulder for the last quarter mile. She wants Jin nowhere near her. She is confused about where she is.

"I DON'T KNOW WHERE WE ARE! THIS DOESN'T LOOK FAMILIAR!" she panics.

"It's okay, girl, I know where we are. I'll get you to where we need to go."

I continue to talk to her… calmly pointing out our destination. "You see… there's my car up there… we're almost there."

"I don't know where we are. Please, I don't know where we are," she panics.

"It's okay, you see my car over there? It's just 40 feet away. Just 40 feet and then you're safe, okay? You remember this house, right? This is Maddox's house."

By a stroke of luck, our friend, Fiera, happens to be leaving Maddox's place as we arrive. I walk with Inari over to her.

"Take Jin to his car," I demand. "Go talk to him and tell him you'll take him to his car. He'll understand," I command Fiera.

Inari gets more excited, "Jin is here!? No! Get me away from him! Get me away from him!" she cries.

I elect to not say goodbye to Jin. I fear that any verbal communication I have with Jin will send Inari into a complete meltdown (as if that isn't what is already happening).

Inari doesn't want to go into Maddox's place. She fears facing the people inside... she doesn't want to go home and face Barry and her grandparents... she suggests Echo's place, but I know that Echo will be sleeping at this hour. We go to my place... I offer her Ada's company... and the company of Ada, we agree, will be the best thing to potentially cheer her up. At the same time, I worry that by keeping her from her friends in Maddox's house, I also helped her sweep the incident under the rug. If I brought her inside, she might have more support, and I worry that she will forgive Jin, and let him continue to hurt her. Did she push him down the hill, or did he pull her down the hill? As Inari's disciple and sycophant, the story I always tell is the story that she wants me to tell. What did I really see?

I start my car. I turn on my headlights. She panics. She doesn't want the headlights to illuminate Jin as we drive by... "I DON'T WANT TO SEE HIM! I DON'T WANT TO SEE HIM!" she screams.

I turn them off... but then point out to her that Fiera's car has already left... "You see? That's her car, turning left up ahead." I wait a couple of seconds, then I turn my headlights on and drive.

When we get to my place, things are a bit calmer. Ada helps. Ada is always happy to see her. I take a video of the giant gash in her head under the bright lights of my upstairs bathroom. It is a huge bump, split open in the middle. It reminds me of a crack in an oversized grape. It is wet, and juicy... but not gushing blood. Inari doesn't bleed like most people.

We stay up for a while. I talk with her about abusive relationships, and I beg her not to return to an abusive relationship. She has a history of abusive relationships. On the surface, it would appear that the cause of her injuries was the result of her hitting and pushing him, but I would never accept Jin's version of events.

"Jin is a 12-year student of martial arts, he should have been skilled enough to not let any of this happen," Inari explains. "The fact that he called upon you to pull me off him at the bottom of the hill was just showboating on his part," she says. "He should have known all kinds of non-lethal takedowns which he could employ to restrain me. He was just trying to make it look like I was the aggressor. I didn't push him down the hill, he pulled me and now I'm completely broken!"

"Please, just don't become a statistic. Don't go running back to someone who abuses you," I beg.

"All relationships are physically abusive," she says.

My mouth becomes agape. It practically drops off my head. "No! Inari... THIS is NOT normal. Most relationships are NOT physically abusive at all... I've never had an abusive relationship in my life. I was threatened with a knife once... but no one has ever put a finger on me... and I've never put a finger on anyone."

"That's not fair," she says.

"What's not fair?" I ask.

"That you were chased with a knife, she should have at least made it a fair fight," she says.

I ponder the darkness of her statement. It is as if she is declaring to me that being chased by a knife would have been okay, had I also been armed with the same. It was as if she craved the chaos in her relationship, and sought to cultivate it.

Inari succeeds at changing the subject. I suspect it is so that she wouldn't have to hear any more lectures from me telling her not to crawl back to him. She keeps drinking. I hesitate to let her, but, on this night, I don't stop her. She probably needs a drink right now, especially after this night. "This is mixed 'for me'," she says in reference to the stiffness of her drink. After a while, she passes out on the floor of my loft. Ada and I sleep next to her, keeping her safe and warm.

Noon rolls around... I'm awake early, *hours* before Inari. I never sleep much... the dog makes sure of it. Jin calls Inari first. When she doesn't answer, he calls me.

I'd been meaning to have a man-to-man talk with him about the nature of my relationship with Inari and we take the time to have that talk *now*. I suppose I could have just scolded him, "how dare you throw Inari down a hill!?" but I did not.

Things are serious, and I feel like part of the reason they fought was due to my presence in her life. I opt to just come completely clean with Jin and try to understand the dynamic that has clearly been building in the air.

Jin acknowledges that he *does* feel jealousy when Inari and I spend too much time together. I ask him about specific incidents... including the night of the Ladytron concert. Specifically, I ask him whether it affected him negatively that Inari had made plans to go to the concert alone with me and then fought tooth and nail to keep him away from going with us. I ask him about his "double take" when he observed us sitting abnormally close together in the bar afterwards.

Jin acknowledges that all those things had been affecting him negatively.

"Has she told you why she befriended you?" he asks.

"Yes," I reply.

"And you believe her?" he asks.

"I do… because I met someone once in much the same way who told me the same thing," I confirm.

"I didn't believe her at first. But then I started reading about it. And I guess there are people like her out there… a lot of them," he offers.

"Well, I called her out that night after the concert, you must know. Even though I am totally confused by her actions towards me all the time… I haven't been *entirely* plotting to overthrow you as her boyfriend. When I told you to get food the other night at the bar, when we were sitting too close, after you left, I called her out, *right then… on the spot… I called her out.* I told her that I got vibes from you that we were sitting too close, and it was putting you off… then I excused myself from the bar and left the two of you alone when you returned from ordering food."

"Yeah, I don't know why, but she seems to be completely unable to read me. She seems completely unaware that the things she does affect me."

"Yes, well… I find that she's right in reading me… *most* of the time. But when she's wrong, which, to her credit, is rare, she is so convinced that she's right, that you can't convince her otherwise."

"Yes, I've found that to be the case," Jin concurs.

Eventually, I concede and concur with Jin: My relationship with Inari does harm to them and contributes to their dysfunction and strife.

"I have to admit that I am really confused by her actions towards me. She says one thing, but then acts another… and if she just wants to be friends, I can accept that, but I need to know what her intentions are *for sure*."

"Well, does she indicate that her intentions are anything but?" he asks.

"Well... not verbally. Believe me, we've had the 'just friends' conversation at least a dozen times... but then she throws me these wild curveballs... these wild signals that just completely fuck with my brain..."

"Like what."

"Well Jin, I asked Inari how she defined 'cheating' and she said, 'kissing or more.' This seems like a pretty basic, well-accepted definition, do you agree?"

"That's how I would define it, yes," he concurs.

"But, Jin, some people are okay with their partners engaging in physical activity, just as long as their partners remain emotionally committed to them. There isn't just one universally accepted definition of cheating," I add.

"Okay, but you haven't been physical?" Jin seeks to confirm.

"No, we don't have a physical relationship. But what we have is the opposite, a completely emotionally inappropriate relationship."

"I'm not really sure what you mean," Jin says.

I hesitate to go too deep. I have lots of stories I could tell him... lots of damning stories... some that would surely break them up for good. My desire to be honest battles with my conscience. Being honest with Jin probably is not the right thing to do. I'm not sure I make the right decision when I begin to confess one of the most damning accounts of our time together, but certainly not the *most* damning episode of our relationship.

"Well... there was this one time... Jin. You remember the night just a couple of nights after she confessed to you that she kissed me when she was blackout drunk?"

"Yes," Jin replies.

"Well… that night… she decided to berate me in front of you… and I said 'that's my cue' and began to leave, remember?" I continue.

"Yes, I remember quite well,"

"Well… that night we went out into the hall. My only intention with being there that night was to spell out *very clearly* how our friendship was going to look going forward. You see, when Inari and I are alone, we are very different than you'd expect. If you saw the two of us alone together, you'd surely be disturbed by it. That night, once we were alone in the hall, we sat on the couch, and the instant I sat down, she got all cuddly with me."

"Okay…" Jin says… seeming a bit choked up on the other end of the phone.

"But I stopped her. I said, 'No Inari, we need to remain 12 inches from each other at all times…because if you let me get any closer to you, I will always…*always*… want more from you… and I will always interpret our relationship as 'more than friends'," I admit to Jin.

"Okay… good," Jin replies, feeling a little bit better, probably feeling relieved that I did what was right.

"But, that lasted for about 45 minutes. *Only 45 minutes!* After a while, I sat on the floor in front of her. I had my arms out in front of me. Then, she crawled her fingers up my wrist… and *she* took *my* hand, and at that moment, I couldn't resist her anymore, so I *held* her hand… *proudly*… then, I gazed into her eyes for what must have been two hours and said absolutely *every romantic thing* that I could possibly dream of saying to her until she eventually fell asleep."

"Okay..." Jin says again... now definitely choked up.

"Then I woke her up and brought her back into your apartment. But I left that night *far, far, far* more confused than I was when I arrived. Do you get it now? And Jin, I have *lots* of stories just like this one, and that's probably not the worst."

I continue, "Look, she's a good girl. She's a good person. She's a great person. And I know she has no intention of hurting me or you. And I know that she loves you. If she were in love with me instead, there would be nothing stopping us from being completely together... but we're not together. There's no kissing or sex or anything... just this incredibly intense, deep, emotional connection. Inari seeks emotional satisfaction from me that she lacks in her relationship with you. I'm sure you've heard her give her speech about the 'three pillars of a relationship'. They are 'physical', 'mental', and 'emotional'. She's missing one of them from you, and she's seeking it elsewhere, Jin. So, if you define cheating as a purely physical act, you're missing part of the big picture."

Jin continues to listen as I speak, "Inari, being an empath, senses how I feel. And I, admittedly, feel very much for her. She knows that she makes me so very happy. She makes me so happy that she is intoxicated by the happiness that she brings to me. My own happiness feeds back onto her, creating this feedback loop that just seems unstoppable. I really don't know what to do about it, but I probably shouldn't allow myself to get caught in this net and I should work on disciplining myself so that I don't end up holding her hands and professing my love to her again."

Jin becomes firmer as if scolding, "Yes, yes, you should."

"You have to understand that one of the reasons I have not cultivated our friendship as much as I could is because I don't want to hurt a friend, and since I have a deep emotional connection with Inari, I care *far more* about her than I *ever care about you*! So if you continue to hurt her, it just makes me not really care very much about whether whatever I'm doing is potentially hurting you, and all of that is easier if we are *not* good friends. So, Jin, if Inari continues to seek things from me, I will give them to her. I WILL CONTINUE TO BE YOUR RIVAL. Positive emotions, such as love, are equally as difficult for me to control as anger is for other people. If Inari seeks some form of love from me, I will obediently provide it… always. You could be the greatest guy in the world, and I still probably wouldn't give a fuck."

Jin should now know that if he wants to keep Inari, he will have to fight her away from me... he changes his verbal posture with me at this point... subtle... but noticeable. I am still polite... he is still polite...

We get back to the situation at hand: Jin's girlfriend is sleeping in my house; bleeding on my floor.

"I don't know if she'll want to see you when she wakes up. I don't know when she will wake up. But I guess from what I gathered from her attitude last night, you should probably expect me to come over and pick up some of her essentials for her. Who knows… maybe you'll see her later…? I dunno… we'll know when she wakes up."

Inari eventually wakes up, and I tell her I am planning to pick up her essentials from Jin's apartment. She agrees that it is best that I go alone, but she insists on riding along. I am hesitant to let her ride along because I fear that, if she rides along, she'll want to go in, and, if she goes in, she won't leave.

And… that's exactly what happens... Inari enters Jin's apartment… I agree to let them chat alone for a few minutes… and a few minutes later, Jin comes out to the couch by the vending machines and tells me that she's decided to stay. Jin takes over nursing her wounds. I think it is very wrong to allow Jin to nurse the wound of the girl he just beat up, but I can't stop it.

I tell him I'll go in and say my "goodbyes" and be on my way.

I enter his apartment to find Inari on the floor, lying on her back. She wants a hug. I hug her against the floor. Then, I pull away from her slightly to look into her eyes as I say goodbye. As I look at her, she takes my hand. "Thank you for everything," she says. I feel Jin's agitation as he paces behind me... it is as if his eyes are about to burn a hole in my skull which increases in intensity as I hold his girlfriend's hand for 20 seconds or more.

"If you need anything, I'm just a phone call away," I declare.

"Thank you for everything," she says again.

Before this day, Jin might have thought nothing of me holding his girlfriend's hand as I said goodbye to her. But now, these things mean different things to him. He has now tasted deceit. He's been deceived by us... I've cheated him. Inari has cheated him. In the end, though, I'll be the scapegoat... and with all that said... I'll probably need a new best friend...

So, after I arrive home, I send Inari a text message:

I think that once you're done talking to Jin about this stuff... things will be different. I went out on a limb and talked on the phone with him for 2 hours this morning... and in doing so... I also destroyed what you and I have. Jin is definitely NOT going to be okay with you and I having alone time together anymore. It saddens me deeply... but ultimately... I hope I did something ultimately good for you... as anyone who loves someone would do.

"But I think you need to call me later... not 'if you want'. You NEED to... even if you think you're just fine."

As I write this... I have not heard a word from her. I worry about her all the time... she can't stop me from worrying... I've worried about her since I met her. I wait, eagerly, for word that she's alright and doing fine and safe.

Who knows what happened after I left? Who knows? Maybe their fighting only escalated after I left. I put serious shit on the table. I felt uneasy about leaving her alone, particularly because I hadn't yet revealed to her the extent of my conversation with Jin. I played a bad game of cards today. A bad game.

Please, Inari, be safe.

Futile battle upon futile battle... I can only influence Inari's decisions... I cannot make them for her. Maybe the best influence I can be on her is to just leave her be. She will make her own decisions. I just hope that I can convince her that *I* am a good decision.

Chapter 40 - Act IV - Loyalty

I feel awful for leaving Inari with Jin on Sunday afternoon and awful for being too honest with Jin. I should have just scolded him as Inari would probably have wanted, "How dare you throw Inari down a hill!" I should have said.

I should have physically prevented her from staying. I should have pulled her by the arm and pulled her away against her will. I had no way of knowing what was going to happen after I left. Maybe their arguing escalated, and they continued to physically brawl with each other. I worry about her, and now that she is no longer with me, I cannot do anything but worry and wait.

Inari returns to her usual routine of ignoring me and leaving me completely in the dark. A couple of days pass before I hear anything. Upon receiving her first call, I feel immediately compelled to reveal the details of my man-to-man talk with Jin. Inari deserves to know everything I said to him and deserves to understand what I said to him and why.

By the time she calls, she's already diligently read Chapter 39. I confront her about whether Jin has been privy to reading the messages and chapters I'd been sending her.

"Are you insane?" she responds. "Do you really think I would let Jin read *any* of that stuff? It is possible that he is aware that some writing exists, but there's no way in hell I would let him read any of it… unless… maybe he's been reading my email."

"I wouldn't worry too much about it," I say. "I quizzed him on some of the details and he seemed to be completely in the dark and unaware of some of the most major events I've written about…. So maybe he only *thinks* he has the full story… I'm pretty sure he doesn't."

"Well, I should probably change my email password anyway. I'm generally not someone to hide anything from anyone. Jin basically has all my passwords. But I just have to tell you that what you said to Jin was *very shitty*."

"Yeah, I know it was," I admit. "I regret a lot of the moves I made. But the biggest misstep I made was in allowing you to ride with me back to his apartment."

"I'm fine," Inari declares, "but in any other scenario, yes, it would be best to keep someone separated after a fight. You don't know what might happen. But either way, any attempts to interfere with a relationship, especially if you think that it might be abusive, are potentially dangerous. You should just stay out of it, you could make things worse, and what you said to Jin was really shitty."

"I know, I know," I say. "I don't know what came over me. I was honest with him, but maybe too honest. I dropped some bombs on him that he wasn't expecting, and frankly, *I wasn't expecting to hear come out my own mouth*, and those bombs could have hurt you pretty badly. I don't know why I said some of the things I said. I frankly wasn't your staunch ally. At the time you were in my custody though, and I thought you were safe, but obviously not safe forever. I worry about you constantly. I should have just said, 'How dare you throw Inari down a hill!' or something like that."

Inari is still sore from her injuries. Yet she is still determined to volunteer at the Haunted Basement. Wednesday, I leave work early in the afternoon and drive across town for the sole purpose of giving her a ride from Jin's apartment to the site.

My experience with painful injuries is limited. But I find that pain from most of the more serious injuries I sustained in my lifetime would subside after 3-4 days. The worst pains would subside in a week or so… rarely did the pain last longer unless permanent damage was involved, like a broken bone, or when I messed up my knees in a sledding accident as a child. For Inari to be in as much pain as she is, 4 days after falling down a hill, must mean that her injuries are pretty severe.

She tells me that upon taking her first shower following the incident, she found herself to be covered in more bruises than she realized… all up and down her body. Through the course of the conversation, it is revealed that she is still extremely unhappy with Jin, now more than ever. I originally figured she had given him a free pass by coming back to him… but is clear that Jin is not using this opportunity to mend his relationship with Inari. The rift in between them grows, yet Inari is still determined to make the relationship work… somehow.

"Eventually he admitted and apologized for pulling me down the hill, and normally I can forgive anyone for anything as long as they show remorse… but I'm not so sure Jin actually feels any remorse for what he did," she says. "He doesn't know that I know this, but I heard a story from someone who was at the Cabooze earlier that night. Apparently, he got up in some guy's face who was giving him shit and was all boasting about how the guy couldn't push him over. 'I've been studying martial arts for 12 years, you can't push me over,' he said. 'Go ahead and try… you can't do it!' Heh… maybe that guy couldn't push him over, but his 110lb girlfriend can, I suppose."

I am disgusted by the story she tells. I hate it when men get all up in each other's faces. It is one of the many reasons I try to distance myself from my borne gender.

I have a story to tell her as well. After the events of the weekend, I bumped into Lucas in the club. Lucas told me that the reason he kneeled to talk to her that night was that Jin was acting like a huge douche in front of everyone. Jin was not actually "singing [her] praises" as he said. Lucas was specifically lying to make her feel better.

Apparently, Jin was boasting to the group about how he treated his girlfriend like shit. "Look at me," he boasted. "I'm an emotionally distant asshole, like my father, yet for some reason, I have this amazing, beautiful, sweet girlfriend. I don't even tell her she's beautiful. I don't tell her I appreciate her, but I have her anyway."

Lucas was so shocked by Jin's words that he felt immediately compelled to try and cheer Inari up who was looking a bit down as she sat on the pavement next to me. "Your boyfriend is singing your praises over there," he said. "He's telling everyone how beautiful you are and how much he loves you," he said.

"I don't believe it," Inari said. "He never says things like that to me," she said.

This past weekend… was a huge clusterfuck. It was another incident in a long line of incidents that now cause Inari to obsessively second-guess her relationship with Jin. She spends much time dwelling upon it during the week and it is basically all we talk about on the phone until, eventually, she just can't bear to talk about it anymore.

"You need to offer me something more than relationship talk," she says.

I take her mission to task. I spend some time making a list. I call it "Yuki and Inari's Spontaneous List" and I email it to her.

It is a list of things that we can pick up and do when we're feeling spontaneous. Inari needs to be spontaneous. Her sleeping issues require it. Plans are incredibly burdensome to her. But really, spontaneity works for me. I'm not a guy who makes plans for much of anything. I like to live in the moment and just do whatever I feel like doing at any given time.

Yuki and Inari's "Spontaneous" List (a work in progress)

1. Dog park adventures
2. Purty Hairz
3. Sewing (I want to learn, and you should teach me)
4. Go to the zoo
5. Go to the humane society
6. Volunteer at the humane society
7. Foster dogs

8. *Tour all the museums in town*
9. *Nature walking*
10. *Photography*
11. *Biking*
12. *Video projects*
13. *Art projects*
14. *Video Game projects*
15. *Video Game playing*
16. *Musical projects that are not depressing*
17. *Cooking*
18. *Juicing*
19. *Party planning*
20. *Fine dining*
21. *Bargain Shopping*
22. *Spontaneous Travelling*
- *Chicago*
- *Duluth*
- *Milwaukee*
- *Black Hills*
- *Bear country*
23. *Camping*
24. *Canoeing*
25. *Costume planning*

Upon receiving my list of 25 spontaneous things to do... she calls me up Thursday afternoon, just before she is scheduled to work at the haunted house. "Your list made me *very* happy," she says with a playful giggle.

And I am pleased that she thinks this way. I want us to start building happy memories together. I offer her a ride to the haunted house, but she says that Jin is getting off work early and is giving her a ride. She's not so sure she will be able to work with her injuries... particularly if they make her wear a mask. The masks tend to rub against her head wound, causing unbearable pain. Jin has offered to take over for her if she gets stuck in a role that she cannot finish.

Later that night, Inari calls me at 2AM. She is crying. She begged Jin to come and pick up her shift at the Haunted Basement. He showed up, but then he just stood around and talked to his friends all night.

"It was horrible," she cries. "They made me wear a mask, and I had to crawl around on my hands and knees and jump up and down off of crates and boxes. He said he would be there for me... but he wasn't! He just stood around all night talking to his friends and just whined and complained about having to be there all night. He treated me like shit! He was out to dinner with his Japanese conversation group, *again*, and was all pissy that I interrupted his evening... even though he *said* he would be there for me!"

I'd been napping... I've got a few hours of sleep in me. I decide that I'll come over and pick her up. We'll find some late-night food. I will do my best to cheer her up and keep the subject to happy things.

I buy her some pancakes. I try to keep the conversation positive... keeping in mind that she told me that I should offer her "more than relationship talk". But it is not *me* who keeps the conversation to relationships... Inari won't stop complaining about Jin all night.

I comply with her topic choice after she clearly chooses to fixate on it. I play along, offering my two cents. Obviously, I don't want Inari and Jin to stay together. But I am never totally militant in my agenda.

"Well, Inari," I contribute, "I told Techna about how I told Jin, point-blank, that our relationship was emotionally inappropriate, and that I was going to continue to be his 'rival' and was not going to stop chasing you. Then I told her that, for some reason, Jin was still okay with you and me spending time alone together. Techna's response to this was without hesitation. She said, 'He must be cheating on her then.'"

"My god, you're right," Inari says. "She's right."

Her mind starts to race, recalling little clues that might suggest that he is, in fact, cheating on her. She has me look up a webpage for "Nonspecific Urethritis", which Jin had come down with a few months earlier and neglected to inform her of up front. The webpage prominently suggests that it is transmitted through sex.

She points out that she found condoms next to his bed, but they don't use condoms because she has an IUD. She also found some little bear in his car that he says was given to him by someone in his conversation group... a little bear holding a heart. Jin claims that she gave them to everyone in the group... "It seems like an odd sort of thing to give the group," she says.

Then there are the nights that he has no consistent explanation for... including a night when he informed her that he was going out to dinner with his group, but "forgot to reserve her a spot". "It's one of those situations where there's limited seating. I didn't think about it, I'm sorry," he said.

"Usually when someone over-explains themselves without being solicited for an explanation, they're trying to hide something," I point out. "If he had just told you that he was going out to dinner tomorrow night and only explained the situation after you *asked* him if you could come along... that would be *normal*. But he chose to explain it all in one shot... that, to me, is suspicious. I was there when he said that to you... and I cocked my eyebrow at him when he said that stuff."

After gorging ourselves on a 3AM breakfast, we park my car outside Jin's apartment, recline the seats back, and talk until sunrise.

She paints versions of him that are not quite as gentlemanly as she painted long ago. She said in the past that one of his good qualities was his aversion to porn. But she makes no attempt at hiding his bad qualities now.

"He hides that he's looking at porn on his computer. Why does he have to give me a separate account? It is like he's ashamed of his internet search history and paranoid that I'm going to stumble onto an incriminating email. Why am I not good enough for him?"

"Well, you're way more beautiful than any girl I've ever seen in any porn video, I must say. I am a man, I've seen the stuff... it's never special, unfeeling, sometimes outright cruel, mechanical. There's no love in porn... so I don't like it," I reply, "but there's love in you. There's no substitute for that."

"Well Jin doesn't love me," she says.

I hate it when she says stuff like that -- when she takes the positive sentiments of love I bring her and merely complains that she's not getting those sentiments from Jin. It makes me feel like my love is worthless.

"Why does he have to look at pictures of other naked girls all the time? He's hiding something, I know it. Why am I not good enough! If he trusts me, then why won't he just give me his password? I have nothing to hide!"

If I were to compare myself to Jin, I would contrast that I've never bought a dirty magazine, nor a dirty video... Certainly, though the internet has many temptations. I'm not a saint, but I'm not nearly as sleazy as I would gauge your average man. I, after all, try to distance myself from my gender. When in a happy relationship, I really have no desire to look at such stuff. Certainly, since meeting Inari, even though our relationship is not sexual, I have absolutely *zero* desire to look at such nonsense.

"Why the hell would a guy ever choose to look at porn when he has *you*?" I ask her. "You're far, far more attractive than any girl who's ever been in a porn magazine or video. I've seen porn before, certainly; I am a *man*, after all. But there's a big difference between shitty porn and being in a beautiful relationship with a beautiful goddess like *you*."

"My attraction to you is a matter of *fact*, Inari. There's no room for opinion here. I should explain it to you from a logical perspective. I want you to believe for certain that I find you more attractive than anyone else on the planet. Seriously, you could put 1000 supermodels in a room and ask me to pick the most attractive one, and I'd pick you every time."

"No way," she says.

"No, I'm serious. I mean… if you put 1000 girls in a room, all of whom, by modern standards, would be considered 'attractive', I would pick you every time. Assuming that no one there is role-playing as someone they are not… in other words, I mean… they should all be being 'themselves'… they should be 'real people'… all in the same room… being themselves. If I met you in that room, I would pick you above every one of them, hands down."

"I still don't believe you," she says. "I'm just a girl."

I joke with her, but I'm serious. "No… let me explain the breakdown for you. Of these 1000 girls, 90% of them would be wearing unattractive footwear. I would be instantly turned off by any girl, no matter how stereotypically 'hot', she is if I met her while she was wearing her running shoes and sweat socks."

Inari laughs generously. "Oh my god, I hate those ugly short, smelly sweat socks!" Inari concurs.

"So that leaves 100 girls remaining. Of those 100 girls remaining, 90% of them would not have any individuality. They'd have nothing to say in their personal bio other than 'live life to the fullest' and no interests to cite other than the enjoyment of 'long walks' and 'camping'."

I continue, "So that leaves us with just 10 remaining. Of the remaining 10, none of them would have your personality. None of them would have your beautiful smile and your angelic aura that communicates true love. They could never convince me that they're not selfish and mean. They could never convince me that they truly care about others and could *never* possibly convince me that they care genuinely about *me*. So you see, Inari. You're the one. I've looked for you my whole life. I've looked long and hard, you see? There's just no comparison. I've never met anyone so amazing as you in my years on this earth, so it will be *impossible* for you to convince me that I'll ever meet a girl like you again in my lifetime. If you're not for me, then, I'm willing to concede right here, that no one is. There's just no way. It is statistically improbable... virtually impossible. If we end this, I will forfeit and live the rest of my life as if my dream girl will never be found. You see how rare you are to me? I mean... even if you told me you didn't want me, I'd have nowhere to go. Where would I go? You're the only one."

The conversation turns to lighter subjects, and for a while Inari pressures me to confess all the details of my fetishes and perversions, accepting them all with an open mind... even admitting that she thinks that my fetishes are "kinda' cool."

We roll around and laugh in the bucket seats of my car... subtly flirting with each other.

But, after a while, her attention dwells once again on her relationship with Jin. She worries about him cheating on her again.

"I wish you cared about me as much as you cared about Jin," I say.

"I do," she replies.

I roll my eyes at her and look away shaking my head. I'd never rolled my eyes at her before. "No... Inari... no... you *don't*."

"I do... but I'm in a relationship with Jin... and I need to see it through."

"I will do my best to respect your relationship with him, but just please understand that this is very hard for me."

We roll over on our sides... gazing over at each other from our respective seats in the car. She gazes at me deeply and I try to hold my gaze on her as long as I can. I slip and look away... but then return my gaze back at her and I gaze and gaze and gaze until *she* finally looks away. Once again, I wish I could just kiss her... but I know I cannot.

She begins to speak again. "Uhhgggh... what am I going to do? How do I fix this?"

"Fix what? Your relationship with Jin?"

"Yes!" she says.

"Wait... after all of this... despite all your complaints... you actually *want* to fix your relationship with Jin?" I ask, surprised.

"Yes," she says.

"Well, I've offered my opinions."

"What are your opinions? What opinions?" she asks.

"My opinion..." I pause. "My opinion is that it *doesn't matter*... I knew your relationship was doomed the day I met you and it is clear to me now that it is *more doomed now* than it *ever has been* before."

"I think it is okay to just go to him and tell him that you think it is not working. I bet that he would understand you 100% if you just said that."

"Nooooooo..." Inari cries. She pauses for a minute, thinking. "Okay... fine... here's the deal... If you can prove that Jin has been cheating on me or *has* cheated on me at any time in the past or *considered* cheating on me at *any time,* I will be done with him. If he cheats on me... we're done."

It is almost 9AM. I need to use the bathroom. She invites me inside Jin's apartment despite my offering to use the public facilities in the lobby of the building. She sits on the couch. I come out to say goodbye. She wants a big hug. I give her the hug she requests.

Then, I hold her hand. "Everything is going to be okay... you're going to be okay," I tell her.

I need to let the dog out before work... so I get in my car and rush across town in rush hour traffic. Inari calls me within minutes after I am on the road and inquires about what kind of software she could put on his computer to break his passwords. I offer to do some research when I get to work, but I don't have an immediate answer. Hacking and cracking isn't really my thing. We have a short discussion about how we might corner him, from hiring a private investigator to paying a cute girl to try and seduce him and report back his reactions.

After I let Ada out for a quick one and two, I immediately turn around and head into the office. I call Techna and talk about party stuff. She asks how things are going with Inari. I tell her the situation. Techna suggests that Inari suffers from "Stockholm Syndrome". I laugh at what is obviously a joke... but not *really* a joke...

"I think Inari probably has a fetish for masochism, and I may never be capable of fulfilling her masochistic urges," I say.

"I don't think she is a masochist," Techna replies.

"If I don't succeed in this mission to prove that Jin was unfaithful, this war will be over, you know. It will be completely futile for me to continue on with this," I add.

"Thank God, I'm getting really sick of her bullshit, Jin's bullshit, and frankly your bullshit," she says.

"Yeah, I know, I'm sorry. I'm learning to give up this fight."

Chapter 41 - Silent Intervention

My time apart from Inari is unbearable. I fully admit that I am completely obsessed with her. If I'm not with her, I'm writing to her, writing about her, or just dreaming of her. I spend most of my time writing… writing text, writing music. I take some time to write her a letter, but I don't have the guts to send it. Then I write Jin a letter. I don't have the guts to send it either. Then I write a letter to them *both*… but I don't have the guts to send it either. So just to be absolutely clear, none of these letters were ever actually sent! But I find it valuable to write my thoughts down and discover ideas of things I might say to each of them.

Jin,

What kind of a pussy are you? You have the most beautiful and sweet girlfriend on planet earth, and you can't tell her this? You can't tell her you love her? You can't tell her she's beautiful?

I am a nervous, insecure wreck of a man... and even I can do that. In fact... I told Inari she was beautiful the day I met her. She practically begged me with her eyes. "I don't hear enough of that," she replied.

I, being an insecure, unconfident man… am told by women all the fucking time that I need to be "confident". It drives me mad... I just want to be "me" and want "me" to be good enough… regardless of whether or not I am confident.

So Jin, if you're such a fucking confident hunk of a man who is supposed to command the respect of the most beautiful girl on planet earth... why the fuck are you too much of a pussy to tell her how fucking amazing and spectacular and special she is?

Why the fuck is it that Lucas has to come to Inari at the Zombie Crawl and tell Inari that you said you loved her?

I asked Lucas about it in private... wondering what the hell that was all about.

Lucas said that you were over there running your mouth about what an emotionally distant asshole you are, like your father... as if being an emotionally distant asshole has earned you the right to have such a beautiful, sweet woman like Inari. "Yeah, I don't ever tell her she's beautiful to her face," you said.

Upon hearing you run your mouth, Lucas went over and kneeled down with Inari and me as we were sitting in the road. "Your boyfriend is singing your praises over there," he said.

Inari replied, "I don't believe that... he never says nice things about me."

"No, he's over there talking about how beautiful and sweet you are and how much he loves you... and I just thought you needed to hear that," he said.

Inari thanked him... she seemed happy to hear it... but, of course, I feel like it is counterproductive.

Why Inari is chasing after you is beyond me... and if she continues to do so... I'm going to have to start dishing out some tough love.

Inari could have any of thousands of more-eligible, more worthy men in this city, and yet she chooses to waste her time on you. What kind of spell you've put on her is beyond me... what kind of potion you use to spike her Cheerios with in the morning is way fucking beyond me.

But you know... when I met Inari, I found it easier to open up to her than any other girl I've ever met in my life.

She is incredibly inviting, incredibly sweet, and cares about people, including you, including me, more than you or I or anyone else deserves.

Why you would choose to dump a girl like her... and why you would choose to bash her head into your kitchen counter... or pull her hair out while you're in bed together... or make up stories about getting mugged when you want to get away from her... or pull her down a hill resulting in a split-open skull and shitloads of bruises and scrapes (while you come up unhurt)... why you would do these things is beyond me.

Furthermore... why she would choose to stay in a situation like that is just as confusing as it is scary.

I have devoted many hours of my life to the simple task of telling Inari that she is beautiful, that I love her exactly how she is, that she deserves to be happy, that she deserves the best man on earth, that she is perfect the way she is. I have devoted hundreds of hours to this task... yet she remains hung up on your pathetic, pussy, ass.... and I feel like she doesn't even believe me when I say these things.

If you don't want this girl, I would take her from you in a heartbeat.

I told you the other day that I'm not changing my posture with your girlfriend... and I told you things seemed to have hurt you... but I hear from Inari that you somehow still "respect" me.

No, Jin, you're not supposed to respect the guy that fucks with your relationship with your girl. It is not normal. I mentioned this to a good female friend of mine and my friend immediately suggested that you must be cheating on Inari. That's how far off your emotional response was!

So, either you pussied out and didn't tell Inari how you really feel... or you really are the emotionless empty robot man that Inari suggests... and regardless of which of those two things are true... Inari shouldn't be attending to your ass... because Inari deserves #1. She shouldn't be cleaning your apartment while she's still recovering from her injuries from the weekend... she shouldn't be the slightest bit concerned about your happiness (when she suggested that she was concerned about your happiness on the phone to me the other night... I about exploded on her).

I keep my promises... and I promised Inari that I would protect her...and that I would never leave her... and I won't. No matter how drawn out and futile this battle becomes... I'm not leaving her as a friend or whatever the fuck our relationship becomes.

I'm going to be around, so you will have to deal with me. I've promised her that I will never leave her. And I intend to keep my promise.

Inari,

As I'm getting to know you better, I begin to see you have a masochistic side to you, and I may never be cruel enough to satisfy it.

Regardless, you deserve someone as legendary as you are. That person is not Jin... nor is it me.

But clearly, our friendship has been "more than" a typical friendship. I admitted this to Jin the other day but somehow, he came out of it unscathed emotionally.... or so he told you.

But I have come to realize that you can be dishonest about things... not just little things, and I believe that of the 3 of us... I am possibly, by far, the most honest among us. This is not to say that I'm calling you a "liar". I only say this to contrast my own honesty and openness compared to typical standards.

You see, my level of honesty here has been quite abnormal... almost inhuman. I've communicated to you not only every emotion I've felt in your presence but virtually every significant thought. Who else have you ever known to pen what is essentially an entire novel for the sole purpose of communicating with the girl he is in love with? In all honesty... I wish I didn't feel so compelled to write all of this. But, nevertheless, I write. I write, because I've never met anyone like you, and I don't believe I will ever meet anyone like you again. This is the most significant story of my life. This is the story that I wish to remember when I am 90 years old. These are the only moments that matter to me anymore.

You need to realize and understand that a girl like you should not have to settle for someone emotionally vacant. And you should realize that you have the capacity to make at least one man on this planet the happiest man in the universe... and that man should fully appreciate and realize that you are the best... not "second best" ... not "good enough" ... but "the best" ... "the best".

I am happy when we're together... I virtually never stop being happy. Even when I'm nursing your wounds, or you're telling me I'm an asshole... I'm still happy. You see, even if you're mad at me, you're still WITH me... and that makes me the happiest guy in the world. That is, until, at the end of the night, you crawl back to this man who couldn't care enough to tell you how beautiful you are... and couldn't feel enough to truly feel like he's sorry for injuring you.

You don't need to settle for second best... or 3rd best... or 4th best... you are fully capable of the best the world has to offer... and the men you're choosing and have chosen are far, far, far from the best.

Thousands of eligible bachelors would foam at the mouth to be with you Inari. You are fucking amazing... and I feel that the only reason you're unable to believe it is because certain bastards don't tell you that often enough or because maybe you seek out men who are going to hurt you.

So maybe I have only one role in your life. Maybe I'm just supposed to be the guy who sits on the sidelines cheering you on, "Go Inari! You're awesome! You can do it!"

Regardless, you know my feelings for you will never fade... even if

I start dating someone else... even if we see less of each other... even if Jin and you get married or some bullshit.

But the next time I see you, I'll have something to give you ... just a token of friendship... and if I ever leave you... you'll know that I will have to come and get it back from you. It is not the kind of thing that anyone passes around on a whim... so as long as you have it... you'll know that I am still part of your life and that I am keeping my promises to you. You'll know that at any moment when you are in peril... I'll always come to your rescue.

And if I decide to end this chase via the strength of my own will... I will, knowing myself all too well, make one last grand gesture, something appropriately big, something huge, something amazing... but I will make this gesture to you postured only as a friend... and when the gesture is done... I will walk away... and if you don't come with... it will be done... the chase will be over. I will be forced to conclude that after such a gesture, if you're not madly in love with me, then certainly, you never will be, because... well... you never wanted to be to begin with, right? I'll seek the strength to forgive and forget... and I'll seek hope in a new direction... and once I've found hope... I'll find new happiness.

Inari and Jin,

So... I think... it is my turn to intervene.

It is a bit unfair, given that there are two of you and only one of me.

And as I told Inari before, "You are not the person to help me; you are part of the problem." The same applies to me...

I am not the best person to help you guys... I am part of the problem.

I may have found myself completely blinded by Inari's brightness... but the shadow of this weekend has allowed me to see a few things a bit more clearly.

You two... Jin... Inari... have issues to work out. You either need to work them out... or you need to go separate ways. I know that neither of you seems to want to end your relationship... but at the same time I want to shake the both of you and scream, "What the fuck!?"

This entire time... I've felt like the asshole among the 3 of us. I've felt like the guy who came in and encroached on a relationship that he had no business sticking his nose into... I felt like the guy that stirred the pot of shit and made it stink 10 times more than it would have been if it had just been left alone.

Whereas it is clear that I've been a problem in this triangle, and whereas it is clear that I've played my role in all the scheming and manipulation that has occurred... right now... to me... it looks like I'm, by far, the most honest person among the 3 of us.

I've written a lot of shit here...

This is chapter 41... within chapter upon chapter of detail upon detail... I've been cut down for my interpretations of events of the past... but even if you take away my interpretations of events and are left with just the factual events... the events themselves tell a big, epic story.

In a rare display of backbone, I'm going to defend myself tooth-and-nail on a couple of points.

1. I didn't just stick my nose into your relationship, I was pulled in. I was pulled in with tact. Granted, when I was pulled in, I came willingly. But it comes to mind that maybe my involvement in your relationship was almost premeditated... planned. I imagine it almost as if one day Inari thought to herself "I'm going to find someone to pull in between Jin and me," found me, and did exactly that. I don't want to attack your character, Inari, this feels quite foreign for me to say, you know... but at the same time... I'm sick of being the pawn. I'm a human being, not a tool or a toy or a drug.

2. I feel like the harder Inari lashes out at me and the more adamantly she denies any wrongdoing... the more she is simply trying to cover up her own mistakes. The hardest she ever lashed out at me was the night I refer to as "Chapter 32". I was confused as fuck... you guys teamed up on me with a brutal assault on my character that night. But later, after I left, I thought to myself that it was all just a fucking game.

Inari, you were waiting for Jin to come home could chew me out in front of him... and in doing so... you put up a smokescreen... she got you, Jin, off her tail. She reassured you that she had no intention of cheating you... she solidified your relationship while using me as a pawn. It was all a show to make sure that Inari didn't look like a bad person. And one thing I've learned about you, Inari, is that whereas you want to "be" a good person. Even more so, you want to APPEAR to be a good person. Maybe that makes you are meant for each other. You're both obsessed over "appearances". The worst lashings I ever got from you, Inari, had nothing to do with anything I did or said to you, but rather... how I made you APPEAR to other people. I feel like half the reason you tell me to stay on the sidelines isn't that you have no feelings for me... it is because you don't want anyone else to SEE that you have feelings for me. You don't want to be seen as a cheat.

But back to that night... Inari was hanging all over you like a monkey... as if she needed to prove to you, Jin, in front of me that she wanted you. I thought at first that it was to make me jealous... to make me want to go away... I kinda felt like crying in those moments. When I finally decided to leave (the PDA was wearing on me), Inari lashed out at me, screaming at me... in front of you. But looking back... it wasn't to make me jealous and go away... it was to make sure that you, Jin, were going to still be around while at the same time making sure that... I... was going to be around.

At the end of the night... it was made quite clear that Inari wasn't going to let me go... she wasn't going to let me stop chasing her.

We were quite different together as soon as we went into the hall and were alone.

Chapter 32, I believe, was all for show, and, now that I think about it... I feel more manipulated than I ever have been in my life.

3. Jin. You haven't been honest. It seems pretty clear to me. You are a very calm, poised guy most of the time, but Inari brings up all kinds of questions regarding your honesty... and you've acted suspiciously in front of me on many occasions that make me believe that you are more of a liar than your politeness would suggest. When people lie, a common mistake they make is to "over-explain" things... and I've watched you do this to Inari in my presence. You can, for example, if you don't want to go to work tomorrow morning, call and tell them you're not feeling well. They'll probably accept your answer outright and let you stay home. Maybe they'll act all concerned and ask you how you're feeling... "Did you catch the flu bug that's been getting passed around?" But if you start to ramble into long descriptions of what your ailments are without anyone caring enough to ask, you give yourself away as lying.

Another telltale sign of a liar is irrational anger when painted into a corner. Humans tend to get angriest when they're confronted by their own mistakes and can't escape them. It is part of a fight-or-flight response. Self-preservation puts them into panic mode and they overreact. Then they do whatever they can to save themselves from a bad situation. When we run out of good explanations, we panic and fight our way out of the corner, or, we "crawl up the wall".

Whether or not Inari thinks you're cheating on her is one question, but it is clear that you have things to hide from her, and your explanations of events that hurt her deeply in the past are still inadequate to her... I personally know of quite a few unsolved mysteries: The mugging incident, the Con dumping, the random group dinner she wasn't invited to, your unannounced, unreported STD test that turned out to be a yeast infection, things she found in your apartment and your car...

Inari has been, at least, physically faithful to you... but if you're okay with me having an emotionally inappropriate relationship with your girlfriend then I question whether or not emotions and human relationships mean jack shit to you.

Inari. You have to stop with your "eye for an eye" attitude. I see you disrespect Jin all the time and I call you out on it... all the time. You have to not be bitter about the little things because they build up until they explode. The best course of action is to always raise concerns as they come... don't let them sit around and slowly come to a boil. Ultimately, Jin's nature is going to be Jin's nature... and you can't change that... nor can he change yours. If your respective natures are not compatible... cut the fucking cord loose now.

Furthermore, I know you have feelings for me... and you know that I have feelings for you because I've basically told you every hour I've known you. If you really had respect for me you'd realize that it is bullshit that you continue to have me wait on the sidelines while you go crawling back to Jin every time he hurts you. You must understand that this insults me and cuts me to the bone. Your weakness is making me strong though... because, I know, that to be with you, I have to be stronger than I have ever been. I know you're not truly weak. We only appear weak after we've been forced to be strong for too long. You've had a lot of bad shit happen in your life, and I have been doing absolutely everything I can do to be strong for you. But I can't just pull you by the arm and drag you away from Jin... you have to make the decision to leave for yourself.

Leaving is the only long-term option. You know this. I don't know when you're going to finally come to terms with it... but I've told you both quite frankly, "You're fucked." I've known you for about 2 months... and in that time I've listened to hours upon hours upon hours of arguments and hours and hours and hours of complaints. By contrast, Luna and I barely had a serious argument for a year.

Laura and I argued maybe once every 3 months for the first 3 years of our relationship. Amber and I argued 3 times in 2 months and then ended it.

When I met you, 2 months ago, I thought you were doomed... and then there was the amusement park incident... and I thought for sure you were doomed... then there was the week when Inari stayed at home and I visited her... and I thought you were doomed every night as I listened to you argue on the phone... and then there was the night when Inari was trying to call me to help her move her shit out of Jin's place... and I thought you were doomed... and then finally there's this weekend where you tumble down a hill after arguing for an hour and then get up and fight like high school jocks... getting up in each other's face and daring each other to escalate the fight to higher levels. Certainly... certainly... I was thinking to myself, at that moment, "They're completely fucking doomed."

But Inari, at the end of all these nights... you crawled back into this situation. And Jin... you crawled back yourself... and I want to shake the both of you... and I want to fucking SCREAM.

I'm now just playing the role of the innocent bystander who gives a shit. It is not appropriate for me to think about myself in the slightest bit at this time...I catch myself thinking about my own needs from time to time... but I quickly discipline myself... I quickly stop myself.

My problems don't deserve to mean shit to me or anyone else right now. If I need to have someone to talk to about my own troubles, I'll find someone other than Inari to talk to... I have plenty of options.

I'm not trying to manipulate you two into splitting up... I'm simply pointing out the obvious...

To quote one of our mutual friends, "I like Inari... I like Jin... but I don't like Inari and Jin together."

Do what you want. Fuck up both of your lives. Hopefully, I'll be around next time there's blood that needs to get mopped up.

Meanwhile, I'm going to at least think about dating other girls. There are plenty of options available to me.

Chapter 42 - Vaguebook

As Jin and Inari feel more distant from me. I feel more and more alone. Often when I get depressed, I write vague messages on social media. It is something I wish I could compel myself not to do. This story isn't really a story about Inari, Jin, and I, you see. It is really a story that is watched and observed and touched by almost everyone we know. They all see what's happening, and they all see it as twisted and bizarre. Feeling defeated, I write a message to everyone I know.

I'm the pinnacle of my life right now. I have so many things going for me... I have a great job that pays well... I have a beautiful house... tons of friends... I am the center of it all... a big change from when I was the computer nerd kid that everyone made fun of... I dreamed of owning a recording studio when I was younger... I have one. I dreamed of many things... and many dreams came true...

So why is it that right now, at this exact moment, I am possibly the unhappiest I've ever been?

I'll tell you why... It is because when you're at the pinnacle of life, there's nowhere to go but down.

It is because "hope" is the zest of life... and right now I have no hope for anything.

It is not that there are no possibilities... it is that there's nothing I want in life anymore... life will never get any better... I will never achieve more than I have... I want nothing... I wanted nothing... nothing but her.

My prophecies have a knack for fulfilling themselves in a timely fashion.

When I met her, I told myself that by October 31, she would not be with this man anymore. I think it is still a possibility... but I don't maintain any illusions that she'll be with me instead... how dumb and naive am I really?

I used to think I was special. I used to think I was special to her. But it is clear that I am nowhere close to the first thing on her mind anymore... no matter how much I love her, no matter how many dozens of hours we spend on the phone, no matter how many sunrises we watch together, no matter how kind I am to her, no matter how devoted I am, or how deeply we gaze into each other's eyes, or how long I hold her hand, or how steadfast I am in protecting and caring for her... I WILL JUST NEVER BE #1.

I kissed her once... and she fainted... then when she woke up the next day, instead of telling me she loved me, she cried and confessed to him... she loved him, not me, despite his emotional and even physical abuses. Then she threw me under the bus in front of him... and yet decided I was still good enough to string along for a while...

And then last weekend... he throws her down a steep hill to meet concrete at the bottom and she gashes her head open... he comes up unscathed and then they fight like jocks. I hold her back while he eggs her on "Come on and hit me... let's solve this with violence!" he says.

Yet despite being there for her and spending the night caring for her... she crawled back to him the next day and is now "over it".

"When it rains, it pours..." she says... and eventually all these clouds will be poured out and all we'll be left with is a massive raging flood to carry us away to new adventures... maybe a new land... a new world... a new planet... I don't know... maybe there will be rainbows... but where there are rainbows, there is rain.

For all the positive signs that I interpreted as dreams-come-true... there were so many negative signs that pointed the other direction. Maybe in her mind she still wants to get away from him... but maybe she's just decided that when she gets away... it needs to be to somewhere else... to someone else... not to me... I am not the savior she possibly thought I would be.

But as I told her the other night... "Even if you tell me, you don't want me... where the hell else am I going to go?"

My love for her is fact, not opinion... and I have no desire to be with anyone else... and I may very well never desire to be with another girl again... because my memories of this incredibly amazing girl who treated me like a champion for just a short time will stay with me until my death and will overpower any feelings I am ever capable of having for another girl in my life.

I feel for her though. She has a curse. To be so amazing is a curse because everyone who interacts with her is conditioned to react to her in an extreme nature... whether it is extreme love, extreme jealousy, extreme violence... her interactions with others are frequently extreme simply due to the simple fact that she is the most beautiful and amazing girl on the planet... and I know that on some level, she just wants to have a normal relationship with a human being that isn't complicated by all these extremes.

But to maintain such a relationship with her, I'd have to take crazy powerful mood-stabilizing drugs that turn me into a "robot" ... like him. And that's what, I've realized just now that she really seeks. She seeks refuge from people who come at her with such overbearing emotions... and that's what her boyfriend, however emotionally vacant and disrespectful he can be, offers her.

I argue that I can be emotionally quite stable... but it is, again, a chicken-and-egg problem. I'd have to "have" her before I could ever achieve this mental state... and whereas I know I can sit atop this mountain, I'm probably not so capable of climbing it.

A few people know that just in the last 2 months, I have, rather unhealthily, drafted 42 chapters of a memoir about the current events of my life, and of her, for whom I've destroyed myself trying to please.

This next party I've titled, "The Kamikaze Ride Ends Here". It is the party to end all parties... it is the final push in my life for something better... before I completely give up on everything.

People tell me I need to "take care of" myself... which to me seems like a "chicken and egg" problem right now because I have stalled. I have completely stalled. And there's no sign that I'll be able to jumpstart my life again as long as my life remains fixated on this obsession.

I am walking dead right now. I have friends... but who among you are really my friends? Who among you can bring me back to life?

But just when life seems to give up on you... miracles happen... and as I write this... I get a random call from a good friend... who's calling for no reason other than to check in on me... as if God or someone told her to do it...

Ohhhh Yuki... find the strength to carry the weight of your world.

Chapter 43 - Fuck It All

I stick to the plan. The plan is to catch wind that Jin cheated on Inari. I talk to Echo on Monday night, hoping to dig up dirt on Jin that indicates that she slept with Jin while he was with Inari. A long story extremely short, I come up dry.

My mission is a failure.

This is done.

I can't do this anymore.

The stiff drinks of Hard Mondays make quick work of my sobriety. And eventually, I find myself drunk texting Inari from the bar.

"Fuck it all," I say.

She calls me up... upset... "You can't text me things like that and not expect me to be concerned," she says.

"Fuck it... it's done... I didn't find anything," I say.

"I told you, you wouldn't," she says.

The previous night, Inari manipulated Jin into thinking that she had cracked his computer password and found incriminating things on it which she demanded he fessed up to, but only succeeded in getting him to admit that he had looked at porn at some time in the recent past. Although she seemed reasonably confident in his character, we did not call off the plan to try and smoke out whether Echo cheated with him.

With Echo unwilling to admit that she slept with Jin while Inari was in New Jersey, my mission failed... my golden opportunity to make a difference failed. I felt like this was the end for us.

"Fuck it all," I say.

The next day, Inari's posture with me seems to permanently change. I think that with me exiting this position in her life, she's reached out to Barry and is attempting to mend her strange friendship with him. She doesn't seem to be interested in any additional drama with me, so I keep my posture very friendly and cheery and try not to burden her with negative thoughts.

I offer to come over, or to talk to her late at night... but as I suspect, she doesn't get around to talking to me. It seems she's not terribly interested in having long conversations with me anymore or seeing me in private. She doesn't answer the phone, she doesn't respond to my texts.

Jin is her man again, for sure this time. I get the feeling that the next time I talk to her, there's going to be some serious verbiage exchanged between us. But Inari isn't the next to call, it is Jin.

"We need to talk," he says.

"About what?" I say.

"It has come to my attention that you've been trying to get Inari and me to break up."

"Do we have to talk about this now?" I inquire.

"We can talk another time as long as it is in the near future."

I say nothing. Clearly, Jin wants to talk now so he simply continues. "What's wrong with being her friend?" he asks.

"That's all fine if that's what she wants," I say.

"Is there somehow any doubt that that's what she wants?" he presses on.

"Well... that's how it seems at the moment... she seems to teeter back and forth all the time. But you know... I don't fucking care anymore... and I'm sick of being spun around in circles all the fucking time. It is confusing as fuck. Her words say one thing and her actions say another."

"I don't appreciate that you're trying to break us up," he says.

"I dunno... what has she told you that I supposedly did?" I ask.

"Basically, we're completely honest with each other, so if you've said anything to her, you can rest assured that it will eventually come back to me. And one of the reasons that she is upset right now is because you've been trying to break us up," he says.

"She doesn't tell you everything, Jin, you only *think* she does! And I don't think you realize exactly how much she tells *me*!" I snap back, finding the emotional strength to argue. "Inari knew I was going to talk to Echo, it was planned. It was very much a group planning activity. Inari basically proposed, straight up, that if I could prove that you cheated on her, then she'd break up with you. It was my mission. She was well aware that I was going to talk to Echo before I did it... we planned it together." I defend myself. "She and I had a long discussion about a lot of things, including whether she could break your computer password, but she ended up just bluffing you in the end."

I didn't mention that Inari suggested hiring a private investigator or getting an attractive girl to seduce him to see how he'd react.

I continue ranting... "You guys have *lots* of issues to work out. And a lot of these old wounds between you are still not healing. Inari has been bringing up these issues basically since the second day I met her... it started with the Con dumping incident, then branched off into all kinds of other areas... including the incident where you footsweep her and leave her bleeding on the kitchen floor."

Jin reacts as if he is on the ropes, stunned... "uh... yeah... that was uh... bad" Clearly, he is surprised that she's revealed that to me.

I continue... "Last week just adds another wound that isn't going to heal between you... yes... for the time being... she seems to have teetered back into your court and Jin is the man! Go Jin!" I conclude sarcastically.

"Inari is a hard one to figure out sometimes... believe me... I've known her for well over a year and I struggle sometimes," he says.

I continue ranting... "Inari knows and has always known exactly what I think and how I feel about things... of the 3 of us, I've easily been the most honest...I've written down every major interaction I've had with Inari, in the form of a 42-chapter book! And you know... she's even, as far as I know, read most of it... *if not all*. I've been honest with her about my feelings, *brutally honest*! Brutally honest about all my scheming, plotting, dreaming, and struggles. But here's the thing that's going to floor you Jin... SHE HASN'T ASKED ME TO STOP WRITING!"

"She hasn't?" He sounds surprised.

"No. I've asked her on multiple occasions if I should stop writing this stuff. I've also asked her if she wants me to stop chasing her, stop whispering romantic sentiments into her ear, holding her hand. She didn't say 'no', Jin. But she refused, outright *refused*, to say 'yes'!"

I continue my rant, "There are no feelings hidden because she has it all in writing... over 100,000 words by now. She's fucking read it. I've spent hundreds of hours with your girlfriend and dozens of hours on the phone with her and listened to hours and hours and hours of complaints about you... so *forgive me*, if it looks to me like you two are on the out-and-out and she's looking for something new! She's only decided to throw me under the bus because I couldn't prove that you cheated on her and now, you're the man again... go Jin! Go get some! I'm sick of it all! I was about to explode before you even called... but now you're pushing me over the edge. Both of you... have pushed me over the edge! You have issues to work out, so go fucking work them out! I just want to go clubbing and get fucking drunk... my kamikaze ride has just about come to an end anyway... so I'm ready to just say 'fuck it all'!"

"Well... I don't think she's throwing you under the bus... or that she's mad and ignoring you for anything you did... it is just that she's really sick and has been sleeping all day, every day, and now Barry is over here working over issues with their friendship."

"I don't know what's going on with her and Barry... she wouldn't tell me."

"I don't know either," Jin admits. "Obviously Inari and I have some things to talk about... but first thing first is to get her feeling better," he says.

"Sounds like both of you want to work out your issues... so fucking work them out and leave me out of it... I gotta go... bye."

I quickly hang up the phone... I hear him say "goodbye" after I pull it away from my ear, but I cannot wait for such formalities as I need to hang up as quickly as possible.

Maybe I'm not an empath, but I know... *I know* how to fucking read people... and I knew this was going to happen.

Is this really a story about an empath? Is it a story about a gullible, emotionally vulnerable man-child, and his relationship with a goddess who looks down upon him and creates realities out of fairy tales? I'm gullible, but not an idiot.

I don't know how this story will end, but at this moment I am damn sure that this story will end like any story, with the words "The End". There is no "Happily ever after" here. This isn't a fairy tale anymore.

Chapter 44 - A Plague of Locusts

Inari eventually gets around to calling me. Inari is ill... she is coughing and sneezing and sore and barely able to talk. Plus, she's got a bunch of drama going on with Barry. There's a lot of shit going on with her right now... but despite all of that, I'm confident that I'll get a call from her after bar close... and I do.

She's quite level-headed, calm, collected. She complains that Jin is, once again, treating her like shit. Two nights in a row she's been ill, and he's not adequately cared for her... and tonight she asks him to pet her forehead and tell her "everything is going to be okay" and he acts angry and blabbers on about "sleep... career... work..." like a dickhead.

"Well, you know, I'd sit next to you and pet your forehead all day, you know, Inari," I say.

Inari just says nothing, like she always does when pressed with an uncomfortable truth or an uncomfortable question.

But her stories of Jin, make me immediately think to myself that this isn't exactly the best way to "work things out" with one's girlfriend. But I do offer to take some blame for the current state of their relationship.

"You realize that he's probably pissed because of the conversation I had with him earlier. I yelled at him fairly passionately."

"What did you say?" She asks.

"I sent it to you in an email."

"I've been ill and haven't been in front of the computer."

"I am too fucked-in-the-head right now to even think about what I said earlier... but I did my best to document as much of it as I remember. But you know... since you're ill... I'll pull it up and read it to you..."

I begin to read the relevant parts out loud... and quickly it becomes clear that I cannot bear to repeat the words that I said to Jin out loud. "Uhh... you know... I don't know if I can read this.... you'll have to pull it up yourself when you have time... I was pretty angry... and yelling."

Our conversation drifts around to various subjects, good and bad, before Inari eventually gets around to pulling up the computer.

"I'm sorry, I haven't been trying to ignore you, I've just been really sick," she apologizes.

To hear her voice makes me feel bad for all the negative feelings of abandonment I had been experiencing for the last few days. When I feel abandoned, the longer the void, the crazier I get... the more I lash out with words and writing. When Jin contacted me, I was in a full panic from abandonment anxiety.

She gradually gets around to reading the previous chapter, where I document my phone conversation with Jin. She is real about it. She objects to little things, big things. Some things, quite directly, hurt her feelings.

"Yeah, I'm not terribly proud of some of the things I said... but I just wanted to be honest and let you know that I said them, I guess."

"But this last line, about how this story will end with a 'The End' at the end of it... it makes me sad. I hope it doesn't mean that we're not going to be friends..." she says, "but... if it came to that... I guess I'd have to understand."

I downplay my emotions on the subject. "I couldn't ever leave you if I tried, Inari. I'm trying to maintain the strength to keep my word the best I can."

I try at least 3 times throughout our 3-hour conversation to bring up the subject of our emotional messiness. Upon sensing that I'm going in that direction she immediately changes the subject to her illness. "I'm just sick and unable to concentrate right now," she says. It is as-if to say that she just doesn't want to deal with the subject... and I respect that she doesn't want to bring up that baggage and leave it alone...

But still, there are plenty of hardcore subjects discussed... new issues with Jin... issues with Barry... drama between Jin and Barry... but for some reason, the subject of *our* drama is the only one off-limits...

It makes sense that she would avoid talking about "us" as it is the only subject we could talk about that would require Inari to answer some *tough* questions. She dodges and deflects, but eventually, I do manage to slip in a bit of confrontation.

"I've made it quite clear to you that we're just friends, Yuki! On several occasions! There should be no doubts about that! I just don't think you've ever had a real good friend in your life, and you need someone like that... someone who will look out for you and stand up for you."

"But Inari, someday I want to marry my best friend... and YOU are my best friend, and this is killing me! Your words tell me that we are 'just friends', but this relationship is abnormal. It is quite inappropriate that I should be allowed to whisper romantic things in your ear all night long. I love saying these things to you. It makes me happy to say these things to you, but it also makes me feel for you in a 'more than friend' way."

"Yeah..." she concedes, "and I'm not sure how Jin would feel about that. But it's just that I don't hear enough of that stuff... and I really like hearing those things from you."

"I enjoy saying nice things to you... and I enjoy taking care of you... looking out for you... even if I only get to see you for 10 minutes while I give you a ride... or deliver your hair products... or massage your feet until you fall asleep... or whatever... I am happy for every minute I have with you."

"I just want you to take care of yourself and someone special will come along," she says.

"I don't want to meet anyone special, because as long as you're in my life, you'll always cast a shadow on any relationship I ever have with a girl... you'll always shine brighter than every other girl in the world because no one compares to you... trust me... I've spent my whole life passionately looking for my soulmate... and no one has ever come close. So, I've got nowhere to go... I don't know what to do."

"I'm sorry Jin is not taking care of you. It is probably my fault, you know," I confess.

"No... it's not your fault... I don't blame you."

But it is like I have to remind her and command her to be pissed at me... "No, Inari... you should be pissed at me right now for the things I said to Jin earlier."

Then she realizes as if she thought to herself, "Oh yeah... maybe I should be pissed," and says to me "Yeah.. you know... I am pissed at you..." and she goes off on a half-passionate tirade before losing energy and puckering out. I just sort of giggle to myself inside at how adorably faint her anger is. I figure that maybe she's just too tired and weathered to be mad at anyone at the moment... and maybe I'll get a more official lashing later. We change the subject back to other things.

We dwell for a long time on Zak. Zak and Jin have a close friendship, and I question the character of anyone too close to Zak. If anyone is poisoning Inari and Jin's relationship it is most-likely Zak, not me.

"Zak is a womanizing prick. He hates women. He treats women like they are the enemy and I've watched him do it many times. I imagine that at some time in the past, a girl hurt him so badly that he's now at war with the rest of them," I declare.

"You'd be surprised at how many men in the scene deal with women in this fashion and the things they say in private," I continue. "One of our mutual friends offered advice to me regarding my fledgling relationship with Amber. He said, 'Think of the most worthless thing that you own, something that you'd have no problem throwing away, and treat her exactly like that thing, and things will work out alright.'"

"That's really shitty," Inari complains.

"Men say all kinds of terrible things about women in the name of 'bros before hos' all the time and it is one of the major reasons I try to dissociate myself from the male gender. But I suppose I have the opposite problem. Placing women on a pedestal isn't exactly healthy either, especially when they are shitty."

Of Zak, I continue, "Zak is quite possibly the darkest and most despicable character in the scene... one of my least-favorite people in the world... and it is all because of his attitude towards women. And if Jin confides in him and maintains a friendship with him, I guarantee you that Zak is giving him quite poisonous advice and it, to me, should call Jin's own character into question. If you subscribe to the notion that 'you are the company you keep', then Jin doesn't exactly keep the greatest company. You know, since I went out tonight all pissed off-and not-so-shy about my disdain for your relationship with Jin, I ranted to a few people I've talked to in the past... and I gotta say, that I haven't received any glowing endorsements of Jin's character..."

"Someone said to me tonight, 'I know you... and I know Jin... and all I gotta say is that Jin is nothing special... and I hope things work out with you and Inari,'" I continue. "I shared with him the story of your tumble down the hill, and he simply said, 'yeah... that sounds like classic Jin... I'm not at all surprised.' Jin's character is looking more and more flawed as I continue to talk to people. One person recalls that he thought that Jin was a total dick to you as far back as Con 2010... to which I was shocked... because isn't that where you met?"

"Yeah," Inari concedes, "And he really wasn't all that nice to me."

"It's a game, Inari! It's a dumb game that men play. You find a girl who is interested in you and you treat her like shit so that she'll work harder for your affections. It breaks my heart that you don't see it!"

Inari offers no explanation for why she would put up with such treatment.

It is now 6AM... "Would you be offended if I got a couple hours of sleep before work?" I ask.

She feels guilty for keeping me up all night, but I assure her that it is no problem... I wouldn't stay up with her all night if I didn't choose to... and I'm used to working on zero sleep.

Chapter 45 - A Murder of Crows

I find myself sleeping a lot. I sleep when I am depressed. My middle school life involved a lot of sleeping. As my *conscious* social life basically involved nothing but constant bullying, I couldn't wait to get home from school, just so I could sleep and let my *subconscious* life take over. I used to get all excited about the kinds of dreams I hoped to have when I fell asleep. My dreams were my only escape from reality. Sleep is also good for making time go by almost instantly... and when you desire nothing more than to sleep through life... you know you're depressed.

Inari calls this morning... it is Sunday... she's at home with Barry who took over nursing duties because Jin failed, apparently, miserably. We talk for two hours, and I do my best to be sweet to her and motivate her to recover from her illness.

She apologizes that she's unable to help me plan my party... I assure her I have it covered... but I have a lot of work to do. After a couple of hours, we concur that I should be getting some serious work done, and we hang up our phones.... reluctantly. But instead of working, I just go back to sleep, just like it was in middle school. I am losing steam in this futile chase, and completely unmotivated to do much of anything but sleep. As I sleep, I just hope that I have good dreams about her. I sleep until 4PM, a solid 14 hours.

I wake up. I watch some TV. I try to motivate myself to program the computer. I have been extremely lazy about preparing for my party. My lights and lasers are still in my car, in fact. I nap some more. Eventually, I decide to call my mom and check up on my dad. There's no answer... so I call my sister.

I don't normally confide my problems in my family... but they're there when I need them. I don't like confiding in them because they usually just yell at me and try to kick my ass into shape and make me feel like my only problem is my own laziness. My sisters, mother, and father are all unique people. We don't really relate much.

My sister, Sandi, treats me no different than I would expect her to. My sister was always the attractive girl that all the guys wanted to be with, so she knows the game of love, as she was once a lying, scheming, manipulative teenager back in the day. She talks my ear off and barely even lets me speak for 2 hours.

"She's in an abusive relationship because that's what she wants. And unless you're going to be an abusive asshole, you're not going to be what she wants. It is psychology 101. I've seen it happen to my student-athletes all the time and I want to intervene, but I can't... because if I intervene, with their boyfriends, or with their families, it only escalates the violence. Oftentimes, they're in abusive relationships because they grew up in abusive families and that's what they're used to... and that's therefore what they seek as adults.

She doesn't want ALL of you, she just wants the parts of you that she chooses to take from you. Your biggest problem is that you've made it too easy to let her take from you. And she just takes the parts of you that she wants and forgets the rest, therefore she *doesn't* respect you exactly the way you are... the only reason it appears that way is because she doesn't want *all* of you!

Furthermore, if she wanted all of you, she'd want to *change* you, and she doesn't *change* you because she doesn't *have to*, because she doesn't want *all* of you. She's just playing you to get what she wants.

You need to come to terms with the fact that she's never going to be your girlfriend, and the only reason it is so easy for her to be nice to you is that *you* have made it even *easier* for her to be *nice* to you... because you don't make any demands of her. You just take care of her, you do what she tells you, you are basically her servant, who doesn't complain, and you don't make her lift a finger, let alone a forearm in return.

I can guarantee you that you're not the only one from whom she seeks this kind of emotionally inappropriate comfort. Unless she decides to get professional help, and she decides that she is done with being in abusive relationships and is ready to actually be with someone who is a good person and treats her with respect... she's never going to get away from him and she's never going to be with you... unless you turn into an abusive asshole and push her down a hill... at which point, this family would disown you... but we know you'd never do anything like that.... so, you'll just have to accept that it is NEVER GOING TO HAPPEN!

She is in this relationship with this emotionally abusive asshole because she wants to be, she chooses to be, she seeks exactly that... and as long as you're none of that, you'll never be what she wants."

I try to state that I know the situation that I'm in... that I know the odds... and they're not in my favor... but I also remind her that 2.5 months is just a blip on the radar in the timeline of life and things need to play out longer before I'll ever have any clue what's going on.

"Jin is obsessed with looking good to his friends... and what he really gets from his relationship with her is just arm-candy to impress his friends. Yet he treats her like shit when his friends aren't around... the events of last weekend are already no longer a secret... they're floating around in the scene... and whereas, in my scene, maybe people don't care much about other people's drama... if a guy puts his hands on a girl and hurts her... people start to care... and people will no longer respect him... he will lose face in front of his peers... particularly when they see them together... and he will not like it one bit... potentially they will both leave the scene and find new friends together? I dunno."

"You need to set boundaries. When you set boundaries and rules for yourself things will start to get better. By setting boundaries you're putting your own needs first. You're taking care of yourself", she says.

She makes a good point... I never thought of the concept of "taking care of myself" as being at all equated with "setting boundaries" for myself.

"By setting boundaries... by not giving her the emotional satisfaction that she unfairly seeks from you, you're taking care of your own needs first and things will get better," she says.

"But she's not unfairly seeking anything... she makes me feel like a king when we're together... I get a lot from our time together," I reply.

"But again, the only reason she makes you feel like a *king* is that it is *easy* to make you feel that way. She only wants what she gets from you in those moments when you give it to her... and when you're not giving it to her... she chooses to be with this abusive asshole. If you're not available or being difficult, she'll get what she needs from someone else, maybe the roommate, Barry."

"It is difficult... because I care about her immensely and I don't want to see her get hurt."

"But, Yuki, she WANTS to get hurt... if she didn't want to get hurt... then she wouldn't be crawling back to a guy who threw her down a hill... in my relationships... if a guy ever got physically abusive with me... I'd be like 'all right... we're done' and get the HELL out of there as quickly as possible and never look back... but she doesn't operate like me... she chooses and seeks out abuse. So as long as she chooses to get hurt... you can't help her... no matter how much you want to... it is her choice to get hurt... and you'll just have to live with that."

"This all just happened so fast... we came together so quickly and intensely... I feel like things just need time to play out..."

"The sooner you get out... the sooner things will get better... things will be worse if you let it drag on for 45 years... I know you don't want to get out... I know you have intense feelings for her... but getting out is the only way to take care of yourself... don't continue to give her the emotionally inappropriate relationship she seeks from you... demand better for yourself."

"I promised her I wouldn't leave her like everyone that came before me... and I want to prove that I am true to my word. And I'm scared that if I do leave her... she'll quickly just find what she seeks from me from someone else," I say.

"If you leave her, and she doesn't chase after you... then she didn't want you to begin with. If she is quick to get what you give her from anyone else, then she's just not there *for you* and she never will be! And I know that's painful... but at least you know that it is the truth and the quicker you know and accept the truth... the quicker you can begin rebuilding your life and solving your own problems."

"I don't believe that she's using me... or that she intends to use me... I think she's just emotionally troubled, and I love being there for her and taking care of her."

"Take care of yourself first. Maybe she *doesn't* intend to 'use' you, I don't really know... but it is her own emotional weakness that leads her to these patterns... she needs to get real help to get over her attraction to abusive men..."

"If I'm not in her life... then how can I help her."

"You can't help her. You can't run yourself into the ground trying to help her... I'm sorry, but the best thing you can do is *go!*"

I eventually get tired of her relentless tirade and abruptly terminate our phone call. The things she said to me do resonate to a degree. I'm not entirely sure that she can pass judgement on Inari without really knowing her whole story.

After nearly an hour of my sister trying to convince me to take care of myself, the only thing I can think of is taking care of Inari.

Would she take care of me?

I know my sister believes she knows what she's talking about, but I don't think she has Inari pegged. Things with her are far more complicated than a simple addiction to abusive relationships. There's something psychologically peculiar about her. I have no time to figure it out right now though. Halloween is approaching.

Chapter 46 - The Wolf Pair

Tuesday night, October 25th, Inari calls me from her grandmother's house, and we get to talking about Halloween costumes. She clicks around on some websites and brings up a site that she and I had looked at and laughed at in the past. It is full of all kinds of flamboyantly gay sexy men's costumes, many of which consist primarily of a thong and not much else.

"What do you want to be for Halloween, Yuki? How about..." I imagine a drum roll as she moves and clicks the computer mouse to pull up a suggested costume, "How about... a COWBOY!" she laughs as I see a photo of a muscle-bound hunk wearing a cowboy thong and a cowboy hat appear on my computer screen... we laugh hysterically as we imagine putting *my* body in something like that. To mess with me she even posts a link to the site on my social media "wall" for all my friends to see. I leave the link prominently and proudly displayed on my profile as if it is a badge of honor. For a while, we poke around at websites, trading links to various costumes.

After an hour or so of this, she declares quite firmly that she wants a wolf costume... one, in particular, strikes her fancy. It is not a kid's wolf costume. It is one of those sexy wolf costumes from a lingerie store. It is skimpy, silver, with brilliant grey faux fur embellishments on the wrists, skirt and mane, and an adorable cute and sexy hood with wolf ears. I bashfully hint at the idea of getting it for her, but I think that it isn't really my job to buy her a hot costume so she can model it only for Jin. I shy away from the idea as she presses me to reconsider. As we sift around for other options, she keeps returning to the same wolf costume. And more and more I dream of how beautiful she would look in it in the flesh, and the idea of being a wolf for Halloween seems to make her so happy, bright, and gleeful. She can't buy it for herself, she's broke. I eventually decide to *consider* the idea, although... *gosh*... it seems really weird and inappropriate for me to spend $450 on a Halloween costume for her. If some other guy spent so much money on a sexy costume for *my* girlfriend, I'd be rightfully angry. The mere fact that she is asking me for this is just another confusing signal to me… but this must be a *positive* signal, right? Yet it all just feels off-balance, as far as I know, even though her relationship with Jin teeters on the edge of collapse, she and he are still "a thing".

"Buy this costume for me, and then we can go out for Halloween and be a wolf pair!" she declares.

A wolf "pair". God. Her deliberate use of the word "pair"… Is that just another bizarrely positive signal she's throwing at me? Fuck! This girl is still trying to reel me in, and I just can't help myself. For now, I try to forget about the idea… even if I am willing to pay for it… it would be inappropriate of me to do so. It keeps this fantasy alive in my head though. I really want to frolic in the night with Inari dressed as a sexy wolf on Halloween weekend! That would be magical!

I leave it alone for the time being, but as we are saying our goodbyes at 5:00AM in the morning, I begin to give in… "We'll figure something out," I assure her. "Maybe I'll check out some local stores and shop around and see if I can't find it cheaper."

Of course, this idea eats at me. I spend the entire day fantasizing about her in this sexy wolf costume. I spend all day looking around, communicating on and off as I shop around. I eventually find a place that sells it cheaper… but… but not in her size. Should I just go "all in" and pay full price? If I don't, I'll surely not have this opportunity to enjoy this moment with her ever again. But she promised that we'd be a wolf "pair". A pair… hmmmmm.

As I continue shopping around town, finally my subconscious thoughts come to the surface. Something must be wrong. If Inari is asking me to get this for her, something must be wrong. I need to ask her some blunt questions.

"Okay, get real with me here. What exactly is going on with you and Jin that suddenly you're asking me to spend Halloween with you as a 'wolf pair'?" I ask bluntly.

"Fuck Jin," she says without hesitation. "He threw me down a hill and is showing no remorse for doing it. I've talked to Barry and my grandma, and I don't think they'll be too proud of me if I crawl back to him now. Barry got all up in Jin's face in my hallway and wouldn't let Jin pass and was like 'You know you gave her a concussion, right?' Jin just said, 'Ok yes, may I pass?' Then as he was leaving said he'd bring over the stuff that I left at his place, and if you or I ask him to stay away from your party, Friday, he would comply."

She talks for the rest of the conversation as if they're done... through... "I can forgive someone if they're truly sorry for what they did... but he is not sorry. He's only trying to save his face... and he's ridiculously trying to convince me that it was somehow an accident and even that maybe I am to blame. He isn't at all phased by leaving me. I even called him today and just left him a voicemail saying, 'It might be nice to hear from you.' But I haven't even heard back."

It rubbed me wrong that she did that. By calling him, she was indicating that she was crawling back to him again... but I guess I understand that it will take some time for her feelings to fade. Yet, I am recharged, that I might possibly have the opportunity to finally, finally have her undivided attention once and for all, and forever. I just want Inari to see the best me I can be. I am excited to show her the kind of person I can be when I have hope for something truly worthwhile and I look forward to our times together. Maybe the plot of this story is what it seemed like it would be all along!

She and I have all kinds of fun things planned for Halloween weekend, and it all starts Friday! Maybe this story will end where it started, with the two of us, petting Ada... alone in a crowd... gazing at each other. But maybe, like so many stories of my life, this story will end in tragedy... I just don't know yet.

Chapter 47 - The Third End

It is the day of "our" Halloween party, October 28, we are both communicating, excited by mid-morning. I offer to pick her up from her grandmother's place to help set up.... but soon, predictably, ominous complications arise.

She decides that she wants to go to the hospital to have her concussion looked at. I offer to take her to the hospital, but she says that Barry will be home from work at 1PM and can take her. I simply assure her that I know how to throw a party and that I'll get all the party preparations done... I assure her that I will support her in whatever she decides she needs to do... and tell her not to worry about helping me with anything.

I prep and prep for the party all day... most of my early morning help bails. I eventually call up our friend Lily and more-or-less beg her to help, but she is so nice that I barely need to beg. I simply offer to buy her Asian food and she's on the job. I clean up the garage with her friend "Jack" and work like mad on music... but despite all the worries I have about party preps... the only worry I really have is whether something is going to come up that prevents Inari from coming to the party... and even if she does come... who is to say that her mood won't be destroyed by Jin?

She wants to go to Jin's place and pick up the boots that she needs for her costume...and I realize immediately that this is a bad idea. I offer many workarounds, including buying her new boots, picking them up from Jin's place myself, and checking with Techna to see if she might have some that are appropriate. But she assures me that Barry will take her over and it will be all good. She'll just run in and out. It is the best option.

The party kicks off... it is a bit slower to start than my previous parties... but once it gets going it is BIG. Twice as big as the previous party. It is an animal house.

Lily comes around with a marker and marks my wrist.

"What's this for?" I ask.

"I'm numbering everyone", she says. She gives me a unique number... #0.

I stumble around all night... I shake hands... I say a few words to everyone I meet. But as the night progresses and she has still not arrived, I get more and more anxious. With my own anxiety building, someone comes to me and informs me that a couple got engaged in my house and asks me to get on the microphone and announce it. I push away the DJ and take over the soundboard. By now I'm so drunk I can barely stand, and my mood is complete shit... I announce myself as the host... "Thanks for coming to my party, even though you all think I'm a fuck-head!" I say. "Congratulations to Chuck and Nancy on getting engaged right here tonight! IT'S FUCKING NICE TO SEE THAT SOME PEOPLE IN THIS FUCKING WORLD STILL KNOW HOW TO LOVE EACH OTHER." I shout into the microphone as the microphone distorts and overdrives the speakers. People cheer. They cheer, but I meant what I said sarcastically because Inari is nowhere to be found. The DJ seems annoyed at me as I speak and tries to grab the mic away from me. We play a bit of tug-of-war before I just let him have it and stumble off.

Still discouraged, 2AM arrives and Inari is *still* nowhere to be found... I try calling her at least 12 times and there is still no answer. It feels like a blatant rejection of me during an important milestone in our relationship/friendship (whatever you want to call it) on a night that was supposed to be important to *both* of us.

I don't know how it happened... but I found myself in my spare bedroom... and on my futon is an old friend... one of the most beautiful girls I've ever known. If Inari was the most beautiful girl in the world, surely Persephone was the second most beautiful girl in the world. She is one of the most fair-skinned women I've ever met, and despite being older than me, looks 10 years younger, dressed in a beautiful lacy, flowing ankle-length classic Victorian dress, she beckons me to sit with her and Techna.

We all make small talk for a bit, catching up with Persephone, who hadn't been seen out in a while. She had recently had a child and was serious about being a mother. I thought she was in a solid, stable relationship with the father, but we never really asked about him.

It isn't long before Techna leaves the room and Persephone complains that her feet hurt, "We need to get one of those freaky foot-fetish guys in here to massage my feet," she says.

"I'm a freaky foot fetish guy," I say.

"No, I mean… you know… one of the *really* freaky ones."

"Well, you know... I'm a freaky foot fetish guy," I say, "I'll show you just how freaky I am!" I massage her feet for a bit and the next thing I know, I am sucking on her stockinged toes, as she laughs at my flirty advances. As she seems to enjoy it, I continue kissing her feet, continuing kissing up her legs, her inner thighs, and then finally I am eating her pussy."

I then put myself completely on top of her, kiss her, and start talking dirty.

"I've wanted to do this for such a long time," I say. "Do you want me to fuck you?"

"Yeah," she replies with a seductive smile and a twinkle in her eyes.

"Yeah? Well, I'm going to do it then… I'm going to fuck you right now." I aggressively take down her panties…" It was all a drunken blur. I don't know how long it took to go from foot massage to full-on sex, but it felt like 30 seconds. People walk in and out of the room on us several times… a couple of times the door hangs open for longer than I want…

"Close the door, we're fucking in here!" I shout.

15 people stand outside the door to the spare bedroom, some need to get in to find coats and purses while we vigorously fuck on the futon, often in full view of everyone. It soon becomes apparent that Techna is very, very upset with me.

She is outside the door, pounding on it, yelling. "Yuki! I need to talk to you, it is super important!"

I take my time, not wanting to stop fucking the gorgeous goth queen under me, but eventually I oblige. I don't remember if I finished. "Wait for me, I'll be back," I say to Persephone.

Persephone complies, but I worry that she will run off.

I find Techna and Daedalus waiting in their car across the street. Techna sits with her legs outside the driver's side door and the door open, looking disappointed.

"Don't you love Inari?" she asks.

"I do very much," I say.

"What are you doing with Persephone, Yuki! Persephone has a *child!* And that child has a *father!"*

"I don't really know what's going on with her and the father, apparently Persephone doesn't seem to care, maybe they're on the outs," I say.

"But don't you love Inari?" she asks.

"I do very much," I say.

"Then what the *fuck* are you doing with Persephone!?" she asks, more aggressively.

"Well, frankly, Inari is not here right now and I'm feeling pretty self-destructive. I mean... I fought tooth-and-nail to get her to come to this party, and despite the fact that she said she was coming, I'm sure that Jin came in and fucked everything up and she's probably off having makeup sex with him as we speak," I rant.

"I mean... it's a pretty fucking simple thing... I bent over backwards just to make sure she'd be here... she's literally the only person I really cared to have at this party... I wanted her to see me at my best... and she DIDN'T FUCKING COME!! It's a pretty simple thing to answer the phone or call me and let me know what's up, but she didn't even do that! It is 2AM! There's no Inari here. So yeah, I'm *pretty fucking upset*! And yeah, I'm *pretty fucking happy* that Persephone is here to make me feel less alone!"

"But I thought Inari and Jin were breaking up and you two were starting something."

"I thought maybe that would happen, but I don't know what the fuck is going on. I am confused, I don't know reality from fantasy anymore. And even if they're done it doesn't mean that she'll give herself entirely to me, who knows, maybe she'll want to be with someone else!"

"I thought she said that if she wasn't with Jin she'd be with you."

"She indicated that if I had met her at some other time and that she was available... and basically if all the planets were aligned that there might be some remote possibility that things *might* be different in a different dimension, on a different plane of existence, in a different reality."

"I just hope that this doesn't fuck up your chances with Inari."

"Why would it? How could it? And even if she found out about it... she has *no fucking right* to object... she's left me hanging for a long time... she hasn't chosen me... she chose Jin over me... and I respect that she's taking her time working things out because I'd want her to do the same for me... but she continues to choose Jin over me... so I can, for the time being.... frankly... do whatever the

386

fuck I want!" I say with a cocky bobble of my head. "If she chooses me, I'll most likely drop everything and run to her... but right now I need her and she's not here and it feels like she doesn't even care one bit... she won't even answer the phone or send me a courtesy text message."

"You're not going to try to 'be' with Persephone then?"

"I don't know and I don't need to think that far ahead. I don't know what's going on with the father and the daughter, I'm just living in the moment."

"Okay then... I was just worried about you," Techna says.

"You should be, I'm in a bad place right now, and I appreciate that you worry."

Techna and Daedalus drive off somewhere. I didn't ask where they were going. I go back into the house hoping that Persephone obeyed my command to wait for my return. I am pleased that immediately I find Persephone... alone.. in the spare bedroom, in the exact spot where I left her.

I lay next to her. We spoon for a while. We continue intense love-making (is that what it was?) for hours. I like that she is so easy to please and seems to be in constant climax when we are together. It makes *me* glow just to know that I can bring her pleasure. Her euphoric cries make me feel valued and confident. Eventually, we fall asleep in each other's arms.... it is nice... she is beautiful as hell and so very sweet to me. It was exactly what the moment required. It made my night to be with her and I even wished a bit that it could continue after this night. But I'm pretty sure we were *both* only looking for a one-night-thing.

At around 6AM, as I am lying next to her, we wake up. We spoon and begin another round of foreplay when Inari finally calls, crying. I roll off of Persephone and answer to hear Inari's sobbing voice. "I just wanted to say I'm sorry, I wanted to come, but Jin is breaking up with me! I'm so lost, and I need your help to get out of here. I need to get my things and go!"

"Are you at his place? I thought Barry was just taking you there to grab boots."

"Yeah, but then he started breaking up with me, he hasn't even told me why yet. I'm just waiting for him to come back so he can tell me why. He owes me a reason, after giving me nothing the last time."

I console her and say the right things. Persephone can hear the entire conversation as her head rests on my shoulder. She begins chiming in, whispering the right things to say in my ear and coaching me on the right things to say. After 90 minutes of trying to calm her anxiety with help from Persephone's whispers, "Tell her you'll go rescue her!" she says.

I echo Persephone. "I'll come rescue you, Inari," I declare. "I'm getting out of bed and leaving right now." I walk out of the spare bedroom door, "Whoa!" I say out loud as I take in the sight of what looks like a pile of worms on the floor... couples making out... slithering like snakes. I step over them as I talk to Inari.

"I need you to go to my house and meet Barry. He's going to give you my anxiety meds. He's expecting you," she says.

"Okay," I say as I change my clothes with the phone on my shoulder. "I'm on my way, I'll stay with you on the phone the entire time okay? You don't have to be alone."

I leave Persephone naked and sleeping in my bed, and I get in my car and go. Did I even say goodbye to Persephone? I don't even remember.

I drive to the northern suburbs to meet Barry, then drive across Minneapolis to the edge of St. Paul, east, to meet Inari at Jin's apartment. We sit by the vending machines as is our usual ritual.

Jin is nowhere to be found. We cuddle and I tell her everything is going to be okay. She flirts with my wrists, as I listen to her cry.

It seems like her relationship with Jin is definitely over... and the only reason she is still around is so that he can tell her all the reasons that they're breaking up... and it sounds like he's pretty firm about things. We talk for hours and hours interweaved with phone calls dealing with party cleanup issues. I sound like a CEO as I issue commands to various friends who are standing by waiting for orders, "Can you send some people up and down the street, collecting any beer bottles and cans that people might have left in the neighbors' yards? I don't want the neighbors to get mad at me. Also, please feed Ada, and get someone to mop the floor. There's a mop and bucket at the top of the basement stairs."

As I deal with business, I touch Inari's elbow to comfort her... I hear the hall door open... and I immediately move my body a couple inches away so it wouldn't appear that we're too close.... after-all... they're not "breaking up" not "broken up". I see Jin in the hall... ... he looks at us then goes back inside. Inari feels like she should continue her talk with him... but asks me to stay because she'll have to be leaving soon.

I wait in the car... thinking she'll be 15 minutes. But 15 minutes turns into 3 hours... eventually see Jin pop out of the building into the parking lot for some reason.

I text him... "are you guys about done talking in there? I've been waiting out here for 3 hours."

"We're almost done," Jin replies. I wait yet another hour before Jin exits the building and comes over to me, still waiting in the car. "Can I let you in my apartment? I understand that you've been looking after Inari and I appreciate that... she was sleeping but right now she's awake."

We go inside and he walks me to the elevator... "I'd hate to impose."

"Impose? About what? How are you imposing?"

"Can you make sure she gets some food in her? She hasn't eaten in 2 days," he asks. "I really love her, and I want things to work out."

"I'm taking care of her," I say. "It is my pleasure to take care of her."

"Thank you," he says... the elevator doors close and he sticks his hand in to reopen them and thank me again... "Thank you, thank you," he says, and then lets the doors close.

I enter his apartment and Inari is out cold... completely sleeping.

I stay with her for a bit... eventually she wakes in a panic... and I act as Barry trained me... I state who I am, where she is, I tell her everything is okay, and I give her a hug.

She apologizes for falling asleep... and states that she barely talked to Jin... and nothing was resolved... I spend some time trying to convince her to pick up her stuff and leave... but she delays and delays until she falls asleep again. I let her sleep... and I sleep on the floor in front of the couch. She rolls over and drapes her hand off the edge of the couch and clutches my forearm and I hold her hand and we sleep for hours... until 1AM. At 1AM I figure that Jin will be returning home... I need to tend to the dog anyway... so I let myself out.

Inari calls me again at 6AM.... things are still messed up... she is still distraught emotionally. After offering several times, she complains that she hasn't eaten in over 24-hours. I offer to bring bagels and take down her specific order. She wants two sesame seed bagels with garlic and herb cream cheese. Jin is still sleeping, and she insists on staying until he wakes up so that they can continue talking. We once again sit by the vending machines and eat. I didn't bring any drinks, and she decides that she needs some water.

"Well we're sitting right in front of a vending machine, so let me buy you something from here," I say.

"No, it's alright, I'll just get one inside," she enters the apartment and emerges a few moments later. "Jin is in the shower," she says.

"Well I have this gig tonight at the Kitty Kat Club, it is going to be super chill, a Sunday night unplugged performance. I scheduled a final rehearsal with the band. How about I come and pick you up later? You can come to see us play. It'll be a quiet little affair. I've even written a song, special for you," I say.

"Yeah, that will be nice, I'm sure I'll just need to get away from this environment, regardless of what happens. But I'm sure I'll just be taking my boxes of stuff and getting out of here," she says.

Things are still rocky and unresolved later in the evening when I return. "How are things going?" I ask.

"We're still done. It's over between us," she replies.

"Let me grab these boxes then and we'll be on our way, I can't be late for load-in at the club, so let's move quickly," I state.

"No, there's no time, we don't want you to be late," she says.

I do not pressure her, but I should have. There are barely 2 boxes of stuff she needs to grab. I could probably get her stuff out of Jin's apartment in just one trip. Instead, she only grabs essentials, her purse full of makeup. She is clearly just trying to keep things at his apartment so that she has an excuse to return.

When I'm not on stage at the club we are very, very close... we hold hands... we cuddle on the couches of the Kitty Kat Club, and she rests her head on my shoulder as if we are seasoned lovers, much in the way Persephone had slept on my shoulder two nights earlier.

I buy her a chocolate shake and fries upstairs from the club, and we take in the scenic views of the Minneapolis skyline visible from the deck of Annie's Diner. As she takes in the first sip she sighs, "No one is ever going to love me for me."

"I love you exactly how you are," I say.

She shakes her head to indicate that she just doesn't believe me. "No, I'm broken. You don't understand all the horror that is in my head. If you knew what goes on in my head, you'd be frightened and repelled, " she says.

"Well tell me what's in your head," I demand.

"No, it's horrible. My head is full of horrible demons. My thoughts are constantly full of trauma and terror. If I told you, you would be scared, trust me. I've had a lot of really bad stuff happen to me in my life, Yuki. Most of it I have not told you about. Most of it I would never tell you about. There are things that I have not told you about Jin that are darker than you think."

"Look Inari, I love you. I just want you to be loved by someone who loves you. If Jin hurts you, you need to learn to get away from him."

"I think I go back to him because his love is the kind of love that I grew up with, constantly being abused by my uncles. In a lot of ways, it just feels like home," she says.

Eventually, it is my turn to play... I play a song I wrote for her after that night she spider-crawled her fingers up my wrist and held my hand on the bench in Jin's hallway leaving me so utterly shocked and confused when I left her in the morning. I didn't try to hide that it was about anything but her. Originally, I called this song "Kissing, Crashing", but 10 years after the conclusion of this book, I renamed it when I realized what the song is actually about. It really defined everything that our relationship was and would become. I had no idea what on earth I was writing about when I wrote it. I just knew that I was confused and in love and that reality didn't feel like reality to me. The feelings were so intense that I just couldn't help but write this.

[to hear the music of Luna and the Destroyer, visit adaloveless.com]

~~Kissing, Crashing~~ Gaslighting

What does it mean, when our eyes meet?
Does it mean that you care about me?
And if it's nothing to you then why
Do I still feel the need to try?

Can't figure out why I'm still kept in the dark
And peering out at things I'm not supposed to see
Your body tells me things that your words just won't say
And I never know the things I'm supposed to believe
What does it mean?

What does it mean when I hold your hand
And walk with you across this land?
Dreaming of rainbows and packs in the wild
and the simpleness of a happy child

These fairy tales don't need to be disbelieved
My eyes can't tell if you're an illusion or what
But the palms of our hands sweat and tell me it's no dream
And fairy tales are real if you believe in them or not
What does it mean?

What does it mean, when our lips touch
And you collapse into my clutch
And when you wake you don't remember much
And I just feel so fucking dumb?

And you treat me like I'm terrible and diseased
And tear me down in public and prompt me to go
Then chase me down the hall and apologize
And let me hold your hand and gaze into your eyes
What does it mean, when our eyes meet?

After my turn is up on the stage, we return to the sofas, much in the same way we were earlier, cuddling in a full embrace, her head on my shoulder.

"I don't know where I should stay tonight. I feel homeless," she says.

"Well, you can stay in my spare bedroom," I offer, but I know she'll think that I have ulterior motives. "You can even claim my home as your home."

"I think I should go back to my grandparents," she says with a sigh. "My grandma loves me. She and Barry, are the only people that truly love me,"

"But I love you too, Inari," she says.

"If you knew the demons in my head, Yuki, you wouldn't."

As I take her home to her grandparents, she passes out in my car on the way. When I wake her up, she once again panics and doesn't know where she is. "It's okay, it's Yuki, you're in my car, you're home with Barry and grandma," I say.

She hugs me like a child who's just seen a monster... she blames the concussion... It started happening after the concussion. I move her essentials from my car into the house. Once again, Barry is sleeping in her bed.

By now, the awkwardness of Barry sleeping in her bed does not phase me. Even though it is the most bizarre friendship I have ever witnessed in my lifetime, I accept that Inari is just "wired differently" than any other human, but she is honest and good and her relationship with Barry is innocent and platonic, but likely as abnormally intense and ours. I prefer to imagine that the intensity of our relationship is special and unique and that someday it will become more. Barry already had his time with Inari. It is my turn!

"We're going out on Halloween, Monday night, Hard Mondays," I state.

"Yeah, I owe it to you after missing your party. We'll finally be a wolf pair for real!" she declares.

"Get some sleep! We are going to have a long night tomorrow. Maddox is having an after-bar party, so be rested up and ready for a long night!"

Chapter 48 - Halloween on Halloween

I maintain contact with Inari throughout the day on Monday, Halloween. She is alert and seemingly upbeat. She seems like she's renewed again, and her vitality fills me with happiness. Maybe she's getting over the fatal state of her relationship with Jin. I stay on the phone with her all day while I shop for last-minute Halloween stuff. The guy who talks to me in the first store I visit is a "furry" and when I tell him I'm looking for a wolf costume, he awkwardly tries to push me onto some black-market dealer friend of his.

"I… I got a guy. He's a lion. He can get you a wolf hat," he awkwardly offers.

Inari, still on the phone with me, rolls around in laughter, because she thinks that furry culture is hilariously pervy. As I drive to the next shop, she still can't contain her laughter, "Oh my god did he really say that! 'I got a guy… he's a lion!'"

I hit a theater costume shop that she recommends in the suburbs and I manage to come out with something that will have to do... a lone, simple, single wolf hat and a cat tail that might pass for a wolf tail. My costume is, well, pathetic compared to the immaculate, sexy wolf costume I bought for Inari in anticipation of tonight. I ponder for a moment at the imbalance of our dynamic, but really this is the night I've been waiting for! I just want to see her and stand next to her with no barriers this time. I want us to finally be together.

I arrive at her grandparents' place. I motivate her to get ready like Barry would have done were he there. I take pictures of her dogs, Scruffles and Aussie who are in their little doggie Halloween costumes… a cute little bee, and a cute little lion! Eventually, Inari emerges as a wolf, and she looks as amazing, adorable, cute, and sexy as she's ever looked... Wow! Just wow.

My heart thumps and I shake my head in disbelief as I give her loving, puppy-dog eyes. "You look amazing," I tell her. She just smiles and poses and beams. She is happy with how she looks.

"Look at me, I'm a cute wolfer!"

Inari's phone keeps ringing. She deliberately ignores it... I know in my heart that it is Jin calling. He's going to ask her if she's coming out to Hard Mondays. I know she's neglecting her phone for this reason, and she knows that answering the phone when Jin calls is going to ruin my mood and my evening.

As we're about to leave I give her a hug, "Inari, you look so damn beautiful! Let's go out and have the night we always wanted to have but couldn't before," I say.

"What do you mean?!" she says in a flirty voice and a smile.

I backpedal... I know, I shouldn't have said that... "I just mean... let's forget about all this drama... and have fun." In hindsight, I feel like I should have said "Let's be together, for real, and take this to the next level... no holding back!"

On the way to the club, I express my concerns about the calls she continues to ignore, "That was Jin calling, right? Jin is going to come to the club tonight and ruin everything tonight, isn't he?"

Inari doesn't say anything, but her phone rings again. She looks at the screen and rejects the call.

"It is Jin, isn't it?" I ask.

Again, she says nothing... but instead, simply hits "send" and calls him back. "Hello sir," she says.

I overhear him on the phone... "I've been trying to call you for a while, and I was just wondering if you were coming to Hard Mondays," he says quite formally.

"Yeah... I was in the shower," she lies, "We're almost there."

He says something else that I don't make out, then I hear him say "I love you."

"I love you too," she says.

"So, Jin's going to be at the club," I state, in a monotone, disappointed voice.

"I guess so."

"Well... this night is ruined already."

"Why is this night ruined already?" she asks as if she really needed an answer.

I roll my eyes, "Because Jin has already ruined it. He's ruined our night. I will bet you a million dollars that I'm going to take three steps into the club, he's going to see you, looking *this* fabulous, in *this* hot wolf costume that *I paid for with MY money* and *steal* you away! I feel like I've just spent $450 on a new sex toy for *him*! Yuck!"

"Jin usually just ignores me in the clubs and talks to everyone else... you've seen it."

"But tonight, he won't! You're dressed like a smoking hot wolf!"

"Jin doesn't care what I wear. He is just happy if I'm naked. Who knows if he'll even be nice to me!? I'm just confused," she says.

"He just told you he loved you," I come back.

"Yeah, I guess he did," she concedes.

"I kinda *don't* want to go to the club now," I say. "You understand that everything changes after tonight, right?"

"What do you mean?"

"When things get futile in my life, I set deadlines. I pick a future point in time, usually a special one, and if I'm going nowhere fast, I stop. I turn. I change course. Tonight is one of those pre-determined times. I chose, long ago, that tonight, October 31, is when everything changes."

"That's just dumb that you would do that," she says.

"Well, I have to do this for me, this has to change, or it has to end," I say.

Inari has nothing more to say. I think she knows she's put me in an awkward position and just stays silent.

It's cold out... I offer her my black faux fur coat to keep her warm while we wait in line. I pay her cover charge, we walk in. She looks left. She looks right. She spins and stumbles. I catch her in a full embrace as if I am dipping her on a dance floor. I quickly turn around and see Jin, glowering, drunk, sipping the last few drops of what was surely a stiff drink.

"I'll catch up with you in a bit?" Inari meekly states as-it it is a question and not a statement. She runs off without any reply from me, with Jin.

As I predicted in the car. 3 steps. 3 steps are all it took for her to find him. As the two of them walk off together, I go away... angry... I need to find someone... anyone... anyone I know... to vent to. My heart is racing.

"I need a fucking drink... I need a fucking drink NOW," I growl.

But no one hears me... the place is a madhouse… a zoo... packed. I get frustrated at the first bar... I go to a second... a third... a fourth… trying to find an open bartender, nervous... impatient... freaking out. Finally, I get a drink from the front bar when Inari reappears behind me.

She is without Jin, so I calm myself a little. "Do you want a drink?" I offer.

"Yeah, but I really want one from the back bar, because they're stiffer back there. This bartender always mixes weak drinks for the ladies," she replies.

I don't complain, but it is a pain. I have to close my tab at the front bar to move my tab to the back and the club is extremely busy. As I push and shove my way to the back bar, Jin follows, and the two of them sit together like a couple, as if nothing happened and they never broke up. I cannot handle this anymore. This is *my* girl! She's wearing my outfit! Jin has her... and presumably a fucking boner.

He attends to his girlfriend better than he normally does tonight... but I sense his mood to be quite grim. I watch, from afar, hoping that there are still big flaws in their relationship. I want them to be over and done with each other, but in time, I see their moods change, they loosen up and she flirts with him as if there's nothing wrong.

I run away from what I see, angry. I yell and scream at people in other parts of the bar, away from them. I am manic, traumatized. I wished I were blackout drunk, maybe I was because I barely recall anything I said to anyone.

I clench my fists... I cuss... I grit my teeth... I shake my head in disbelief... in anger. It was a mood that I have only shown a few times in my life. Eventually, I pretend to be calm and collected, even though inside I am absolutely steaming, when Azena chats me up with a seductive inflection in her voice.

"So... that's a nice house you have... do you live with...uh... roommates?" she asks.

"No, I live alone," I reply, robotic and without feeling.

"Oh... well... that's an awfully big house for one man," she teases seductively.

"Yeah... I guess... it's an awfully big mortgage payment too, unfortunately..."

"Well, I'm having people over after bar tonight and you're welcome to come along."

"I'm supposed to go to Maddox's with Inari, but who fucking knows if that's going to happen now. I'll tell you what... If I don't leave with Inari... I'll go home with you."

Azena scoffs as if offended that I'd choose Inari over her and is put off by my aggressive mood.

I lighten my tone... "No, no... I didn't mean it like that... I just mean that I've committed myself to other obligations, but if Inari decides that she doesn't want to go to Maddox's, I'll go to your place... I'll come over okay..."

She is unimpressed by my backpedaling... I just walk off, because I'm unimpressed by her gold-digging... and I have no more gold to be dug up anyway. The last of it went into Jin's wolf costume.

I stumble around more... Jin and Inari are now in the firebar eating French fries, sitting together. Inari leaves for a moment to grab water from the other room, and I take her chair and speak in a surly nature to Jin.

"So, Jin... how's it going?"

"Pretty good... pretty good," he says.

"Oh really... I heard that the first thing you said to Inari when you woke up Sunday morning was 'I'd hate to say this, but I don't think this is going to work.'"

"Yeah well, a lot has changed in 24 hours."

"Oh yeah? What's changed?"

"No offense, but that's between me and Inari."

"Oh, I see. Well, you know... we have plans later... and I hope we keep them."

"Like what?" he asks.

"No offense, Jin, but that's between me and Inari."

He gets up from the chair abruptly and stomps off; he leaves Inari's purse behind. Dutifully and attentively, I hold onto it, like any boyfriend who would be trusted with his girlfriend's purse. A few minutes later, he realizes it is missing, and he comes back and takes it directly from my hand... "Thanks!" he says, and briskly walks away.

I stumble over to the restroom area, where I find Zak. I'm still very angry.

"I heard you'd been talking shit about me," he says.

"Oh really... what did I say?"

"I heard you think I'm 'sleazy'" he says, hushing his voice so as not to project any negative sentiment about himself into any eavesdropping ears.

"I don't think I ever used that word exactly, but to be totally honest, you and I just have to agree to disagree on certain things. And I don't really agree with your sexual politics."

"My sexual politics are none of your business!"

"Well, you know, Zak, you sleep with lots of women, you kick them to the curb, you hurt them, you toy with them, you steal them... I think it's greedy because I'm really a one-woman kind of guy. I figure that at some time in the past one of them probably hurt you really badly and now you hate the female gender."

"Whatever you might have heard about me is a lie. And you only think you know my views on relationships!" he snaps.

"Fine whatever, I really don't even fucking care right now... I'm just sick of this bullshit with you and Jin and Inari... fuck all of you. Really Zak... FUCK ALL OF YOU... Inari didn't even come to my party!"

"Well... I would have shown up for your party if I didn't have a thing that night."

"Who do you think I am? Am I some kind of little middle school, head-gear-wearing, zit-faced, unpopular dweeb who spent his birthday with his grandma and Aunt Suzie? My party was spectacular, why the fuck would I care if you did or didn't come? I DON'T CARE! I don't think you really understand. If you didn't come it was your loss... I honestly don't even remember who did or didn't show up because there were so many people there."

Zak seems to get it now and changes the subject abruptly. "Jin and Inari never broke up," he states plainly.

"That's not what I heard. I heard that he broke up with her like 5 times this week."

"Yeah, well that's what she says... that's what *she* says... that's what *SHE* says!" he repeats with increasing animation, posturing to defend his friend from his "liar" of a girlfriend. "She's a really skilled liar, you know!?"

"Zak, Jin packed up her shit in boxes and left them by the door. I was there... I saw the boxes with my own eyes... her SHIT was

PACKED UP and WAITING FOR HER AT THE DOOR and I
SAT AROUND ALL WEEKEND outside his apartment waiting
for them to finish their 'talking'. Do you have any idea how
fucking fatiguing that is? All damn weekend! So, tonight I fucking
came here with Inari, and she takes 3 steps into the club… Jin sees
her in the hot wolf costume that *I bought* for her so that *we could
be wolves together*… he pops a boner… and decides he wants his
girlfriend back! This is EXACTLY HOW I PREDICTED IT
WOULD HAPPEN! SO FUCK ALL OF YOU! I DON'T
FUCKING CARE ANYMORE! I WANT TO FUCKING DIE and
I WANT THE FUCKING WORLD TO BURN WITH ME!"

I dream up some other "brilliant" things to say, but just as I am
about to deliver my next onslaught of words, a short gay man
approaches Zak who is blocking his path.

"Can you get out of the way, please!?" he asks.

This straw breaks the camel's back, and Zak loses control. He
starts screaming at this random little gay man. "Fuck you! I'll get
out of the way when I want to, punk!" The shouting quickly turns
into a scuffle, pushing and shoving. The bouncers come and break
them up, but the bouncer in my opinion bounces the wrong guy.
He should have bounced Zak. Zak was in the wrong. Zak stomps
his foot on the ground as the little gay man is dragged away,
throwing hand signals back towards him, and I hear the tinkle of
shattering glass as Zak stomps on the ground, shattering a glass
from the bar. Our conversation is now done.

Jin eventually leaves Inari with me like he's been known to do. I
calm down a bit, as I know now, at least, that she's coming with
me to Maddox's party as originally planned... but the drama of the
evening has worn on me immensely.

The bar closes. As we're standing outside... Zak finds Inari. He
reaches his arm out straight and braces himself on the exterior club
wall and looks down upon her as she leans away from him, "You
should thank Yuki for the wolf costume," he says forcefully.

She says nothing in return, just emits a blank, fake half-smile, like she does when someone hits her with an awkward statement or question to which, despite her impeccable skill at navigating human relationships, she has no response that will spin the cold facts in such a way to paint her in a warm immaculate light. Despite enduring months of torture, I am still 100% on her side, and I make it clear with my body language that his comment is definitely not cool, cocking and shaking my head. Thankfully his tantrum is short-lived. Zak turns, walks off, and says no more.

We make it to Maddox's place... my mood is still in a drag... I can't deal with my feelings of being jacked around earlier in the evening. But I try to remind myself that Inari is here. "This is good! This is what you want!" I tell myself. But I know she's just here out of pity now.

I stay near her... I am lethargic... I lay on the floor as Klara, possibly the 3rd most beautiful girl I've ever met, comes over and straddles me as I lay on the floor. I've never seen her be so forward with me, but maybe she's just flirting after spending the night in my spare bedroom while Persephone and I had wild sex, and maybe she just wanted a taste, after the slimy man who was trying to get with her didn't satisfy her. I almost think she wanted to 1-up Inari or make Inari jealous. Despite that she places her danger zone right on my danger zone and rotates her hips seductively in an effort to get me aroused, succeeding to a degree, I make it clear with my body language that I am not really interested in having her straddle me on the floor, particularly in front of Inari. I grab her hips and push her off of me. On any other night, I might have gone for it.

Axel, another random staple of the scene who has had very little involvement in this story, is leaving and gives vibes as if he'd like to offer me advice. With a flick of his head, he beckons me outside.

"You know I had a close friendship with Inari. I feel like you're at the point I eventually got to. You need this relationship to become real, or you need for it to back off. I get it, man. But when I was with her, she didn't have Jin or Barry or anyone else, so this is different," he says.

"Well, I have no choice. I have to see where it goes, and at this point, I'm just along for the ride," I reply. "I don't know what the nature of your relationship with her was, but I make no assumption that it was the same. You and I are different people, and my relationship is deep, deeper on an emotional level than I have ever had with another human being. I have no choice but to appreciate and love everything about her for that reason."

"Jesus, man, this girl has you in a spell!" he says, "Do you even know your own reality anymore, or are you just living in the reality that she feeds you? Be careful to take care of yourself, and set your own boundaries, and take control of your own life. She will do what she will do, regardless. When she goes back to Jin, she's *not at all* thinking about you, you see?"

"I don't know. It is what it is. It is after midnight. It is November 1st. I put a deadline on ending this madness. The deadline has passed, this is over."

I thank him for his advice. Axel leaves for the night and I return inside and lay on the floor a bit longer.

Inari goes down into the basement, alone. I follow… although I don't sense she is too interested in having me follow her. I make an appearance on the dance floor then retreat behind some curtains to a room they set up with bean-bag chairs and a round table. It was a popular spot to hang out and smoke pot. She comes looking for me but she refuses to come in and sit with me. Instead, she just socializes while others pass a bowl around the table. She and I both say "no thanks" when it is passed to us.

Eventually, the party winds down and Inari wants to take her boots off. I offer her a foot massage, and she offers me her feet. I am just excited to have the privilege to touch her sometimes. We use this time to talk about serious stuff. It turns into another "just friends" conversation and echoes all of our previous "just friends" conversations from the past.

"It's officially November 1st. Time is up. I will stop this," I declare. "You have no sexual attraction to me. I just have to accept that... and accept it, I will."

"It's not that," she says, "it is just that I don't work like most people..."

"I get it, I get it... it is fine."

"What do you want from me, Yuki," she asks firmly.

"I want... I want to be with you and build a life with you."

"But I don't understand... there is nothing romantic between us... there has never been anything romantic between us... I don't understand where all this imagined romance is coming from!"

"I don't know what this reality is that you're trying to push on me! Do you not see the romance in our relationship? It has been explained a thousand times. Our relationship is abnormal! You agreed to this! Jesus, do you know how abnormal it is for me, or anyone for that matter, to write you a *god damned book*? Do you know how much work it even is? I have worked my ass off to prove my love for you, and you soaked up the rays of my love so much that you must be sunburned under all that makeup! "

"You're emotionally weak... and I need someone who is emotionally strong... I can't be the strong one in the relationship. I will break you... because... I'm damaged," she replies.

"I am a strength multiplier, Inari. If you give yourself to me, I will multiply your strength 1000 times and show you how strong I can be! But if you give me zero, I have zero to multiply, which is just zero! If you think Jin is strong, you're living in a fantasy. Look at all the stupid, weak things Jin has done to you! Just because Jin is enough of an asshole to ignore you and make you feel like shit, doesn't mean that he is strong! I'm sorry, but when a guy gets upset and whines and even gets *angry* or even violent about stupid, small things, *that* person is *weak*. Yes, I am sad, upset, and feeling betrayed right now, but you must understand that this is *big* for me, right? You and I are a *big thing!*"

She scoffs, and rolls on her side... she's annoyed with me, "We are nothing. I'm just a girl," she says.

I lay next to her... "Hey, it'll be okay. Yes, everything changes tonight. We'll see each other less, but you know that I'll still drop everything for you when you need it... when you ask for it... always. I'll always be here for you, but I have to stop chasing you, I have to stop worshiping you like a deity."

"The idea that I'll get to see you less makes me sad, Yuki. I love you, but I just wanted to get through today without any drama. I wanted to have a good time and not think about all the fucked-up things happening in my life... I just wanted to forget about it all for a night."

"I'm sorry... I'm done... we're done... you're okay... this is what you want. You want me to be over you... so it is a *good* thing you realize, right?... it is what you want... it is a good thing."

She falls asleep... I sleep next to her, nuzzled against her for what I assume to be our final night together. Someone turns out the lights in the room... we're completely in the dark now and alone.

I try a few times over the next couple of hours to wake her so I can take her home. She mumbles incoherently in her sleep. She mumbles, "It's okay to leave me here." But I know better. "Don't worry about me," she squeaks, but I know better.

Eventually, the time to leave truly comes, and I lift her by the shoulders, as I learned to do so many times before. She snaps awake in a panic, "Yuki! Yuki!" she shouts. She hugs me in panic as if running from the devil. I am flattered that she is coherent enough to immediately know who I am, and not assume that I'm Jin or Barry like she sometimes does.

"It's okay... you're at Maddox's place...we're in the basement... you're fine," I say.

"There's something on top of me! There's something on top of me! What is it? Get it off of me!" she says in a panic.

"There's nothing on you...look... you're fine," I say calmly.

She quickly comes to and with a renewed burst of energy we go upstairs to say goodbyes. Inari actually seems quite vibrant and happy, despite just waking from a nightmare in a panic. I first go home to let Ada out into the yard. I open the car door so Ada can say hello, one last time, then, I drive Inari home to her grandma.

She invites me in, the sun is already high in the sky. We bond with her grandma like a family, talking about the night and the fun costumes we saw.

As I'm leaving, we break away from her grandmother, and I say romantic, sweet nothings to her one last time… like I always did. She glows. She beams a smile. I feel like I should be kissing her again… like she's begging me to. As we slowly make our way to my car door, I give her a big hug... again… and again… and again… and again… and again… and again… but she just looks at me with these eyes... as if begging me to kiss her. But I do not.

I go to work, but I am unable to concentrate. The events of the night eat away at me, I cave in and call to get some things off my chest.

"I just have to say that I was really mad at the bar. I was really angry. I know I kept my cool around *you*, but you must know that I was fuming and foaming and angry and vengeful when you *weren't* around, and I let my anger reach other people. I was angrier than I'd ever been in my life. I feel like you jacked me around last night, and honestly, I'm still angry at you."

"I respect that. I'm sorry you feel that way," she says. "The last thing I would want to do is make you feel disrespected."

Asserting my anger seems to have earned her respect.

"I'm really sorry for letting my anger get the best of me. I understand you just need to get well, to heal. You don't need any drama from me or anyone else. I'll put my 'deadline' bullshit aside for a while, and just concentrate on helping you heal."

Her conversation turns to doubt about Jin. She talks like she's going to leave him. She talks like she is going to press charges against him. "I might need you to file an affidavit," she says. As we continue to converse, I feel more and more confident that she's over him. She's done.

"Why don't you come to my neurologist appointment tomorrow?" she asks. "It is important to document what happened with my head injury. It's important that the doctor hears from a witness, and you know... my brain... You're the only witness. I don't even know my brain is working right now, so you have to tell him your observations."

The next morning, I get up early, 5AM, and meet Inari and her grandmother at her doctor's appointment. The sun has not even begun to rise as I arrive at the hospital. I am just happy to be by her side, even if it is just a boring doctor's appointment.

Having rolled out of bed so early, my hair is a mess. Inari is annoyed with me for showing up with messy hair. She frantically tries to fix my hair, in the waiting room, but her anger is not enough to quell the happiness I feel to just be by her side. I just smile and beam at her as she frantically brushes my hair before they call her name.

"You're adorable even when you're mad at me," I say.

"No, Yuki, this is not cool," she says.

"I'm just always happy to be near you, Inari, even if you're mad at me," I reply. I look over to see her grandmother smile back at me. Her grandmother seems to know that I actually love her.

Being here for her reminds me of the time when we sat in the ER, snuggling, and I remember the feelings of onlookers who must have thought we were intensely in love as we held hands and waited for the nurses to call her name.

When we get into the doctor's office. She portrays Jin as a serious, violent, abuser. She tells him the story of being thrown down a hill by him with all the embellishments she can conjure and all the omissions that might make her look bad, always hinting that maybe there are still things that he's done to her that she is refusing to admit.

The doctor dutifully pokes and prods her, trying to smoke out the facts. Is her relationship with Jin safe?

"Maybe I should just send someone over to his apartment to get my stuff," she suggests with a sigh.

Being her disciple, her sycophant, I simply echo her versions of the events, leaving out the details that might cast any doubt on what actually happened. Somewhere in my brain, I know I have doubts, but I want so badly for there to be no doubts. I want so badly for Inari to be a perfect deity. My head and heart are completely hers. I smile at the idea that she's found the conviction to move on from him and maybe move *to me*.

Chapter 49 - "Chapter 49"

But what do I know, right? Stella, Maddox's girlfriend, calls, concerned. She fears for Inari being with Jin. She got an invite from Inari just moments earlier. Apparently, they are planning a potluck together.

I am a bit surprised that she'd be doing anything with him. Inari is supposed to be finding the strength to get away from Jin... planning a party with him concerns me immensely. I decide I need to talk to her immediately. She answers on the first ring. As I make small talk with her, she immediately senses gloom in my voice.

"What's wrong, why do you sound so gloomy?" she asks.

I hesitate to tell her, just making more small talk, and more and more she gets angry.

"Yuki! Stop acting all depressed and stop spreading shit about me! You are making me look like a slut in front of our friends and it is really hurting me! I heard you said all kinds of nasty shit Monday night and you're making me look like a horrible person!"

"Look when I talk about you, I hold you in the highest regard and highest concern! But yes, I did feel like you really jacked me around on Monday, and I might have gone off the rails, but that's not really my concern right now,"

"Okay, what is your concern then?" she asks.

"You're planning a party with Jin. Do you think this is healthy? I'm trying to keep you safe and take care of you, and you're following him around like a lost puppy!"

"Look, the only reason I'm going to this party is that if I don't go, then I'd have to uninvite all my friends and Jin would have to replan the event with only his friends. And you see, if more of my friends are there, I'll have to spend less time interacting with certain individuals… get it?" she says.

"But if you want to split up with him, you should just cancel the party," I return.

She immediately changes the subject, like she does when she simply does not want to talk about an uncomfortable subject anymore.

"Things are fucked up, Yuki! I keep getting cornered in clubs and parties by people demanding to know what's going on between you and me. This is really damaging my reputation. You're making me look like a slut! I am not a slut! There is nothing romantic between us, Yuki! Nothing!"

"I'm sorry," I concede, "I feel like I've just nuked our friendship. But I've always maintained that we have no physical relationship."

"Even if you tell them that," she returns, "they'll put one-and-one together and just make assumptions on their own! And right now, I feel like everyone thinks I'm just the slut who is cheating on Jin and this is not the case!"

"But Inari, I don't really have to say anything to anyone! All they have to do is look at us! Look at us! It didn't look good when you whisked me away during the Zombie Crawl and we went off into the darkness arm-in-arm without even saying goodbye. I looked up at the train, and saw our friends looking at us in absolute shock! So many people see us just gazing at each other all night and they just ask me about us. I assume they ask you too! I assume they ask Jin! All they have to do is look at us, and they will form their own conclusions, regardless of what reality actually is!"

Despite fighting back, I feel weaker and sleazier than I've ever felt before in my life. My own lack of self-control on Monday seems to have emotionally hurt, challenged, and threatened her. It is probably even *my* fault she is back with Jin now.

413

"Stella confronted me today," she continues, in another rant. "I heard that, *apparently,* Techna and Daedalus crashed at Maddox's place last week, instead of yours, because they were sick of hearing you talk about me all the time!"

"Well, that's not what happened. That's not why they stayed at Stella's, but I suppose that was the easiest thing to tell her," I hint, naturally expecting Inari to press for more information.

"So, what happened then? Why *did* they stay at Stella's place instead of yours?" she asks.

"Something different. Uhhhh… something different. I've written it down. It's Chapter 47. I have not given it to you yet."

A normal girl would have immediately snapped, "Yuki, I'm so sick of you and your goddamned book! Give it up! Stop all this writing and obsessing!" But Inari is no normal girl. She does not ask me to stop writing. She does not ask me to stop worshipping her. It is confusing. It is so confusing. It is as if she wants me to worship her while hating it all at the same time.

I revert to my disciple state, I grovel. "I hold you in the highest regard, Inari. I've always sung your praises and portrayed you as a magical, perfect person. If anyone was ever portrayed negatively, it was Jin. Jin was always the demon. Jin threw you down a hill! Jin mistreats you! Jin hurts you! Jin is the aggressor, and you are the victim who needs to find the strength to come to terms with your fears! Nobody deserves to look down upon you. If they do, I will fight for your honor!"

"You just want to parade me in front of your friends like a trophy! You wanted to dress up like a wolf to make it appear to everyone that we're together when we're *not!*" she says.

"Well, the 'wolf pair' thing was your idea, Inari!"

"No, it was not. I didn't say that!" she denies.

"Yes, you absolutely suggested it, and literally begged me to buy you the wolf costume, despite my protests and concerns that it was inappropriate," I continue to affirm.

"I don't know what you thought you heard! Maybe you were drunk or something! I don't know. Whatever you thought you heard, you didn't hear... or misinterpreted to mean something profound and romantic when it was really just nothing! I just meant it like, 'Hey, Yuki, let's be a wolf pair!' or something like that. It was nothing more than friendly, ever! You always misinterpret things!"

Knowing that Inari will never allow me to accept reality without her disfavor, I stop the argument about who suggested the wolf-pair idea and never mention it again, to anyone. Clearly, the costume incident was the most damaging of our relationship so far. Rumors, flying around, that I spent hundreds of dollars to make her sexy for Halloween, would make it difficult to stave off the rumors of her being a "slut". I don't want to lose her favorable treatment, so I bury the facts. She saves her reputation.

"Look, I don't need to parade you around like a trophy! That's Jin's way of doing things! I don't care if anyone else is around Inari. I don't want to make it *appear* that we're together. I just want us to *be* together! I don't care if it is only you and me, alone! Look, I'm sorry I've hurt you." I profess, removing my argumentative tone. "I shouldn't have done that. Forget about my problems. You have bigger problems, and your problems are my number one concern."

"You need to take care of yourself, Yuki," she says.

"I need to retrain my brain. No matter how many times you tell me, or how firm you are with me... and no matter how clear you are that we are just friends... my brain just doesn't want to believe that it is supposed to be that way. My brain is so sure that we're supposed to be together... that even the slightest gesture of kindness from you makes me fixate on you... it is like a broken record... skipping... replaying the same thing over and over... and I can't help but want to be with you... and I can't believe that it will never be... my brain won't let me believe it! I feel so confused! So completely... BRAINWASHED!"

What she should have said here was, "Yuki... it will never be... get over it now." And if she had said those words, the repeating melodies in my brain would jolt ahead to the next track and I'd be on my way... but at the end of the conversation, *sigh*, she simply cannot let me go. I practically invite her to say "Yuki, go away now." But she won't do it. I invite her to concede that she and I will never be more-than-friends but she... ..... she just won't do it. And since she won't do it, she leaves the tiniest thread of hope. Just enough to keep me confused and her lapdog. Just a thread.... the tiniest thread... just a tiny little thread of hope... and that's all I need to end up dreaming about her every night.

"Do you want me to go away and leave you alone, Inari?" I ask.

"Right now... my brain is all injured and I can't think straight... and I'm just trying to fix myself and fix my brain and take care of myself... and when all of that is done... only then will I take a look around and see what happens next," she says dodging the question.

"See a therapist, Yuki! They can help you. Maybe, when you're feeling down, you should just... I don't know... Write!" she says.

(Oh look here I am ... writing.... again.)

"I write when I'm feeling down too, you know," she confesses.

"May I read some of your writing?" I ask.

"No. I write for me and me alone."

I feel a little betrayed that she will not share any writing with me, especially since I've shared everything I've ever written with her... confessions... professions. But hang on... that's not entirely true. I have not shared *everything* with her, that 47th chapter is still locked away.

After I get off the phone with her, I immediately feel compelled to confess Chapter 47 to her. I message her and offer to tell her the real story if she wants to hear it.

I think about the night for a moment. Persephone's presence and all the great sex, love, and togetherness would have been absolutely the greatest moment of my life had we connected at any other period of my life outside this tiny sliver of time I have known Inari. But, Inari, my goddess, master, guru, deity, or whatever you want to call her, overshadowed everything, and to me, the most beautiful part of the night was that *Techna saw the love I had for Inari*. Inari was more important to me than anything in the world. Whatever Inari asked of me, she would get. Techna's heart was pure enough to ask me the *right* question, *right away* when I met her and Daedalus outside across the street that night... "Don't you love Inari?" she asked.

To which I replied... "Absolutely I do."

I ponder over what Inari's reaction to Chapter 47 will be. There are two possible reactions she would have to the news of my encounters with Persephone... and both of them are bad. If Inari is angry at me, then well... it is bad... and if Inari doesn't care... then... well... it is just as bad. Either way... it is just bad. But I suppose there could be a 3rd reaction of... mild disappointment... followed by some kind of emotional jolt of understanding. Maybe she would be disappointed that I moved on. Maybe that would lead her to reach *back* at me... *completely*. Maybe she would understand I actually *can* wield the attention of one of the most beautiful girls on planet earth. And maybe she will, therefore, see me as a powerful man... a man who can wield *her*.

But as I've concluded so many chapters before... I conclude this chapter as if it is the end. Turn the page... is there a Chapter 50? I don't know... you tell me! While you're there, reach back in time and tell me not to do whatever it is that I'm about to do! Tell me not to fuck up whatever it is that I'm about to fuck up!

Chapter 50

Today is Saturday. Today is the day that Inari and Jin are hosting their party, and there is nothing I can do about it. I see it as a symbolic rekindling of their relationship, and I feel like I just can't let it happen. I have to stop it, somehow. But I know that any attempts to stop it will only backfire. It is early afternoon, and I am already on the verge of a panic attack. I've already sent Inari two text messages, simply out of the hope that I could acquire her attention and inspire her to call me. I WILL NOT SURVIVE THIS NIGHT without damaging my reputation, my relationship with Inari, or my own physical body… I KNOW THIS TO BE TRUE. I'm going to flip out. I feel it. It is boiling, rumbling. Things are going to be bad, very bad. It is only early afternoon and as each minute ticks by, I feel my nerves crescendo just a tiny bit more.

It is a familiar feeling. I've felt it before. It is the same feeling I had the day I threw Amber out of my house at the beginning of summer as I sat around waiting for "douche bag Brad" to leave. It is the same feeling I had when I gave Luna flowers on her birthday while she disappeared for 3 days with another guy. It is the same feeling I felt when Laura disappeared for an hour during a party on a "walk" with this *same man* a few months later. It is *not* the feeling of failure, but the feeling of *anticipating* failure.

Maddox's girlfriend, Stella notices me online posting random things that gave me away as needing attention. She strikes up a text conversation "You do OCD the same way I do," she says.

I… I… am freaking out. I confide in Stella. I confide in her in such a way that she must think that I am the weakest and most pathetic man on planet earth. I don't cut down Inari, I remind her that we are and never were anything more than friends, but I remind her that I'm completely in love with her. She offers me much advice, but she doesn't take sides.

I rant in a crazy frenzy… I am scared… "You must understand that I'm going to drive myself crazy just wondering what the hell happens today. I WILL NEED TO KNOW. I WILL NEED TO KNOW IF IT IS OVER BETWEEN US. I WILL NEED TO KNOW."

It is true. I will obsess over every minute of the day, wondering what is happening across town at every given moment of the day and night while I sit alone at home. I imagine Jin and Inari finally happy again together, holding hands, kissing, entertaining friends, laughing. As the night progresses, I will imagine them returning upstairs to his apartment where he ravages her like he's never done before. Yet I… I will be sitting at home, alone… staring at the walls… with no one to keep me company except for my dog, Ada. I will go crazy… I will do something drastic.

I continue to talk to Stella in panic, and eventually, she gets pretty firm with me. "Yuki, STOP THIS! This must STOP," she says. "You're in love, yes. She is a friend, nothing more. But become the best 'you'. You need to get out of the house for a bit. Get outta' your head… into new thoughts."

"I understand. I will find a way to stop it." I say.

Stella's words are true. I *must* stop this feeling from getting loose. Where do I go? Persephone! I remembered that I got an email from Persephone. Persephone is the right companion, at the right time, I realize. She is completely unaware of all the details of my summer. She doesn't know how bat-shit-crazy I'd gotten. Persephone, right now, at this moment, is now a necessity. She only knows of me to be the bold person who ravaged her all night a few nights ago.

She recently sent me a long message, but I acted rather aloof because my head and heart were still wrapped around Inari's finger. Persephone is good, great, immaculate even. Persephone is beautiful, smart, ambitious, stable, and functional on so many levels that Inari is not. I realize, I not only have to reply to Persephone, but I have to reach out, as a confident man, in the most tactful way I can possibly play it. My execution from here on out has to be flawless. I have to reach Persephone, and I have to reach her tonight.

I reread her message from days ago, which I had mostly ignored. In it, she expressed how she was looking at her email history of two years ago from around the time I first met her.

Back then she ended up inviting me to an after-party. It was my first after-bar party since venturing back out in the scene. The vibe of that party killed my mood. It reminded me of the environment that I lost Luna to 10 years ago. At the time I still hadn't reconciled with Luna, so I honestly feared that I might even bump into her on that night. I didn't want to come off as being upset to her, even though I was hurting inside as I watched Maddox and Persephone openly fornicate for hours in a 3-some with a 3rd transsexual woman while drunk and popping ecstasy pills. She later confronted me at a club about it, "You didn't appear to be having such a good time at the party," she said, expecting me to talk to her about my feelings.

Initially, I just brushed her off, unable to find the words to say out loud, but later I thought about it, then tried to set the record straight in a message.

Hey,

I've gotta set a record straight before I come off as an asshole.

Being at the party Saturday night brought up some bad feelings from my past that I will NOT elaborate on. All that shit was nearly 8 years ago now, so it is not really a problem. It just made me a bit sad... sad enough to not be able to fake a smile long enough to meet a bunch of new people. I know I certainly wouldn't want someone I barely know dumping a bunch of drama on me. So, I'm not going to do that on you, that would suck.

I write this just because I don't want to come off as someone with drama issues. Drama at parties is never fun.

I'm not so sure anyone there could accept me the way I am. In fact, I'm willing to assume that everyone there already doesn't. I am the true definition of an outcast. I am an outcast, even to the outcasts. I do not fit into any band of rebels and never have when I tried. I could cite specific examples, but another time and only if you decide you care.

There's who you WANT to be, who you CAN be. But being who you CAN be is not always aligned with what you WANT. And sometimes the pursuit of those things that you "can have" or "want to have" can lead to unhappiness.

Thus it all circles back at you in a downward spiral. You know... I've got certain cards to play, and I can only play the cards I have. And some of my cards might not beat the next guy's cards, therefore, sometimes, but not always, that also means that I just can't win.

I really think that you are a very beautiful person in every sense of the word. I hope I get a chance to get to know you better. I'm sure I will to a degree. Maybe you'll be around Monday night.

Yuki

But that was two years ago. Different drama was on my mind back then, I was just out of an 8-year relationship with Laura, heavily isolated, and being thrown back into a scene that I regarded to be unclean... a "cesspool" I called it. Now, this cesspool is all my own. I am the master of the scene... and a master of the cesspool. My fiancée, Laura, had stripped me of my identity. She made me feel as if who I was, on the inside, was unclean and an embarrassment to her.

I was in the process of learning to express my inner self *outwardly* and the Goth scene was the community that embraced and welcomed me. In a way, I was "coming out" much in the way someone who is gay might come out. But I am merely a simple heterosexual man who thinks that the world should be a bit different than it is.

So much has changed since then. I have found so much optimism since then, but if you had just met me, you'd never know it, because, in this scene, which is already full of gloom-and-doom, I still feel like I'm the gloomiest person in Minneapolis.

I have to play this right. I have to connect with Persephone, and it has to happen *tonight!* I decide to play the role of the guy who's become self-realized, a man who's found himself, his image, and doesn't give a fuck what anyone thinks... I act the part well.

Persephone,

I finally actually went back and read what you were talking about from 2 years ago. Well... I gotta say... that as I've opened up and expressed my true self more to people... I've become a much happier person. And whereas I thought that people might frown upon my freaky hair and the way I dress... I've found that it makes people actually respect me more... mothers on the street introduce themselves to me on the street because their daughters want to meet the guy with the colorful hair... or even police officers compliment me on the way I dress... It is really quite strange to me, and this is quite contrary to what I was raised to believe growing up in a homogeneous small town. These days, it is win/win for life.

I hope your daughter is well... and I hope everything is well for you as well. I know you'll bring her the best life you can. You're one of the most level-headed people I know. Sometimes I lose my head off my shoulders... I kinda envy those who keep it together all the time.

Persephone's reply:

I know exactly how you feel about the hair, the clothes, and just, in general, expressing myself. Luckily for me, it was midway through High School that I figured this out. It completely turned my life around from being a shy and unattractive nobody. You never really realize how insecure and repressed most people are until you are able to express a little charisma and confidence. As long as you don't become one of those brooding-in-a-corner-weirdoes, people, as you say, will come up to you on the street. People befriend you seeing that you have the ability to influence others and you'll even be even more powerful if you actually have some brains in your head. It's always been a big help in the workplace for me.

My daughter is doing so well...although her dad turned out to be an emotionally unstable narcissist. Aw well... these things happen, and you move on. He does love his daughter and does take care of her.

It's scary to think that I am one of the most level-headed people you know. I feel like most of my interaction with friends is done in a crazy drunken state. I guess that is sort of why I disappeared for a while. I had this idea of being married and having kids, because even though I love parties and drinking; it tends to bring out a lot of anxiety afterwards and it was getting too hard to control. Anyway, it was great to be back out again. It seems like I missed a lot of changes in your life while I was gone. I'm slowly trying to work socializing back into my life, so hopefully, I see you around more at Zero, Hard Mondays, etc... or if you ever recover from your last house party and decide to have another one. If you read to the end of this thank you for letting me ramble on.

I ask her if she wants to go out later. I was planning on hitting Zero. She replies that she was thinking about hitting Zero too, but she's concerned that with other events going on elsewhere tonight there will be hardly anyone there.

"Well, as long as I have you there, I'm happy," I say.

She and I meet at the club. We loosen up with a drink. Zak comes over to us as we're close to each other and he presses himself into our conversation like he typically does when he wants to steal a girl away from a man she's talking to. He smiles really big and exclaims "Persephone!" as if saying her name with the right inflection and smile was enough to get her to sleep with him. He can't help but smile the biggest and brightest Cheshire smile I've ever seen him smile as he prepares, once again, to try and steal the woman I'm talking to away from me in mid-sentence as I speak to her.

I think to myself, "No, Zak, you asshole, not tonight!" Then, at that moment I take her hand and let him know that she's mine. His Cheshire smile, which I had thought couldn't get any bigger, grows bigger yet. So, I take it a step further; I move my hand around to her hips, and I stand proudly in front of her, and I kiss her like a real man kisses a woman. I don't know how long Zak stands there before he retreats, emasculated because I am too busy kissing her. I press her against the bar… caressing, touching until I ask her if she wants to get going a little bit early before bar close.

"Yeah," she replies with a smile, a glow, and a twinkle. We leave together, I take her to bed, and we fuck each other in just about every way possible all night long. She reaches orgasm upon orgasm… she just never seems to stop orgasming it seems, and I love that about her. As a man with empathy, I want to know that I am pleasing her, and she makes it vocally well-known as she screams out "Oh my god, you're so fucking good!"

We finish, exhausted, and she falls asleep on my shoulder. I glow to be with her, and I believe that maybe she cares about me in a way that is a bit deeper than a "fuck buddy". I wonder if I have won myself a lasting companion, but I do not impose any ideas on her, yet I win for tonight. I have survived without hurting myself or offending Inari and instead I may have helped myself greatly. Maybe I even helped Persephone.

As days pass, my willpower to contact Inari fades. Chasing her is exhausting, frustrating, futile, and pointless. I enjoy my time with Persephone and overcome my desire to obsess over Inari. Sometimes, I catch myself thinking it might be unfair to Persephone that I carry around this baggage… but I remind myself that time will tell me what it is that I really want from Persephone… and who knows… maybe we will actually become quite close. All is fair in love and war, as they say.

I'm left in the dark, so I naturally figure that Inari is not calling me because there is simply no reason for her to do so. She typically calls me only when she needs me… or when I'd act so desperate as to make her worry about me (if I'm lucky). But now, she's only worried about herself and even if I were about to drown myself in my bathtub, she'd be too wrapped up in self-repair to notice. Her self-interests clearly still reside entirely with repairing her self-interests. I see things differently now. So many days pass that I lose count, but I still lethargically make an effort to contact her. There's still not a word from her. Finally, one day, it is not *she* who contacts me but Jin. He sends me an email... and due to its contents, I figure that Inari has asked him to scold me on her behalf.

Yuki,

I'm writing this with the hope and assumption that your actions recently have been only uninformed and not malicious. Getting right to the point, please stop talking about Inari and me. To anyone. At all.

Inari and I have a good, happy relationship. We've got a few things we're working on, but that's between the two of us and no one else. We love each other and are happy together, so please do not try to come between us.

By talking about us or simply venting your emotions to mutual friends of ours, you are making both Inari and I look bad. In particular, you are making Inari look like she is cheating on me, which of course is not happening. You are really hurting her, to the point where she does not want to go out in public because of how many people are approaching her to ask about the situation. She is dealing with some difficult medical issues, and her doctor has specifically told her to avoid emotional stress during this time. You are causing her a tremendous amount of stress and pain. Please stop it.

Inari told you everything she did because she trusted you to be a good friend and keep it to yourself. I think she feels quite betrayed by your actions. I know I do. I don't ever make advances on my friends' significant others. And even if I thought someone I had NO interest in was dating a bad person - I might mention it once but would respectfully keep my mouth shut after that. That's part and parcel with treating your friends like the adults they are.

Please don't misunderstand this message: I don't hate you and I do want to be your friend. Inari wants the same. That can only happen, though, if you completely drop your infatuation with her. In addition to the obvious, this means stopping the inappropriate, emotionally charged venting to a number of people in our social circle.

Please take some time to think this over, and if there's anything you would like me to clarify, just ask.

-Jin

I am furious that Inari would send Jin to do her dirty work for her. I reply back. I am angry. I type as fast as I am angry, spouting out a tirade of words.

Jin,

Inari should be well aware by this point that I am seeing someone else. So, therefore, if all your assumptions are correct about her, then she should feel emotionally relieved more than anything.

Regarding Inari, she admits to being emotionally weak. I was with her when she went to her neurologist and watched her concede that maybe she should just send someone over to your place to get her stuff so that she didn't have to deal with you again... she's been quite conflicted, but of course, at this point in time she seems to be on "Team Jin"... I can't fathom what kind of spell you have on her... and whereas, yes, I care very much whether I make her look bad, don't think that I feel the same about YOU, Jin.

She conceded that her family and Barry would all frown upon her if she crawled back to you, and she's well aware that I will as well.... but you know... I'll always be here when she needs me. So yes, I was disappointed that she can't seem to get away from what I see to be a bad situation... and if I ever hear of her getting injured again... well... we'll see who shuts up next time.

You've managed to convince her that she's been lying to herself and that her accounts of the events on the night in question were false. Basically, you're using her love for you as a weapon against her, and that I will never support, sir. I think you're more interested in saving your own face than loving your girlfriend, who, in my opinion, is the easiest girl on planet earth to love.

My "poor" conduct probably just brought you closer together, so "You're welcome!" Maybe I was played by her in such a way to cause this exact scenario. It is all complex and confusing... more confusing than you realize, Jin. This is not at all cut and dry. Regardless, Jin, I hope that she learns to break free from her self-destructive patterns... with relationships... and with friends.

So, one last thing... when you decide to worry about the emotional trauma she's going through... maybe you should think about the emotional trauma that YOU just put her through. Stop and think... regardless of what she decides to do with herself, her emotional situation right now is rather lose/lose.

I wish I could help... but obviously I'm incapable. I did the best thing I could think to do... FOR HER. I moved on... FOR HER. I will spare you my interpretation of her emotional reaction when I told her I would do this... because I've been cut down far too many times for misinterpreting things that seemed so night vs. day to me. I guess I'm not as in touch with reality as everyone else or something. I have been told to forget, unsee, un-hear, un-feel things so much these last months that I don't really know what is real and what is not because what is remembered isn't always what was real.

So, I think, Jin, that the actual real reason Inari is not so willing to go out in public, is because she'd have to face the music with people who don't understand why she went back to the guy who gave her a concussion among other injuries. I think it has very little to do with anything regarding our friendship. I mostly kept secrets until you caused her a brain injury. Once that happened, I NO LONGER FELT LIKE KEEPING SECRETS from anyone... and that's when shit got out of hand for you and everyone. If you didn't throw her down a hill, Jin, all of these secrets would probably still be locked up.

Yuki

Jin replies once again. His reply is as-if he didn't even fucking read anything I said to him. It addresses none of the points that I made.

Yuki,

Pardon me for being unclear. Your emotions are out of control and your behavior recently has been completely inappropriate. I think it would really be best if you saw a therapist to work on these issues, Yuki. I say this because I'm concerned. Please look into it.

If this is something you refuse to do, fine. It's your life. Inari and I are both seeing someone, and it really does help. Regardless, if you insist upon spreading further drama then I must respectfully ask that you not contact either of us again.

Jin

I really don't like this guy now. I don't like people trying to convince me that I'm crazy! I had an emotional response to a stimulus that was designed to evoke an emotional response! My response may have eventually been extreme, however, the direction of the response was quite normal. That's not *me* being crazy, that's me being *driven* crazy

Jin,

Well… I don't think that my emotions are at all out of line. Particularly for wanting to stand in the face of someone who physically hurt someone I care about… and for getting frustrated that this person let herself crawl back to him.

Barry might stand in your face in Inari's hallway and want to beat you up for the shit you pulled… but in comparison to most people, I'm actually quite chill, collected, and passive, compared to most men… including you. Remember when you shouted at Inari, "Come on, let's resolve this with violence!" Well… I didn't do that Jin!

You did! In my eyes, you'll never be a saint, Jin.

But I'd take a bullet for Inari, and that includes a bullet from YOU.

You can posture all politely like you're taking the high-road or something, but really, you're not. You're just obsessed with looking good for other people... and I couldn't care less how neither I nor you look. I'm not "obsessed with appearances". But it is in your best interest to leave me alone and not fuck with me and simply allow me to move on the best I can. Hopefully, I'll remain distracted enough to not give a fuck about you and Inari.

I could say some things that would save my own face... but I'm sure that Inari would rather I kept my mouth shut about certain things. I realize that in acknowledging that I should "keep my mouth shut" that I'm also implying that there are things still hidden in this story that could be said, but WILL NOT be said. I still keep things hidden because I never want to make her look bad. You're both kinda' obsessed with appearances really. The worst lashings I got from her weren't for things I SAID or DID, but for ways I made her APPEAR. That is an important observation.

Let me just say to the both of you, that if you want to preserve your relationship and forget about it all... don't press me to say anything more. Forgive, forget, and let these massive hemorrhages that you've inflicted upon each other heal... forget about the past... work on your future. I've got the past documented in over 100,000 words... let me dwell upon it like you know I'm capable.

My friends tell me "It's time to let it go" ... It is.

I send the email, and literally at that exact second, Inari calls. "Hi Yuki, how are you, I miss you," she says in a tone of voice intended to pacify me.

The pots and pans banging and clanging in the background clearly give away that Inari is currently with Jin, and he is cooking like he normally does. She must have figured that since Jin was incapable of bringing me into an alliance with them, she would use her spooky charisma to get the job done herself. I imagine a scenario where they both stand together, reading my email exchanges with Jin. Inari might just roll her eyes and just say, "Jin, you're doing this all wrong, let me take care of it."

On some level they're just trying to go about their lives as a normal couple, trying to do damage control to their reputations.

"Yuki, you need to stop this obsessi…" she says.

"I'm seeing someone else," I say, cutting her off.

She seems to stop dead in her tracks, and I can practically hear her heart shatter on the other end of the phone, but at this point, I don't care in the slightest bit about her feelings anymore.

"Who are you seeing?" she asks. "I don't believe you! You're just trying to get a rise out of me, and this is ridiculous, it's not going to work, you realize!"

I pause and stay silent for a moment.

"Who are you seeing?" she asks. "Tell me!"

"Persephone," I reply.

"I don't think I know Persephone," she says.

Moments of silence pass, before I continue, "She's one of the fashion designers. Since there aren't many fashion designers in the scene, and since I thought Jin ran a 'fashion company', I figured the two of you would know who's who in the business, but … apparently *not*. In fairness, she's been away from the scene for a bit, but she's one of Techna's best friends."

"What does she look like? Is she fat? Is she ugly? Are you just taking advantage of this girl to get revenge on me? Because if you are, that's despicable and you should be ash…"

"Persephone is gorgeous!" I exclaim with a bright cocky smile that she can surely sense, even though our conversation is over the phone.

Inari stops, dead in her tracks. An even longer silence pervades the conversation. I imagine her calculating her next move frantically like a chess player, playing speed chess. If Persephone truly is a powerful queen, then Inari's ability to cast a spell on me is next to nothing! Inari is in the final throes of this game, trying to find a way to avoid checkmate with just a rook and a pawn.

"Persephone is absolutely gorgeous! One of the most beautiful people I've ever met! Incredibly, incredibly, hot, and sexy! She's very prominent, respected, tall, thin, beautiful, dark, mysterious, and fashionable!"

"Well, Yuki, you know… if you're doing this to try and make me jealous, just keep in mind that it doesn't work with me." Inari declares firmly.

"It is just the right thing, at the right time," I say. "I need her; she needs me… right now it is mutually beneficial. Importantly, she knows nothing of what happened during the summer. She's not been around to witness any of the craziness between you and me. Upon becoming reacquainted with her, I've shown her only my most confident, outwardly expressive, bold, strong, strong-willed, and competent self. None of my weaknesses are in the way (yet). But time will tell if we grow into anything more. Inari… THIS is the 'me' that I wanted to show YOU, but you wouldn't let me. You've only seen this crazy, worried, lovesick, plotting, scheming, but brutally honest person. I am a different person when I actually have someone to properly love. I've been stuck… like a record skipping... as I've said... and I needed a little help to get the needle to jump back onto a forward-moving path."

I continue, "Look, I've done all I can for you, and then some. So I have to move on! But I want you to know that meeting you and loving you have been easily the most beautiful experiences of my life! I still think that you are magical and amazing. And I am going to remember these moments for a long, long time."

"But I'm just a girl," she whimpers.

"No," I reply, "No you're not, 'just' a girl. These weeks, hours, days, and moments with you have been the most important of my life."

"But I'm just a girl," she whimpers again.

"In all honesty, Inari, after everything you and I have been through... no woman on planet earth scares me or intimidates me anymore... only you. No one I have ever met has ever meant as much to me as you have. It drove me crazy, and I lost control. You warped my reality, my memories, and my senses, spinning me out of control in a tornado of confusion! This kind of thing can never happen to me, to us, to you, or to *anyone* who stands across from your laser-beam eyes... ever again!"

"But... I'm just a girl," she whimpers again.

"Look, I'm going to go now. This is what you want. This is what we need. I'm not going to bother you anymore. And whereas you'll be getting fewer calls and texts from me going forward, don't think for a minute that it means that I don't want to talk to you. I will gladly offer you all the companionship you seek from me... and I will gladly drop everything and anything I'm doing when you need my help. I'm merely trying to respect your space."

A truce.

I cannot be in the middle of Jin and Inari's drama anymore. I cannot rescue her. I stop my email tirade with Jin and Jin stops his as well. I decide that I need to walk away... and I can't look back at all.

Despite having originally decided that Persephone and I are too busy to see each other until next week, we cave. We simply *cannot wait that long* to see each other. I find myself at her house on Friday night. I go over and make an attempt to spend "quality time" with her. I try to talk to her and get to know her more than I had in our previous encounters. We eventually forfeit conversation and instead watch movies.

As we sit in silence, holding each other, I realize how this experience contrasts the last few months. It is calm. It is quiet. In the last few months, I hadn't bothered to watch any movies. The only movie night Inari and I ever had was the night when Techna sewed in my spare bedroom, and I rubbed Inari's feet for 3 hours. Movie nights are a rather antisocial exercise, and Inari and I were so capable of just gazing at each other for hours on end, whispering sweet nothings to each other, and holding hands. This time with Persephone, however, is normal. This is peaceful. I don't have to fanatically pump all my energy into worshipping her and appeasing her.

Persephone and I make love as we watch some random superhero movie and then she rests her head in my lap on the sofa for a while and we have a simple conversation. My phone rings. I pull it out of my pocket, accidentally answering it without looking at the name. I am in mid-sentence with Persephone, when I realize that it is Inari. I assume that she feels a jolt to know that I truly am with someone else, and my time with Persephone was real, and not just a lie to make her jealous.

She is emotionally weak, crying, whimpering, but she says she's doing better than she has been the last few days. She notices that I appear to be busy. "You should be with your girlfriend right now, I'm sorry for interrupting."

"But I'm not leaving you like this," I say.

"I told you, I'm doing better than I was. I'm sorry I didn't get back to you," she says… still in a weak, whimper of a voice.

I assure her that if she needs anything, I'm here for her. But she insists that I get back to Persephone. After several attempts at offering my attention to Inari, I give up.

"Okay, I will do as you suggest. I will finish what I'm doing here, but when I'm done, I'm going to call you, and I hope you answer, okay?"

"Okay," she says.

I make Inari wait for me to finish my night with Persephone. I devote myself to Persephone for as long as I can, repeatedly making love to her over and over, as has become our routine, but even as Persephone falls asleep on my shoulder, I cannot help but think of Inari. At 3AM I declare to Persephone that I must leave…

"There's no reason you really have to go quite yet," she says.

"I have to volunteer in the morning, and I need to prepare beforehand. There will be another night," I say.

I kiss her goodbye and I leave the house. I start my car, but before driving off, I call Inari. She answers on the first ring. It seems she's been waiting for my call. We talk. We talk until sunrise… again… one last time. Then, Inari disappears from my life for what feels like a long, long time.

The End.

Epilogue

Ten years would pass before I actually understood what drove me to write a book covering a mere 90 days of my life. No other time in my life ever inspired me to write a book, before, or after. You may think me to be a naturally obsessive, crazy stalker, and narcissist after reading this, but I must implore you to understand, again... no other 90 day period of my life was quite like this. I have my own serious issues with depression and emotional dependence, but I am confident that I am too humble to be a narcissist.

Things with Persephone were temporary, lasting just a few months, but those few months were important in my ability to escape Inari's immediate grip on me. The awkwardness of dealing with her baby, and especially the 'baby daddy', eventually broke down the facade of confidence that I put up to initially win her affection. We went our separate ways without even saying a word about it and just faded from each other with no real drama. We occasionally got lunch together for the decade that followed, and never talked about the time we spent together.

Eventually, when I found myself alone again, Inari reemerged, but with another, newer man, Ken. She used Ken to arouse feelings of jealousy in Jin, and shortly thereafter, Jin had finally had enough. They split up, permanently, once and for all. Inari was now in the predicament that she had invited Ken to move from another state to live with her in her grandparents' house. From the outside looking in, I watched as Inari escorted him through hell, making him her servant, leading him to believe that he was her boyfriend, living in her room, sleeping in her bed, at her grandparents' house, with Barry still around. Many of these episodes might be worthy of another book someday, but writing books is hard, and getting people to read them might be even harder, so time will tell if this story ever sees light. I almost never finished even this very book because she read it and tore it apart, telling me it was a "piece of shit", then convinced Ken to pressure me to bury it. I buried this book for 10 years and did not look at it, read it, or revise it. I hope that if you made it this far, you have a slightly better opinion of it than she did.

Ken would drive her out to spend time alone with other "friends", engaging in sexual excursions of which it took me 3 years to get her to confess. In truth, she never really 'confessed', but rather began to just accept the statements I dropped into conversations regarding those times, thereby affirming my assumptions about what was actually going on. There was a period of close to a year, when I saw Inari weekly, but refused to talk to her because of how she was treating Ken, now a friend of mine, who actually *did* things for me (as opposed to offering me mere *words* as currency for favors).

Barry eventually abandoned her, marrying the first woman who would have him. Inari suggested, "He doesn't even like her that much." I'm sure that statement is just her way of demonizing Barry for leaving her. Barry does not communicate with Inari anymore. Inari says it is because his wife won't allow it. Inari clearly misses whatever Barry brought to her, but I've never talked to Barry about it. On some level, I wish I knew more of his story.

My parties got too big and too dangerous to continue throwing. Without the social status associated with them, people stopped saying "hello" to me everywhere I went, and I spent most nights at a bar, sitting alone, looking grumpy and unapproachable.

I hit rock bottom for a time after my father died. My dog, Ada, died one month later, leaving me with massive debt from vet bills. Inari, despite calling me her "best friend" for the entirety of these 10 years, was never by my side to console me during these events, but Ken was.

Inari, even when in the background, was still a very prominent figure in my life. Even if we only saw each other occasionally, as she disappeared into a cave for months or years with whoever she was seeing at the time, whenever Inari needed me, I sprang into action.

If she called when I was across town at a concert with friends, I would abandon my friends, leave the show, and go meet her.

If she called me at 7:15 in the morning, in a daze, after a long night of partying with creepers who tried to take advantage of her, I rolled out of bed and jumped in my car to go rescue her.

If she called when I was out on a date, I would abandon my date and go see her.

If her boyfriend got mad at her and abandoned her in a restaurant at 11:30 at night with no way home, I went and sat with her, and shared drinks and food with her, getting her home safe at the end of the night.

On so many of those nights, we behaved as we always did. I listened to her vilify and demonize her boyfriend, usually some kind of sociopathic businessman. I would shower her with compliments, affection, and love while we often sat in my car, just parked outside his house. I typically rubbed her back and feet, and held her hand, until 8:30 in the morning, long after sunrise, going to work on no sleep. This was our routine, for well.. around 7 of those 10 years. To Inari, I was her "best friend". She frequently told me she loved me. She frequently told me that I was the most important person in her life. She would beg and plead with me to understand that she regarded me to be *even more important* than whatever boyfriend she had at the time. I wanted to believe her, but I couldn't help but point out the obvious.

"Inari, I'm not the most important person in your life. I'm not even sure I'm #2. Did you call me up yesterday and ask me how my day at work went? Did you check in with me and let me know that you made it home safe from that party you were at last week? No. In fact, I don't even know what you did last week, because you said nothing to me. You could have been buried under a mountain of cocaine in some crack den… you wouldn't be checking in with me… but you check in with Adam, your boyfriend. What you're telling me is bullshit."

Despite my complaints, Inari simply repeated her sentiments, for years. She told me that I was #1, more important to her than anyone else in the world and that she loved me more than anything or anyone. Whereas my logical brain did not believe her sentiments, my emotional brain did. It kept me drawn to her, fixated, and completely devoted to her.

In reality, she wasn't around. She didn't care that I was stewing, alone, in my lonely house, watching the paint chip off the walls, trolling the internet and dating sites trying to find someone who would spend a day with me. I spent most of the decade being "friend-zoned" by multiple women, often devoting myself to one at a time, while ignoring all others, never to achieve any status other than "friend" or "buddy". I began to hate this word, "friend", with increasing ferocity, and I would cringe anytime I heard it from a female, especially when it came from Inari's mouth. Some of the other girls gave me the "run around" for years while I bought them drinks and fancy dinners.

Sexual encounters with random women happened occasionally but rarely. They were always short-lived and uncommitted, despite my intense desire for a committed relationship. I was giving up on dating and going out. Attempts at dating were futile until I stumbled into Vee, who took an instant liking to me. She was previously married to a woman and had two children with her. Our first date was amazing, and she would move into the house I originally bought with Laura, where Amber also once lived, within a year. "Amber's Room" became the children's room. Eventually, we got a new dog, a Samoyed, completing our queer family. By no coincidence, we named the dog Yuki. It was a strange experience for me to be with a woman who actually *did* things for me, had a powerful job, and wanted to build a life with me. At the age of 41, this would be the *first time* in my life that I ever had such a dynamic.

There was love and passion. Things were mostly okay with us, but we fought as people do. The children had typical behavior problems that we didn't always understand how to navigate, I couldn't get her to ditch her ugly shoes, and she tried to control all the finances, but we always worked things out.

2020 arrived and Covid 19 hit. The kids were forced to homeschool during the pandemic. The "other mother" lived in the neighborhood where George Floyd was murdered by police, the neighborhood burned during the riots, homeless encampments started appearing in her backyard, and heroin needles started appearing on their front doorstep. The kids came to live with us 100% of the time. The "other mother" came to help homeschool them every day. My house became a pressure cooker, but everything was being worked on and worked out. "We just need to make it through the pandemic," I told Vee, "Then... we'll be alright."

In the middle of the summer of 2020, Inari called, frantic, crying. "Yuki, I need your help! I don't know who else to call! Adam is dumping me, and the doctors think I have uterine cancer!"

I hadn't heard a word from Inari in a year, maybe more. But, like I always had been conditioned, I dropped everything, went to rescue her, and brought her home. The kids loved her. She slept on the floor with the new dog as her pillow.

Over the next few months, we made it a regular Monday night thing to go to The Saloon for drag shows. "Hard Mondays" were canceled long ago, but it reminded me of the good times I used to have there. After, she and I would stay up all night, parked in front of my house, talking in the car, much like old times. Vee would wake up for work at 4:30AM and we would still be sitting there. Usually, I just listened to her whine about Adam all night. Eventually, Vee got tired of it and planned an excursion, a vacation, to Arizona without me. It was clear that she was going out there with the intention of cheating on me (and she came back with an STI), but by this time things were so intense with us that I didn't care and my intense friendship with Inari always cast a shadow on everyone else, so if all that happened, I don't blame her at all. I invited Inari to spend the night at the house for 4 straight nights while Vee was away. It was around that time that Vee announced that she would be moving out just after Christmas.

I continued regular outings with Inari, eventually, we found ourselves intensely making out in the car after a night at the bar. I stayed with her as long as I could, drove her to her own car, where she slept with the heat cranked. Concerned and missing her long after sunrise, I returned to check on her. She was sweating from how hot it was in there, makeup running down her face, but we kissed some more before I kissed her a final goodbye. She drove home. She never mentioned the incident again.

Eventually, an MRI was performed, and Inari was put on a priority list to have an emergency hysterectomy. It was thankfully determined that the massive mass in her uterus was benign, but that week, her grandmother was diagnosed with lymphoma. I dedicated myself to helping Inari recover from surgery and helping get her grandmother to chemotherapy appointments at the Mayo Clinic, paying for hotels as needed.

Inari and I spent virtually every day together in the first half of 2021, while the world was mostly on lockdown, the venues were all closed, and restaurants served only take-out.

She spent all her time fixated on Adam, the businessman who dumped her, however… and seemed to not care that I was being good to her. If I said something nice to her, her response was always "Adam never said that to me."

Eventually, I snapped, "I'm really tired of hearing about Adam! I am going out on a limb to be here with you every day and bring you burritos and make sure all of your needs are taken care of, and all you can do is moan about how much you miss Adam! Why can't you just appreciate me instead?" I demanded.

"Yuki, I didn't mean to offend you. You mean more to me than anyone in the world. You're my friend!"

(There was that word, "friend", again.)

"No, this is not a friendship! This is different from friendship. This is an amoeba! This is something else! I don't do the things that I do for you just for some random friend! If I wanted a 'friend', all I'd have to do is go to a bar or a grocery store or whatever and say, 'hey I'll be your friend, now let me take care of all your needs, buy your drinks, and pay for these groceries, and rub your feet until you fall asleep every night!' Easy peasy! Do I do that? No... this is NOT a friendship. I do these things because I love you, and I've always loved you, and there's never been an illusion!"

"But there's nothing romantic between us, there never was," Inari complained.

By this time this very book was buried for 10 years, and her intense manipulation had rewritten my reality so deeply that *even I* believed that there was never any romance between us. I didn't employ ammunition in the argument that I could have used: about the time we made out in my car, or the morning after, or all the weird, graphic backrubs I routinely gave her while kissing her neck and talking dirty to her. I didn't bring up any of the events from 10 years ago, I just accepted the reality of her statement. I accepted that "there was never anything romantic between us". I always parroted that exact line to Vee over the years. At the time, I believed it, myself.

"You don't have to do anything for me anymore, Yuki," she said. "I'll get what I need another way."

I left Inari that night, and she seemed to get immediately to work replacing me. It was maybe only two days later that Inari was spending her time with another man, a man from her therapy group. Apparently "nothing" was happening between them, but I knew in my heart that she was lying to keep me loyal. She broke up with him quickly because he had children that would steal his attention away from her and Inari wanted to be the sole object of his attention.

Then Gary came along.

Finally, Lewis, I'd had enough. After she flaked out on our dinner plans for two days in a row, I found myself driving her to an event, where I paid her cover charge and bought her a round of drinks when Lewis showed up, and it was immediately apparent that this was *not* their first date. I immediately pounded 5 mixed drinks and stormed out of the venue. She followed me outside where we argued for 30 minutes. I went in to close my tab, pounding another mixed drink, finding her and Lewis, one more time, embracing. As I left, I stood firmly in front of them I gave them both hand signs with a firm "fuck you!" attached.

I stumbled off to another club, sending her angry texts full of every four-letter word I could think of only to find myself aggressively fornicating with a girl I knew on the dance floor, eventually ending up in the women's restroom, in a stall. I had to carry her home that night… to her husband.

After the bars all closed, I called Inari and she answered. We argued and argued for hours, but it ended with more aggressive, intense screaming. Volleys of every four-letter word I could conjure flew out of my mouth at her. She disappeared for 3 days without answering or even viewing a single text message I sent her and I became increasingly worried. My mood constantly switched between apology and anger and intense self-loathing. During those 3 days, I went absolutely insane, calling her grandmother and even Adam, her ex-boyfriend, worried about her whereabouts. Was this Lewis guy into drugs? Was she OD'd in a basement somewhere? She wouldn't even let me know that she was alive. It felt deliberate. She knew I loved her, there were no illusions. She was punishing me for leaving her cult. 3 days later she emerged, unshowered, after spending every night with Lewis. She invited me over to talk, but it was clear that we were at an impasse. She offered to drop her pursuit of Lewis if I continued being her friend, but I didn't believe her. It was all a lie. She told me that I was the most important person in the world to her, that she loved me more than anyone, but I just didn't believe her anymore.

"If I was the most important person in the world to you, you would have at least let me know you were alive at some point in the last 3 days. There's no way this is true. You would have reached out to me. You would have been desperate to reach out to me, just as desperately as I was trying to reach you! You see, you *are* the most important person in *my* world. There's a stark contrast between how you regard me and how I regard you. We are at an impasse. This friendship, this amoeba, is over." I declare.

Stressed out, fatigued, and physically losing weight, I reached out to an old friend, buying him dinner, and telling him the story of what's been happening to me in 2021. I am barely getting into it when he interrupts me and says, "Dude! That's gaslighting!"

"What the fuck is gaslighting?" I asked.

"Gaslighting is where one person manipulates another person so badly that they end up rewriting their reality, look it up!" he said.

I search on my phone and up comes an article pointing out the red flags associated with relationship gaslighting. Inari hit all eleven red flags out of the park.

1. Withholding what is valuable to you
2. Words without action / words not matching actions
3. Controlling sources of information
4. Denying provable realities / rewriting versions of events
5. Making weak promises, unkept, upon completion of certain tasks
6. Vilifying defectors
7. Positive reinforcement used as confusion
8. Using confusion as a weakening mechanism
9. Aligning people against each other… "they're all liars"
10. Wearing down slowly with time
11. Blatant lies

"Holy shit! Oh my god! I had no idea!" I bury my head in my hands for what must have been an eternity, just repeatedly saying things like "I can't believe it! This is so bad! This makes so much sense now!"

All 11 red flags were knocked out of the park, beginning with the day I met Inari 10 years ago. I felt duped, cheated… like my whole life had been turned upside down. I returned home, extremely depressed. When I'm depressed, I often work on music or listen to old tracks. I found the track I wrote when she spider-walked my arm and held my hand in the hall of Jin's apartment building. Upon listening to the lyrics, I realized that the song I wrote is entirely, entirely, about gaslighting, in every single word.

Zeroing in on the idea that confusion can be used to trick the brain into accepting a reality that is not real, I realized now that this song is entirely about how Inari employed tactics of confusion, actions not matching words, words not matching actions, outright denials, lies, and intentionally vague, plausibly deniable statements to control me, put me to task, and keep me working for her.

Gaslighting – by Luna and the Destroyer
[hear it at adaloveless.com]

What does it mean, when our eyes meet?
Does it mean that you care about me?
And if it's nothing to you then why
Do I still feel the need to try?

Can't figure out why I'm still kept in the dark
And peering out at things I'm not supposed to see
Your body tells me things that your words just won't say
And I never know the things I'm supposed to believe
What does it mean?

What does it mean when I hold your hand
And walk with you across this land?
Dreaming of rainbows and packs in the wild
and the simpleness of a happy child?

These fairy tales don't need to be disbelieved
My eyes can't tell if you're an illusion or what
But the palms of our hands sweat and tell me it's no dream
And fairy tales are real if you believe in them or not
What does it mean?

What does it mean, when our lips touch
And you collapse into my clutch
And when you wake you don't remember much
And I just feel so fucking dumb?

And you treat me like I'm terrible and diseased
And tear me down in public and prompt me to go
Then chase me down the hall and apologize
And let me hold your hand and gaze into your eyes
What does it mean, when our eyes meet?

I began frantically researching gaslighting and applying what I've learned about it to all the events of the last 10 years. The term comes from a play, turned movie, called "Gaslight" where a man, a murderer, "love-bombs" a woman and marries her, intending to steal her family jewels. His goal is to convince her that she is crazy, get her committed, and obtain power of attorney over her so that he can search for the jewels unabated. He attempts to convince his wife that she stole things and removed a picture from the wall but simply doesn't remember, because she is a crazy kleptomaniac. He tells her that footsteps she hears in the attic and the dimming gaslights in the house are all her imagination. He questions her sanity and talks down to her causing her to clamor and claw to re-win his affections. Her constant struggle with accepting reality blinds her from seeing the truth, that he is manipulating her, as she works and tries to frantically restore the feelings of love he offered her in their initial whirlwind romance.

Upon researching various manifestations of gaslighting, I determined it was essentially a cult brainwashing tactic. It was a way to get your followers, your disciples, to look to *you alone*, a guru, for truth, enlightenment, and love. It is used by cult leaders, dictators, mob bosses, and corporate bosses to get their underlings to work tirelessly for them… and yes, it works in romantic relationships too.

I eventually reached out to Ken, who slept in Inari's bed for two years, while doing her bidding, now vilified and demonized by her for the purpose of preventing me (or anyone) from communicating with him. Ken seemed to know the truth, no wonder she didn't want me to talk to him. Ken acquired a whole library of books in the fallout of their relationship. He hands one in particular to me and encourages me to highlight the things that stand out. It's called "Stop Walking on Eggshells" and it offers advice on how to get your life back when someone you care about has borderline personality disorder.

Borderline personality disorder is something I had heard about but ignored. Jin accused her of having BPD when they broke up. Others did too. I had no idea that Ken was also pointing to BPD as Inari's ailment. I was living in Inari's reality, so I never bothered to research any red flags about her until now and was trained to ignore information that came from her defectors. At the beginning of the book, Ken loaned me, is a 30 question mix of Narcissistic and Borderline traits that, if observed, point to either NPD or BPD, both dangerous afflictions to befriend. A score of 12 is cause for concern, a score of 16 is extremely concerning. Inari scored a 17 composed almost entirely of BPD traits. She would have scored 100% of the BPD traits if she had children, I'm sure, because a few of the questions concerned children, yet I could not mark them due to the fact she has none.

BPD individuals are very often "natural gaslighters". They gaslight the people close to them out of necessity, not necessarily malice. They figure out how to do what they do because they're constantly feeling empty, in fear of being abandoned by those they love, and simply figure out what works for their survival. This makes them gifted liars and spinners of half-truths.

I now know too much. Inari had to be real with me. No more lies. No more half-truths.

The next time I talked to Inari, she tried speaking to me the same way she had for the last decade. Clearly, she wanted me, needed me, to stay in her life. She was willing to spend hours on the phone with me to beg and plead with me to stay as her friend, but only on her schedule. After all, I wasn't the only person she needed to "groom". Grooming her relationship with Lewis now clearly meant more to her than I ever would or could matter, despite my intense love and devotion. For the first time, I called out her actions as outright abuse… psychological abuse… psychological domestic abuse. "You're a domestic abuser, Inari!" I told her outright. She attacked my reactions, telling me that I was "too sensitive" and "too emotional" and "had no right to feel the things that [I] did", but by now I knew that all those things she was saying were what's called "reactive abuse" and were straight out of the gaslighting playbooks I'd been reading. I came armed with valuable phrases to shut down any of her attempts to gaslight and invalidate me.

"You're not allowed to justify your abuse of me, by judging my reaction to it."

"I don't have to justify my discomfort of your mistreatment of me."

"You don't get to dictate how I feel in response to your abuse."

"You don't get to decide my standards for what I tolerate. I do."

"I'm not interested in having a conversation where you invalidate me and my feelings."

Inari was completely unable to defend against these phrases and her arguments and justifications for her behaviors towards me are completely shut down. "If I ever sit next to you, hold your hand, or stand across from you again, it is going to be because you've clearly and directly and unambiguously asked me out on a date. If that's never going to happen, then I never want to see you again."

"Oh, so you're saying that you won't be my friend because I won't let you fuck me then?" she snapped.

"It was never really about that. Granted, I absolutely wanted all of you, completely, but it was more about building my life around someone that I cared about more than anyone else on the planet, more than I cared about anyone I've *ever* cared about. It was about building *our* life... together. But now that I see things more clearly, I realize I was just your lapdog, your servant, your bitch. I'm not your bitch, Inari! Not anymore. I dropped everything I was doing to come rescue you, whenever you needed me, at any time during the last decade! Now, finally, when I need something simple, you're too busy to lift a finger, let alone a forearm! I left my relationship of 3 years, and her children, just so that I could come take care of you, and here you are believing that you were just entitled to receive and never give anything back!"

"You didn't really do that much for me," Inari replied.

I was shocked at her blatant disregard for how much effort I and everyone else had put into taking care of her for the last decade. I sold my Bitcoin to pay for her needs in 2021. She was 37 years old! Her grandparents kept her kitchen clean and the fridge full of food that she merely complained was "too sweet". She did very little to help her grandmother deal with cancer but was certain to inflate its importance in order to paint herself as some kind of generous personal care assistant, who was selflessly helping her elderly grandmother take care of herself in old age. Inari's grandmother was very able-bodied and capable of taking care of herself for the most part. Inari mainly sorted pills once a week and spent much time complaining to me about how her grandmother did nothing but yell at her all the time. What I observed, actually, was Inari verbally abusing her grandmother on many occasions while her grandmother calmly tried to redirect her.

"You are a bottomless pit of need, Inari!" I scolded. "No matter how much I or anyone does for you, and no matter how much we all tell you we love you, it is just never enough. This is like a bottomless pit that I dump everything I have into, and, in the end, nothing ever comes out... it just disappears into an abyss, a void."

"You don't have to give anything to me anymore, Yuki, I'll find it from somewhere else," she replied.

I think that this statement is sad, pathetic, and cruel. She was telling me that I was just a source of "supply" that she could easily replace with the next sad sap that came along. But nothing could stop me from caring about her. I encouraged her to get the right help. I know that deep down in her heart, she doesn't *want* to destroy the people closest to her.

"On some level, it is nobody's business, but it seems to me that you're not being forthcoming with me about your psychological conditions. After asking around, and recalling conversations I've had over the last decade, I found out that I'm not the first person to point out your horrendous gaslighting behavior, and, if your therapists are not treating you for the right thing, then they're doing you a disservice."

"What do you think it is that they're supposed to be treating me for then?" she asked.

"I'm not the first person to say this to you. You know what I'm going to say," I replied. "Look, it's none of my business, I'm not trying to get you to confess or anything, it's not about me pointing fingers at you and saying 'Haha! Look! I got you!' In fact, I'm hesitant to say anything because the textbooks suggest that even accusing you of having this condition will absolutely, potentially break you! It could potentially shatter you into a dissociative state, causing you stress to no end and maybe you'll lash out at me seeking revenge, or even become suicidal. But you've heard this before, from Jin, from Ken, and from at least 3 or 4 other mutual friends."

"I still don't know what you're talking about," she replied. "Do you think I'm a narcissist?"

"No, I don't think you're a narcissist, but if you are, you're an extremely 'covert' narcissist. We all have a certain level of narcissism in us, and you score reasonably low on that scale. I'm talking about borderline personality disorder."

"They tested me for that and concluded that I didn't have it," she replies.

"Well, they can't diagnose you with something if you lie to them. As I think I've established and documented here, you have a real serious problem with lying and spinning half-truths in order to paint yourself as the victim. I even wrote a song about it, years ago, where I used the metaphor of dancing and spinning to describe your inability to make a statement that wasn't spun to paint yourself in the most perfect light all the time. Look it up, it's called 'Truthiness'. I've sorta known this all along, I realized, but I just wouldn't accept reality, because you had me so deeply indoctrinated into your cult. I imagine your therapy sessions to be entirely focused on overcoming traumas of bad shit other people have done to you, but you also need to look at the bad things *you've* done to *other* people!"

"No, they did a test that there was no possibility that I could cheat on," she replied.

"Look," I sighed, frustrated, "It doesn't matter. This has nothing to do with me, and everything to do with you getting the help that you need. It explains a lot: your claims of being an 'empath' can actually be attributed to a symptom of BPD. People with BPD are hypersensitive to facial expressions, and therefore are naturally attracted to sociopaths, like you were attracted to Jin's dead, robot eyes. It explains that phenomenon I called 'the feedback loop', your dissociations, the cutting behavior, your need to put your friends above your romantic relationship, keep someone like Barry around as your 'constant', and the high-conflict nature of your personality. I feel like you've spent so much time in the mental health system that you should already know this, and I'm absolutely baffled as to why you're pretending like this is new news. You're a smart girl, Inari. Maybe if you get the help that you *actually* need, you'll stop destroying the relationships you have with the people who are closest to you. No matter how much anyone tells you that they love you, you will never believe them. You always need more because you constantly feel empty inside. All of this is also straight out of the textbooks."

We agreed to have one more conversation in an attempt to preserve our friendship. I offered to remain her friend under the simple condition that she call me, before midnight, armed with a single story about something she did wrong in her life. "We're all perpetrators and victims, Inari. Nobody is only a victim! Tell me a story about when you were a perpetrator! Did you cheat on a test? Did you punch a kid needlessly on a playground? Tell me one thing, anything, anything simple."

She called at 11:55PM, and for over 5 hours I pressed Inari to confess a single sin. She could not, even as the sun began to rise early in the morning. She didn't know how to see herself as a perpetrator of anything, she only knew how to play the victim.

That would be the last time I ever heard anything from Inari, ever again.

Thank You

Thank you for reading this book. I am glad I managed to hold your attention until the end. I never intended to be an "author" at any time during my life. I still don't consider myself an "author"… I'm just a guy with a story to tell. I hope that there weren't large parts of the story that were confusing.

Facebook loves to shove memories in my face, particularly ones from 10 years ago… a nice round number. Throughout the summer as I revised this book, old memories were being thrown in my face from the days past. Photos from the Zombie Crawl and other meaningful and traumatic moments were being fed to me all summer contributing to my sadness.

The PTSD I experienced from her discard was real. Maybe you've been through worse, and if so, I feel for you, and sometimes I feel like an imposter. But in my own heart, this trauma was real enough that I woke up every morning dwelling upon these events. I dwelled upon them all day. I dwelled upon them as I went to sleep at night. I just couldn't help but work on this writing… and I just wanted *someone* to hear what I had to say. Not *everyone*, like an attention-seeking narcissist, but *someone*.

I spent a solid year of my life simply ruminating on these events, barely able to function. I couldn't work for months following her discard. I couldn't even do basic things like… watch television… because it would only interfere with the thoughts in my head and drive me mad as if I were watching *two* televisions at the same time with the volume cranked. The only thing I seemed to be capable of doing, was revising this very book… and drinking.

It was a challenge to re-open this book after 10 years. All the events in this book are real-as-remembered, but my recreations of some of these events are likely flawed by the entropy of time. The dialogue is largely dramatized for the purpose of character development, but the key pieces of dialogue are burned into my memory as if they were spoken to me just moments ago. I can still hear Inari whisper her seductive things into my ears and the inflections in her voice when she called me up sobbing, "I had no idea! I had no idea how serious this was!" or Jin's "Let's resolve this with violence!" or when he invited Inari to push him down the hill in his Irish accent. I am quite certain that all of the key dialogue was completely verbatim and truthful in both content and spirit.

I sought therapy, a new thing for me, and EMDR therapy helped. I aggressively sought to change my circumstances, managed to go on a few dates, and even had a short-term "illegitimate" relationship after Inari's discard of me. But as I wrote earlier, illegitimate relationships drive me mad, and, currently, I just trade traumas between "Inari" and another girl, a severe alcoholic, gambler, smoker, and dealer who seemed to be trying to build a cult of her own, but in her own unique way. Luckily I did not get in too deep with her... I learned my lesson to a degree.

As I finish this book, the cold Minnesota winter is upon me, and I only wonder what is next, if anything, for me. The end of my romantic life feels like the end of my life in general. As I said at the beginning of this book, I was searching for Inari since I was a child, but she is now gone, certainly now, forever. I demanded that she block my phone number and all my social media accounts, and she reluctantly agreed during our final conversation. She has not reached back in many months now, and I'm quite positive she never will.

Love is a powerful weapon. We don't expect people to *not* scream when guns are fired at them. We don't expect people to *not* cry at funerals, or *not* cheer when they win a million dollars. Do not expect me to just be able to shut down these feelings of love, just because *her* love for me was a twisted manifestation, like a gun shooting blanks. Like running from a falling building, Inari's love compelled me to run... not *from* her... but *towards* her...

Thank you for enduring this and enduring me. *Please join me at adaloveless.com for discussion and music.*

- Ada

Printed in Great Britain
by Amazon

71660319R00274